The Bookshop by the Beach

By
JC Williams

You can subscribe to JC Williams' mailing list and view all his other books at:

www.authorjcwilliams.com

The Bookshop by the Beach copyright © 2020 J C Williams

All rights reserved. No part of this book may be reproduced in any manner without written permission except in the case of brief quotations included in critical articles and reviews. For information, please contact the author.

All characters appearing in this work are fictitious. Any resemblance to real persons, living or dead, is purely coincidental.

ISBN: 9798667318040

First printing September 2020

Cover artwork by Paul Nugent

Proofreading, editing, and interior formatting & design provided by Dave Scott and Cupboardy Wordsmithing

Chapter One

Libby pressed her hand up against the bus shelter, using it as support so she could raise her left leg. Her new pink Converse trainers were cutting into her Achilles tendon something dreadful, and each step felt like electricity surging through her foot. The decision to dress without ankle socks was, presently, proving to be the wrong one.

"Aww, hell," she said with a grimace, looking up to see how far she still had to walk. Peel Promenade wasn't particularly long, maybe half-a-mile or so, she reckoned, though she'd never actually measured it. But even more than several steps right now would prove to be a challenge. She reasoned that the laces in her new trainers must be too tight, and so she made her way towards the wooden bench inside the shelter so she could re-lace her shoes and maybe give her feet a little breathing room. She'd not stepped more than one pace inside the bus shelter however when the overwhelming stench of stale urine slapped her in the face, a result, perhaps, of some well-lubricated revellers caught short the previous evening waiting for the last bus home. She couldn't spend the day in a pee-stained bus shelter, as she needed to open up her shop in precisely sixteen minutes, she confirmed by glancing at her watch. The thought of sitting down to adjust her trainers and perhaps relieve the discomfort was no longer quite so appealing, so she figured she'd simply suck up the pain rather than take the risk of sitting down on the bench, and with that, she sallied forth once again.

This was her third journey up and down the promenade that morning. She was embracing the balmy weather that had been forecast by sporting her new red Ditsy floral dress, which she felt was for mornings such as this. She had entertained the notion, back at the house, of wearing an Audrey Hepburn-inspired hat to complement her sunglasses, but in the end had thought better of it, preferring to show off her newly styled hair instead, and leaving the hat on her bed under the watchful gaze of Catticus, her cat, and donning just her sunglasses.

The casual observer might have thought Libby was simply out for a morning stroll, enjoying the warm summer air, and perhaps planning what the weekend may have had on offer. The casual observer's assumptions would, however, have been entirely wrong, with the vision of twenty or so burly rugby players conducting a morning training session on the beach providing a bit more insight into Libby's current motivations.

Libby planted her foot down, setting off again, and staring straight ahead in order to give the impression that she was completely ignoring the men on the beach and that the men on the beach were most certainly not-at-all the reason she was traipsing up and down the promenade with as much an air of casual sophistication as she could muster. She flicked her eyes to the right, but the now-sweating men were unfortunately still too consumed in their morning training session to pay her any heed, which, regrettably, had also been the case on her previous trips as well.

Every step was agony, but Libby would, no matter, do her best to maintain her composure and air of sophistication. She was, after all, a lady of impeccable breeding…

"Shit… shit… bastard… aww, shit… bloody trainers… shit…. ah, shit…" she muttered each time her foot hit the pavement.

Libby still had a few minutes before work, and with one foot now soon in danger of needing amputation and the second foot not far behind, she hopped up onto the wall which ran alongside the promenade separating it from the beach. Perched up there, she swung her leg around, enjoying a panoramic view of the peaceful Irish Sea. This vantage point would also allow her to be seen by the group of men on the beach. It had to. After all, she'd spent seventy quid on this new summer dress, and she'd be damned if it wasn't going to be admired. Libby adjusted her

CHAPTER ONE

sunglasses, pretending to focus her attention on something or other of significance off in the distance, so that when the rugby team turned to admire her understated beauty — which they inevitably would — she'd appear tantalisingly aloof. After five minutes or so of this, however, the fascinating thing she was pretending to look at was becoming distinctly tedious and the rugby team, to the best of her knowledge, hadn't glanced over in her direction once. Fearing her mission was heading towards failure, dashed on the rocks like a mussel or clam dropped by a gull from high in the air, she offered a strategic cough in the team's general direction in furtherance of her goal... but not one inquisitive head turned in her direction. "Bloody useless, this lot," she said, before conceding it was perhaps time to get her stylish arse to work.

"A-ha!" shouted someone very near to the wall where Libby was sat.

It was so sudden and unexpected that Libby gave a fair bit of a start, began to wobble, and had to brace herself lest she topple off the edge like Humpty Dumpty.

"Caught you!" came the phantom voice, surprising Libby once again, as if the first time hadn't given her enough of a fright as it was.

"What the...?" said Libby, instinctively jumping forward this time, straight off of the wall, her feet planting firmly into the sand. She spun round to locate the owner of the offending voice, but there was no one there. "Hang on, I think I *know* that voice," she declared after a pause, recognition dawning. "Where are you, you silly twit?" she asked, moving forward and peering over the wall.

Freya, who had been squatting to conceal her arrival, glanced up with a broad grin. "Let me guess..." she said, taking a draw on her vaping device and then letting go a plume of sickeningly sweet smoke. "Is Luke on the beach, by any chance, amongst the others? I know you fancy him."

"*Pfft*," replied Libby, shaking off the very suggestion, but then, "I wouldn't know, would I? I'm just soaking in the view before I need to open up the shop, aren't I?"

"Bollocks," Freya answered, releasing another plume. "You're even wearing a new dress, if I'm not very much mistaken. You've really put some effort into this affair, haven't you?"

"It's not an affair!" Libby protested. "Don't call it that!"

"You know what I meant," Freya replied, smirking. "But, still. You'd like it to be one, now wouldn't you?"

"Whatever," answered Libby, fighting the smile she could feel emerging, not wishing to give things away so easily. "Anyway. Why are you out and about so early this morning? I didn't think you were working today," she added, attempting to shift the conversation over to a different topic.

"I hadn't planned on it, but I got called in," Freya explained. "What can I say? I'm indispensable, I suppose."

"Hmm, well you *are* good at what you do, I'll give you that," Libby had to admit. "And those doughnuts of yours are how I met you, after all."

"It's lovely to be appreciated," Freya replied.

"It is, isn't it?" sighed Libby. "And I've spent the last twenty minutes walking up and down the promenade trying to get appreciated, haven't I? But these blokes—"

"And the one bloke in particular?" interjected Freya.

"Alright, fine. And the one bloke in particular, yes," admitted Libby. "And he must be stupid or something. I mean, he's not even glanced over. Not once. And I'm a wonderful kisser, right? I've been told this. It's my *thing*. And I've not seen him for two weeks, and he's not even called? Really? What's that about?"

"Wait, hang on, so you kissed him?" asked Freya. "When was this??"

"Well, sort of," replied Libby.

"Sort of? How can you *sort of* kiss somebody?" enquired Freya.

"I saw him out at the pub a few weeks ago and we chatted," explained Libby.

"Yes...?" asked Freya.

"And I think it went well," said Libby.

"And...?" asked Freya.

"And I think it went well," said Libby again.

"So when did the kissing part happen!" Freya demanded.

CHAPTER ONE

"Okay, well that part I only dreamt about later that night," Libby admitted.

Freya just shook her head in disappointment at this, not even bothering to reply.

"So you see? I did sort of kiss him," said Libby, answering Freya's non-answer.

"But if you only *dreamt* that part, then how's that supposed to make him want to call you?" said Freya, pointing out the obvious weakness in Libby's reasoning.

"He should just *know*," pouted Libby, crossing her arms over her chest.

"Hmm. Well, call me crazy, but I'm not sure parading up and down the promenade like a peacock is going to convince him," Freya observed, going in for another lungful on her vaping device. "I think that gives the impression you're a bit, I don't know... desperate, maybe? Bordering on crazy, even?" she said. "Nice dress, though."

"It is, isn't it," declared Libby. "My new trainers are killing me, though. Honestly, you might need to carry me to the shop."

"I did see you walking ahead of me a bit earlier, Libby, and it wasn't a pretty sight," remarked Freya. "You looked like you'd had a bit of an accident, if you catch my meaning."

"An accident?" asked Libby. "Like I'd twisted my ankle?"

"No. I mean an *accident*," Freya clarified. "Like you couldn't make it to the loo in time."

Libby pressed her hand against her forehead. "Aww, bloody men. I'm sick of them. I only wanted to get Luke's attention, and I thought my new dress would help," she moaned. "But it looks like I've totally wasted my money, and it was money I couldn't even really afford to spend in the first place."

Freya bobbed her head up and down knowingly as she listened, as if she had all the answers. And, in fact, "If you wanted to get Luke's attention you should have just whapped your tits out," she said, providing one such answer.

"*Whapped?*" asked Libby. "I'm sorry, but what does that even mean?"

"To get them out," explained Freya. "To unsheathe them from their bonds. To unleash them from their fabric prison. To—"

"Yes, I get it," said Libby, getting it. "But, sorry, I'm not getting my tits out on the beach at this time of the morning. Before work. And sober."

"Well then, I'm all out of ideas, and I need to get to work. So you're on your own, I'm afraid," Freya told her. "Pop in later and I'll treat you to a nice custard doughnut or two, all right? It'll make you feel better."

"Thanks. Maybe I will," said Libby, turning back around to face the beach.

"I know how you could get his attention," suggested Freya, still crouching down behind the wall, hidden from view from those on the beach. It was very much like a Cyrano de Bergerac-inspired scene.

"You're still there?" asked Libby. "I thought you said you had to go? And that you were all out of ideas?" Libby pointed out.

"Yes, but a thought just occurred to me, now didn't it?" Freya *also* pointed out.

"Oh?" said Libby, her interest piqued. "Do tell?"

Freya turned so that she was facing Libby. From her position of cover, she stretched herself up so that she could sneak a peek over the top edge of the wall, just enough to afford her a view of the beach. She paused for a moment, surveying the scene, and then declared, "Right, then. If you want to get a man's attention, Libby, what you need to do is be strategic."

A hint of a smile appeared on Libby's face. She cocked her head slightly, intrigued, tucking a few strands of blonde hair behind her ear, and curious as to what sort of advice Freya might have to offer. "Strategic in what way?" she asked of her friend, hopeful she'd be receiving some serious advice from Freya this time, something actually useful. "What did you have in mind?"

"Like this. Here, I'll show you," replied Freya. Freya stretched up a little more, raising her chin so that she could speak over the top of the wall unobstructed. "SHOW US YOUR WILLY!" she hollered, yelling it out at the top of her vocal range, before very rapidly lowering her head out of sight quicker than a homesick mole.

On the beach, a rugby ball dropped to the sand. At least eighteen sweating heads turned to identify the source of the voice,

CHAPTER ONE

and as Libby was the only person situated near to the group, all eyes were now upon her.

"Is everyone looking at you now?" asked Freya, from her position of safety behind the wall.

"Yes," replied Libby, through clenched teeth and a forced smile.

"You're welcome," whispered Freya.

Freya's approach had been unorthodox, but Libby couldn't knock the results. Those four shouted words of Freya's had achieved what a seventy-quid dress and a pair of stylish-but-crippling Converse trainers couldn't. Libby tried her best to retain her composure despite the obvious reddening of her cheeks she could feel, finding something interesting further on up the beach she could pretend to focus on again. Somewhat flustered, she reached for her handbag until she remembered she didn't have one. "Freya?" said a grinning Libby, her jaw fixed and her lips unmoving, speaking as if she were a ventriloquist. "Don't think I won't get you back for this."

To take her mind away from matters of the heart, Libby settled in behind the counter of her shop with her morning coffee. She cast her eyes around the room, doing a visual sweep and quick inspection of the books on display, which were perfectly aligned on their shelves with not a one of them even a single millimetre out of kilter. This was because she'd straightened them all only the day before. And the reason they were still organised like this was that no customers had been in since. Not a single one. Not even someone looking for directions. In the past forty-eight hours, in fact, the only people that'd walked through the shop doors were the postman, Freya, and of course herself.

Still, it was Saturday morning, and looking very much like it was going to be a glorious day in this lovely seaside town of Peel on the Isle of Man. The first sunseekers were already starting to stake their claims on their little section of the sand for the day, and with the more adventurous among them already daring to dip their toes into the gentle waves rolling in even though the water had yet to be warmed by the sun's rays. A day such as this had all the ingredients to make for a prosperous afternoon for the town's various businesses, and Libby could certainly benefit from one of those.

But there weren't any customers yet. And so Libby picked up some reading material she'd started in on the night before. Now, as the proprietor of a bookshop, a love of the written word was pretty much a prerequisite for the job. But she simply couldn't get through what she'd been attempting to read the previous evening. Not one to give up on the printed page, however, she took a sip of her coffee and soldiered on, continuing where she'd left off. And yet each page was an arduous struggle, and the effort was such that as she lowered her reading material once she finally managed to finish it, she also lowered her head, placing it down onto the countertop, and releasing a pained whimper as she did so. Yes, as far as credit card statements went, this was one that would most certainly not enter Libby's best-seller list. "Aww, what the actual hell," she said, now bouncing her head on the wooden surface.

"Wait, hang on," she said, pausing her head-bashing for a moment. There were certainly a lot of numbers to be taken in from what she'd just pored over, but one set of numbers in particular brought a sudden realisation in Libby's mind that something was perhaps amiss, that something wasn't what it ought to have been. She lifted her head back up, retrieved the statement from the counter, and then ran her fingers down the debit column. "One hundred and seventy pounds!" she wailed, looking at the paper in her hands, then glancing down at her pretty new dress, and then looking back at the paper. "You were only supposed to cost seventy pounds! Why are you not *seventy* pounds?" she said, throwing the floral-themed fabric presently covering her figure a furious look of contempt, as if this were entirely the dress's fault. "You didn't even bloody do what you were supposed to do!"

It wasn't that Libby was useless with money, it's just that she didn't have any. Which, then again, it could be argued, to some extent did make her useless with money.

CHAPTER ONE

Back at her old job in London, she'd earned a much higher wage, of course. The problem there, however, was that so much of her earnings went towards paying rent that there wasn't an awful lot left, not nearly as much as she would've liked. While there were elements of London city life she'd found appealing, these were limited mostly to the social aspects. And she did like the food. What didn't motivate her to haul her bum out of bed at five a.m. each morning, however, was the commute to work each day. An hour of being dry-humped in a sweltering tin can with rarely any available seats to be had was not the best way to start your morning, and the thought of repeating the process for the evening commute at the end of a long day at work was never one that brought Libby any joy.

Still, if you'd have asked any of Libby's friends back over in London if they would have envisioned her running a book shop in the Isle of Man as her next career choice, they'd have thought you somewhat bonkers. Yet that's exactly what Libby was now doing. Her commute to work currently entailed a ten-minute walk (and thirty minutes when you're trying to impress a man on the beach, as it should happen) from her gran's house nearby. And rather than the commute being an arduous pain in the tits as it once was, it was now one of the things Libby enjoyed most about her day and looked forward to. Peel was a picture-postcard seaside town. Sure, it wasn't quite the tourist destination it once was, back in its heyday, but it did have a nostalgic charm that still managed to attract its fair share of people flocking to soak up the sense of a bygone age. And now Libby made it her home as well, and The Bookshop by the Beach was Libby's new office.

Libby's quality of life had definitely increased as a result of her move. But as quickly as her quality of life was increasing, by contrast, the contents of her bank account were decreasing. The concept of living to one's means was one she was familiar with, of course, but one she was yet to embrace — as evidenced by the number of entries on her credit card statement. Also, it didn't help that her means weren't what they used to be, either. When her gran had pitched the idea of running the shop to Libby, she had indeed been spot-on about the quality of life on this pretty little island in the middle of the Irish Sea. However, where she may have stretched the truth, just a mite, was in regard to the amount of passing trade who utilised the services of a quaint little bookshop next to the beach. Oh, that, and also her stories of tripping over attractive men at every corner, such was their availability. Gran could be somewhat flexible with the truth, it would seem, when it served her purposes. But Libby loved her dearly, and she was pleased to be able to keep an eye on her now that Grandad had passed away, so there was that. Perhaps the only downside to this living arrangement was that living with your gran wasn't exactly up there on the list of desirable traits a gentleman might necessarily be looking for, despite the fact that Libby was drop-dead gorgeous, with impeccable style, wit, and charm. Oh, and modest to boot as well.

"Morning!" put forth Libby, with a polished enthusiastic perfection, when a potential customer finally, blessedly, came through the door. "Lovely day for it!" Libby added. She didn't know what *it* might be, but people tended to fill in that blank themselves. Of course, Libby hoped the woman would find it a lovely day for buying books.

The mature lady hovered just inside the doorway, allowing her eyes to adjust from the bright sunlight outside. "I need a roll of film for my camera," she announced after a long, lingering moment, removing her sunglasses and slipping them into her quaffed hair. She didn't move up to the counter as she said this. She maintained her position by the door, and called out to Libby as if Libby were her servant.

Libby chuckled and politely awaited a follow-up that didn't arrive. "*Ehm...*" she replied after a moment, sweeping her hand across the interior of the shop to introduce row-upon-row and shelf-after-shelf of books by way of explanation. The woman didn't speak, and Libby was useless when it came to silence, feeling the need to fill it. "Do people even still use film in their cameras?" she asked, shrugging her shoulders.

"I do," declared the woman abruptly. "I need a roll of film for my camera," she repeated, rummaging in her bag to locate her purse. "Twenty-four exposures should suffice, as I just want to get a few pictures of the castle," she said, producing her purse, and then pointing through the window to Peel Castle across the

CHAPTER ONE

harbour, even though Libby was of course well familiar by this time with the location of Peel Castle and didn't really need it pointed out to her. "And don't you be trying to upsell me to thirty-six exposures, either," the woman added, emphasising this directive with a stern, wagging finger.

Libby exposed her teeth, with a vacant grin, like she had a touch of wind. "Sorry, we don't sell film. We're a bookshop. We sell books," she said, wondering what could possibly have given the woman the impression a bookshop would be selling camera film, or *anything* other than books for that matter. "We do have books about cameras, though. And photography, also, if you're interested?" Libby suggested helpfully.

"What? Don't be silly. How on earth am I supposed to take a photograph of the castle with a book?" came the immediate rebuff. "You're not making any sense," said the woman. "So you don't sell rolls of film, then?" she asked, appearing unconvinced Libby was telling the truth, as if Libby might be able to produce a roll of camera film if perhaps she just looked hard enough.

"No, madam," said Libby, as politely as she could. "No film for cameras here, I'm afraid. Just books. Also some greeting cards and postcards and such," she added. "But, no, as far as camera film goes, I'd have to say that's a *negative*," Libby remarked, giving the woman a wink, and hoping she might be appeased to some extent by a bit of gentle wordplay.

"So why did your friend up the road tell me you did?" the woman replied, frustrated that she'd been misled, and Libby's attempt at humour washing right over her.

"I'm sorry you were somehow given the wrong impression," offered Libby, assuming an apology was the quickest way to draw this conversation to a close. "Wait, did you just say my friend up the way?" Libby asked, the woman's words to that effect suddenly registering.

But the woman wasn't listening to Libby anymore. She was tut-tutting, tucking her purse back into her bag, and turning to leave. "No use if you want film for your camera," she said to a couple coming through the door just as she was going out, her voice dripping with disdain.

As the film-seeking woman had spun around and exited, Libby caught a glimpse of a bakery shop bag, held in the same hand as the woman's large handbag and so previously out of Libby's view behind it. This only confirmed Libby's suspicions. *"Bloody Freya,"* she muttered under her breath. *"I should've known."*

As it should happen, whenever Freya had customers of hers mention in passing something or other they were looking to buy — items she knew darned well a seaside bookshop would have no business selling, mind you — she would often send them Libby's way. She did this, in part, to help get people through Libby's door. But she did this, also, for the sake of her own amusement at the stories Libby would tell her later. So far this year, for instance, Libby had received enquiries for Irish black sod turf for burning in the fireplace (the Isle of Man was in the Irish Sea, yes, but it was not Ireland), Isle of Skye whisky (again, wrong island), a solar panel for a VW Campervan, and a 12mm ratchet-strap automobile cargo tie-down, amongst other things. In fact, only the week before, a rather excitable chap had come in looking to purchase a pair of ice skates, despite the fact that it was the start of summer. Still, Freya made the most amazing custard-filled doughnuts and, as such, could usually be forgiven.

Once the couple that had come in were taken care of, and with no other customers immediately present, Libby took the opportunity to step outside and soak up a little sun. She would never tire of the view from her shop, and she enjoyed standing outside the front door watching the world go by, on occasion, striking up a friendly conversation with those out enjoying their day. She also loved to watch the kiddies squealing with delight on the beach. It reminded her of visits to stay with her gran and grandad in the school holidays when she was a little girl. And judging by the number of ice creams she saw being enjoyed today, and on many other days, she wondered if perhaps she weren't in the wrong line of business!

But books were her passion, as she'd always loved to read. And in fact this was why her gran had suggested Libby taking over the shop. And not only did Libby love to read but recently she'd even started to write, using the frequent lulls during her day to begin penning a novel of her own. She was surrounded by books

CHAPTER ONE

daily, row upon row of them. *How hard could it be to write one of my own?* she'd thought. Much harder than she had imagined, as it would turn out. Still, the struggle, and the realisation of how difficult it actually was, only made her appreciate that much more the contents of the product she sold. Hers was a labour of love, and likely never going to be a literary classic, but it was something she very much enjoyed.

Fortunately, business soon picked up as morning changed to afternoon. A steady stream of actual customers, as opposed to those sent under false pretences, kept Libby busy. And more importantly, it kept the shop *till* busy. It'd been relatively quiet of late, and an influx of cash was just what was required to keep Libby's spirits lifted. Freya also popped in on her break to deliver a couple of her signature custard-filled doughnuts, freshly made. So, her earlier shenanigans vis-à-vis Camera Film Lady were of course immediately forgiven. In the thirty seconds or so she was in the shop, Freya had also managed to convince Libby that staying in for a quiet night was absolutely not happening, and that going out for a bit of fun would be a far better option, much healthier for the soul, and who was Libby to argue with such sterling logic?

The custard doughnuts called out to Libby for over an hour before she finally had a free moment to avail herself of one of them. She devoured half of one of these delectable beauties in one ravenous assault, leaving a perfect half-moon shape in the remaining half as she moaned in delighted satisfaction. In typical fashion, of course, the door opened and a customer walked in just as she was tucking in, and to her abject horror — as, cheeks full, she must have looked like a squirrel with a good-sized load of acorns in her mouth — it was Luke. She wiped sugar crystals from her chin, and unable to speak as a result of the amount of doughnut presently filling her gob, she waved in his direction.

"Hiya, Libby," Luke said, returning the wave.

"Luke!" gasped Libby, after quickly swallowing hard, as Luke made his way to the counter. "So. What are you up to?" she asked by way of casual conversation as he presented himself before her, despite the fact that Luke was wearing a pair of running shorts, trainers, and a running vest, thus rendering the answer as to what he might be up to fairly obvious.

"Oh, just out for a run," replied Luke, throwing his thumb over his shoulder in the direction of the out-of-doors, where he had in fact been running.

"Training this morning? And now a run? Are you trying to put me to shame?" Libby asked amiably.

"Well, it's good to keep fit, I reckon," replied a smiling Luke. "Anyway, I did see you this morning, by the way. And heard you."

"Ah, yes. That wasn't actually..." Libby began, not entirely sure how to clarify the situation to him, or even if it was worth delving into.

"I liked your dress, also!" Luke entered in, saving Libby the trouble of deciding whether to attempt to explain the whole beach debacle thingy or not. "I mean I still like it, of course," Luke felt the need to point out. "It's not as if I stopped liking it or anything."

"What, this old thing here?" said Libby, running her fingers through her fringe as she looked down at the dress she was wearing, and taking back in her head the negative reaction she'd had to the price tag. It was now completely worth every penny that she'd not yet repaid.

Unfortunately, when she ran her hand through the front of her hair, Libby completely forgot that she was still holding onto half of a doughnut with that very same hand...

"You've wiped..." said Luke, motioning to her face, where there was now a gooey yellow snail trail across the top.

"What?" asked Libby, feeling her forehead, as indicated, for confirmation.

"From your doughnut... it must be... it's custard, I have to assume...?" offered Luke.

Libby did the only thing that made sense, the only thing she *could* do under such a circumstance: she took a finger, wet it with her lips, and then wiped the custard off her forehead with it. Then, she placed the custard-laden fingertip into her mouth, sucking it clean, and pulling her moistened finger from her mouth at the conclusion of this task with a pop. "I hear it's good for the skin. Excellent for anti-ageing," she joked nervously, trying

CHAPTER ONE

to play off like this little facial faux pas of hers was no big deal, even as she died a little inside from the embarrassment.

"Is that so?" said Luke, eyes going wide.

"Oh, crap! Oh my god, I didn't mean..." she began, realising what she'd just said, and what she'd just done with her finger, and how all of that very likely must have come across. "Ah... anyway, how can I help?" she asked, feeling her cheeks turning crimson, and very anxious to move the conversation along to something else, anything else. "What I mean is, how can I help as far as...?" she said, motioning to the sea of books around her.

Luke glanced around him. "Ah. Right," he replied. "Well, you see, your friend Freya pounced on me as I was running past the bakery shop just now. I basically got shanghaied, I guess you could say, as she can be rather persistent and persuasive, as it turns out, and she actually suggested popping in to see you. She said you might be able to help?" he said. "And so, well, here I am," he concluded, holding his hands up in the air, palms raised, like a priest about to consecrate the Eucharist.

Just when Libby thought the man of her dreams was there to speak with her, he then presents Freya as his only reason for being there. *Ah. Marvellous*, she thought to herself. *Another one of Freya's gags.*

"Marvellous," Libby said again, but out loud this time. "And what's our Freya suggested you pop in for?" she went on, her words drenched with sarcasm. "A tin of tartan paint, perhaps? Or a left-handed screwdriver, maybe?"

Luke took a cautionary step back, away from the counter, confused by Libby's sudden change in tone, and unsure about the nature of her current line of questioning. "No. No, neither of those things," he told Libby. "I'm here for a book, actually. Because... this is a bookshop...?"

"Ah. Sorry about that," answered Libby, snapping back to a more normal demeanour.

"I told her I was thinking of doing a half-marathon, and she mentioned that you had some useful books on training," Luke elaborated. "Are you... okay?" he added.

"Sorry. Yeah. See, Freya's got this thing she does where she..." Libby began, but then decided against going into it. "In fact, never mind," she said. "Here. Let me show you where they are, those books you're looking for."

She emerged from behind the counter and found herself breathing in the scent of him. He'd just been out for a run, but good god he smelt so good, she thought. "Just over here," she announced, leading the way. She sang the words, which took her a little by surprise. "Just there. Everything you need to get fit. Not that you're not, of course. I mean you're very fit. Fit as in healthy, I mean, not that you're fit as in *fit*. Although, that is... I mean... oh, bugger," she said, fumbling desperately. "I'll leave you to browse, then, shall I?" she suggested, taking her leave and retiring to her position behind the counter again.

Bloody hell, thought Libby, back at her station. *So much for sophisticated and charming, woman.* She left Luke to his own devices, allowing him to sort through the available books at his leisure. She used the opportunity to check her forehead for any remnants of custard she may have missed from earlier, but she couldn't stop herself from glancing over in Luke's direction. Repeatedly. *Stop staring*, she scolded herself. *Make it a little more bloody obvious, why don't you.*

"I'll take this," Luke said eventually, placing the book he'd chosen on the counter. "Oh, wait, I haven't got my wallet," he added, patting his pockets and suddenly realising they were empty. "Sorry, I hadn't planned on coming in until I was waylaid by that Freya. I mean, not that I didn't want to or anything. I just hadn't planned on it today, you know?" he explained, patting his pockets down for a second time, even though he knew by now there was nothing there.

"Don't worry, just take the book with you and pay me later," Libby told him. "And don't try and run off on me," she joked, pointing to his running outfit. "After all, I know where you live," she said. "Whoops, I mean, I *don't* know where you live. It's just a figure of speech," she quickly backpedalled, worried about how what she'd said might have sounded. "I'm sorry, this happens when I have too much sugar. It sends me a bit, you know..." she explained, twirling her finger in the air beside her right temple.

CHAPTER ONE

Luke smiled politely. "I'll drop the money off soon, I promise," he promised. "Listen," he said, giving his chin a quick rub, "I don't mean to be cheeky, but I wondered if—"

"I'd love to!" replied Libby instantly.

"You'd love to?" asked Luke uncertainly.

"Absolutely, I'd love to!" Libby reiterated, but then, blushing, realised Luke hadn't even specified yet what the thing was that she was so readily agreeing to. It could've been anything, after all. She didn't know.

Luke pointed to the white bakery shop bag sat off to the side on the counter. "I noticed you have what I'm assuming must be a spare doughnut there, is what I was going to say," he told Libby. "And, after what you said about sugar making you a little crazy, I thought I'd help you out by maybe taking the other one off your hands...?"

Libby pressed the bag forward. "Well in that case, then, I'd *love* for you to have this doughnut," she replied, giggling like someone who'd just made a right fool of themselves, or like someone who'd had too much sugar, or both.

"She's right, you know," observed Luke.

"Who is?" asked Libby.

"Freya. She warned me that you could be a mite bonkers," explained Luke.

"Oh she did, did she?" replied Libby, making a mental note to bring this up to Freya later on.

"Look, I don't really want the doughnut," said Luke, gently pushing the bag back across the counter. "I was actually going to see if you wanted to maybe go for a drink sometime...?"

"Hmm, I don't know. Are you going to be dressed like that?" enquired Libby, cocking her head sceptically, pleased at this favourable turn of events but playing it impishly coy.

"No, I'll be dressed in proper clothes on the occasion," Luke assured her. "And I might even have had a shower as well," he added, with a smirk.

"In that case, then..." Libby answered him. "In that case, I would be inclined to take you up on your fine offer of a drink sometime. Yes, I think I should like that very much, in fact. A drink would be splendid."

"Splendid, is it?" remarked Luke with a chuckle. "Splendid indeed," he agreed. "Hang on, what's this? Are you writing something?" he asked amiably, suddenly noticing the open notepad on the countertop. Even viewing them upside down, Luke could tell that the words filling the pages didn't appear to be business-related.

Libby flicked her head back. "*Splendid* is how us book types talk," she joked, at the same time as snapping her notepad shut. "It's just a hobby," she said, tucking it away behind the counter. "So anyway, what are you training for?" she asked, shifting the focus back onto him. "Some sort of marathon, you mentioned earlier...?"

"Yes. The Peel half-marathon," replied Luke, jogging on the spot to emphasise the point.

Libby rolled her eyes. "Ah. *Half*-marathon, is it?" she teased. "I've done loads of those, myself. But if it's not a *full* marathon, then it's hardly worth getting out of bed for, now isn't it?"

"Ah, so you've done these before? It's not too late to sign up, if you're interested," Luke informed her happily. "I can put your name down for you, if you like?"

"Sign up?" asked a startled Libby. She hadn't expected Luke to call her bluff like this, as she'd only been joshing him. "Oh, em... I might have been over-egging the pudding, somewhat," she confessed. "I mean, I haven't actually..."

"There's also a five-kilometre race as well," offered Luke. "We could be training partners, if nothing else?" he suggested, dangling the carrot.

Libby glanced at Luke's well-toned legs, and then back up to his smiling face. "All right, I'm in," she said, raising her hands in submission.

"Cheers," said Luke. "I'll give you a ring about that drink, yeah? Oh, and of course I'll pop back in to pay for this," he told her, holding up his new book.

"Sure, sure. Sounds good," said Libby, clenching her fist in a celebratory *yes!* motion the instant Luke turned his back and headed over towards the entrance door.

"Oh. And, Luke?" she said, calling after him. "Can you put me down for two places on the 5k run?

CHAPTER ONE

"No problem," Luke answered. "You, and...?"

"Me and Freya," said Libby, rubbing her hands together like a Bond villain.

"Freya?" asked Luke. "She runs as well?"

"No, she doesn't," replied Libby. "But she bloody does now."

Chapter Two

Libby peeled open one eye. The narrow strip of sunlight breaking through her curtains was agony as it burned into her retina, but she couldn't bring herself to turn her head for fear that moving her head in any way, given her current condition, might possibly produce results even more unpleasant. She pulled her duvet up over her face in an effort to provide relief from the sunlight, but as she did so her elbow brushed up against something lying beside her. Something large. Much too large to be her cat, Catticus. She froze in panic, as she definitely did *not* recall having come home with anybody the night before. She lowered the duvet ever so slightly, opening her other eye as she did so, so that she was now fully sighted. Without turning, she snuck a furtive glance from out of the corners of her eyes, dreading what she might find, wondering whose head might be revealed resting on the pillow next to her and praying to all that was sacred that it was vacant. There was indeed someone there. But, fortunately, it was only Barney.

"You scared the bejeezus out of me, Barney!" exclaimed Libby in relief. She took hold of her oversized stuffed polar bear and gave it an affectionate embrace. "Don't mind my stale breath, Barney," she told Barney. "Last night, Aunty Freya thought two drinks somehow meant ten," she explained. "My goodness, what *is* that?" she added, wincing. "Barney, what in heaven's name is that hullabaloo, do you have any idea?" she asked her bear. But, sadly, Barney had no answers to give her.

Pneumatic drills and such had invaded Libby's dreams. When she'd awoken, she just assumed it'd been a remnant of the one too many drinks she'd had. And yet, even now, the noise persisted. She hoped it would disappear, but it didn't. They were either building a multi-storey car park next door, or her gran was up to something at this ungodly hour... which turned out to be not so ungodly as she thought, actually. *"Ten-thirty?* That can't be right," she said, struggling to focus on her bedside clock through the sleepybugs still in her eyes. "Oh, fiddlesticks," she moaned. Libby was an early riser by nature, so the realisation she'd slept in on her one day off a week wasn't greeted with much enthusiasm.

Libby threw the duvet off, relieved, at least, that she was the only one under it — present polar bear company excluded, of course — and headed off to find out who or what was making the persistent racket she found so vexing to her ears and to her hungover noggin.

Down at the base of the stairs, Libby peered up the hallway towards the kitchen, where it was becoming apparent that this — judging now by the increased volume coming from that very direction — was the source from whence the mystery noise was originating. She took a step closer, and she pressed her hand to her mouth as her gran's bum appeared into view, just for a millisecond, before disappearing as quickly as it arrived. Libby didn't know whether to be alarmed or amused. But as she got closer to the kitchen, and as her head cleared from half-sleep to full wakefulness, she realised the noise she was hearing was in fact music. And, along with the tempo of this music, her gran's bum was keeping time, appearing and disappearing from view in measured beats. Intrigued as to what the rest of Gran might be up to, aside from merely the bum portion, Libby approached with caution so as not to startle her, taking up a position resting against the doorframe, where she waited for the dance music that was playing in the kitchen to come to its natural conclusion before venturing to speak...

"I'd say those look very much like my gym leggings, if I'm not entirely mistaken?" offered Libby, whilst admiring the dexterity she'd just witnessed of a woman who was due to turn eighty later that year.

CHAPTER TWO

"Oh, hello, dear. You're finally up?" said Gran, by way of a greeting. "Anyway, yes, they're very comfortable," she declared, giving the waistband on the leggings a twang. "I wasn't sure if they weren't perhaps a little too figure-hugging, though, which is why I thought I'd close the blinds over."

"Very considerate of you, Gran, especially with Amorous Andy living across the way," said Libby. "Him catching a glimpse of you doing a workout wearing skin-tight Lycra, at his advanced age, could well have been enough to see him off."

"Amorous Andy? Why do you call him that?" asked Gran. "He's just lonely, is all, poor thing."

"And randy," Libby pointed out. "Very, very randy."

"Ah. Fair point," Gran conceded. "And speaking of which, you were quite late coming in last night, I noticed," Gran added with a mischievous grin. "Did you pull?"

"Did I...?" asked Libby, somewhat confused.

"Pull," repeated Gran, waggling her eyebrows.

"I'm sorry, I don't..." replied Libby, uncertain as to how to respond, and wondering if Gran was implying what it very much seemed she was implying.

"Is that not what you call it now?" responded Gran.

"Has anyone *ever* called it that?" asked Libby with a gentle snicker. "But, no, Gran. No, I didn't, to answer your question."

"Libby, you're blushing," Gran told her. "I can always tell when you're lying to me, young lady, and your blushing makes it obvious," she pointed out. "So spill it!"

Libby smiled. "You read me so well, Gran," she replied.

"You *weren't* blushing, actually," revealed Gran. "But now you may as well tell me!" she said, giggling.

"That's a dirty trick, Gran!" protested Libby, but laughing as well. "Anyway, I'm too hungover to go into details, Gran," she went on. "Although, honestly, there really aren't any details to go into, I promise. I *do* have an upcoming date, however, if you absolutely must know, though the specific day and time is yet to be determined."

"Oh?" said Gran.

"Yes," replied Libby. "Suffice to say, he's athletic and extremely good-looking. And, he of course has the most impeccable taste in women."

Gran gave her a wink. "Atta girl, Libby. Never forget for a moment how special you are."

Gwen Tebbit, or Gran, as Libby liked to call her, on account of her being her gran, was a simply beautiful and delightful person. Libby completely adored her. Gran was also completely crackers, of course, but that was part of her appeal as far as Libby was concerned. She was the youngest old person that Libby had ever known, with an infectious energy and enthusiasm that just made folk around her into nicer people. She had a zest for life that was rare to witness in someone of her advanced years. One day you might find her in Peel Harbour engaged in a paddle-boarding lesson, for instance, and the next she'd be learning how to carve tree trunks with a chainsaw! Every day was a new challenge for her. She was inspiring.

"There's coffee there in the pot, Libby," offered Gran, who was stretching off at present, straight-legged, touching her toes like a gymnast. "Help yourself, dear. It looks like you could use some," Gran added, now upright and reaching up towards the ceiling.

"I think you're definitely right about that," agreed Libby, pouring herself a generous cup from the percolator. She held the cup in her hands, letting it warm her fingers, and held it up to her nose to take a sniff. "Mmm... that's so good," she said, closing her eyes, inhaling the welcome scent, and enjoying the wonderful aromatherapy the coffee was providing.

"Remember, you promised me a walk and an ice cream today!" Gran reminded her. She had both of her hands on her hips now and was twisting from side to side.

"Don't worry, I haven't forgotten," Libby assured her, even though she only remembered it just now as Gran had said it. "I just need toast with lots of butter, and then a good shower," she told her.

"Don't forget to slather on the Marmite!" said Gran.

"In the shower? Gran, that's just weird," Libby answered. She may have been slightly hungover, and also not fully awake yet,

CHAPTER TWO

but Libby could still provide her gran well enough with a gentle ribbing when an opportune moment presented itself.

"It's got loads of B vitamins! It's good for you!" insisted Gran, apparently unconcerned as to whether Libby should be eating it or applying it to her skin as an all-over body wash.

"I'll have to take a pass on the Marmite, I think," declared Libby. "Never did get a taste for that stuff. Sorry."

"Suit yourself, but all them B vitamins is good for vigour!" replied Gran with a shrug. "Anyway, I'm going into the garden for ten minutes on this," she said, picking up her skipping rope from one of the kitchen chairs. "Does wonders for your arse," she declared happily.

"I hope you've got a sports bra on, Gran, otherwise Amorous Andy is going to think all his Christmases have come at once," advised Libby with a smirk, and adding, "That is, if he doesn't keel over from a heart attack!"

"Hey, if you've got it, flaunt it," said Gran, with a suggestive wiggling of her wiggly bits.

Libby deposited two slices of bread into the toaster and, as she waited for her toast to pop up, briefly considered taking up Gran's lead and stretching off, but she decided the stretching could wait at least until her second cup of coffee was had. With morning callisthenics ruled out for the time being, her thoughts drifted instead to the night before. She'd been hoping, despite it being strictly a girl's night out, to bump into Luke the previous evening. But she supposed, on reflection, that it was just as well she hadn't. After all, she didn't want to appear over-eager and scare the poor fellow off. And she even had a hazy recollection of telling Freya something to that effect, that she'd planned to play it cool. Yet even with such sentiments having been duly expressed, she couldn't even wait until the toaster had done its job before her phone was unlocked, just to, perhaps, see if she'd had a text from a certain someone.

There weren't any from Luke, as it turned out, but there were a handful from her female friend.

Freya:
> Is that what you call playing it cool…!??

"Hmm," murmured Libby, chewing her lower lip. This opening salvo from Freya had certainly piqued her interest. *What did I do?* she wondered. She was also impressed that Freya was up this early on a Sunday morning (early for Freya, that is) to send such a text until she realised it was sent at 03:26 and so, in fact, likely on her way home from the night before.

Freya:
>You better not have texted him!

With this second message from Freya, Libby was starting to read between the lines. Perhaps she hadn't played it quite as cool as she recalled, having been under the influence of copious amounts of prosecco as she was? Afraid of what she might find, she went to her outbox instead, praying there weren't any texts to Luke there amongst her sent items. There weren't, which was good news, as was the sound of the toaster popping. She set her phone down and attended to her toast, applying a generous application of butter whilst the bread was still warm. She placed the toast on a plate, and then returned to the kitchen table. Once settled back into her chair, she took a bite of toast, and then picked her phone back up. She went back to her inbox, where she knew another seven unread messages from Freya awaited. Freya could be quite the author, it would appear, when pissed and wandering home.

Freya:
>You said you were going to play it cool. Your words.
>But telling his mate you wanted to have all of Luke's babies is not that!

"Oh, bugger. Did I actually say that?" Libby wondered aloud. She looked up at the ceiling, narrowing her eyes, trying to recall the events of the evening before. Libby had to admit Freya had a point. If she had indeed said that, then such a declaration of intent wasn't exactly indicative of playing it cool, now was it?

The next several messages from Freya were gobbledegook, consisting of random numbers and letters, likely as a result of all the alcohol consumed getting the better of her. But then there

CHAPTER TWO

was one final message in which Freya seemed to regain clarity, forming actual intelligible words again. Libby was apprehensive about opening it on account of the all-caps lettering she saw in the preview pane. But finally she did, and braced for impact.

Freya:

> AND I CAN FORGIVE YOU FOR MANY THINGS LIBBY. BUT SIGNING ME UP FOR A RUN!!!!! ME RUN?????? WTF!!! HOW AM I SUPPOSED TO RUN FOR ONE MILE!!! YOU WITCH!!!!

Libby sucked in air through her teeth. She didn't know why Freya thought the race was only one mile. A little white lie on her own part, maybe? A simple misunderstanding on Freya's? Either way, she'd worry about how to break the news to Freya that the race was actually 5 km rather than one mile a bit later, maybe a little closer to the time. But the good thing for now, at least, was that she'd not drunk-texted Luke. And whatever she may have told his friend, well, she just had to hope he was too inebriated the previous evening to recall it anyway.

She did have a vague recollection of something a little more innocuous being discussed the night before, something to do with running and training. And, indeed, this would explain the Couch-to-5k app having been downloaded to her phone. And it would also explain why her socks and trainers had been placed strategically at the foot of her bed, which she must have done as a visual reminder of her intention to commence with Operation Get Fit upon awakening. But, no, this was more of a Couch-2-Couch day, she decided, with slippers on as opposed to trainers, and maybe watching a few films on the telly. The only venturing outside that she'd be doing today, aside from the walk and the ice cream she'd promised Gran, was perhaps a trip to the local shop for some lovely chocolate Hobnobs. After all, who would ever start a fitness regime or diet on a Sunday? Rather, that's what Mondays were for, it seemed to her. And, also, if she was going to start a training regimen soon, she'd need to get her strength up, she reckoned. And so that's where the chocolate Hobnobs came in — she needed to properly fortify herself! It was pure Science, it was.

Gran dabbed at her eye with a sleeve of the thick, comfy cotton dressing gown she'd changed into, and with her bright pink gown matched in colour by that of her equally comfy plush slippers. The exercises and walk a little earlier had given way to rather more of a lazy Sunday afternoon, and the two of them, her and Libby, both appeared to have been consumed by the sofa such was their current relaxed state. Also largely consumed at this point was the supply of chocolate Hobnobs, with the package placed between them now nearly empty. The pair of them were almost like twins. Granted, they were separated by more years than Gran might perhaps care to admit, but their corresponding blonde hair and hazel eyes were most definitely from the same bloodline.

"I love watching An Affair to Remember," remarked Gran. She sighed, and then after a long pause she said wistfully, "He was always my dream man." And then she sighed again.

Libby wanted to smile but she couldn't. She had to employ her ventriloquist skills again, on account of the face pack she'd just recently got up to apply (in part to prevent herself from eating any more lovely, lovely chocolate Hobnobs), a face pack that would likely have cracked if she moved her cheeks too much. "Who? Cary Grant?" she asked, teeth clenched together, her lips barely moving, and this reply being in reference to the film they were watching.

"Your grandad," answered Gran. "Your grandad looked a bit like Cary Grant. And whenever I watch this movie, I can't help but think of him. A proper gentleman, he was. Always opened the door for me wherever we went, never cursed. I don't recall him ever raising his voice to me, either. Not even once. A right proper gentleman. I'd have to say they broke the mould when they made your grandad, Libby."

Libby reached over and patted Gran's hand. She missed her grampy as well.

"You just couldn't help but love the silly old sod, now could you?" added Gran, welling up once more, and necessitating a

CHAPTER TWO

further dabbing about the eyes with her free hand not currently being patted by Libby. "I shouldn't watch these Cary Grant films, Libby. They always bloody set me off!"

Libby gave her Gran's hand a gentle squeeze and then released it, allowing her gran to use both hands now in order to mop up the tears, as it was now becoming a two-sleeve task.

It'd been five years or so since Bert passed away and whilst Gran tried her best to present a brave front, Libby knew the loss of him tore her up inside. Libby herself had nothing but fond memories of her grampy, and with this treasure trove of pleasant memories primarily centred around idyllic days spent on and around the beach. He could, for instance, she recalled, build the most wonderful sandcastles, that both she and all of the other children on the beach would marvel at. He also always had a tale to tell, and through the naïve eyes of a young child every story he told was to be taken at face value and not to be questioned as anything besides the complete truth. As she grew older, she did of course begin to harbour doubts as to whether her grandad did in fact invent the world's first space rocket as he claimed, or, for that matter, whether he really did discover the Isle of Man as he always told her, planting a flag on its shores upon his arrival and claiming it for the Tebbit family. But, at the time, she swore blind to her friends that her grandad was King of the Isle of Man, and she, by extension, a princess!

Trips to the Isle of Man as a girl had always generated a mix of emotions for her. At the start of the summer holidays, waiting with her parents at the ferry terminal in Liverpool, she was fit to burst. Endless days spent by the seaside awaited, and their journey of several hours across the Irish Sea, once aboard the ferry, simply could not pass by quickly enough. She willed that ship to get a wriggle on and deliver them to their destination in Douglas, for every single second spent on the beautiful island where her grampy may or may not have been king was precious to her. Her parents would accompany her, enjoying a portion of their summer on the island, and then, going back to work, they would allow Libby to stay a few weeks longer to be looked after by her doting grandparents. Even now, if Libby were to close her eyes, she could still see her parents waiting there at the ferry terminal, come to collect her at back-to-school time. She was thrilled to be reunited with her parents, of course, after what to a child seemed like a very long absence from their company, but her departure from the island was always an occasion tinged with sadness at having to say goodbye to her grandparents and returning to her rather more ordinary life in the UK. Friendships, adventures, and further wonderous discoveries would have to be put on hold, yet again, until she could return to the island the following year.

"So how's that book of yours coming along, dear?" asked Gran once the film was over and the mopping-up exercise with her dressing gown sleeves complete, bringing Libby out from her reminiscing and back to the present.

With Libby's face being tightened up from the drying mud mask, she answered Gran's question with a simple shrug of the shoulders and a grunt. Also, she didn't really know what to tell Gran anyway, because the truth was, the book wasn't going as well as she'd hoped it might. She enjoyed the romantic notion of being sat in a bookshop, penning her bestselling novel between customers, with a lovely view of the beach and the sea through the shop window. But the reality was, she was finding it a bit difficult. She was onto the third draft of her regency romance novel by now, for instance, and still, reading it back to herself, she was struck by how many times she'd used certain words and phrases like *heaving bosoms, buxom, desire,* and *throbbing* this and *throbbing* that. The book was, by her own reckoning, pretty much rubbish. She'd likely have given it up some time ago if not for the enthusiastic support and encouragement of the select few friends and family members she'd told about it, who were all genuinely interested in the progress of her novel and keen to learn what headway she'd made on it. After several months of effort, however, all she had was a notepad full of scores and scores of crossed-out and rewritten lines that still weren't entirely to her satisfaction. In frustration, she'd even switched over from writing to doodling at one point, spending several hours and multiple attempts at illustrating her leading man, replete with a washboard stomach that you could grate cheese on. But,

CHAPTER TWO

unfortunately, she was even less of an artist than she was a writer and so the results of this exercise weren't pretty. As far as the writing, though, she was nearly ready to perhaps call it a day and resign herself to the art of selling books rather than the art of creating them.

"Your grandad wrote a book, Libby, did I ever tell you that?" asked Gran. "It must run in the family, writing books."

"Hmm?" said Libby, perking up. This was news to her. She prodded one of her cheeks tentatively, feeling out the state of her constricting mask. Nearly there. But she couldn't wash it off quite yet. And so, without speaking, she simply waved her hand to Gran to encourage further explanation regarding this new information.

"I thought I'd mentioned it to you before, no?" answered Gran. "I suppose I didn't, then," she went on. "Well, anyway, when I say a book, it was more of a journal, really. A series of them, actually. I thought for certain I'd told you about these, Libby?"

Libby shook her head in the negative, but appeared very interested, and so Gran continued.

"Well, it was certainly a surprise to me at first as well," said Gran. "Would you believe that we were married for thirty years before he'd even mentioned he'd written them? He was worried about me reading all his innermost thoughts, the big dafty that he was." Gran drifted off just for a moment, a twinkle forming in her eye at the thought of her beloved. "It's been a fair few years since I last read them," she continued. "But you can have a read of them yourself, Libby. If you like?" she offered. "It's nice to read through and witness the transformation of him being a youngster and then turning into the gentleman he became. Oh, and there's also a bit in there about how we met," she said, tapping the side of her nose. "Although I don't want to spoil the ending for you as to how that particular bit turned out," she added with a gentle laugh, before suddenly looking more serious.

Libby could see Gran was in imminent danger of welling up once more at the memory of losing her husband and, worried her gran's dressing gown sleeves didn't have too much more absorption capability remaining in them, reached out to take Gran's hand again to comfort her. But Gran shooed Libby's hand away and smiled.

"I'm fine. I'm fine, dear," said Gran. She cleared her throat, pulling herself together, and then continued. "Well, anyway, apparently, he'd kept a diary when he was a lad," she went on, brightly. "But it was only when he was in his late teens that he started up again."

It looked like Gran was about to say more, but Libby was pressing her cheeks like she was examining a freshly baked sponge cake for doneness, and, finally satisfied that it was time, got up to head over to the bathroom. She held a finger in the air, indicating for Gran to please hold that thought for a moment, pointed to her masked face, motioned in the direction of the bathroom, and then mimed the opening of a book in her hands and nodded towards Gran encouragingly.

"I'll go and fetch them while you chisel that hardened muck off of your face," said Gran with a laugh, taking Libby's meaning, as she was quite good at the game of charades.

And then, fifteen minutes later and reappearing rather rosy-cheeked...

"I look much fresher now," declared Libby as she re-entered the room, and happy to be able to speak normally once again. "If I'd had a better night's sleep, I'd be positively radiant!" She then reclaimed her spot on the sofa near her gran, and noticed the books resting there on Gran's lap like a sleeping cat.

Gran offered the journals a fond, gentle caress, before then handing them over to Libby. "These are very special to me, Libby," she said. "Take good care of them while they're in your possession, yes?" she asked.

"Of course. Yes, definitely," Libby assured her.

"Right, then," said Gran, satisfied. "Well, now that our Cary Grant session is over, I'll need to get changed out of my dressing gown and get ready for my hot-yoga class!"

Libby took hold of the journals and, with Gran now off to prepare for her upcoming yoga class, handled the books like a historian entrusted with sacred texts. There were four in total, A4 in size, with cream paper held in black hardback binding. Aside from a little damage to the corners, they were in remarkably fine

CHAPTER TWO

condition considering their age. She lifted the one on the top of the pile, opened it up, and instinctively placed her nose inside to take a whiff of history written on the pages. The first thing that struck her, upon pulling back and taking a good look, was the uniformity and neatness of the handwriting on display. The spacing was cramped, though, as if maybe paper were a rare commodity in those days, which, who knows, perhaps it was.

Libby didn't expect it, but before plunging ahead to read anything yet, a cold shiver ran through her, accompanied by a sense of guilt from the fact that she was about to pry into somebody's most intimate feelings. Perhaps this was why her grandad had kept the writings to himself for so long. She closed the journal for a moment, out of respect, and held her hands flat against the cover, knowing that her grandad, as a young man, had held in his hands the same object on many occasions. In a way, she could feel him, the two of them linked, through the book. It was a comforting thought, and it brought a smile to her face. She was just about to open the journal back up, then, and delve into its contents when...

Her phone, resting on the arm of the sofa, lit up. She winced, wondering if it was Freya, eager to regale Libby with another description of something else embarrassing she'd said or done the evening before. "Oh, fudge!" she cried, upon picking up the phone and seeing Luke's name there on the screen. There was nothing wrong with receiving a text from Luke in and of itself, of course. It could generally be considered quite a good thing, in fact. But in relation to the horrifyingly embarrassing things she'd said the night before, she couldn't help but wonder if word of her wanting to have his babies — and not just have them, but have *all* of them, no less — might possibly have reached him. Was he texting to express grave reservations about further associating with such an obvious madwoman?

Libby opened the message with one eye closed, fearing the worst, but was put at ease as she read on by its casual, friendly tone, and with nothing at all about having babies in it, thank goodness.

Luke:

> Hiya, Libby. Just thinking of you. I believe I promised you a drink, yes? How's Thursday night? I'm off for a run just now. Hope the training is going well!

Libby lowered the phone with a relieved, contented grin. The training was going fairly well, she felt, even though it hadn't yet commenced, as such, necessarily. She *had* managed to download the running app onto her phone, though, and that was a good start, surely? No need to rush into things, after all. Baby steps! And the actual *training* portion of the training would begin the following day. Most likely, that is. Probably. If the weather was good.

Yes, life was looking pretty rosy for Libby right about now, she reckoned. Her skin was flawless at present, she now had an upcoming date, and by this time next week, being entirely optimistic, she'd be effortlessly running 5K without breaking a sweat. Granted, her credit card bill was a bit of a grey cloud hanging overhead, but what was the point in having a credit card if you didn't use it?

Libby turned her attention back to the collection of journals in her possession. She looked briefly heavenward, in search of permission to continue. "Grampy, I'm sorry I'm about to start reading your journals," she said. "Is this okay? If you don't want me to read them, just send me a sign, all right?"

Libby's eyes ventured around the living room, out through the window, and then back into the living room, glancing about. No apparitions appeared, no lightbulbs blew, and no flash of lightning was seen outside nor crack of thunder heard. Libby took this as permission enough to read, and a partially hungover Sunday afternoon seemed as good a time as any to tuck in and make a start of it.

"Now then, Grampy," she said, opening the first of the journals, and placing her finger on the initial entry and reading the date listed there. "Right, then, Bert Tebbit. What were you doing in the year nineteen sixty-three, on the fourth of January, on a Friday?"

Chapter Three

"They *call* it a 5k, Freya. But as you've said yourself, it's only a mile, and so not at all as bad as it sounds," offered Libby by way of clarification. She felt the need to offer up some kind of explanation or other, as the distance could be seen right there plain as day in bold lettering on the entry form Libby had given her.

By her own admission, maths had never particularly been one of Freya's stronger subjects in school. Libby was still concerned, however, that Freya would still see straight through the bogus explanation she was providing regarding the true distance of the race they were about to start training for. But while Freya did seem somewhat sceptical, she appeared to accept Libby's nonsense nonetheless, at least for the present moment. And so, with that, the two of them were soon dressed in their running gear and limbering up outside the bookshop.

Libby wasn't ordinarily much of a runner, really, but she was something of a gym bunny, at least, and so her general fitness was fairly decent overall. The same couldn't be said about Freya, though. Freya wasn't fat, necessarily, but she did refer to herself alternately as *cuddly*, *fluffy*, and *doughy*, and this was not for no reason. She'd made several bold statements over the previous few months, in fact, about hoping to lose some weight. Libby was more than pleased to help her friend out in this respect, and reckoned training for this upcoming race provided the perfect opportunity for Freya to shed a few pounds. The fact that it *also* provided the perfect opportunity for revenge on Libby's part was just a happy coincidence! But while Libby was busy stretching out her hamstrings in preparation for their run, Freya was more concerned about other things being stretched out...

"Oi, these leggings aren't see-through, are they? Or are they?" asked Freya, turning to look at her own rear like a dog chasing its tail. "I'm worried they're maybe spread a bit too thin, if you know what I mean? You think I should have got a larger size, Libs?"

"I'm sure you're fine," answered Libby. "Besides, nobody cares about what you look like when you're out exercising," she offered. "More than anything else, people just feel guilty because they're not doing something themselves."

"You sure?" replied Freya, not entirely convinced, and craning her neck for a better view of her posterior region. "Because I'm pretty sure you can see my knickers," she observed, causing the approaching man walking his dog to slow his pace considerably.

"Ladies," said the dog-walking man cordially, tipping his hat, and holding his gaze a little longer than his wife would likely have approved of had she been present.

Freya, her spirits buoyed by both the warm summer's evening and the dog-walking man's eyes lingering admiringly on her bum, launched into an enthusiastic series of star jumps... but her energy levels very quickly showed signs of immediate strain, as did her bra. "Bloody hell, I'm going to knock myself out with these two," she said, looking down cautiously at her chest.

"Are you not wearing a sports bra?" asked Libby, who'd moved on to a series of calf stretches in her own warm-up routine.

Freya shook her head in the negative. "How could I be? I don't even own one," she said. "But, yeah, now you mention it, it might have been a good idea, because I'm in real danger here of giving myself a couple of black eyes on this run!"

"Well I do appreciate you agreeing to this, Freya, unforeseen hazards notwithstanding," replied Libby sympathetically, and dipping down into some deep-knee bends.

"Agreeing? Funny, but if memory serves, I seem to recall you signing me up without my consent...?" chided Freya, narrowing her eyes in playful reproach.

CHAPTER THREE

But Libby was pretending not to hear Freya just then. Now finished with her stretches, Libby clasped her hands together in front of her, raising her chin up, and taking a deep lungful of the salty sea air. She looked like a choir instructor, ready to lead her group of students into song. As far as inspiring backdrops went, you could certainly do a lot worse than this pretty seaside location, she thought.

"We'll head towards the castle. Just there," suggested Libby, pointing to the huge castle in the distance, not too terribly far away, in case Freya might have somehow forgotten there was a large castle nearby, and where precisely it was located. "The route I have in mind, we'll head out from here, straight up, then take a left, detouring by the quayside, encircling the harbour, and following that road until it comes back up and around to the castle. Then, we circle round the castle, and then retrace our steps until we're back to where we started. Sound good?"

Freya curled her lip, not particularly liking the sound of this suggestion at *all*, as it should happen, and being rather horrified by the length of the proposed route, actually. But, after a long pause, she acquiesced with a shrug. "All right. Go on, then," she responded, inviting Libby to guide the way.

"Tally ho!" said Libby, leading the charge, first on the narrow pavement outside the shop and then, after looking both ways, crossing the road and heading towards the walkway on the promenade. With the warm evening air caressing her cheeks, she could already feel the calories starting to burn off. She glanced over her shoulder in order to offer up some words of encouragement to her running companion carrying steadily on behind her...

... And was surprised to find no one actually *there* behind her. "Freya...?" asked Libby uncertainly, wondering if she should be worried that something might have happened to her friend, or if, rather, she should be cross that Freya had possibly skipped off and made a hasty exit and furtive getaway while Libby hadn't been looking.

"Over here! Man down!" Freya called out.

Libby then caught sight of her, not yet past the pub three doors up from the bookshop, with one hand of Freya's propped up against the phone box there and her other hand held behind her lower back. From the look on Freya's face, Libby could tell that something was terribly amiss. "Oh my goodness! Hold on, I'm coming!" shouted Libby, making haste towards her stricken friend's position.

"Medic!" cried Freya in response.

"What's wrong? Have you hurt your back??" Libby asked upon arrival, concerned for her friend, as Freya was in some obvious distress. But, upon closer inspection, Libby could see that Freya wasn't rubbing her lower back at all as she'd initially thought. Instead, she appeared to be rummaging around back there, dipping her hand into her nether regions. "Freya, what on earth are you...?" she began.

"My bleedin' knickers have ridden right up my bum and are cutting me like cheese wire! I need to fish them out!" exclaimed a distraught Freya. "Maybe... maybe we should head back and call it a day?" she asked tentatively.

"Nonsense!" insisted Libby. "Just pull the fabric out of your arse, soldier! C'mon, Freya, we've totally got this! This run doesn't stand a ghost of a chance against us!" she cried, rallying the troops, as it were.

"It's not ghosts I'm worried about," grumbled Freya. But with knickers retrieved and put back into place, they were soon on their way. Freya was puffing like a steam train by the end of the promenade, but at least she was giving it a go. As for Libby, she kept her mind occupied by daydreaming about Luke, imagining the two of them out on a training run together, working up a bit of a sweat as they jogged along, and then perhaps stopping at a little café for a glass of something cold, at which point Luke would naturally confess that he'd been admiring her from afar for months, this whole time smitten, and that...

"Medic!" shouted Freya, once more.

Libby turned around and, once again, Freya was not behind her. By this time, they'd moved away from the promenade and to the quayside, where the boats moored in the harbour bobbed gently on the ocean waves, and Libby had been so lost in her thoughts that she hadn't noticed Freya wasn't faring quite as well as she was. In fact, Freya was now on all fours, and causing the passing traffic, much like herself, to slow to a crawl. "Are you okay there, luv?" one concerned motorist called over in concern. "Do you need assistance?"

"Yes, you can give me a lift," moaned Freya, without raising her head. "To the hospital!"

"I've got this, but thanks," said Libby, having returned to her afflicted ally, and gesturing the helpful motorist on with a friendly, appreciative wave. And then, "No woman left behind, Freya!" Libby added, addressing her fallen comrade now, and extending a hand to her.

"I can feel a pulse in my tongue," declared Freya, using Libby's help to right herself. "And with all the bouncing around my boobs are doing, my nipples have been rubbing against my bra like bloody mad. I need ice cubes!"

"Ice cubes on your nipples? How kinky!" laughed Libby. "But are you sure it's the right time for that?"

"It's always a good time," responded Freya, laughing as well.

"Alright, let's walk for the rest of the way," suggested Libby. "That'll allow your breathing and your pulse to return to normal, and at least we'll still be getting a little bit of exercise as we go along, more leisurely though it may be, yeah?"

"Sounds good," Freya happily agreed.

"And just think, keep in mind that this is the worst you're ever going to feel," added Libby, accentuating the positive. "Because you're going to get stronger each and every time you go out for a run! Am I right?"

"Wait. *Each* time, did you say?" replied Freya, not liking the sound of Libby's words so much anymore all of a sudden. "You mean there's going to be *other* times as well?"

"Sure, you're my training partner, aren't you? And we're totally going to smash that 5k run to pieces!" proclaimed Libby enthusiastically.

"I don't like running," came Freya's prompt and very much less enthusiastic reply.

Freya trudged on like a moody teenager who'd been asked to rake up the garden leaves instead of, say, playing on one's Xbox, as any sensible person should prefer. Thirty-six agonising (as far as Freya was concerned, at least) minutes later, however, and their inaugural training walk/run had managed to finally reach its conclusion, and it couldn't be more welcome a conclusion in Freya's opinion. Returning to their point of origin, the Peel town centre, it was mutually decided upon that some form of liquid refreshment was in order. A stylish and somewhat cleverly named juice bar called The Orange Peel had just recently opened, catering to the health-conscious and those eager to fill their bodies with nutritional goodness, and this was Libby's first choice. Directly opposite was the beer garden of the Red Lion, and this however, at Freya's firm, unwavering insistence, was where she and Libby ended up, sat outside, and enjoying a pint of cider apiece.

"I didn't like that, Libs. I can honestly say, I didn't like that at all," Freya informed her friend. "With the jostling about from all that damned exercise, it feels like my internal organs aren't in the right place anymore," she declared, taking a large, palliative slug of cider in order to soothe her innards. "Bloody hell, I'm not going to be able to walk properly tomorrow, I don't think," she moaned in despair

"You did absolutely amazing, Freya, all things considered. I'm really very proud of you," Libby replied encouragingly. "So how are the nipples?" Libby asked, wincing sympathetically.

"I think I've got third-degree burns," answered Freya. "I can feel the heat radiating from them," she said, peering down the front of her top. "I think they're going to need a bit of TLC later on. Would you like to—?"

"No, you can do that yourself!" Libby said with a laugh, not allowing Freya to finish her sentence, and entirely mistaking her meaning.

"I meant do you want another pint, silly!" Freya corrected her friend.

"What? But we haven't even finished our first one yet," Libby pointed out.

"Maybe *you* haven't, but I have," said Freya, downing the rest of her pint in one go. "See? All gone," she declared triumphantly. "Time for another!"

CHAPTER THREE

"Freya! We've just been for a run to try and get ourselves into shape, and here you are quaffing pints like a madwoman!" Libby protested.

"Yes, but it's refreshing, innit?" said Freya with a shrug and a cheeky, unrepentant grin.

Libby sighed. "Fine. Go on, then. Yes, please," she said, giving in without further arm twisting required, and feeling guilty about it but not so much as to decline Freya's offer. "Unlike you, I'm still working on my first," she noted. "But I may be done with it by the time you come back with the second."

"And if you aren't, then I'll just have to drink yours as well!" offered an ever-helpful Freya.

Libby eased back into her chair at the outdoor beer garden, watching the world drift lazily by. The setting sun offered up the last of its warming rays, which Libby gratefully accepted. There were certainly worse places to live, she mused, stretching contentedly like a cat next to a roaring fire, and then taking another sip of her cider. Her reveries were interrupted, however, as a small Jack Russell dog arrived on scene, travelling up the pavement running alongside the outdoor seating, and stopping to take notice of one of Libby's trainers, giving it a good sniff.

But it was not an interruption that was unwelcome. "Hello there, little guy," Libby offered, leaning forward and reaching down to pat her new furry friend. "Aren't you a cute little..." she began. But with teeth suddenly exposed, and followed by a growl that was rather brash and impertinent for a creature of such diminutive dimensions, Libby cautiously pulled her hand back, very slowly, not wishing to make any sudden moves that might set the discourteous little imp to biting.

"Hulk! Stop that!" shouted the dog's owner at the end of its extended lead, catching up to the dog, and then pulling the wee blighter a safe distance from Libby's feet. "Sorry about that. He's a grumpy little bugger when he's hungry, and..." the fellow went on, but abruptly trailing off. "Oh. Oh, it's you. Hello, Libby," he said, standing before her now, his tone suddenly acidic. "If I'd realised it was you, I might not have leapt to your defence quite as quickly as I did," he added.

Libby rolled her eyes. "Hello, James," she replied, addressing him in a manner that was not the slightest bit friendly. "And I should have known it was your dog immediately, as soon as it started growling, as the two of you have so similar a disposition," she observed. "Nice name for the dog, by the way," she remarked drily. "Is it meant to be ironic?"

"Come on, Hulk, let's go," replied James, without bothering to answer Libby directly, "I wouldn't get too close to her anyway, as you don't know what you might catch. She might have... might have... bookworms or something!"

And with that, James turned on his heel and whisked Hulk away before his canine companion could get even angrier and, like its superhero namesake, burst out of his clothing (which, in this particular case, as it should happen, was an adorable ickle wickle tartan doggie vest). Or, then again, James's hasty retreat could just as easily have been attributed to James being angry at himself for flubbing that last insult of his so very badly.

"Bookworms?" said Libby in response — and with her face screwed up in a mixture of confusion and derision — though it was uncertain if James could even hear her by now. "Did you seriously just say *bookworms*? You great gormless twit, that doesn't even hardly make any—"

"Your best mate bought himself a pet rat?" asked Freya upon her sudden return, placing two pints of golden cider on the table as she watched James move off into the distance.

"It's a Jack Russell terrier. And a particularly ill-mannered Jack Russell terrier, at that. Much like its owner," said Libby. "And he's most certainly not my best mate."

Freya sat down, glancing up the street at the retreating figure of James once more. "Hmm, I don't know, ill-mannered he may be. There's something about him, though, don't you think?" she considered aloud. "Kinda sexy nerdy, it seems to me. *Sexdy*," she said, coining a new term. "Or, *nerxy*, perhaps," she added, now on a roll, and pleased with her own wit.

"Are you kidding me?" replied Libby. "Freya, he parts his hair on the side, has glasses, and was wearing a t-shirt with bloody Men in Black on it, for crying out loud. I wouldn't exactly call

CHAPTER THREE

that nerxy," she said, adding, "Well, I mean, I would never call *anything* nerxy. But, you know."

"Well, first of all, there's nothing wrong with parting your hair on the side. And there's certainly nothing wrong with wearing glasses, either, if you need them. So you're just being silly there," responded Freya. "And as for the shirt, I think it was the Green Hornet he was wearing, actually, if I'm not mistaken."

"Which is even worse," commented Libby. "So, what, you like him or something?" asked Libby. "Do I need to remind you that *nerxy* devil of yours nearly put me out of business not too long ago?"

"Do I like James? No, I wouldn't say I *like* him, necessarily," replied Freya. "All I'm saying is that he does possess a certain charm about him that some women might find appealing. Not *me*, of course. But *some* women."

Libby shook her head in disbelief. "Freya, he owns a comicbook store, for god's sake," she said, as if that should be explanation enough as to why no woman in her right mind would ever find him the least bit appealing. "And a comicbook store that he tried to relocate to *my* bookstore, I might add, in case you've already forgotten," Libby continued. "In fact, that dirty rotten scoundrel, need I remind you, Freya, that…"

But Freya didn't appear to be listening.

"Oi! Freya!" shouted Libby, snapping her fingers to rouse her vacant friend, who seemed to have drifted off, as she was looking into the distance at present, her eyes glazed over. "What are you doing? Are you still thinking about him?" asked Libby.

"Maybe a little bit. Yes," Freya admitted, her eyes returning to focus. "It's the glasses and side-parting, I reckon. I think it's maybe a Clark Kent type of thing?" she suggested, raising her pint glass to her mouth.

Libby didn't have many enemies, but James was one of them. Well, enemies would perhaps be too strong a word. But it would be fair to say that if they'd still been young schoolchildren, for instance, James would most assuredly not have been receiving an invite to any of Libby's birthday parties. And for Libby that was pretty much as serious as things could ever get, as anyone and everyone would normally be welcome to attend.

Libby's current interaction with James had begun several months prior, during a time in which losing her shop had most unfortunately been a very real and frightening prospect, with the business that her grandparents had set up and operated for over forty years in danger of going tits-up on her watch. A fellow retailer, James ran — and continues to run — a small shop on the outskirts of town, where he sells comics and other such related merchandise. With his regular clientele at his bricks & mortar location, along with flourishing online sales as well, he was doing well for himself. He was doing well enough, in fact, to warrant an invitation from the local council to become a small business mentor. And this in fact had been Libby's introduction to James as, amongst other duties in his mentoring capacity, he would occasionally pop round to the other shops in town to offer his advice, with her shop included among them.

At first, James had been pleasant enough, and Libby was grateful for any useful tips on offer. But she couldn't shake the uneasy feeling that there was perhaps something more to his visits than that. It was the strange way he looked around the shop while he was there, as if he was sizing the place up. And then when he started throwing comments into the conversation about how he was outgrowing his own shop, and how he wished he had a shop as spacious as Libby's, well, she knew she wasn't just paranoid. With his father being Libby's landlord, and with her rent in arrears at the time, she couldn't help but feel she'd allowed a fox into the henhouse by granting James such access to her shop. And then, indeed, her suspicions were in fact realised when she was issued an eviction notice from James's father, with James coming in the very next day with a tape measure, measuring things, and completely abandoning any pretext of trying to help her. He'd obviously wanted the place for himself since the first time he'd stepped inside and checked the place out, it seemed to her. Libby had been devastated at the prospect of closing the shop. But the thing that hurt the most was having to tell her gran that the shop would soon be closing its doors after so many years in business. Some sleepless nights followed, but fortunately, a very timely uptick in trade around Christmastime had saved the day — and with it having been much busier

CHAPTER THREE

around the holidays than usual, even — allowing her to settle her arrears and forego eviction. After that, business had been relatively slow during the first few months after the winter holidays had passed, as they often were, but things fortunately picked up again with the warmer weather and the resulting influx of beachgoers and tourists, again, as they often did. Thus, she'd managed to stay afloat. But the lessons learned from all this were that, one, she needed to up her game and not be complacent where the business was concerned and that, two, James was not one to be trusted and was most definitely not her friend.

But Libby didn't wish to think any more of James at present. She ran her thumb around the rim of her glass, a gentle smile emerging. "I've been getting to know my grandad this week," she said, moving the conversation to more pleasant a subject.

Freya narrowed her eyes. "Your grandfather? Is he not dead?" she asked, never one for sugar-coating a question.

"Well, yes. But Gran let me have his journals to read through," offered Libby by way of explanation in regard to her apparent ability to communicate beyond the grave. "It's funny, I feel a bit like an archaeologist discovering an ancient tomb for the very first time. Well, not that my grandad's been dead for that long, I mean. It's more that I have that same mix of emotions they must feel as they examine all the ancient artefacts that have laid hidden away for so long, you know? On the one hand, I almost feel guilty for violating my grandfather's privacy. But, on the other hand, it's fascinating and exciting to learn about his life."

"What, like a diary, you're saying?" asked Freya.

"Pretty much, yeah. But in the form of larger journals. Several of them, in fact. I'm only into the first one so far," Libby explained. "Well, the first one we've still got, I should say. He wrote some when he was younger, but those are sadly lost. But then he began writing them again in his late teens, and these are the group that still exist. It picks up, in the first of them, when he's eighteen and just starting his first job."

Freya leaned forward in her seat. "And?" she asked, her interest piqued.

"And what?" replied Libby.

"And so what have you discovered?" answered Freya, adding, helpfully and instructionally, "Obviously, don't skip the good part."

"Well, he's just been offered his first job, as I said," Libby told her, smiling at the thought of how happy he'd sounded in the journal entries, pleased as Punch.

"Yeah...?" pressed Freya. She nodded, raising her eyebrows, and licked her lips in anticipation. "Doing what?"

"Something in printing..." Libby replied, searching her memory. "Em... typesetter, maybe, I think it was?"

"That's it?" replied Freya.

"Yes, I think that's it," confirmed Libby.

"No. I mean *that's it?*" asked Freya. She eased back in her chair, entirely underwhelmed over this revelation that didn't turn out to be really that much of a revelation. "That's a bit disappointing, Libby," she said. "The way you built that up, I thought you were going to say he worked for MI6 or something, or was maybe getting ready to rob a bank," she went on. "Something a little bit more impressive or dramatic than just a rubbish typesetter."

"No. No secret agent work that I'm aware of," Libby replied with a shrug. "Nothing of that sort to the best of my knowledge," she said, taking a sip of her cider, and then staring at the glass as she set it back down.

"Sorry. It *is* pretty cool that you've got these journals of his to read through," offered Freya, softening her tone. She could see what these writings meant to her friend, and she felt slightly guilty. "And it'll be interesting to see what he becomes later on, yes?" she added, trying to be a little more supportive.

"Ah. But I already know what he becomes," Libby answered. "Because I'm now running his bookshop," she happily pointed out, smiling. "But it's going to be interesting to read about him meeting Gran. So there's that. I do feel like, in a stupid sort of way, that I'm prying. Do you know what I mean?"

"It's not stupid at all," Freya assured her. "It's nice that you're getting to know a side of your grandad that you wouldn't have known otherwise, I think," she said. "You know what's a bit sad, though?"

CHAPTER THREE

"Braveheart!" replied Libby in an instant, with no hesitation whatsoever. "Bloody English soldiers," she added, closing her fingers into a tight fist. "Every time I watch that film, I always hope somehow it's going to turn out differently in the end. They should make a new version, with an alternate ending, where—"

"Every time with you and Braveheart!" said Freya, laughing, and seeking to derail this current Braveheart-related diatribe — only the latest out of many that had come previously — before this particular one could gain steam.

"Well it bears repeating, now doesn't it?" replied Libby with a cheeky grin.

"No, what I was *actually* going to say was sad... aside from Braveheart, of course..." said Freya, continuing her earlier point. "Is that people probably don't write journals much anymore. Everything's digital nowadays, you know?" she went on, waving her hands animatedly. "People live their lives on social media. No one writes anything down on paper anymore. And journals, like the ones you're reading, well, they've got no chance, do they? What are we going to leave for future generations? Some daft, stupid pictures online with more bloody filters than a water purification plant? I mean, and speaking of these pictures, half of those people don't even look anything like themselves! God help them if they go missing and their family members provide their most recent picture, right? Wouldn't have a snowball-in-hell's chance of finding them, what with those stupid Bambi eyes and whatnot. Or what about the ones with the doggy nose and ears? How ridiculous are those?"

"Wait, didn't I just see you post one of those the other day?" interjected Libby.

"That's not the point!" Freya protested, smirking.

"Oh? And what *is* the point, then?" asked a grinning Libby.

"It doesn't matter!" replied Freya. "Anyway, look what you've started, Libby. You've got me on a rant!"

Libby eased Freya's pint glass further towards her, feeling she'd benefit from another dose of cider right about then. "Here, it'll calm your nerves," she suggested.

"I suppose it will," replied Freya in response. "I suppose it will at that," she agreed, taking a large somewhat-less-than-dainty sip. "Ah! Better!" she declared, once that was sorted, restorative tonic having been successfully delivered. "Now. What were we talking about again...?"

"I think I might write my own journal when I've finished reading my grandad's," Libby considered aloud. "Imagine how nice it would be for my grandchildren to be able to read about my life in years to come?"

"Yes. Absolutely riveting material," said Freya, with a comical roll of the eyes. "After all, who wouldn't want to read about the two of us working every day, single, and then going to the pub once a week on the weekends?"

"I'm sorry. Hang on. Did you just say *once* a week?" interrupted Libby. "Since when has it ever been once a week? And this makes it two times," she said, waving her hand across the beer garden where they were presently sat. "Two times, *so far*, in a week where we're supposed to be training!"

"Well, usually one time, on the weekend, if you consider the entirety of the weekend as being one single trip...?" Freya gamely suggested.

"Fair enough," replied Libby with a chuckle. "But, anyway, I take your point about my journal perhaps not being too terribly exciting to read. Still, it'd be nice to have something for them to physically pick up and hold in their hands, something where they could actually smell the ink on the pages. Also, the thing with a journal is that it's pure, yeah? And by that, I mean the information you put in it is raw and unfiltered. You're telling the complete truth, as near as you can. And of course that's what I hope to get from Grandad's journals — the clear, unvarnished truth. Or the truth as he saw it, at least, through his eyes."

Freya nodded. "It's always good to tell the truth, Libby," she said, in a loaded kind of way. "For instance, how old did you tell Luke you were, out of curiosity?"

"Ah. Well. Sometimes a slight extension of the truth, or an omission of the truth in this case, isn't such a bad thing. Besides, what's my age got to do with anything?" said Libby, smiling over the rim of her glass as she took a sip.

"It's just a for instance. No special reason I ask," replied Freya, enjoying another sip of her own cider.

CHAPTER THREE

"I'll reveal my age, maybe, once we've had our second date, I suppose," Libby put forth. "Because there's certain to be a second one, mind you, once he realises just how fabulous I am."

"Naturally," Freya answered.

"Anyway. On the subject of truth," continued Libby, "I could totally see your knickers through those leggings, by the way."

"You could?" asked Freya. "Why didn't you say so? Why didn't you tell me?"

"Well I'm telling you now, aren't I?" Libby rightly pointed out. "And what kind of a friend would I be if I didn't?"

"You could have told me *before* I went to get these drinks, at least," Freya was quick to mention. "I had half of the pub turned around and staring when I was stood at the bar!"

"Well now you know why," Libby advised happily. "Anyway, you can get something more suitable before our next outing," she added. "Something that doesn't show your arse off to the whole world, right?"

"Our next outing?" Freya said with a whimper. "Please don't remind me there's going to be a next time."

"All right. I won't remind you there's going to be a next time," replied Libby.

"But you just went and said it again!" cried Freya.

"Right. And also, on the subject of telling the truth..."

"Yeeeesss?" replied Freya, uncertain where this was leading.

"You know how I told you that 5k race of ours worked out to be about a mile?" answered Libby. "Yes. Well. About that..."

Chapter Four

4th January 1963

I've done it! Letter received today and Mum cried as she was so proud – Art college here we come. I'll miss getting a regular wage but if I spend any more time working in a printers, I'll go insane. Be a bit strange going back to a classroom and I still don't know what I want to do for a job but at least I know what I DON'T want to do.

I saw THE absolute perfect suit in the Harrow Bros shop window on the way to work. It's teasing me every morning and every night as I walk past. Grey, double-breasted slim fit. Just like Sean Connery wears.

Me and the boys are invited to the re-opening of the Red Lion on Saturday. Wish I had the new suit as I'm certain Helen's going to be there. Might need to tap Dad up for a loan on it, although I'm not sure I should press my luck as I'm already hoping he's going to help with some money when I'm at college as it is.

7th January

Head's still killing me. The Red Lion seemed like it was in as much of a desperate state as it was before it shut for re-furbishment. Still, Helen was there as expected. She was looking lovely. I spent the whole night buying her drinks and being the perfect gent. It cost me a fair amount of dosh, which was fortunate at least for the dodgy-looking biker who eventually swept in when I was in the loo and ended up taking her home. I saved him a bloody fortune. What an idiot I am, and my mate Terry took great delight in taking the piss. Helen did however seem impressed when I described to her the new suit, at any rate. Can't wait to get that suit. Plan B required for my future love, on the other hand, as I'm pretty certain Helen is not it.

Going to look for a scooter with Terry tomorrow. Wanted a car but my bank balance doesn't. Car might get me laid quicker than a scooter, but can't afford it. New suit will absolutely get me laid, though.

15th January

Helen waved to me today, which was nice. She was on the back of her new boyfriend's motorbike. I hope they'll be very happy together. Arsehole. Him, that is, not her. Okay, both of them, actually, now I think on it.

Shouldn't have gone out last night as I'm skint again. Gran's birthday tomorrow so my 'suit saving fund' will be diminished as I want to take her out for a slap-up lunch to celebrate. She deserves it.

16th January

Six gins Gran had. Six!!!! She may be getting on in age, but she can certainly knock them back still! I was struggling to keep up. She does make me laugh and is mad as a box of frogs. Told her I had a girlfriend. She always presses the point when she's drunk as, in her words, I'm not getting any younger, and felt like I had to give her something. Didn't want to let her down, so a little white lie doesn't hurt? She asked me her name and I had a mind blank. So I started to say Helen, for lack of anything else coming to mind. But then I remembered Helen on the back of that motorbike, and I didn't want to say Helen. So it somehow ended up coming out of my mouth as Helga. And, thus, I now have a girlfriend called Helga. Wasn't sure if Helga's a

CHAPTER FOUR

German name or Scandinavian. Could be either, maybe? Dunno. So when Gran asked what Helga did, I covered all bases by saying an au pair and part-time masseuse. I think I quite like the sound of this Helga of mine, actually! Just hoping Gran can't remember me telling her all this. Otherwise, I'm going to have to ask Terry to wear a blonde wig and stuff a few socks down the front of his shirt.

It was a great afternoon with Gran, but the suit fund has taken a hammering. It's also not helped by the fact I've now actually bought a scooter. Suit will just have to wait a little longer, I suppose. Terry thinks the only thing holding the scooter together is the rust, but what does he know? He's not a mechanic.

26th January

Bloody scooter broke down on the way home from work. Bugger. Just noticed previous diary entry about Terry. I think I'll just tell him I was struck by a lorry or something and that's why it's out of commission already. I had to push the thing for over a mile to get home. I split my good trousers in the process and I now have a three-inch tear directly up the crack of my arse. Mum's on the case. I was going to go around and demand my money back for the scooter but the guy who sold it was an evil-looking bastard so I think I'll give it a swerve and take it to the garage. I've now got no motorised transport, no girlfriend, and now an unwanted air vent in my good trousers.

I'm thinking of going to the Isle of Man TT races in the summer. Terry's not keen but I love the racing and I'm sure I can talk him around. Mum's sister owns a shop and lives over there so can put us up, so we'll only need the boat ticket and beer money. I was hoping to bring my scooter over but that's not looking likely. Still, it's a few months away so plenty of time to get the old girl fixed up. And speaking of old girls, I mentioned the trip to Gran and now she's wanting to come with us as well. Not exactly sure having Gran tagging along is going to improve our pulling abilities but we'll have a laugh. Don't think she'd fit on the back of the scooter but as the thing is currently in pieces that doesn't matter for now.

4th February

Terry's mate, Greasy Barry, is going to have a look at my scooter. Terry said he knows what he's doing and is cheap. He'll need to be as I've not got any cash. Gran, god love her, has said she'll pay to get my scooter fixed.

7th February

I thought Greasy Barry got his name from being good with engines or something. Not so. It's on account of his hair. Barry is a fishmonger by day and engine tinker by night. He's cheap for a reason and the reason being he's bloody useless. Three hours he spent looking at the scooter and it's now in pieces on our garage floor. Mum came in twice to check that the chest freezer hadn't gone on the fritz and all the fish in it spoiling because the smell of haddock was so strong. Barry, the cheeky sod, also wanted paid even though he accomplished nothing. I gave him half a tub of white emulsion we had laying about by way of payment as he happened to mention he was going to paint his living room, and he seemed happy enough with that thank f---.

17th February

I've been working on a portfolio for art college. Watercolour mainly. I love getting out in the country, sitting under a tree and painting. It takes me away from everything. I've parked the idea of a new suit for the time being. I need to save every penny for college. Hopefully I can get a couple of commissions for artworks?

CHAPTER FOUR

18th February

I think I'm in love!!!

A girl on the bus noticed my sketchbook so I showed her a couple of pictures. She was beautiful and smelt like fruit. Strawberries, I think? I believe her name was Gwen, but it was a bit noisy on the bus. I asked her twice but couldn't hear well enough to be sure what she said. I just looked at her gormlessly as she told me. She must reckon I'm a complete plum (speaking of fruit). She said she works at The Crown on Saturday nights. I did catch that part. It wasn't an invite, really, more a statement of fact. Still, I've got a funny feeling we'll be heading on over to The Crown on Saturday night. She was lovely. As she was getting off the bus, I shouted over that I'd be happy to paint her. I don't know why I did that. I've never done that. She must think I'm some sort of weirdo. She was lovely (it must be true as I've said it twice). She looked like a film star. I think I still need that suit. I hope she doesn't think I'm a weirdo.

22nd February

I didn't tell Terry and the boys why I wanted to go to The Crown as they'd have taken the piss and said something to her. Turns out her name actually was Gwen, so I'd got that right after all. And the other thing I was right about was the fact she was lovely and looked like a film star. A bit like Natalie Wood, I reckoned, after getting another good look at her.

I didn't get to speak to her that much. Well, the only way I could speak to her was when I was ordering drinks.

Terry knew something was up when I offered to buy the first three rounds of the night.

Cost me more than I could really afford but it was worth it. I was half-drunk by the time I'd finished two minutes worth of total conversation with her.

She said she liked my paintings, so I said I'd take her out for a lesson and show her how to do it. She said yes. SHE SAID YES.

It's not a date, exactly, but it's as good as a date. I think? God, she's lovely. I think she might even be a bit older than me. I said I'd take her down to the river and show her how to do a pen and ink wash. She didn't have a clue what I was on about, but I had just smashed three pints in a very short amount of time so it might not have come out as intended.

I've got a date. Well, sort of. The only problem is that I said I'd pick her up on my scooter. A scooter that has more pieces laying about than a jigsaw factory.

I'm not sure what to wear to take a girl for a painting lesson. I might ask Gran as she's pretty good at this sort of thing. Of course I'll have to tell her first that, sadly, it's over between me and Helga.

Gwen is lovely.

Chapter Five

Freya walked up to the entrance of Libby's bookshop, glancing through the broad front window to see if Libby was behind the counter. She wasn't, but the lights were on so Freya figured she must be inside. "Bloody door," said Freya, struggling to release a hand on account of the largish white box she was carrying. Instead, she extended her right elbow, using it to press down on the lever door handle whilst trying to avoid spilling the contents of the box. Once the door latch was released, with great dexterity and balance, she eased open the wooden door with her hip, with the box in her hands remaining upright and intact.

"Thanks so much for the help with that door, Libs!" Freya said. "I know you're in here somewhere, and here I am only delivering my very best friend something special!"

Libby peered through a gap in one of the bookshelves she was presently stood behind. "What's that? Something special?" she enquired, removing a book to widen the gap and enhance her view.

"Ah! There you are!" replied Freya. She set the box she was carrying down onto the counter and extended her arms to the offering, introducing it like a gameshow host revealing a new item for contestants to bid on. "Yes, indeed! Something special!" she was happy to confirm, patting the top of the box, but very deliberately not giving away the secret as to its contents. "You'll have to guess what it is!" she teased.

"Well, just taking a wild stab at it here, I'd say... it's a cake?" proposed Libby, returning the book she was holding back into place on the shelf and ambling over to where Freya was standing for a closer look.

"Hey, no fair!" Freya protested unhappily. "How'd you know?" she asked, rather disappointed that the surprise was revealed before the box had even been opened.

"Elementary, my dear Watson," said Libby, raising a finger in the air. "You do work in a bakery, after all. And this box, right here, judging by the size of it, is of the type one tends to place a cake in. And so logic thus indicates that the contents of said box must include cake, or, at the very least, something very much cake-like in nature."

"A-ha!" declared Freya.

"A-ha...?" asked Libby, wondering why Freya was suddenly looking quite pleased with herself.

"But you don't know *why* I've brought it here," replied Freya, placing her arms across her chest triumphantly.

"Hmm," said Libby, mulling this over for a moment. "Okay, so it's not my birthday," she mused, thinking out loud. "But you *do* know about my special relationship with cake, the incredibly strong bond the two of us share, me and cake that is, and how famously we get on. So... if I were to hazard a guess, I'd have to say... you brought it here because you love me and want me to be happy...?"

"Wrong!" Freya shouted, even though Libby was standing right next to her.

"Wrong? What, you mean you don't love me and want me to be happy?" Libby pouted.

"Of course I love you, you dumbhead," answered Freya. "But that's not the reason!"

"Oh. Well... I dunno, then," replied Libby with a shrug of her shoulders.

"Open it!" suggested Freya, pleased that a small element of the surprise remained, at least.

"Hmm, interesting," said Libby, merely bending over and giving the box, and whatever contents might have been inside, a good, preliminary sniff.

"Open it!" Freya said again.

CHAPTER FIVE

"It *is* for me, you say?" asked Libby, stroking the lid of the box affectionately.

"OPEN IT!" exclaimed Freya, the suspense killing her more than it was Libby.

"All right, all right, relax," Libby replied with a laugh, giving in, and not wishing for her poor friend to have a stroke. She pressed her nose closer, peering through the inch-or-so gap she created. "Is that...?" she asked, opening the lid of the box further to afford a complete view inside. "It's a doughnut!" she declared, with an excited squeal. "But... I thought it was a cake? Only... it's *not* a cake," she said, trying to work out just what it was exactly that she was looking at and admiring. "It's... *sort* of a cake... but a doughnut as well...?"

"A bloomin' *big* doughnut!" Freya declared proudly, looking over her friend's shoulder at the masterpiece she'd created. "It's a doughnut cake! A doughnut so big that it's a cake!"

"It's the size of a dinner plate," marvelled Libby, staring at the beautiful, wondrous thing her friend had made. "I think you've really outdone yourself this time, Freya. I could bloody kiss you!" she added. "But... that still doesn't explain...?"

"Here. This might help," replied Freya, handing over a small envelope, the type you might expect to accompany a delivered bunch of flowers.

Libby eased open the envelope and released the piece of paper from within on which there was a hand-written note. "I'm sorry about my dog trying to hump your leg," read Libby, reciting the note aloud. She gave out a nervous laugh, assuming this to be some sort of stupid Freya-type joke she wasn't getting. "I don't understand. You don't even have a dog," she said. "You're weird at the best of times, Freya, but this situation is even starting to surpass the time you suggested we streak at that charity football match."

"It's not from me, you nutter, and anyway you should have streaked with me as it was very liberating," remarked Freya, raising aloft her rather generous bosom in both of her hands in order to emphasise the point, before releasing a finger to then aim at the paper. "It's from James," she said. "Anyway, I've got to get back to work just now," she added brightly, turning towards the door, and appearing quite happy to leave her friend in suspense and without the benefit of further explanation.

"James? Ew, gross," Libby responded, wrinkling her nose. "Why would he do this?" she asked, following Freya to the door and not letting her get away so easily. "And his dog wasn't even trying to hump my leg, either! It was just sniffing my shoe!"

"I don't know. Maybe James is just projecting? Maybe that's what *he* wants to do?" suggested Freya.

"Ew. Just... ew," replied Libby. "Freya, how could you even be a party to this?"

"Well, he came into the shop and paid for it," Freya answered with a shrug. "I just work there, remember, so it's not for me to refuse business. Still, I did try to make you something special I thought you'd like, yeah?"

"A giant custard doughnut cake, yes," Libby told her, "which I'll now forever associate with the thought of James humping my leg. So thanks for that, Freya. You've just ruined my favourite thing, custard doughnuts, forever!"

"You're welcome!" Freya replied cheerily, turning to leave once again.

"You're not going to help me eat it, at least?" asked Libby, but it was the type of question that was clearly not supposed to be answered in any other way but a firm no. "Hang on," said Libby. "Is this not a bit odd?" she asked, causing Freya to pause and pivot round to face her again. "I mean, the last time I saw James, it was not exactly a pleasant conversation we had," she went on. "I thought the mutual dislike we held for each other was fairly obvious. And after that evil so-and-so tried to get me evicted from my shop so he could take over the location for himself, the last thing I want from him, the *very last* thing, is tokens like this. Surely he knows this? The whole thing is just weird, isn't it? I mean, is he stupid or something?"

Freya laughed. "You're talking about a man, keep in mind. All men are stupid, are they not?"

"Hmm, fair enough, you've got a point there," Libby conceded, laughing as well. "But, still. Even so."

CHAPTER FIVE

"Maybe he secretly fancied you all along, and that's why he was being a Grade-A arsehole?" proposed Freya. "Know what I mean?"

"Um... not really?" replied Libby.

"Okay, like, back when we were little kids at school, and a boy would punch your arm? Like that," explained Freya. "They'd punch your arm even though they actually really liked you, or *because* they actually liked you, as boys, being daft as they are, don't know how to express emotions properly. And so even though they like you, it comes out looking like the opposite."

"Ah. I see what you're saying," Libby answered.

"It's because guys are dumb! Nothing they do makes sense!" said Freya. "So the only way to make sense of their actions is to remember their actions make no sense," she offered sagely.

"Fair enough," said Libby again with a chuckle.

"Or maybe he's simply trying to make up for being a dick? It could just be as simple as that," Freya added. "You'd be surprised how many times my baking skills are called upon in service of someone trying to make amends for being a dick."

Libby pondered, for a moment, the options presented to her. "You don't think he *likes* me, though, do you? You know... like *that*?" Libby called after Freya, who'd started up the pavement on her way back to her own shop.

"What do I know? I don't claim to have all the answers! Most of them, yes! But not all of them!" Freya shouted back over her shoulder. "Anyway, don't eat too much doughnut cake, as you'll need to get into your disco knickers for your date with Luke later on tonight!" she added, and with no attempt to lower her voice in view of those passing tourists or locals out enjoying an early morning stroll. "That is, of course, before he tries to get you back *out* of your disco knickers!" she said with a cackle, evidently pleased at her own wit. And then she was off.

Libby stood outside her shop door, watching the retreating figure of her friend, and considering in her head the horrible, horrible possibility that James might like her. She shook her head, trying to clear that notion away, and she thought of Luke instead as she headed back in. She'd put on a kettle and make some tea, and she'd have some of that delicious doughnut cake, she decided. She'd focus not on who'd sent it, but on simply enjoying it for what it was, and whose loving hands had made it. Yes, a very large slice of custard-filled doughnut cake would soon set things right, she reckoned.

As it should happen, Freya's earlier playful admonition had, in fact, turned out to be rather prescient after all. Not the comment about Luke liberating Libby from her disco knickers, that is, as she hadn't even left the house to meet him at this point. But, rather, the prediction that she might wolf down far, far too much of that delightful doughnut cake.

Libby was, at present, stood only in her knickers, and daring bravely to look at her reflection in the full-length bedroom mirror. But her expression turned despondent at what she saw. "Aww," she moaned, looking at her rotund belly, "I look like I'm four months pregnant." She spun around slowly, like a rotisserie chicken on a skewer, affording herself a view from every possible angle, hopeful that one such angle might prove to be a bit more flattering than the last. But, sadly, none were.

"Curse you, you crazy, rubbish funhouse mirror!" she shouted at the mirror, as if it was somehow the mirror's fault for what she saw. Still, she held her current side-view pose for a long, lingering moment, caressing her belly with the palms of her hands, intrigued by what she might look like if she *were* actually four months pregnant. The irony was not lost on her, however, that no bloke in their right mind would want to get close enough to her to make that happen looking as she presently did, at least in her overly critical opinion.

The problem was, not only had she polished off much more of that obscenely delicious custard-filled doughnut cake than she should have that morning, but she'd then made short work of a spicy chicken wrap for lunch as well. And then, later, she'd been distracted by Igor the ice cream man on her short walk home, and had given in to temptation there also. If ever there was a deserving occasion to throw on her shapewear knickers, then this evening must surely have been it. But the education

CHAPTER FIVE

provided by Bridget Jones was not lost on Libby, and so she'd opted for something a bit more attractive in the undergarment department as opposed to perhaps something more slimming and stomach-flattening. Still, there remained the matter of her outerwear, and this was proving most vexing a problem to solve. So much so, in fact, that...

"Are you still alive in there?" asked Gran, tapping on Libby's door in concern after not seeing her for some good while.

"I'm fat, Gran!" declared Libby in despair. "And I don't know what to wear! I've tried about fifteen different outfits and they all look awful!"

"Pish-posh! There's nothing *of* you, Libby!" said Gran through the door. "But, if you are feeling a bit bloated," she said kindly, "then you know what to do, don't you?"

Libby walked over to the door and opened it a crack, peering out, and eager for whatever advice Gran might have on offer. "What? Star jumps?" asked Libby, figuring ten minutes or so of exercise couldn't hurt.

"No, no. Breasts," Gran put forth.

"I'm sorry. What, now?" asked Libby, uncertain she'd heard her gran right, even though they were nearly face to face.

"Breasts," Gran reiterated, confirming that Libby had indeed heard her correctly. She went on to explain: "You can't take two inches off your waistline with a few minutes' worth of exercise. But what you *can* do is add two inches onto your cleavage! And trust me, if you do that, and then undo an extra button on your shirt as well, there's not a chance that this boy's eyes will wander down far enough to notice how fat you are. And not that you *are*, mind you. You just *think* you are. But, still, if you're worried, then there's my advice."

"So... pad my bra, is what you're saying?" asked Libby, trying to work out Gran's meaning.

"Exactly!" affirmed Gran. "I think I used chicken fillets once, when I first started dating your grandad," she offered helpfully.

Libby pressed out her bottom lip as she contemplated this. Not the part about the chicken fillets, as that would be a bit messy, and also a waste of good chicken. But the idea in general of bolstering her boobs in one form or another.

"Thanks, Gran," said Libby. And then, once Gran was on her way, leaving Libby to her own devices once again, Libby was back in front of the mirror. Buoyed by Gran's words of worldly wisdom, she cupped her hands around her modest pair of boobs, pressing them together so that they looked like two bald heads sat in a prison of fingers. "Hmm, you know, this just might work," she announced to her mirror self.

And so, several more outfit changes later, Libby was on her way, headed to the rendezvous point of La Mona Lisa, the local Italian restaurant, looking absolutely fabulous in her forgiving jeans, low-cut top, and a bra that pushed up more than it held in. No coat was required on account of it being a balmy Isle of Man summer's evening. Luke had offered to meet her and escort her the short walk from her house over to the restaurant, but she figured she'd use this time instead to compose herself and perhaps give herself a final little bit of a pep talk to not make a complete and utter idiot out of herself, and so told him she'd meet him there. As she enjoyed the warm sea breeze stroking her perfectly styled locks, she winced at the painful recollection of the last date she'd been on, during which time she'd quaffed several glasses of red wine for some Dutch courage. As for making a complete and utter idiot out of herself, she'd only managed to go and fall asleep in the women's loo, now hadn't she? Her date thought she'd ditched him, and he ended up leaving. The restaurant owner, alerted by one of the staff at closing time about a pair of feet seen under the door of one of the bathroom stalls — and with no response forthcoming from the owner of said feet despite repeated verbal issuances of concern — feared the worst, and so called the police. The police, after receiving no response through the stall door either, had been fully prepared to break it down in order to retrieve the unconscious or perhaps even lifeless body. Someone suggested unscrewing the hinges, a power tool was retrieved, and they'd just started in on this solution when suddenly they heard snoring from behind the door. Libby did wake up in time to make it out under her own steam, which was fortunate as she'd fallen asleep with her knickers round her ankles. She didn't see Frank, her date, again. It was her first date with him and also the last. Since then, she had, at

CHAPTER FIVE

least, made a concerted effort to cut down on her drinking, aside from the occasional overindulgence thanks to Freya's insistent arm-twisting.

"Ah, my-a beautiful lay-dee!" said the friendly, charismatic proprietor of La Mona Lisa, Luigi, in his thick Italian accent, once Libby arrived at her destination and stepped inside. "You look-a like a million lira!" he told her, singing the words as he smacked his fingers against his lips. "But I no see-a any take-it-away order for-a you this-a evening, Miss Libby," said Luigi, running his finger down his notepad.

The Italian charm was always laid on rather thick, and Libby wasn't entirely convinced anyone could be *that* Italian, but she was always happy to lap up the praise nevertheless. "No, no," she said, glancing through to the seating area. "I'm not here for any takeaway tonight, Luigi, I'm here for a sit-down meal inside the restaurant this time."

"*Meravigliosa!*" said Luigi. "Your-a crayzee friend is no-a with you, though?"

"Freya?" asked Libby with a laugh. "No, I'm meeting a boy. A real boy," she told Luigi. And she instantly wondered, as soon as the words came out of her mouth, why she'd referred to her date as a boy, like she was at primary school, and also why she'd felt the need to specify that it was a *real* boy as opposed to... well, she wasn't even sure what.

"Ah! Very good!" Luigi answered agreeably.

"In fact, there he is," said Libby, spotting Luke and pointing over to his table. "There's my Pinocchio," she added with a giggle, in joking reference to her awkward 'real boy' comment, but Luigi just stared back vacantly.

"Ah," said Luigi, moving the conversation swiftly along. "The gentleman said he was-a waiting for a special lay-dee, but I no know it was-a you. I escort-a you to your table, Miss Libby," said Luigi, humming a melodic tune as he weaved his way through the tables in the dining area, leading the way, and offering a cordial smile to his other patrons along the route.

"*Signora,*" he said, pulling her chair back and inviting her to take a seat as soon as they arrived at their target. "You like-a the *vino?*" he asked "I find-a you an extra special bottle, yes? *Bellissima!*"

Libby gave a discrete glance across the table to see what it was that Luke was drinking, which appeared, upon visual inspection, to be a soft drink. Her mind also flashed back to the unhappy sound of a drill taking the hinges off of a toilet stall door. For both of these reasons, she said, "No, thank you, Luigi. I'll just have a mineral water with a twist of lemon, please?"

"Very good, Miss Libby," replied Luigi.

With Luigi having then bustled off to get her drink, Libby turned her attention to Luke. "You look very smart," she said, tilting her head and appraising him approvingly.

Luke, for his part, didn't scrub up too badly at all, was Libby's considered opinion, with his crisp white shirt contrasting nicely against his lovely sun-kissed skin. The ambient light from the flickering candle in the centre of their table twinkled on his blue eyes, eyes which were presently transfixed by Libby's bountiful cleavage, Libby couldn't help but notice, and a fact Libby was only too happy to observe. *Good suggestion, Gran*, she thought.

"You look very smart as well," said Luke. "I mean, you look nice. Very nice!"

Libby bit her lower lip, as she'd once been told it looked sultry. Or was it seductive? She forgot which, exactly. But, either way, it was something she saved for occasions such as this. Luke had handed her a menu, just now, but she didn't need to look at it. She already knew what she wanted.

"You know what you're having?" asked Luke, to which Libby nodded. "I take it you've been here before, then?" he asked.

"Yes, everything here is delicious," Libby answered. "And I'm pretty sure I've already made my choice," she added, exaggerating the chewing of her bottom lip, and narrowing her left eye slightly.

"Oh. Are you okay?" asked Luke, his voice full of concern. "Is there something in your eye?"

Seductive wasn't working out so well, not nearly as well as Libby had planned. "Here, hand me that menu again," she said, so she could at least go through the motions of deciding what to order, although honestly she really did know what she wanted as she always got the same thing. After two or three minutes of scrutiny, she peered over the top of the menu. "You know what you're having, Luke?" she asked, as if looking for suggestions.

But, at this point, Luigi reappeared, placing Libby's drink in front of her and then offering a gracious bow. "You-a going to have-a the usual, Miss Libby?" he asked, notepad in hand and issuing forth a friendly wink.

Libby hesitated, wondering whether to continue the pretence of attempting to decide what she wanted, but it was pointless. "Yes please, Luigi," she said, giving in. "But make it a small one this time?"

"Excellent-a choice for the lay-dee," said Luigi, putting his pencil to work. "One *diavola* pizza, small-a this time, with-a the extra spicy-a sausage, and-a with-a the usual side-a of-a the chips to keep it all-a company," he sang, tapping the point of his pencil down in a theatrical flourish at the end of transcribing Libby's order. "And-a for you, *signor*?" he said, turning to Luke.

"Just a house salad, please," Luke answered, pointing to his own selection on the menu.

"Excellent choice, *signor*," said Luigi, scribbling on his order pad, a contented grin on his wobbly, ruddy chops.

"A salad?" said Libby, once Luigi had moved away. "Are you trying to make me look bad, mister? Usually it's the woman who orders the salad," she teased.

Luke held his hands up in defence. "No, no, sorry, not at all," he said with a laugh. "It's just that I'm in training, so trying not to get too carried away," he explained. "But it's nice to see a woman with an appetite," he added. "Perhaps I'll help you out with a slice or two of your pizza, if you like?" he suggested. "Or a handful of your chips?"

"Not if you want to keep your hand!" replied Libby, feigning offence at having to share her food. "I'm just joking, of course. You can always eat anything of mine any time you want," she quickly reassured him. But then, horrified at how saucy that might have sounded, she immediately changed the subject. "So, em... how *are* you?" she asked.

"Nervous, if I'm being honest. I always get nervous on first dates. In fact, I even turned up an hour too early because I forgot what time we were supposed to meet," confessed Luke. "This is my third vodka-and-Coke as I've sat here," he said, tapping his finger on the side of his glass. "Well, Diet Coke, at least," he added. "I *am* in training, after all," he said, smiling.

Libby smiled back, but then opened her eyes wide in sudden realisation. "Wait, hang on," she said, pointing across the table to his glass. "That's got vodka in it, you said?"

"Yes," Luke answered. "Why, do you maybe want something stronger than—?"

"Yes, please!" said Libby without hesitation, not even letting him finish. "Red wine," she told him enthusiastically.

Luke laughed, a gentle, good-hearted laugh. "No problem," he said amiably. "When Luigi or someone else comes back, we'll sort you out."

"Thanks," answered Libby. "I won't drink too much. But, heck, no sense being a teetotaller if I know you're drinking as well."

First dates were never the most relaxed of affairs. You were putting yourself out there to be judged, and with the constant fear of rejection ever-present. There was concern about whether the other party would even turn up in the first place or, if they did, whether they would end up looking for any excuse to make a hasty exit and bring the date to a premature conclusion. It was an emotional rollercoaster ride looking at the face of your date and trying to gather some indication that they were remotely interested in you or if, rather, they were in point of fact mentally arranging their washing basket such was their abject boredom. Presently, with Luke, it seemed like it was going reasonably well. They'd spoken before, of course, and they certainly knew by now that they liked each other. But this was their first proper date, and so how it could've turned out in the end had been anyone's guess. But, again, it looked to be going along fairly well, all things considered. Libby *did* have a habit of often prattling along at pace, and with the nerves of a first date thrown into the mix, she soon found herself going ten to the dozen. As they passed the time waiting for their food to come out of the kitchen, she was encouraged, though, by the periodic appearance of Luke's white teeth as he smiled at the punchline of her jokes like the dutiful date he was, and, currently, she was just coming to the conclusion

CHAPTER FIVE

of a (she hoped) humorous anecdote that she anticipated he would likewise appreciate...

"And that's why I thought the capital of the Netherlands was called Hamster Jam!" she told him, laughing before she'd even got to the end of her sentence.

"You're quite mad," remarked Luke, smiling broadly. Then he glanced up to Luigi, who had reappeared and was stood before them.

"This is-a for the special lay-dee," Luigi announced, revealing a long-stemmed red rose from behind his back. He presented it ceremoniously to Libby, who graciously accepted, offering it a courtesy sniff before placing it on the table next to the glass of red wine she'd managed to obtain a bit earlier.

"Sorry about that," whispered Libby once Luigi had removed himself from their presence again. She pointed to the rose and leaned closer. "I mean, I bet they'll add the cost of that to the bill, right? I think it's some sort of scam where restaurants give out a crappy, expensive-looking rose like that, as if the woman is actually going to be impressed by it or something."

"Oh," replied a dejected Luke, not making eye contact. "Actually, em... well, it was actually me that brought it along," he went on, forlornly. "I'd asked that Luigi chap to bring it to you. I thought it would be romantic. I'm, ah... I'm sorry you didn't like it."

Libby blushed, squirming in her seat. "No, no, I do!" she said, immediately changing tack, and suddenly appearing very fond of the rose, which she now lovingly picked up. "It's beautiful, but it's just that I wasn't sure that... that..." she floundered, unsure how to wriggle her way out of this embarrassment.

"I'm joking," confessed Luke, a crooked grin across his face. "That was nothing to do with me at all," he told Libby, bringing her anguish to a grateful end.

"Oh, you right bastard. Don't think I won't remember that," said Libby, smirking back, and placing the rose back down onto the table. But her attention was diverted momentarily as she spotted a young lady heading their way, food in hand. "Ah, this could be our dinner," said Libby rubbing her hands together in anticipation.

"Good evening," said the polite server upon reaching the table. She placed the modest but delicious-looking salad instinctively in front of Libby, and then prepared to deliver both the pizza and chips to Luke's side of the table.

"Sorry. Excuse me," said Libby, holding up her hand like a policeman directing traffic. "But the salad is for my friend," she said, passing Luke's salad over to him. "The rest of the order is just here," she advised, patting the newly cleared spot in front of her.

"Ah. My mistake. So sorry," said the young lady apologetically. "I just assumed that…" she started to say, but trailed off for fear of causing any offence. "There we go, madam," she said, placing Libby's portion of their table's order in its proper place. It didn't leave an awful lot of white tablecloth still visible over on Libby's side.

"I've not eaten a thing all day," offered Libby by way of false explanation, looking up to the server from her bounty, briefly over to Luke, and then back again at the server.

The young lady passed no visible judgement, although what she may have thought privately was anyone's guess. "Enjoy your meal," she offered with a cordial, gracious smile, and then took her leave.

"Wow, I really hadn't expected it to be quite so big," marvelled Libby, taking her plate and transferring a slice of the pizza over to it. "It's one thing when you order it in a box for take-away, you know? But it looks so much larger laid out in front of you," she remarked. "So you're going to help me with this, right?" she asked of Luke, wagging her finger between her pizza and chips.

"You're certain I won't lose any digits?" Luke teased.

Libby laughed, then assured him, "Yeah, all joking aside, I'm definitely going to need some assistance here."

"That does indeed look good, I have to admit," said Luke, eyeing Libby's food admiringly. "I may relieve you of a slice or two," he readily agreed. "I've been trying to eat a little more sensibly, in general, now that I'm in training for the upcoming race," he went on, making pleasant conversation. "I wouldn't ordinarily take a half-marathon so seriously, but all the lads at the rugby club are putting in a friendly wager. They've all thrown a hundred quid

CHAPTER FIVE

into the hat, and the fastest race time takes all. So, as you can imagine, there's a fair bit of dosh up for grabs, and hence me eating salad," he said. "Well, salad and maybe just a slice or two of pizza," he added, correcting himself, and giving Libby a wink. "Anyway, how's your own training going for the 5-K race?" he asked, probing around his bowl and spearing a chunk of tomato and green sweet pepper along with a forkful of lettuce.

"Mmm," offered Libby as a temporary placeholder, her jaw being presently occupied in processing a slice of pizza. She held her finger to indicate a response was forthcoming. "Great," she said eventually, whilst wiping a dribble of tomato sauce from her chin. "Yeah, I'm really into this running thing."

"Great! What's your PB at present?" asked Luke.

"My... PB? What, you mean, like, peanut butter?" Libby replied, her mind really more on food than on racing at the moment.

Luke laughed, assuming Libby was being silly. "No, seriously. What's your personal best?" he asked.

"Ooohhh, my personal best," Libby said, laughing along and playing like she'd only been joking when really she hadn't. "Hmm, okay, let's see, then... personal best, uh... that would be..." she said, stalling for time, trying to come up with some sort of figure that might sound reasonable, as she hadn't expected to be put on the spot like this. "Well, I think it was... nineteen minutes and change?" she offered, hoping this to be suitably impressive and yet at the same time plausible and realistic.

"Wow!" said Luke, pressing out his lower lip. "That's seriously impressive! Nineteen minutes?"

"And change," Libby pointed out, quickly realising she must have miscalculated her fictional time, and hoping to mitigate the damage as best she could.

"Still," said Luke. "At that sort of pace, I imagine you'll be near the top of the women's leaderboard for the 5k, yeah?"

Libby nodded along, but panicking inside, figuring she now needed to manage expectations here. "Maybe it was miles I meant? I always get the two mixed up," she said, immediately backtracking. "Ah, yes, that's it," she said confidently, "it was nineteen minutes and change for the five-*mile*, not the 5k."

"Well, even so, if you can run five miles in that amount of time," said Luke, "then they should put a saddle on your back and enter you in the Grand National!"

"Em... chips?" asked Libby, pushing her chips towards him in a desperate distractionary manoeuvre. Fortunately, it seemed to work, with Luke raising his fork and skewering a selection of the tasty little devils and then plunging them into his mouth. But, sadly, Libby's sense of relief was not to last for very long.

"Oh, I meant to say, my mate Ryan saw you out the other day and he said you were looking good," Luke offered, unfortunately changing the subject to something even more squirm-inducing as far as Libby was concerned.

Libby lowered her head as a rush of embarrassment flooded her cheeks crimson. "Oh, crappity," she said. "I was really kind of hoping he wouldn't remember."

"Not remember you were looking good?" asked Luke. "I'm not sure I follow."

"No, I mean about him seeing me in general," explained Libby. "And, more specifically, the part where I told him I wanted to have a certain someone's babies," she elaborated, her cheeks turning an even darker shade of red.

"You said you wanted to have Ryan's babies?" replied Luke, smiling politely like the dutiful date he was, but a fair bit confused.

"What? No. I said I wanted to have *your* babies. All of them, in fact," Libby answered, but immediately regretting it because, from the look on Luke's face, it was obvious he had no idea what she was talking about. Worse yet, he wasn't saying anything in reply. He was just raising an eyebrow.

"Wait, hang on," said Libby, realising she'd made a terrible mistake on top of an already terrible mistake. "Your mate Ryan. Is that not the one who's got those stupid stripes shaved into the side of his head?"

"That's him," confirmed Luke.

"Oh, sorry. I mean, that's your mate, isn't it? I shouldn't say he's stupid-looking," Libby answered apologetically, afraid she was digging an even deeper hole for herself.

CHAPTER FIVE

"It's okay, I agree. Those stripes *are* pretty stupid-looking," Luke told her with a chuckle.

"Thanks for that, at least," replied Libby. "But... if that's Ryan... then that's not the mate of yours I was talking to last Saturday night, was it?"

Luke shook his head. "I don't know anything about that," he said. "Ryan was on the beach with his girlfriend a few days ago and saw you out running," he told her. "He said you were looking strong and travelling along at a pretty good clip."

"Ah..." Libby faltered. "Well... it's just... okay, then, as far as the other thing I was... I didn't... I mean, I was only..."

But she'd broken her shovel on the hole she'd dug. "Okay, look, I can't actually run 5k in nineteen minutes," she confessed, reasoning on a diversionary technique away from all talk baby-related. "Probably closer to forty, actually," she admitted. "Maybe fifty, after I've had this lot," she added with a sigh, twirling her finger around in indication of her pizza and chips. "It's going to take me a few extra trips to the gym to work it off, that's for sure. Anyway, I'm sorry, I just prattle on when I'm in social situations and a touch nervous."

"Nervous?" asked Luke.

"Of course. Nervous, yes," said Libby. "I can be a bit of a..." she began, looking for the most accurate word of what she could be. "A nincompoop, I guess. Wait, no, not a nincompoop, that's not right. A clutz, maybe?"

"A clutz?" replied Luke. He didn't seem convinced.

"Well, a verbal clutz, is what I meant," Libby clarified.

"Ah," said Luke with another chuckle. "Well I think it's endearing," he assured her, taking her hand in his across the table. "Besides, Freya warned me in advance that you can be a complete disaster at times. So, fear not, you're just living up to my expectations."

"She said that, did she? And this is meant to be reassuring somehow?" Libby answered, with a smile which told Luke that she wasn't really offended.

"Yes, and yes," Luke replied with a laugh. But then he turned more serious, tilting his head this way and that, and staring at Libby's face lovingly, longingly...

Or so it seemed to Libby. She squeezed his hand and looked back at him in eager anticipation, certain that something very romantic was about to issue forth from his lips.

"Libby...?" he said.

"Yes?" she replied, giving his hand another gentle squeeze.

"Only..." he said.

"Only?" she replied expectantly.

"Only you've still got a bit of tomato sauce on you," he said, motioning to her chin. "Just there. I think it's starting to dry out at this point, so..."

"Ah. I need to go to the bathroom anyway," she said, pushing her chair back and getting up. "Thanks," she told him.

As far as romantic words went, it certainly wasn't what she'd been hoping for. Still, she'd take what she could get, she supposed.

Once in the bathroom, Libby pressed her face closer to the mirror. The tomato sauce on her chin wasn't a small spot like she'd thought. Luke had been too polite to say so, bless his heart, but it was actually a huge bloody splodge is what it was. With a firm fingernail and some splashes of water from the sink, it was soon taken care of, however. Following that, she straightened up and assessed herself in the mirror once more. At least her boobs were holding firm, she was happy to see. The push-up bra was a mite uncomfortable, but it did produce the desired effect. She looked admiringly at her own figure. She'd never contemplated breast enhancement, but she was certainly pleased with the present, temporary increase to their apparent volume, even if they were starting to hurt a bit from the restrictive nature of the bra. She maintained eye contact with herself in the looking glass for several seconds. "Right, you. Stop being such a nob," she said, aiming an accusatory finger at the face staring back at her. "Relax and be normal. It's going well. Or at least, well-*ish*," she said, closing her hand into a fist and offering her twin in the mirror an encouraging fist pump. "Okay. Nice talk," she told her reflection.

Libby had a quick wee and, on her way out the door of the loo, reached behind her back to adjust her bra strap a little, and then gave her boobs a fluff with her hands. With her face sorted, her

CHAPTER FIVE

bladder lightened, and her boobs bountiful and brilliant, she took a deep breath and then started to make her way through the dining area over to her date. She felt good as she walked back to their table. And she must have looked as good as she felt, also, she thought, as it didn't go unnoticed by her that several pairs of eyes zeroed in on her as she walked past. Even Luigi, on the phone as she came abreast of him, looked like his eyes were going to pop out of his head as she brushed by. Sure, she was a bit of a car crash on occasion, but when she pulled out all the stops Libby was able to carry off an elegant air of sophistication, she felt confident, such that any man would surely be proud to be seen out with her.

"Ah, you're back," said Luke, as Libby sat down. "I hope you don't mind, but I took the liberty of procuring the desserts menu for us while you were gone, and..." he began, looking up from the menu.

But Luke didn't finish his sentence. His mouth continued to move, but no words came out. And then, eventually, his mouth stopped working altogether, his jaw just hanging open. Before he had time to compose himself, however, Luigi, who'd finished his call, came bounding over with a fresh cloth napkin to intervene.

"Hey-a, Miss Libby," said Luigi, holding the unfolded napkin up in front of her like he was performing a magic trick. "You 'ave a... how-a you say... disrobed atta-the-function."

Libby stared back, wondering where this was going, as she quite liked magic tricks. Although, with Luigi's thick Italian accent, she didn't really understand his banter, it being an odd sort of banter for a magic trick.

"I think you mean wardrobe malfunction, Luigi?" suggested Luke, finding his voice again.

"*Sì*, that-a too," replied Luigi.

Libby followed Luigi's gaze, where she was met with the sight of her left bosom, a bosom which was unfortunately presently issuing forth from the confines of her top. "Egad. I am undone!" she exclaimed. It was no wonder that all eyes had been on her, she thought, what with her having paraded through the length of the restaurant like a bloody stripper.

"Thank you, Luigi," she said, as Luigi continued to hold the napkin up to spare her modesty while, horrified, she adjusted herself and rehoused her wandering boob. "And I'll take another glass of wine, if you don't mind?" she asked, at the conclusion of putting all her bits back in their proper place.

"Certainly, Miss Libby. I think you could-a use one," agreed Luigi, and off he went for that very purpose.

Libby placed her elbows on the table and cradled her face in her hands, looking forlornly at Luke. "I *thought* I'd felt a bit of a breeze," she said. She shook her head, sighed a deep sigh, and then told him, "I'll completely understand, Luke, if there isn't going to be any second date."

"You're joking, right?" came the reply. Luke, for his part, was struggling, unsuccessfully, to hide his cheeky grin. "We've not even had dessert yet, and I've *already* managed to cop an eyeful. So, yes, of *course* there's going to be a second date!" he declared happily.

Chapter Six

3rd March

I don't quite know how the hell this has happened, but Terry's only managed to get himself a girlfriend. Nice she is as well. Most of the guys have now got themselves a girlfriend apart from me. I'm pleased for Terry and all, but it's starting to feel like I'll be the single one forever. We're still going to the Isle of Man TT races in June! I've bloody told Terry that if he thinks of backing out then I'll... well I don't know what I'll do exactly. Probably sulk. Gran has confirmed that she's still willing to go with me to the TT races, but I think I'll need to manage her expectations and that she is a Plan B at this stage as I'm hoping Terry doesn't let me down! There's always the chance that I'll have a girlfriend of my own that might want to come with me.

The scooter is running like a dream! One of Dad's mates is a mechanic. An actual mechanic, rather than someone who thinks that they're a mechanic just because they own a spanner like the last plonker who looked at it. Also, my dad's mate doesn't smell of fish, so there's that as well.

So, I've now got transport to pick Gwen up for our (sort of) date. The only problem is that I've not seen her since to confirm our (sort of) date. She's not been working this week and doesn't seem to be home when I phone. The phone just rings and rings and no one answers. Ah, I was stupid even thinking about it. I mean, she looks like that and I look like, well, not as good as that.

I'm going to die single.

Still, only a few more weeks working in a shite job before I'm off to art college.

She was lovely was Gwen.

5th March

Well, today was supposed to be all about horseracing. Yup, a grand day out had been planned for a day at the races with all the boys. Beers, gambling and more beers and it would have been a great day out had I'd not agreed, instead, to drive Gran and her three friends to Southport for the day. I need to start writing things down when I agree to them as I'm useless at remembering what I've said I'd do. To be fair we did have a right laugh. Bloody cold mind you!! Not sure what they thought they expected by going to the great British seaside in March. One of them brought a hipflask with them and once that was polished off there was talk of skinny dipping. I love my gran, but the thought of seeing her and her friends au naturel, well, it doesn't bear thinking about.

I remember family trips to Southport when I was a kid. Gran reminded me today about the time I got particularly scared on the Ghost Train ride and peed myself. Gran told her friends that I was sixteen when this happened rather than my actual age of five or so, so they took great delight in teasing me about that all afternoon. They all laughed and called me pissy-pants. Cheeky old devils!

All in all, I suppose, the horses wouldn't have been as much fun anyway, I reckon (who am I kidding), and it would have cost me a fortune. Gran and her friends did feel guilty about me missing out, but I told them I was still spending the afternoon surrounded by a load of old nags anyway so

CHAPTER SIX

it wasn't all too bad. Not sure they entirely appreciated the sheer brilliance of that joke. Ah well.

Gran and her friends are completely crackers. I had to lie down for an hour when I came home as they'd completely worn me out and I was possibly also suffering the effects of hypothermia.

8th March

I AM GUTTED. Terry said he saw Gwen with some shaven-headed bulldog in the main street today and that they were holding hands. It's stupid really– I don't know why I feel this bad about it as I've only spoken to her a couple of times. I really liked her. The boys are heading out tonight (without girlfriends) but I couldn't face it in case they ended up in The Crown and I made a fool out of myself by seeing Gwen after several pints. She doesn't even know I fancy her, but a few of the boys do. Wish I hadn't said anything to anybody.

I need to finish my art portfolio for college, but I've just lost the appetite to paint or draw. It'll come back soon.

Gran could tell I wasn't myself today when I went to see her. She knows me so well and correctly figured my glum mood was as a result of a girl. She just told me that I would find the person that I was meant to be with. She cried because I was sad, and she didn't want me to be sad and that nearly made me cry as well. Ah, who needs women in their life just now as there's sure to be dozens of beautiful women at art college.

Scooter is running like a dream, at least, so every cloud and all that.

12:26 a.m. – Terry just threw a small rock at my window on his way home from the pub. He missed the first few times as he was very drunk so the neighbours will love me tomorrow thanks to the noise he was making. The stupid bugger scared the hell out of me.

But he wanted me to know that Gwen was asking where I was!!!!!!!! Seems she was looking forward to her painting lesson and wondered why I hadn't called. I guess I must have taken her number down wrong? But Terry gave me her correct phone number, and I could kiss him for it. We must have looked like something from Romeo and Juliet what with him throwing stones at my window and me peering out like a lovestruck maiden blowing him a kiss as gratitude.

3:00 a.m. – I can't sleep. Why would she want me to phone her and take her out painting if she's got a boyfriend? Oh god, what if she's just seeing this as a painting lesson and here I am thinking that she likes me? Ah, women. I'll just play it cool when I phone her tomorrow I suppose. Oh who am I kidding, I couldn't play it cool if I lived in an igloo.

9th March

What the actual hell just happened? Mum and Dad fancied fish and chips so I said I'd go and pick it up and also give me a chance to go out for a spin on my scooter (it's running like a dream still). It's not easy to hang a carrier bag on the handle but I've mastered it. So, I put the order in for the fish and popped out to peer in the tailor's window which is on the same street as the chip shop. There I am imaging how I'm going to look when I can afford the suit when I was snapped out of my daydream by a woman screaming. I near on shit myself I can tell you. I turned in the direction of the corner shop where the noise came from and saw a scruffy looking lad wearing a leather jacket coming sprinting up the pavement toward me. I caught a glimpse of some old dear lying flat on the ground outside the shop behind him. This lad had a handbag tucked under his arm which I quickly figured didn't belong to him. My brain was telling me to jump back and let him past, but I didn't. I still don't know why I didn't. Instead, I swung my scooter helmet in the direction of his head and connected perfectly, nearly knocking him clean

CHAPTER SIX

out. Now, this woman on the floor and the rightful owner of the bag, well, she only turns out to be the mum of the guy who owns the tailoring shop. The owner's been cashing up for the day when he heard the noise and came running out. He's recognised me from being in his shop so often and I've only had a right result. He's going to let me take the suit as a reward and I can pay it off in instalments. I get the suit and can take the next twelve weeks to pay it off!!!

I came home without the chips which I forgot so I had to head back out for them. Still can't believe I nearly knocked that prat out. I think it was maybe imagining myself in the suit looking like Sean that done it. Maybe I'll turn into an international sex symbol, or even a superhero when I wear it? Gwen might like that.

I've just had a thought. It was nice of the tailor and all, but I did just get his mums purse back and so he could have just given me the suit? Ah well, I still get the suit which is a proper good result. I need to head around there tomorrow to get it properly fitted. I might see if he can throw a nice pair of shoes in as well.

New suit, local superhero and I've got my first date(ish) with Gwen tomorrow. Scooter is still running like a dream so maybe things are on the up!?

10th March

I went to pick Gwen up on the scooter with my painting supplies in my rucksack. I only forgot a bloody helmet for her, didn't I? I was supposed to try and borrow a spare one for her but I sodding well forgot all about it! I then had to go back home and pray that mum was able to lend me her car – which she could! Mum's car has never been driven so quick as I wanted to make sure Gwen didn't change her mind – which she didn't!

I took her down to the canal as planned and showed her some pen & wash watercolour techniques and we painted the narrowboats. She's funny and great company. Though in typical Bert Tebbit fashion, I made a prize melon out of myself. I took a paintbrush from my bag and the crochet love heart that Gran made me when I was a kid must have been caught on it. Gran had given it to me as a good luck charm when I was playing the Cowardly Lion in a school play. Mum tonight confessed that she popped it in my bag to bring me luck. Anyway, when it flew out of my bag, Gwen picked it up and was looking at me like I was some sort of psycho declaring his undying love. I had to tell her it was a gift from my gran, and I wasn't sure why it was in my bag. I don't know if she thought it was endearing or a little sad.

I deliberately didn't pry into her love life especially after the crocheted love heart incident, but she did mention that she's recently broken up with her boyfriend. She said he's been a bit clingy since and was trying to get back together with her but there's absolutely no chance of that happening.

Like a true gent I offered to take her for something to eat. After we both ate, and after I'd polished off a very nice ploughman's lunch, I realised that my wallet was in the under-seat storage on the scooter. A scooter which was at home, in front of my house and miles from where we were now. Gwen ended up having to pay. Ah, I'm such a tool. I've been planning this all week and I go and forget the helmet and my wallet. The only thing I didn't manage to forget was the love heart from my gran even if I didn't know it was there!

To move the conversation away from my stupidity I figured it was a good time to tell her about my heroic escapades, about how I selflessly tackled a vicious (he could have been!?) mugger and returned an old lady's purse in the process. Gwen seemed suitably impressed by this and told me I was very brave! I thought that was encouraging,

CHAPTER SIX

but on reflection my mum used to say the same thing if she was taking a splinter from my finger.

I wanted to ask her if she'd like to go on a proper date, but I didn't have the nerve. I really like her, and the thought of her saying no would be crushing. Plus, she'd probably worry that she'd end up paying again! (she won't)

We had a wonderful day and she's so easy to talk to and unbelievably pretty. Lovely eyes.

I said I'd give her a call if she wanted to try painting again as she was actually very good. I don't know if she likes me. As in LIKES me. Or just likes me as a painting friend. I think I'm a wee bit afraid to find out.

Anyway, need to go to sleep.

Damn. Just realised that she's still got the love heart that Gran made for me. That's good, I suppose, as it means I'll have an excuse to see her again in order to get it back. Oh, wait, I wonder if she thinks it was a gift? It wasn't meant to be. What if she thinks I'm... (GO TO SLEEP BERT!!!)

Gwen is lovely.

Chapter Seven

Libby had come to the realisation that running a business was a constant struggle. It seemed that everyone had their hand in your pocket, figuratively speaking of course, at every opportunity, whether it be water rates that needed paying, or tax, or suppliers, or advertisers, or shoplifters or bank managers or landlords, et cetera. And then, in addition to that, there were the long, long hours as well. To make any money from a shop, you had to physically be there and make yourself available to the paying public. Sure, when it was busy, and the till was ringing, it was a fantastic job to have. You were your own boss and all the net profits were yours to keep and do with as you pleased.

But the till wasn't always ringing, of course. And booksellers, like many other businesses, were under constant threat from wider market forces such as internet-only retailers. Online shops, who often didn't have the same fixed costs, made life exceptionally challenging for those who operated in the bricks & mortar world. It inevitably resulted in many shops either going bankrupt or having to drastically change their business model. Fortunately, at least for Libby, there was a core group of consumers who still liked to purchase their reading material from a physical shop. These types of valued customers relished the opportunity to browse in person so that they could actually pick a book up, hold it in their hands, look it over, flip through the pages, enjoy the cover artwork, and take the time to read through the back cover copy before they were finally, hopefully, enticed into making their purchase. For these people, buying a book was an *experience*, and one that couldn't be replicated by simply clicking the "Add to Basket" button on any particular shopping website.

Not that Libby was hostile towards internet shopping in general. In fact, far from it, as often the internet was her only shopping option available on account of being constantly in her own shop. And, indeed, for a shop to flourish in this competitive environment, business owners had to be savvy! They needed to change with the times and adapt their business to cater to and take full advantage of the changing tastes and buying habits of the consumer who, after all, had a myriad of purchasing choices and avenues available to them. And yet, to address this very real threat to her standard old-fashioned business model, Libby had, to date, done a great deal of nothing in this regard.

Though Libby talked a good game, the truth of it was that she'd been burying her head in the sand for some good while. For someone relatively proficient at navigating the internet, she didn't even have any online presence for her own bookshop to speak of. And whilst the prospect of a website had certainly been considered, well, the act of considering it in and of itself was about as far as that option had ever really progressed. Instead, the survival of the business to date was as a result of passing trade, which naturally increased during the summer months and also with key shopping events such as Christmas.

The winter months were generally long, however, and with passing trade solely dependent on those regulars who'd perhaps not embraced online shopping themselves, preferring instead the physical shopfront, business was markedly reduced during these lean months to a bare-bones minimum at best. And, at worst — as Libby had encountered only too recently — it was reduced to such an extent that the ship was in danger of sinking entirely. For these times, then, when sales slowed and the public were not coming to *her*, Libby had to take her wares to *them*. She knew this. And she knew it wasn't just a matter of keeping things afloat during the lean months, either, but of keeping sales robust all year round as well. And she knew the first step in the journey towards greater success was to create a website. She absolutely *had* to get off her arse, no two ways about it, and embrace the opportunities that online commerce could bring to

CHAPTER SEVEN

her business. And, owning a bookshop as she did, she even held several books in stock on this very subject, in fact! The problem with these books, however, was that they were an awful lot of pages to go over, collectively, and would take no small degree of effort on Libby's part to read through. As such, it was, most certainly, a confounding conundrum of the worst order.

Still, in full knowledge that the survival of her business could hinge on her efforts, she resolved to attend to the matter at hand forthwith, and plonked her bum on the seat behind the counter of her shop, armed with a mug of coffee in case intermittent boosts of caffeine should be required. This was now a girl with a steely determination to drive her business forward. One book amongst the handful she'd gathered in front of her caught her eye and was the one she took hold of first. It could have been the intriguing title: *Online Marketing and How to Totally Kill It!* Or, alternatively, it could well have been the handsome and sharply dressed chap with the healthy tan on the front cover that may have had some bearing on her decision. Either way, this was important, and she was going to "totally kill it!" just like the title of the book had said. Yes, this was truly a pivotal juncture in her journey towards improvement. She pressed on, eagerly, with a renewed spirit of determination, with staunch indefatigability, with a steadfast, dogged, unyielding persistence, with robust, enthusiastic vigour, with...

"Oh, who am I trying to kid?" she said, closing over the turgid tome after merely eighteen seconds or thereabouts. She pushed the pile of books to one side in defeat, and she immediately felt guilty for falling at the very first hurdle. She loved to read, of course, but good fiction was more her game, and this sort of reading material she had in front of her right now wasn't exactly in that vein at all, sadly enough.

Libby's eyes wandered through the front window to those folks on the beach opposite enjoying the last of the day's sun, and she thought it was worth keeping her door open for another twenty minutes or so should there be a last-minute flurry of shoppers. As Libby waited patiently for any potential customers who might arrive, she flipped open her laptop in order to crack on with her decidedly limited investigations regarding how to drag her business, kicking and screaming, into the modern age. *"E-commerce business in the Isle of Man,"* she typed into the web browser's search engine, and then scrolled through the results.

"Hmm," she said to herself, clicking on one of the links before her, and then another, and then another still. It quickly became apparent that one business appeared very prominently indeed whenever she typed any combination of words relating to Isle of Man shops and online trade — that shop being The Stand-Up Comic, which was owned by none other than the nerd with the side parting, James. His online presence appeared on virtually every search result, and whilst she turned her nose up for just a moment she could not fail to be impressed by what she saw. Every link she clicked on presented attractive imagery that drew you in and left you wanting to learn more about his business. Libby knew very quickly that emulating this impact was the way forward for her own shop. There were links to his website, his eBay store, Amazon, and numerous YouTube videos of him hawking his wares, and it was, to be fair, deeply impressive. And, curiously, if you were to believe your eyes, the images of his physical shopfront revealed it to be roughly the same size as Harrods. Yet Libby had once been inside his shop, and she most certainly didn't recall it being anywhere close to as large as it looked to be in the photos she was seeing. She once had a similar experience with online dating, which had included similarly misleading promotional photos, but that was another story. Carrying on, Libby read through an assortment of customer feedback comments for James's business and noted that these were from customers all over the world. "Hmm," she murmured to herself once more, for she was now suitably intrigued. James had successfully marketed himself to the world, and it wasn't lost on Libby that James was likely making money taking orders even as he slept.

Libby definitely needed to get in on this action, she was of no doubt. And why spend hours and hours attempting to digest volume after volume of boring marketing instruction when she could find someone gaining success locally, and simply try to copy what they were doing? It made perfect sense, as far as she was concerned, and was a much more appealing strategy than

CHAPTER SEVEN

slogging through a load of dry reading material. First order of business, then, was trying to work out how he made his little seaside shop come across like a huge department store. And the only way to do that, she reckoned, was for her to venture over to the other side of town and have a good nosey through his shop window.

And so, with this vague approximation of a plan of attack formed, Libby printed off several choice pictures of James's shop captured from her internet investigatory activity. Step One in her masterplan was to compare his actual shop against images in hand. She wanted to see what sort of creative photography James might have employed to give the illusion his shopfront was much grander than it actually was, hence making it so inviting to prospective online customers. If she could work out how he'd done it, then this could be a tactic she might also employ for her own online presence. She hadn't given up on the attractive fellow on the cover of the book she'd recently set aside, however, not entirely at least, thinking she might come back to him at some point. "*Kill it!*" she scribbled across the top of one of the pages of printed-out images, as a reminder to herself to revisit the title at some later date.

With the beach now more or less vacant and the last of the potential customers headed home, Libby locked up for the day. Now buoyed with a fresh sense of commercial optimism, she took one last look around her shop before setting off on her way to the other side of town and James's shop.

En route, Libby reflected on her relationship with James. At one stage he seemed pleasant enough. Likeable, even. But she just couldn't forgive him for trying to muscle in on her business and secure her shop for himself. Because of this, James was not to be trusted, and was, in her considered opinion, a colossal cockwomble. His dog was rather cute, she had to admit. And of course it wasn't the poor dog's fault that its master was a great giant get.

Not wishing to think any longer about James, Libby turned her attention instead to her surroundings. The arteries of Peel were a series of narrow lanes and roads that intertwined with one another and with most ultimately ending up leading out to the glorious seafront. The quaint houses that lined the streets hadn't changed for ages, giving Libby a nostalgic sense of what the area would have looked like many generations before. It was easy to lose yourself soaking up the history that oozed from every brick, Libby thought, and if you closed your eyes it was easy to imagine the commotion of the bustling seaside markets of days gone by, along with the persistent pounding of a blacksmith's hammer. While tourism had suffered on the island in recent times due, in the main, to affordable overseas travel, for those who ventured to this charming little rock in the middle of the Irish Sea, they were rewarded with an idyllic charm seeping from its every pore as they stepped into this picture-postcard island location. Overall, Libby was very happy she had decided to call it her home.

Soon enough, Libby was on the other side of town and arrived just before her destination. She took up a tentative position of cover behind the phone box on the pavement opposite to her target. She glanced down at the printed-out images in her hand, and then across to the shop. "Definitely looks more impressive online than it actually is," she said with an indignant sniff.

James's shop was modest in size, situated on the corner of the street. The two front windows displayed a plethora of action figures, comics, t-shirts, and other assorted items a comic book sort of nerd, she supposed, if they were stood in her place, would be licking their lips over (if she was being kind) or maybe even the windowpanes (if she was being especially unkind). It was difficult for Libby to see through his merchandise and into the shop proper from her position to check if the lights were off. It was well after five p.m. by this time, and she reasoned that the shop would very likely be closed, but from her current vantage point she couldn't be absolutely certain.

Libby paused for a moment to consider her present actions. She harboured nagging concerns in regard to James's motivation for buying her that doughnut cake as he'd done. Was there a romantic undercurrent inherent in his gesture, she wondered? If so, her presence here now, if observed, may give out the wrong impression. Aside from this, there was also further incentive for her to avoid detection in that she was one shopkeeper trying to

CHAPTER SEVEN

steal ideas from another. This was industrial espionage! Or as close to even approaching some dubious semblance of industrial espionage as one might ever expect on a sleepy island such as this, leastways.

"Right, then. Nothing ventured nothing gained, I suppose," she said, egging herself on. She was here now and may as well complete her mission, she reasoned. She took one final glance up and down the road and then, with the coast clear, ventured forth. She lowered her head as she crossed the street, trying to remain as inconspicuous as any covert operative should. It was devilishly exhilarating, though, this skulking about, and as her heart thumped in her chest she began whistling. Well, to call it a whistle was being generous, as she'd never been terribly good at whistling to begin with, and being nervous as she was right now didn't suddenly make it any better, either. As such, it was a rather lame attempt to remain casual and inconspicuous, as these things went, and would probably have had the exact opposite of the desired effect had anybody actually been about. She was reminded of that bit about a tree falling in a forest and then wondered to herself, similarly, *If a Libby is whistling, very badly, in the middle of the street, and there's no one around to hear, is she really making a fool of herself?*

Now just outside the shop, having successfully navigated the crossing of the street, Libby was relieved to see the shop was, in fact, in darkness as she'd hoped. She made her way over to the entrance on the corner of the plot, where the front door was set back from the pavement in an alcove. "Oh, my," she said, startled, as she was greeted by a life-sized image of Spider-Man painted there on the smooth brick.

She'd seen the Spider-Man themed painted entranceway online already, but this was one instance in which seeing the thing in person was even more impressive, with the online photos not doing it justice. The whole thing formed a sort of mural. First, there was Spider-Man crouched down on the right-hand wall of the alcove, palm out, with him shooting that webbing stuff from his hand. On the wall opposite, to the left of the door, was depicted the subject of Spider-Man's attention — a slightly portly fellow, looking angry and menacing, with multiple metal arms sprouting out his sides. Libby searched through her memory to recall this multi-limbed chap's name. She knew it had something to do with his having four limbs too many. She wracked her brain and, finally, satisfied, decided he was called Professor Cephalopod. Yes, she was certain that was it, or, at least something very much like it. Behind the characters, and crossed up and over the doorway, was the backdrop of the New York skyline. As an added flourish, Spider-Man's webbing was made out of string, glued to the wall, giving the whole thing a bit of a 3-D effect. The webbing started from Spider-Man's wrist, shooting over in Professor Cephalopod's direction by following the one wall, a section of it crossing over the door, and another section of it picking up on the other side and then continuing across the other wall until it reached its target, Prof Ceph himself. While comics were not her thing, whoever had painted this scene was someone with obvious talent, Libby had to admit, as the whole affair looked absolutely smashing. She could easily appreciate the artistry involved in creating the scene, not to mention its ability to capture the attention of passersby and entice them into entering James's shop.

    She pulled the printed-out pages from her pocket once again and settled her eyes upon the particular images of the shop's interior for review this time, in order to compare them up against the reality. With the shop in darkness, and confident she had only Spider-Man and his chubby Professor friend for present company, Libby stepped up to the door and pressed her nose to the glass, taking a gander inside. Even with the lights off, Libby was impressed with what she was still able to make out. She could see an assortment of action figures, of every conceivable superhero, and row after row and shelf after shelf dedicated to a vast selection of comics, books, and anything and everything comicbook related. It was flippin' nerd heaven, is what it was. And not only that, but it amazed her as to how many goods could be so jam-packed into a shop so modest in size. It was like looking into a Tardis, and she couldn't believe it possible there could exist so bloody much *stuff* inhabiting such a relatively small space.

CHAPTER SEVEN

Today's brief exercise in espionage had certainly been worth the time, Libby felt, as it gave her an insight into what could be achieved by properly utilising limited resources. Even so, with her own shop having six or seven times the floor space, she could easily understand why James might have been so eager to get his hands on it. As successful as he'd been with what he had available to him, she imagined he could well accomplish much, much more with a shop as large as hers.

Pleased with the fruits of her present labour, Libby placed her printouts on the floor of the entranceway and removed her phone from her back pocket. *A picture or two for market research*, she said to herself, pressing her phone up against the glass. But just as she was about to capture a few shots...

A small dog abruptly appeared on the other side of the glass, barking its wee head off. Libby jumped back in fright. But then she took a couple of deep breaths to calm herself as she realised that, one, the dog couldn't reach her through their mutual glass partition and, two, it was only Hulk.

Calmer now, Libby leaned against the wall of the alcove in relief, as she listened to the Jack Russel's incessant, yet harmless, yapping.

"Hush now, it's all right, little guy, it's only me," she said in the direction of the door, hoping to calm the wee fellow down, as he was probably just as frightened as she had at first been. "Who's a good boy? That's right, *Hulk's* a good boy," she continued, in her most soothing manner. But it didn't seem to be having any effect. "Hulk, it's me," she carried on, trying once more. "You remember, right? We've met before. You like me. Or you like my trainers, at least, yeah? Em... good boy?" she said, adding a cheery thumbs-up in for good measure, figuring it couldn't hurt.

Pacifying the dog didn't seem to be working, and Libby was also worried that where the dog was, his master was probably not too far away. James could well appear at any moment from the stock room, for instance, in response to the ruckus, and discover her there. There would be questions. And it would be awkward. And Libby reckoned it was as good a time as any, then, to be on her way. She went to move, only her progress hit a bit of a snag... in the very literal sense. She was stuck to the wall. She could pull away an inch or two only, with something holding her fast.

Libby took one hand and felt around behind her, and it soon became apparent what the situation was: she was ensnared by Spider-Man's webbing. The problem was, as it should happen, her expensive and not-yet-paid-for — but stylish! — leather belt. It was adorned with silver decorative fandangles fastened on, strewn along the entire length of it, and the string that was Spider-Man's webbing, she could feel, was entirely caught up in this ornamental frippery. She could only imagine that Professor Cephalopod, watching on, must have been very pleased with himself that he was presently not the only evildoer to run afoul of his nemesis Spider-Man's crime-fighting efforts.

"Ah, hell. This was definitely not at all part of the plan," Libby moaned, wondering what to do now, how to get herself out of the current mess she was in. With sufficient force, she felt fairly confident, she could free herself — but that might mean ruining James's impressive mural, or, even worse, damaging her newly acquired designer belt that was on its first outing. Placing her phone back in her pocket, she moved both hands behind her back, but without being able to see exactly what she was doing, it was impossible to make any real progress. And the distraction of having an overexcited Jack Russell barking madly away didn't exactly help matters, either.

Libby was amazed that James hadn't yet appeared but was grateful for small favours, at least. With little to no success disengaging her belt, the only thing for it was to remove it from about her person, which she did... or at least tried to. With the string tangled up in it as it was, she couldn't slip the belt through her belt loops, and so the only thing she managed to accomplish was to tangle herself up even more — while ripping a good portion of the string from the wall in the process, though, even so, still not detaching herself completely. It was an entirely hopeless affair.

"Can I help you?" asked James, suddenly appearing on the pavement in front of Libby, bag of groceries in hand. The tone of his voice made it clear, however, that he was none too pleased at Libby's shenanigans. He looked her up and down, and then

CHAPTER SEVEN

looked the wall behind her up and down as well, surveying the damage.

"James!" replied Libby, like they were long-lost friends.

"Libby, what are you doing here?" asked James, after quieting his dog.

"Oh, you know. Just hanging about," Libby said casually.

"Yes, I can see that," replied James, narrowing his eyes, and looking at the state of Libby's belt and its present attachment to his wall.

"I, erm... I just came to thank you for the cake...?" she said, changing tack, spontaneously conjuring up a lie that she hoped might impress.

"By destroying the entrance to my shop?" he asked, placing his shopping bag down. He stared at her impassively for a long moment, unmoved, and then leaned in close to her.

"Hey, hold on there, mister!" replied Libby, reflexively placing her hand up before her face. "Just because I'm a captive prisoner at the moment doesn't mean you can just go and take advantage of me!" she scolded him.

"Oh, don't flatter yourself, Libby," said James with a sigh, reaching past her and releasing her belt from its web-based incarceration with relative ease. "I used to be a Boy Scout. I'm good with knots and such," he explained, in response to Libby's look of amazement. James went quiet for a moment or two. "Is this vandalism because you're still cross with me over that whole putting-you-out-of-business nonsense?" he asked her eventually, cocking his head reprovingly.

"What? No, of course not!" replied Libby, putting her belt back in place and attempting to sort herself out. "Why would you even think that?" she asked, laughing nervously.

James pressed his glasses up his nose, glancing down to the printouts Libby had laid on the entranceway floor, with the top page bearing the words *"kill it!"* scrawled there, plain as day. "It's just, I couldn't help but notice..." he told Libby, nodding in the direction of the paper.

"Notice what?" asked Libby, not immediately seeing what James was seeing.

"What *is* all this? Surveillance photos or something?" James demanded, pointing to the ground.

Libby squirmed, her jaw lowering in hopeful expectation of a plausible explanation issuing forth that did not arrive.

"Well?" said James.

"No!" replied Libby. "Well, yes. Though not really. I mean, okay, sort of, I guess…" she conceded. "But you should totally take it as a compliment!"

"Kill it?" said James, reading Libby's own words aloud. "Really, Libby, don't you think that's a bit over-the-top? I mean, what, you've come to kill me? Or to kill my dog? Are you really that desperate for revenge?"

"What… wait… no! No, of course I'm not here to kill you! Or your dog! Or even hurt you at all!" Libby floundered.

"Well I should hope not," said James, crossing his arms over his chest. "But seriously, though, why *are* you here?"

"Ah, well, actually, if you must know," Libby said with a sniff, as if it were all James's fault for getting the wrong impression, "I'm just trying to up my game when it comes to promoting my shop online," she told him. "I was doing some research into the matter, reading *lots of books*," she emphasised, giving a wipe of her brow for effect. "And I also did loads of research online. And looking at the images I came across online, I couldn't help but notice how professional your business appeared, and also how impressively presented it was."

"Uh-huh," said James, moving his hands from across his chest and now placing them on his hips.

"And so I wanted to come and take a look for myself, that's all," Libby concluded. "So no killing today, I promise!" she said, holding two fingers out like a gun, and then carefully holstering her imaginary weapon to show James that there wouldn't be any murder or mayhem on the menu this day.

"Libby, if you needed advice, all you had to do was ask," said James. "I'd be happy to help you out."

"You would?" asked Libby, relieved, but also a little confused. "But I thought…?"

CHAPTER SEVEN

"Libby, I'd love to see any business on the Isle do well," James answered. "If our economy here is thriving, that can only be a good thing."

James appeared sincere in his offer, and for a moment Libby felt a wave of guilt — guilt from the fact that she'd badmouthed both James and his business to all and sundry, and guilt that she thought James was trying to put her out of business when here he was just now willing to offer his help in making her business a success.

"I'm sorry," offered Libby. "When the shop was going through a lean phase, I accused you of being a complete bellend. I was, perhaps, judging you unfairly? But still, you have to admit—"

"It was *shyster*, if I recall," said James, gently correcting her. "Although you may have called me a bellend as well for all I—"

"*Complete* bellend, actually," Libby entered in, providing a gentle correction of her own."

"Right, you may very well have called me a complete bellend also," replied James, before adding, "But, yes, as to your other point, you may have been premature in the conclusions you'd drawn. I'm not half the villain you make me out to be."

"Yes, but you can see how it looked, can't you?" asked Libby. "You were in my shop nearly as much as I was! Checking the place out! Measuring it up!" Libby submitted. "And as if that wasn't enough in itself, I also heard you started selling some of the same books as me! What were you trying to do, give me unfair competition or something? That's some dirty pool, mate. I mean, what exactly were you playing at? You're a comicbook shop, you don't even sell novels and such."

"Why are we stood out here?" replied James, not directly answering Libby's diatribe. "Look, you've come this far, so I may as well bring you in and show you the shop, yeah?" he said not unkindly, adding, "I've actually still got some of those titles you sell on a shelf inside collecting dust."

"A-ha! So, you *were* trying to go into competition with me?" Libby asked accusingly, rearing up. "Right, so you admit it, then! You *were* trying to—"

"Do you ever shut up?" asked James, shaking his head. "Did you ever think about exactly *why* a bloke with a comicbook shop would suddenly start selling chick-lit cheesy romance novels and the like in his shop, when that's *not at all* the sort of thing he sells?"

Libby's face went blank. "Because... you were trying to put me out of business...?" she offered weakly, shrugging her shoulders.

"No. That's not it," James told her. "And you can take them all back as they're not selling for me, either."

"But..." Libby began, though not knowing what else to say, as she was at something of a loss.

James unlocked the door, using his foot to gently move a lively, animated Hulk, now wagging his tail, from his path. "Can I offer you a cuppa?" he asked Libby, but Libby stood rooted to the spot.

"I don't bite," James assured her. "And Hulk has had his fill of human flesh for the day already, so he won't bother you either, I promise."

"Hang on," replied Libby, a puzzled look on her face. "What did you mean when you said I should take all those books back? I mean, the *back* part, specifically. You're not making any sense."

"They're your books, Libby. Or at least they used to be," James answered her.

Libby didn't say anything. She looked thoroughly confused. And this was because she was in fact thoroughly confused.

"I wasn't trying to put you *out* of business. I was trying to keep you *in* business," James explained. "Libby, I knew you were in trouble when you couldn't pay your rent to my father," he went on. "My old man's not a mercenary, but he needs tenants who can pay their rent. Which is why he suggested I move in when you moved out. It's harsh, but, that's business. Anyway, that's why I started to buy stock from you, so you'd have more money to pay your rent."

"Buy stock from me?" said Libby, not any less confused. "But you didn't... I don't have any recollection of... I mean I think I would remember you buying stock from me...?"

"Ah. Well. Not purchased from you *directly*, necessarily," James explained further. "Not exactly. See, it's not as if you would've taken charity from me, would you? So I sent a group of friends round to buy your stock in order to help you out," he elaborated.

CHAPTER SEVEN

"And I only put them up for sale in my own shop in hopes of at least recouping my costs if I was able. But they haven't sold, as they're not the sort of thing my clientele is really interested in," he said, pointing in the vague direction of one corner of the shop in which presumably the books were sat, forlornly collecting dust. "As I said, you're welcome to take them back if you like."

"I think... I think I would have taken charity?" Libby offered somewhat apologetically. "Now, so let me get this straight..." she added, finally following James into the shop, and with the cogwheels in her brain turning and clicking into place. "That sudden uptick in business I saw at the time, that was down to you?"

"Well, not entirely, of course. But to a large degree, yes," James told her.

"But why would you go to all that trouble and expense for me?" Libby asked, bending down to give Hulk a good scratching of the ears now that she was inside, with the dog having received her eagerly, presenting himself happily before her for a good round of petting.

"Because I'm a nice guy!" replied James.

But Libby remained slightly sceptical, and she pressed the point further. "It just doesn't make sense, James," she said. "Sure, it's nice to be nice and all, but why would you go to such expense to help me out, and why didn't you tell me at the time?"

"Tell you at the time...?" James asked, chuckling, shaking his head from side to side. "You're joking, right? I did try to talk to you a number of times, actually, Libby. But by that point you'd launched a one-woman campaign to besmirch my character all over town, and, Libby, you're actually fairly good at besmirching when you want to be."

"Oh," replied Libby. And she continued to attend to Hulk as she said this, as petting the dog was easier than trying to come up with something more to say.

"Look, what I'd wanted to tell you at the time but failed miserably in doing so," James carried on, "is that I enjoyed popping in to see you, okay? I looked forward to calling in for a chat on my way to work. Did you never notice that your shop isn't *actually* on my way to work?"

"Oh," Libby said again.

99

"Libby, what I'm saying, in case you haven't figured it out already, is that I'm rather... well, I *would've* been rather fond of you, I mean, if I'd been given the chance," James told her, laying it all out there.

Hulk was enjoying the generous amount of attention he was continuing to receive whilst Libby sought to formulate a reply she knew she couldn't put off forever. "James, with hindsight," she said eventually, looking up from her current canine consort, "I'm sorry I misjudged you. I have to say, what you did for me was very sweet and kind, and you truly helped me through a particularly rough patch for the shop. Thank you. Honestly, thank you so much."

"Yes, well that's more like it, I should think," James replied with an amiable chuckle.

Of course Libby had purposely left the subject of James's professed feelings unaddressed, conveniently leaving them to one side. And in furtherance of not addressing it, "Well, I should probably leave you to it, James. And I've got a training run I really ought to be doing right about now, as I'm getting ready for a race at the end of the month. You wouldn't be a runner, by any chance?" she said, changing topic to something else entirely. Not that she expected a comic shop nerd to be into running or anything similar, but it was simply the first thing that popped into her head.

"A bit of one, yes," replied James. And, in response to the look of surprise on Libby's face, elaborated, "I can't say I'm very good at it, mind. But I did manage to complete the half-marathon last year."

"Oh?" said Libby, as she'd honestly not expected this.

"Yep. And dressed as Wonder Woman, no less," James added proudly.

"Wonder... Woman...?" asked Libby incredulously, as she had *truly* not expected this.

"To raise money for charity," James quickly added, lest Libby get the wrong idea. "Besides, Wonder Woman totally rocks!"

"Oh... kay?" said Libby.

"She totally kicks ass!" insisted James. "Have you not seen the recent film?" he asked.

CHAPTER SEVEN

"No. No, I haven't. But don't worry, no judgement here," Libby replied, laughing affably.

"I've signed up for this year as well, but we'll see," James told her. "Anyhow, we should go for a coffee to discuss a strategy for your e-commerce enterprise, yeah? What do you reckon?" he asked, escorting her from the shop.

"We totally should!" said Libby, smiling encouragingly, while cheekily mimicking his language.

In truth, Libby wasn't entirely certain that the two of them getting together would be an especially wise course of action, given James's previous — and still current? (she wasn't sure) — feelings for her. She'd agreed out of politeness, as it would've been rude not to. And she just might take him up on his offer, as she definitely did have use for his advice. But she wasn't sure how she might go about following through whilst at the same time navigating such potentially dangerous waters.

"And once again, I'm sorry for any misunderstanding, James," she added. "You know, about the shop and everything."

"Cheers. It's fine," replied James. "All it took was you stalking me to clear the air," he joked. But then he paused for a moment, chewing his lip. "There is one thing, Libby," he ventured, but then waved the thought away, dismissing it. "In fact, forget it," he said, reconsidering.

"No, what is it? Go on," Libby told him accommodatingly, but just hoping it wasn't something romance-related, as that could easily turn things exceptionally awkward.

James was clearly struggling with what he was about to say and weighing up whether he ought to continue. "Well, it may be none of my business, Libby, but..." he said tentatively.

"But?" asked Libby, not sure she liked the sound of this.

"But I was out with Hulk the other night, and I saw you with that rugby player fellow," James revealed.

"Luke?" Libby answered, her expression hardening somewhat. "What *about* Luke?"

"Yes, that's the one," James answered, his manner suggesting he'd known what Luke's name was but just hadn't cared to say the name aloud. "As I said, it's none of my business. But that fellow, Libby? He plays rugby, sure enough. I hate to tell you, however, that it's not just on the rugby pitch where he *plays the field*, so to speak… if you take my meaning?"

Libby didn't take his meaning. Not then. Not at first.

"I'm sorry to tell you this, Libby," James continued. "I don't know Luke all that well, truth be told, but I do know a few of his mates. And what I hear from them is not good. Luke has a reputation as a bit of a ladies' man, you see, and I'd hate for you to be the subject of one of the bawdy types of tales I've heard one too many times. Libby, you're too nice a person for that."

"Oh," said Libby.

"I hope you don't think I'm overstepping the mark?" James offered. "Only I wanted you to know that he generally has several women on the go at any given time," he added indelicately, wincing for Libby's benefit as he said this.

"Oh," said Libby again.

"So… yeah," said James.

Libby smiled to brush off the suggestion that this news would bother her, but of course it did. Very much so. She could feel her bottom lip begin to tremble and, as such, decided it was definitely time to take her leave before any waterworks should commence. "No, it's fine. Anyway, I must…" she offered, mustering up a response, weak and aimless as it was. She gave James and Hulk both a wave goodbye and then off she went.

She succeeded in retaining her composure only until the bottom of the road, whereupon some tears escaped despite her best efforts. "It's just hay fever," she said for the benefit of a kindhearted passerby who stopped to see if she was all right, before waving him politely away.

Alone once again and able to collect her thoughts on the way home, she came to the realisation that she still liked Luke, even now, despite this current revelation from James. Still, she had to admit to herself that she couldn't claim to know Luke half as well as she thought she did, with James's news being a bit of a rude awakening for her and a huge slap in the face.

"Stupid cow," she muttered to herself, wiping away the excess moisture from her cheeks.

CHAPTER SEVEN

Her legs were like jelly, so she took a detour into an empty bus shelter and collapsed there on the wooden bench inside. She cupped her hands around her face and sobbed.

"Oh, you stupid, stupid girl," she said, her voice breaking with emotion. "Libby, you stupid girl."

Chapter Eight

Fenella Beach, an intimate sandy cove sat under the protective eye of the ancient fortress of Peel Castle, was one of Libby's absolute favourite locations on the Isle. And it was a challenge to make it onto that shortlist because as far as beautiful spots on the island were concerned there were certainly plenty to choose from. It was a popular destination on a summer's day, and it also afforded a lovely view, on a summer's eve, of the setting sun over the sky above Peel.

At this sublime setting, Libby had unofficially adopted her own section of rock a short descent along the shallow cliff face just beyond the edge of the public car park. It wasn't exactly like climbing down from Everest, though still required a surefooted approach to reach, however. But, once the way down was safely navigated, the spot offered a lovely place to relax and watch over the beach. On one previous occasion, Freya had rather cheekily christened the location "Dwayne Johnson" — on account of her longstanding desire to "sit on The Rock," as she'd then remarked. Libby should not have been surprised at Freya's saucy wit. And, the name had stuck.

"Dwayne" was, ordinarily, a social sort of rock, in that it was a place where Libby enjoyed a glass of something, often along with Freya, languidly watching the children squealing with delight on the nearby beach below, or casually observing some of the more adventurous folk taking their paddleboards directly out onto the Irish Sea.

Libby wasn't being overly social on this particular evening, however. The warm orange hue of the setting sun was, as usual, providing a splendid backdrop. But Libby was sat alone, staring vacantly off into the distance. It'd been three days since James's unpleasant revelation regarding Luke's lothario-like ways, and she still felt a sickening knot in her stomach. She rationalised it all as Luke just being a good-looking guy and simply doing what most men, in her experience, were born to do: namely, to make her life a complete and utter misery. She couldn't shake the embarrassment, though, of knowing she was likely the subject — amongst similar others — of the typical locker-room banter amongst Luke and his mates sharing details about their latest conquests. Mercifully, in Libby's particular case anyway, it hadn't reached the stage where she'd become another notch on Luke's bedpost. So there was that, at least.

Presently, something caught Libby's attention, something approaching, something close and zeroing in on her position. She raised her hand and, without even needing to turn around, gave a little wave and said, "Oh, hello, Freya."

"Oi! ... How... did... you... know...?" replied Freya, as she gingerly progressed down the steep rocky path from the car park, pausing between every word she spoke with each careful step.

"I could hear you," Libby answered. "When you're concentrating on something, like clambering down a rockface, for instance, you breathe heavily through your nose. So I could tell it was you," she explained. "Also, I could smell you!" she said, turning now to look at her friend.

"Hiya, Libby," said Freya upon final arrival. "And hello there, Dwayne," she added, having a seat and then patting the rock fondly. "And I take it you mean you could smell *these*?" asked Freya of Libby, presenting a steaming hot portion of chips. "I called round the house when you didn't answer your phone, and your gran informed me that you'd gone for a walk. I figured you might be here, and likely in need of chips with extra vinegar, and so here I am," Freya told her. "And if you *didn't* end up being here, well then, I'd just have to eat the chips myself, wouldn't I? So, it would work out quite well either way, you see," she declared happily.

"Thanks. But I'm not really very hungry just now," said Libby, along with a shrug, and then a sigh.

CHAPTER EIGHT

"Things must be serious if you don't want chips," suggested Freya. "Are you sure you don't want any?" she asked, holding the chips aloft and bobbing them up and down in the air like a little boat rising and falling on the ocean's waves, trying to lighten her friend's spirits.

In response, Libby emptied the wrappers from her pockets for Freya's inspection. "Oh, there's no problem with my appetite in general, sadly, as you can see," she answered. "Two Hobnobs I ate on the way here. And the rest I polished off once I got here. The entire packet," she said in reference to one of the empty wrappers. "I've also made significant inroads into a supposedly family-sized bar of Mint Aero," she added, in reference to the second empty wrapper in her hands. "And by 'made significant inroads' what I mean is that, regrettably, I ate the whole bloody thing. So, yeah, my appetite is unfortunately really quite healthy even if the food itself isn't."

"Ah, well if you don't want any, then, as I said, I'll just..." Freya responded, pulling the chips in close to her own person, and away from Libby.

"Get those little beauties back over here this instant!" Libby demanded, reaching in and snatching them up. "You're my best friend, and so you should know when I'm only trying to convince myself of something and failing miserably!" she advised, giving Freya a sort of friendly glare. "Thank you! Thank you!" she said as she popped one chip into her mouth, and then another.

It was unclear as to whether Libby was talking to Freya or the chips at this point, whether she was thanking Freya, or thanking the chips themselves for being so delicious, as Libby appeared to be addressing the chips directly as she spoke.

"We all know it's impossible to refuse chips!" Libby added, flaring her nostrils and taking in the tantalising aroma. "They smell absolutely *divine*," she observed contentedly. And, again, it was difficult to tell if Libby was talking to Freya at this stage or if she was speaking specifically to the chips, because she stared lovingly at the chips themselves as she was complimenting their heavenly scent.

"You okay, Libs?" asked Freya, worried for her friend. "I mean, you're not here to, you know...?" she said, nodding her head down towards the remaining section of cliff beneath where they were currently sat. She was half-joking, but half-serious as well, for she honestly was concerned. "I feel like, as your friend, that I should just double-check, yeah? I mean, I know you're depressed at present."

Libby followed Freya's line of sight, looking down to the rolling ocean waves a short distance away. "What? Jump into the sea? No, don't worry, of course I'm not going to jump. Plus, it's only about, what, ten or fifteen feet to the water? And knowing my luck lately, even if I *did* want to top myself, I'd probably just end up floating anyway," she said. "Mind you," she continued, whilst availing herself of another chip or three, "I *have* eaten two thousand calories or more in only the last half hour alone, so I suppose, now I think on it, I'd sink like a bloody stone!"

"Seriously, though, Libs, you know I'm here if you want to talk, right?" offered Freya.

Libby smiled. "I know. And thanks for that. But I'll be fine, Freya," she answered. "I know I shouldn't let men get to me like this, but they all seem to be the bleeding same," she went on. "I'm nearly thirty, Freya and I'm still attracting complete arseholes. I thought I'd left them all behind in London and I held out the romantic notion that all the men over here would be charming gents who'd each be climbing over one another to be with a girl as wonderful as me. I suppose I'm just feeling a bit stupid, if I'm being honest," she said. "Ah, men," she sighed, taking another couple of chips in hand. "Who bloody needs them, anyway? All they do is fart, clog up your bath with hair, snore, talk endlessly about footy, and... and..." she put forth, searching for yet another example of how useless they could be.

"Disappoint in bed?" Freya suggested helpfully.

"Exactly," replied Libby. "Who needs men when you can have chips!"

"Chips never disappoint," remarked Freya sagely.

"No they do not," Libby couldn't help but to agree, plunging her current handful of the tasty little devils into her mouth with reckless abandon to emphasise the point.

But despite Libby's current enthusiasm and the brave front she was presenting, it seemed apparent to Freya that Libby had

CHAPTER EIGHT

not *entirely* given up on men in favour of chips. "So, have you heard from Luke, at least?" she asked.

Libby shook her head in the negative. "Not a call, text, or anything in three days," she answered. "And I suppose this only proves James correct, now doesn't it?"

"Oh? How so?" asked Freya.

"Well, I reckon Luke's moved on to his next conquest, hasn't he?" replied Libby. "Because I didn't become his latest notch after our first date, I expect he's set his sights on someone who's more of a guarantee, as it were."

"Hmm," said Freya, considering this. "Still, you *did* show him your boob before the end of your first date, even if it was an accident, though, am I right? So that can only be a good thing in his mind," she pointed out. "Anyway, I take it you've not tried calling him?" Freya asked. "It could be as simple a thing as a misunderstanding, couldn't it? I mean, as far as who was meant to call who next or what have you?"

"*Call him?*" protested Libby. "He's out trying to bonk half the town, by all accounts, and I'm supposed to *phone* him? Besides, I'm the one in a mood with him, aren't I? So I shouldn't have to phone him. That's not the way these things work."

Freya offered a noncommittal shrug of the shoulders. Her friend was upset, and so Freya was willing to overlook Libby's confused logic, along with her use of the word *bonk*. It was a word that Freya thought consigned to history — rather like the contents of her chip carton that Libby was managing to make remarkably short work of. Freya tried, failingly, to suppress a burgeoning smile as another thought then came to mind. "So how's James?" she asked offhandedly.

"*So how's James?*" asked Libby, repeating Freya's own words. "And what's *that* supposed to mean?"

"What?" said Freya with a laugh. "I don't mean anything by it. And you're the one who brought him up," she replied, using her hand to conceal her grin which had now changed to a crooked smirk. "Ahh, sunset's nice tonight..." she added, looking out to the lovely view, as if to change the subject.

"*Nothing's* going on with James," Libby assured Freya, in no uncertain terms.

"Okay. If you say so," replied Freya, still keeping her eyes on the unfolding of Nature's glorious spectacle.

"I know what you're doing, Freya," Libby answered. "James is just helping out with my e-commerce strategy and whatnot," she told her. "That's it!"

"And *whatnot*," Freya replied, her crooked grin now turning into a broad smile.

"Freya!" Libby shouted.

"So, the chap who's *just* helping you with your e-commerce strategy and whatnot has been around to your shop, what, three times in two days, I think you told me?" Freya advanced.

"He needed to take photographs for the website!" exclaimed Libby.

"Right. And this also being the chap who recently confessed to having feelings for you, previously?" Freya was only too happy to point out.

"It's all professional and above board," declared Libby. "And it's five times, not three," she admitted.

"What is?" asked Freya.

"James. He's been around five times," Libby responded.

"I thought you told me yesterday it was three times?" asked Freya.

"I told you that in the morning," Libby answered. "He was in twice after that, later the same day."

"I see," said Freya, arching an eyebrow.

"He wanted to evaluate my merchandise presentation skills!" insisted Libby.

"I'll bet he did," said Freya. But she could sense the elastic band she was stretching was just about to snap, and so didn't press this gentle teasing to the point of breaking. "We can get a pint of cider when we're done here, if you like?" she proposed, charting a course away from the topic of James.

"Yes," replied Libby, without any sort of hesitation at all. "You know…" she added, steering even further away from the subject of James, "You know how I was reading my grandad's journal?"

Freya nodded her head, inviting further details.

CHAPTER EIGHT

"He's really so sweet," Libby went on. "Well, *was* so sweet, of course," she added, correcting herself. "Randy little so-and-so when he was younger, though!"

"Oh-ho. My kind of fella," Freya entered in.

"But it's cute reading about how he met my gran, you know? How he's desperately trying to woo the woman of his dreams," Libby continued.

"I wonder if he does…?" asked Freya, only half paying attention, as her mind had drifted off, temporarily, thinking about that pint she'd suggested a few moments before.

"Of course he does, Freya! How else would I even be on this earth talking to you right now if he hadn't!" Libby had to remind her.

"What? Oh, sorry, I was thinking about…" Freya replied. "Ah, never mind. Sorry. Back in the room now. Go on, then."

"It is a curious thing, though, to be able to read his journals and follow along with the journey he's taking when I know what the eventual outcome is going to be, even if I don't know the exact details of how he gets there in the end," Libby carried on. "It's like watching a movie where you already know how things will end, but you just don't know the twists and turns of how it all leads there. Do you know what I mean?"

"Like Titanic?" suggested Freya.

"I suppose so, yes," agreed Libby. "Except without the terrible bit at the conclusion, of course."

"Of course," granted Freya.

"But, yeah," continued Libby. "In the case of Titanic, we all know what's going to happen in the end, but we don't know the precise journey of Jack and Rose before they both meet their respective fates. So I suppose it does feel in that respect a bit like I'm reading about Jack and Rose. Which is sweet, in a way."

"Only I hope your grandad was a better swimmer than young Jack was!" Freya offered.

They both laughed. And then the two friends sat in quiet reflection for a long moment, there on Dwayne Johnson, enjoying the last gasp of daylight on another beautiful summer's eve on the Isle of Man.

"Thanks," said Libby eventually.

"For what?" asked Freya, rising to her feet, hands raised to the heavens for a quick stretch.

"Just for being you," Libby answered. "You went out of your way to find me when you knew I was a little down in the dumps, and I do appreciate that," she offered. "Give us a hand, will you?" she added, reaching up.

As Freya pulled her chip-laden friend up to her feet, she smiled as a thought occurred. "Just think, Libs. In a few years, someone could be reading *your* journal."

"Oh, *that'd* certainly be a treat for them," Libby answered with a smirk. "Single loser with a failing business, who keeps eating too much, even though she's supposed to be training for a race? Quite a tale it'll be, for sure." Libby bent down to pick up her wrappers and the now-empty chip carton, letting out a groan as she did so. "Bloody hell, I think you'll need to push me around in a wheelbarrow at this rate," she advised.

"What, for the race?" asked Freya. "So it's now a wheelbarrow race, then, is it?"

"It well could be!" said Libby, patting her belly. "There aren't any rules saying it can't!"

Freya placed an arm around Libby. "Everything will turn out all right, Libby, you'll see," she offered kindly, giving Libby's shoulder a gentle squeeze. "I mean, so what if Luke hasn't ended up being the man of your dreams as you might have hoped? You'll find Mr Right eventually, sure enough. You may kiss a few frogs along the way, yes, but one of them will turn out to be a Prince!"

"If you say so, Freya," answered Libby, trying to look to the positive.

"Chin up!" instructed Freya. "Don't forget, your grandad is single now at the point you're reading, yes? When he was writing those entries of his he might well have thought he'd be single forever, mind, and just look how that turned out, right? And as for your business, well, I'm sure with the efforts you're now putting in that you can turn things straight around."

"If you say so, Freya," Libby said again. "If you say so, it must be true, yeah?" she then said, with the inclusion of a hopeful smile this time.

CHAPTER EIGHT

Freya gave Libby another encouraging squeeze. "Just think, Libby..." she said, taking her free hand and sweeping it across the horizon. "Your grandkids could be reading about *your* love story one day. Like Jack and Rose! Only instead of Jack and Rose, it'll be the story of James and Libby!"

"I'll throw you over this cliff in a minute!" said Libby, pulling away and offering her friend a playful punch on the arm. "And in this rubbish analogy of yours — rubbish because James is in it! — if it's not the Titanic, it'll be the bloody Lusitania!"

"No, no. Never. Now come on, Rose, let's go and get this pint," concluded Freya. "Night-night, Dwayne," Freya added, blowing a kiss to her favourite section of rock. "See you soon."

"A pint it is," said Libby, in full agreement, at least in regard to this particular suggestion specifically. "At least now you're finally making a bit of sense!"

Chapter Nine

3rd April

I'm turning into a minor celebrity around these parts, as it should happen. Today, I received a hand-delivered letter from the mayor's office inviting me to the town hall for their annual civic awards ceremony. According to the fancy formal script, I'm going to be one of the recipients of a bravery award for tackling that thief. The lettering was embossed and everything. With gold leaf! Mum and Gran must have visited every house within at least a mile radius to show the letter off to anybody who was even remotely interested and even to those who probably weren't.

Earlier, I had a third painting lesson with Gwen today. The letter hadn't arrived at that point so I couldn't tell her about it. Anyway I'd finally gathered up the courage to ask her out on a proper date, but just as I was about to, she only went and mentioned her ex-boyfriend. My heart sank for a moment and I nearly spilt paint all over myself. I thought she was going to tell me she was getting back with him, but thankfully it's just the opposite. (That's good!) Apparently, he is acting like her bloody shadow, can't really accept that it's over between them, and is, in her words, a bit of a pain in the bum. I'm pleased that she was confiding in me like this, but at the same time, by telling me about such things, I'm wondering if she sees me as one of her girlfriends? (That would be bad!)

I might have a quiet word in this fella's shell-like, just to tell him to back off! I can do that, can't I? I AM getting a bravery award after all.

Just had a thought. I could invite Gwen to the award ceremony!! I should have my new suit by then as well. This could be perfect timing.

I reckon I'll phone her tomorrow and ask her. What's the worst she could say!?

Well, okay, granted, the worst she could say is no. Saying no would definitely not be good. Still, nothing ventured, as they say, right?

3:15 a.m. – Wait, I can't just invite her to an awards ceremony with my family as our first proper date, can I? Maybe that would be a bit odd? I mean, most first dates would consist of a trip to the cinema and then perhaps a stop at the chip shop on the way home, that sort of thing. Or then again she might think accompanying me to the awards ceremony is the coolest thing ever?

Sod it! I'm going to phone her up in the morning and suggest taking her out. Not to the awards ceremony. Not yet at least. But for something a little more informal first.

Hmm, but where? Where shall we go? Cinema? Or something else?

Well, I suppose I'll worry about where we'll go once she says yes. Maybe something will come to mind?

Hang on, what if she says no? I shouldn't like that very much, her saying no. Dealing with rejection is a real bugger. If only I wasn't feeling all these bloody feelings! Blimey, this never used to happen. It doesn't seem all that long ago that all I was worried about was my stamp collection, that being my largest concern in life.

Right. Stop bothering me, brian! I need to sleep!

CHAPTER NINE

Ugh, I just realised I misspelt brain. Who's Brian? There's no Brian here! I meant brain. I just called my brain Brian. Bloody hell. I definitely need to sleep.

4th April

Well, it turns out that Gwen doesn't even really like painting all that much! After I'd finally mustered up the nerve to phone her but then stammered down the phone for what seemed like an eternity, I finally, eventually, got round to asking her out. Her response? "Took your blooming time, didn't you? I've had to go on pretending to like oil painting for three odd weeks now!"

To be fair, she wasn't the most diligent student as evidenced by her saying it was oil rather than ink wash. But she didn't dislike painting, necessarily. She just wasn't as keen on it as she'd led me to believe, she told me, as it was simply an excuse to get to know me better. She's a right crafty one, she is.

Anyway, she said yes!!! About the date, I mean. Though I wasn't really fully expecting her to say yes, if I'm being honest, and so when she asked where I was going to take her on this date of ours I was at somewhat of a loss. Consequently, I just pulled an idea out of thin air. Because of this impulsive response, I now need to find out if there is a circus performing anywhere nearby, as it should happen! And she got very excited when I suggested the circus as well, so I can't exactly back out of it. What was I even thinking? Why the blazes did I suggest the circus???

While I had her on the phone, I also told her all about my glorious letter from the mayor and promised I'd let her see it. Which, on reflection, possibly sounded a little lame and rather came across like a school pupil bringing something in for show and tell? She might be impressed by it when she sees it, though, one never knows.

Anyhow the important thing is that I've got a date with Gwen!!! She is lovely, if I haven't said that before. I think I've said that before. Still, it bears repeating. She is lovely.

And as if that wasn't enough of a brilliant day already, I've also booked the boat passage for me and Terry to go to the Isle of Man TT races. His romance is on the rocks again, so it looks like it's just going to be the two of us, which is fine with me. I better speak to my Auntie Norma and make sure it's okay that we stay with her when we go over there, just to confirm. She's quite a bit older than my mum, so hopefully having two beer monsters like me and Terry won't pose too much of a problem. Hmm, I wonder if Gwen likes motorbike racing? Perhaps she might like to come along as well?

7th April

Gwen not only held to our date but also seemed to quite enjoy it. I couldn't find a circus anywhere, but there was a special offer on at the zoo, so we went there instead. I might have seen an advert in the paper, which made me think of animals and suggest the circus in the first place?

She looked stunning when I picked her up, and she even called me her hero for getting an award from the mayor. I puffed out my chest, raised my pecker proudly in the air, and said it was nothing. Also, I must be getting braver because I plucked up the courage to ask her if she wanted to come along to the civic ceremony and she said she'd love to!

I bought her a giant stuffed polar bear which, on reflection, wasn't the best idea to do quite so early in the day as I had to lug the large furry chap around with us from then on, and it was a fairly warm day. Ah well.

She laughed at my jokes, which was a result, as they are often awful. I don't think she was just being polite, though, or at least I hope not. And I did manage to really split her

CHAPTER NINE

sides when we arrived at the monkey enclosure, though to be fair that really wasn't my doing. See, just as I was reading the sign that warned the public to beware of one Derek the Defecator, I had the misfortune of finding out firsthand this wasn't just a friendly nickname the lads had given one of the primates. No sir it was not. And it turns out Derek can hurtle faeces at the same velocity as a bloody discharged bullet. The projectile exploded on my tee shirt, so it did, with several fragments of the dried excrement also landing in my hair in the process. Gwen laughed, the zookeeper laughed, the coachload of school kids on a day out laughed, and Derek himself seemed particularly pleased with himself also, the manky little maggot.

Fortunately, the zookeeper was kind enough to help me brush myself off. It seemed like he was used to doing this on a regular basis, as he had a cloth at the ready for just such purpose.

The good thing that came about from the whole incident, however, was when Gwen gave me a lovely sympathy hug. She seemed very gentle and delicate about it, though, and strangely so in fact, until I realised she was just being careful I was completely clean from bits of poo before she leaned in for it!

And as if a hug wasn't brilliant enough in itself, she gave me a peck on the face as well, I'm pleased to report. I was very sweet, she said, protecting her stuffed polar bear from harm as I did during the assault. What I didn't tell Gwen, of course, was that I'd very nearly used the bear as a shield! It was just pure instinct, is what it was, and I'd only managed to catch myself at the very end, tucking him behind my back at the last possible instant. And it's a good thing I did as it resulted in that kiss! And it never would've happened without Derek, so I reckon I should give credit where credit is due. Right, so thank you, Derek, you cheeky little devil!

14th April

Sorry, diary. I see it's been a week since my last entry, and I feel like I've been ignoring an old friend. But just loads of things going on, and I've been neglectful in writing it all down. I will try harder in future, I promise!

Gran had been pestering me to meet the new girl that, as she's put it, has brought a twinkle to my eye. Is it that obvious???

I wasn't sure if I should, as I didn't know if it might be a bit too daunting or off-putting for Gwen at this early stage to make the rounds meeting the family and all. Anyway, I suggested it to Gwen and she said she'd be honoured, as it turned out. So I went ahead and introduced the two of them a couple of days ago, and Gwen even baked a wonderful spiced banana cake special for the occasion. Gran adores banana cake, as it should happen (or any kind of cake, really, now I think on it) so that naturally went down very well with her. They spoke like old friends for over an hour, so I don't know what I was ever worried about.

Afterwards, I swung by my house to introduce Gwen to Mum and Dad as well. And again, similar as she did with Gran, she knocked them bandy. Dad's gushing appraisal of her was that she was, his exact words, a cracking lass. Mum was quick to echo this sentiment, though seemed sad when I mentioned the banana cake as we'd not brought any along with us from Gran's.

As far as the trip to the Isle of Man, it turns out Terry's on again off again romance is now firmly back on. Who knew all that was required for true love to flourish was the offer of a two-week all-inclusive holiday in Benidorm? (Which I've no idea how he can even afford, mind.) Anyhow, that means I'm now stuck with a spare boat ticket for the ferry, and also left wondering once again if I should ask Gwen if she fancies coming on holiday with me. But I dunno. I've only had a quick cuddle and a peck on the cheek so far and

CHAPTER NINE

so a holiday might be a little too much to ask at this early stage?

Right. Civic ceremony tomorrow! The suit arrived today, and I've even bought a new pair of shoes to go with it which Dad, being the brilliant dad that he is, kindly showed me how to polish to an extra gleaming shine as well. I tried on the whole kit and caboodle tonight to see how I looked, and I do look rather dapper even if I do say so myself. And I DO say so myself, though Mum was happy to verify it also.

Unrelated, I need to start thinking about art college. I need to complete a portfolio as part of my course, and I've not been giving that as much attention as I should. I see art college as the ticket out of my dreary career in printing, so I must and will knuckle down. BERT YOU WILL KNUCKLE DOWN!!!

16th April

I'm officially the bravest person in town because the mayor himself told me last night and I also have a certificate confirming it. My head was bloody thumping this morning from too many celebratory drinks. It was such a good night and my new suit certainly didn't disappoint what with me getting several compliments and a couple of admiring glances from some older ladies. Gwen also looked unbelievable – like a film star – and smelt amazing, like strawberries, as she always does. I wonder if it's some kind of perfume she uses, or if she just naturally smells like that all the time?

Mum, Dad, and Gran were exceptionally proud of me, and Gran made a point of pointing out to everyone at the drinks reception that I was her grandson. I think Gran – no, strike that, I KNOW Gran – had too much to drink as she started getting rather flirtatious with the mayor and at one stage tried to take his mayoral chains off from around his neck. He was a good sport about it, at least, and

I'm not entirely sure he wasn't rather enjoying the attention anyway (up until his wife returned)!

I walked Gwen home afterwards and it was my turn to kiss her on the cheek this time. She smiled and said I cleaned up quite nicely and looked grand in my new suit.

She is so lovely.

18th April

Tonight's headline in the local press!

Local Hero Commended for Tackling Thief

I think Mum must have purchased every bloody paper she could get her hands on so she'd be able to distribute a copy to absolutely anyone she knows, on account of yours truly being on page four. The photographer at the awards' reception took a belting picture of me where Gwen was hanging proudly from my arm. The boys down the pub are going to be impressed when they see it in the paper. Oh, and the mayor was beside me there also, come to think of it. I expect the lads will be impressed seeing me stood there with the mayor, so there's that as well. The photo and accompanying article filled nearly half a page. Well chuffed am I.

On another matter, I now need Terry's romance to remain on track as Gwen has agreed to come to the Isle of Man with me. Not that the bloody rotter would have been getting the ticket back from me anyway after deserting me for a Benidorm trip (that I'm certain he can't afford in the first place).

I do hope that my scooter is up for the journey, as I've only ever ridden a maximum of about five miles in one go, so I'll be praying that an Isle of Man road trip won't be a test too much.

1:46 a.m. – Laying here awake and a thought just occurred. What do I do about the sleeping arrangements when we're

CHAPTER NINE

on the Isle of Man? I've only ever pecked her on the cheek, so it's not like we're intimate or anything. Oh god, I don't even know how to bring it up. What if she thinks I'm some sort of moral degenerate trying to get her into bed? And what's Auntie Norma going to say about me bringing a girl over instead of Terry, I wonder? Given Auntie's age, she might be old-fashioned and offended by that sort of thing? There's not a ghost of a chance I could get a hotel to stay at either, as I imagine they're all booked up months in advance for people attending the races.

2:23 a.m. – On consideration, sharing a bed with Gwen would be rather nice, I should think. Certainly much better than sharing one with Terry!

Argh, need to put such thoughts away. Must go to sleep.

Will absolutely do some painting tomorrow, right? Right!

19th April

I went painting after work as these lighter nights are a godsend to get out and about. There's a field only about ten minutes or so away from our house with the biggest oak tree you've ever seen. Must be hundreds of years old, I expect. Sitting under it, you get the most inspiring view of the valley, with rolling tree-lined hills any way you look. It's the most idyllic setting you could imagine, perfect for painting any number of scenes from under the tree or even painting the tree itself. I phoned Gwen up this morning to see if she wanted to come along as I know she'd love it up there. Yes, I know she's not as keen on painting as she first made herself out to be! But, as I say, it's lovely up there. Her mum said she was busy when I phoned, though.

Strange.

Or maybe it isn't? Maybe it's nothing.

I'm sure it's nothing. But I've been dwelling on it for most of the day. I wish I didn't overthink things quite so much like this. People can be legitimately busy after all and there's nothing wrong with that and it doesn't mean they don't want to be with you.

Although maybe I'm coming across as too overeager? Am I pushing too hard? Expecting too much?

Bert, don't be stupid. Stop overthinking this, you bloody eejit.

20th April

I'm completely gutted. The smoke didn't wake us all up, but the sirens surely did. Three fire engines were outside at about five this morning. Woke the entire street, in fact.

Some complete wanker only went and set fire to my scooter in the rear garden. It's a complete write-off. And the bike was leaning against the shed, so it's destroyed most of that also. The only positive is that the fire was extinguished before it reached the house.

I'm fuming that someone could do this. Why would someone do this?

Not only that but it's evening now as I write this down and I've still not heard back from Gwen, which tops off a thoroughly awful day.

21st April

The police paid us a visit today. They suspect the arson attack might have something to do with the thief that I tackled, revenge, they're thinking, and that the filthy blighter has probably seen the newspaper picture from the awards ceremony and tracked me down. What a comforting thought! The officer told me this particular fella is well known to them already and is, in their own words, an unsavoury character.

I needed my scooter to go to the TT races!

CHAPTER NINE

Most if not all of Dad's garden tools and such have also been destroyed in the fire to the shed, so he's unhappy about that as you can well imagine but of course thankfully doesn't blame me.

Still nothing from Gwen. I phoned her again, but her mum said she was out. I'm starting to think that asking her to the TT races was a bad idea? Maybe it was too much too soon?

How can I go from being on cloud nine last week to this? Feeling completely terrible.

22nd April

The police came around to confirm that they'd spoken to the thief about the fire. They said that he's currently on police bail awaiting trial for another matter, but they're now fairly certain it wasn't him that started the fire, at least, due to him having a cast-iron alibi for that particular time period. That's not to say it couldn't be one of his dodgy lowlife friends what done it, though, perhaps even at this wazzock's direction, and the police advise that we should all be extra vigilant. They'll also send a few extra patrol cars this way throughout the night, they assured us, so grateful for that.

I've suggested to Gran that I'll move in with her for a few days until things settle down. It might be being overly cautious, but I just don't want to think of her on her own in case one of this idiot's friends is on a revenge mission or something. Mum and Dad also think it's a good idea too. Gran was delighted at the suggestion. She's not frightened, necessarily. She can handle herself in a fight, she tells me! But she's happy enough to spend some more time with me, she says.

Still nothing from Gwen. I tried phoning her house again, but there was no answer this time. I mentioned to the police that she was included in the picture at the civic ceremony, just in case she might possibly be in any danger because of it. They said they certainly hoped the culprit wouldn't sink that low, but also said they'd check in on her periodically to be on the safe side. Again, grateful for their efforts.

Should I go over to Gwen's house myself? I'm concerned for her, of course. But then again if she's given me the boot then it just seems a bit sad on my part and I'll end up making a right fool of myself, won't I?

HAS she given me the boot? Were we even a proper couple?

Oh bloody hell. I can't see me getting too much sleep tonight.

23rd April

I've moved into Gran's spare room. I was thinking about bringing some sort of weaponry along with me, such as my old cricket bat, or a golf club or summat, just for the sake of protection. Gran advised me not to bother, though, as she could easily disable any attacker or assailant, she told me, rendering them in a state of complete agony should the need arise. I thought this was all a load of good-natured bollocks, mind you. But when I got here, she explained to me how it was done. She even demonstrated with a knitting needle, showing me how to go about it, and said she could do the same with any manner of ordinary household objects. Blimey, where did she learn skills like that? Does Gran have secret military training?? Bloody special forces??

I wasn't sure if she was having me on in an effort to make me feel better or what, but let me tell you she sure looked convincing brandishing about those knitting needles of hers and I certainly wouldn't like to be on the wrong end of them! Just for peace of mind, though, I have taken the

CHAPTER NINE

liberty of positioning my grandad's old walking cane near to the front door. One can't be too careful, after all. It's made of some sort of hardwood or other (cherry? walnut?) and is fairly heavy, the cane, so I could inflict some serious damage with it I reckon should an appropriate opportunity present itself.

Gran's been baking so hopefully while I'm here, however, the only thing in danger of being waylaid is my waistline.

Nothing from Gwen. I've phoned once from here, and I've also called home three times over the course of the day to check and see if she might have tried to reach me there. I think Mum must have been getting a bit fed up with me by the end of the day, to be honest, with all the pestering.

24th April

The police came to see me in work today and I now know why I've not been able to speak to Gwen all week. They checked up on her, just as they'd promised, only the outcome wasn't good. It wasn't good at all. Not even the least little bit.

I can't believe this even as I'm writing it.

The police have informed me Gwen is in a bad way and has been in hospital. They told me she was viciously assaulted after finishing work at the pub the other night and ended up with several injuries including a broken jaw! When she's able, they'll need to take a report from her.

For the love of god, who would do something like this to a beautiful gentle soul like Gwen?

They don't know who was responsible, which explains why her mum was rather evasive on the phone. Jesus have mercy, I hope her parents don't think I could be in any way responsible for it?

Who the hell has done this to you, Gwen???

Oh Gwen. My wonderful, lovely Gwen!

Chapter Ten

Libby plonked her bum down on the sea wall opposite her shop. She hadn't slept much the previous couple of nights, what with matters of love and business both playing on her mind, and so her morning coffee was today an extra-large. She'd likely be requiring at least several trips to the loo before lunchtime because of it, she reckoned, but she needed a pick-me-up to get her mental engine shifted into gear for the day ahead.

As for said matters of love, she'd still not heard anything from Luke. Not that she wanted to in any way, shape, or form... or at least that's what she told herself. Deep down, though, she'd harboured the notion that he would come begging for a second chance once he realised what an utterly momentous mistake he'd made in not realising how fortunate he'd been to be even in with a shot with such a catch as she. Granted, after a fitful night's sleep, she probably wasn't looking as glamorous as she usually did right about now, but that was nothing the flagon of coffee in her grip couldn't sort out.

She adored this time of the morning, the quiet solitude after those commuting to work and the kids going off to school had come and gone. It was still a little too early for the majority of the tourists and other beachgoers to have taken up position on the sand, so Libby had the beach pretty much to herself. She sipped her coffee, enjoying the gentle, hypnotic sound of the waves lapping the shore, the gulls circling round overhead, and the smell of the briny sea air.

She could only relax for so long, of course, as she'd need to open the door of the bookshop in a bit. She pivoted on the wall so that she was facing the shop, the sight of the shopfront bringing a smile to her face. It was a charming Olde-World style structure with weathered wooden panelling, panelling that was a challenge to maintain on account of the often-volatile Irish Sea being only a stone's throw away but certainly worth the effort in upkeep. She read the name, there on the sign on the front of the building — The Bookshop by the Beach — and still had a hard time believing it was all hers.

Her current vantage point put her in mind of a picture she'd seen on her gran's social media page, as she suspected it was taken from right about that very spot. She placed her oversized coffee cup down onto the seawall and retrieved her phone from her handbag, unlocking the screen and using her index finger to swipe to the camera roll, opening up Gran's image of the shop that she'd saved to her phone. She held up the phone, comparing Gran's photo with her own view, confirming that this was indeed the spot from where Gran's photograph was taken.

Libby sighed contentedly, cradling her phone in her lap now, and studying the image on the screen. There was Gran and Grandad, outsized pair of scissors poised and ready for action, blades hovering above a yellow ribbon placed across the entrance. They looked proud as Punch, definitely well chuffed! And the crowd of friends and well-wishers gathered together there as well had smiles all around. The image had definitely captured a joyous occasion, of that there was no doubt, and in fact Libby could make out champagne flutes in many of the onlookers' hands, all of them clearly eager to toast to the success of the excited shopkeepers. Everyone's obvious enthusiasm in the photo warmed Libby's heart, and it made Libby happy to see her grandparents so happy. If Libby needed any additional motivation to make a success of this business, there it was. All Libby had to do was just look at all the beaming faces in that photograph to give her the required boost. And while it wasn't champagne she was drinking today, Libby raised her own beverage in the direction of the shop as those people so many years earlier had done, happily joining in on their toast. "Cheers, you lot!" she said, before pressing her coffee to her lips.

CHAPTER TEN

Libby glanced at her watch, swinging one leg back and forth from the knee like a pendulum keeping the beat and marking time. It was still fairly early. She wondered to herself what Gran might be up to at this very moment. In the midst of some workout routine, perhaps?

Gran had joined a social club on the island, a social club which catered to the rather more mature demographic. Yes, Gran was now an official card-carrying member of the Lonely Heart Attack Club which, amongst several initiatives on the go, also had an activities club called the Silver Sprinters. This energetic bunch would meet as often as they could manage, for whatever endeavours that might possibly be dreamt up. It was quite the vision to see twenty or so pensioners performing a wide array of activities, be it a Tai Chi workout on the beach, for instance, or something more pulse-quickening like roller-blading up and down the promenade. It was a delight for Libby to see her gran so active, and the folk at her club had smashed the stereotype of the elderly sat at home in their robe and slippers. No, this lot liked to keep busy, and were, for the most, an inspiration to demonstrate that advancing years were not a barrier to having a bloody good time.

Libby drained what contents remained of her cup, and could practically feel her pupils dilate due to the caffeine overload. And, then, they dilated a second time, as...

"What the? What's all this, then?" she said, straining her eyes to get a better look at what very much looked, coincidentally, like Gran herself coming right Libby's way. It was indeed Gran, Libby was soon able to confirm as the figure got closer, but what on earth was she doing? Libby pushed herself down from the wall and raised her phone, which was now in record mode to capture the moment. Libby chuckled. "Mad as a hatter!" she remarked merrily, for no one's benefit but her own, though possibly capturing her observation on the audio portion of the video she was recording in the process.

Dressed in a purple Lycra catsuit, most women of Gran's age would be quite happy for a gentle stroll, no hurry at all, soaking up the seaside setting, and perhaps contemplating at leisure what the day ahead might have to offer. Not Gwen Tebbit, however, whose arms were spinning like a windmill as, skipping up the promenade with her rope, she was advancing at a fairly impressive rate of speed. As she approached, her cheeks puffing like a steam train, she received a less than inconspicuous ogle from a young lad in a car the colour of an unsightly shade of faded green and with an overly loud exhaust in desperate need of repair. The spotty teen propped his elbow on the frame of the open window, leaning out and smiling as his car drew level with what he must have thought was a 'hottie' out for a morning run. His jaw fell, however, as did his foot on the accelerator, when he realised that what he was seeing wasn't a young hottie at all, but rather a much-more-mature-than-anticipated hottie.

"Did you see that? He was totally checking you out!" Libby called over to her, proud that her gran had the ability to still turn a head or two.

Gran's spinning arms came to a halt with the grace of a swan landing on a tranquil lake, gathering up the skipping rope in her hands, all in one fluid motion. "In the green car?" she asked, freeing one hand and offering a cheerful wave should the lad be looking in his rear-view mirror. "Oh, it happens all the time," she added to Libby with an assured sniff.

"Oi, so what's with the skipping rope, Gran?" asked Libby. "I don't remember you leaving the house with it this morning. Did you nick it from the club?"

"Not nicked. Borrowed!" replied Gran. Gran casually draped the rope over her shoulder, and then leaned over, placing her hands on the seawall beside Libby and using it to stretch out any lingering knots in her legs. "It was a Rocky-inspired workout today," she announced.

"It was, was it? As in the boxer, Rocky?" asked Libby.

"Yes, that's right," replied Gran, still doing her stretches. "Ten minutes shadowboxing, ten minutes jogging, and then a vigorous skip to the Rocky theme tune," Gran explained.

"Ah," replied Libby, nodding approvingly.

"Right. And I still had a little petrol left in the tank. Which is why I took the rope with me, you see, and carried on with the skipping part," Gran explained further.

CHAPTER TEN

"A-ha," said Libby. And then a thought occurred to her. "So. Have you punched any slabs of meat on your way here, then?" she asked. "I mean, in keeping with the overall Rocky theme?"

"Not yet, but there's still time! Good idea, in fact, as I'll need to walk past the butcher's on the way home, yeah?"

"Very good, then," Libby replied with a laugh.

Gran pushed herself off from the wall, straightening herself up. Then she glanced about, surveying the scene, examining her surroundings as if just now realising where her rope-skipping excursion had led her. "Right. What should we do for breakfast?" she asked. "How about we get some waffles?" she proposed. "Yes. Waffles and syrup. Most definitely," she declared, answering her own question with confidence, the matter apparently settled.

"Hmm. I could definitely see myself eating some waffles," agreed Libby, happy to oblige. "I still have a bit of time before I need to open the shop, and all I've had so far this morning is coffee, so that sounds good to me."

"Off we go, then!" replied Gran.

"Off we go," echoed Libby, and then adding, as an afterthought, "Come on, Mr Balboa. We'll also see if we can find a flight of steps for you to run up!"

The smell of bacon and other general fried grub filled the air at the Cosy Café. Libby sniffed her hair, wondering if she might just have to take another quick shower before work in order to wash away the grease that was likely clinging to every strand. She smiled uneasily as a plump chap in a stained white t-shirt busied himself by wiping down the table next to them. The cloth he was using for this mission was even grubbier than the table he was attempting to clean. Still, he appeared to enjoy his work, shaking his bum in time to the music playing over the radio and giving a glimpse of his builder's bum each time he leaned over, hips gyrating.

Libby averted her eyes, directing them back toward her gran. "Why are we here again, Gran?" whispered Libby through a forced smile. "I mean why here, specifically?"

"The waffles are to die for," replied Gran happily.

"So's the hygiene levels," offered Libby, shooting a quick glance over to the wobbling bum cheeks gyrating only a very short distance away from their table. "I just didn't have this down as your sort of eatery?" she said, her attention focussed once again on Gran.

"It wasn't, but then one of the girls put me on to it," replied Gran. "Trust me, Libby. Once you try these waffles, you'll know what I mean."

"If you say so," Libby answered with a shrug, pleased enough to be sharing Gran's company of course, but not so convinced about this whole waffle business.

Gran then waved politely to catch the attention of the fellow Libby had noticed, rag in hand, beside them. "Heya, Brian," said Gran to Brian, the owner of the jiggling buttocks and also, as it should happen, the café.

"Ah! Ready to order, then? And what can I get you lovely ladies?" asked Brian, now stood before them with notepad in hand and one of those little blue pens that you'd only usually only find in the bookies.

"We'd like some of your delicious waffles, Brian," announced Gran.

"Not a problem," replied Brian, scribbling away. "Would you like them with our very special, extra delicious syrup?" he asked cheerily.

Gran giggled in a manner that surprised Libby. "Yes please, Brian," Gran tittered like a schoolgirl.

"What's special about the syrup?" inquired Libby, innocently enough, and genuinely curious. "Is it the real type of maple syrup? I mean, as opposed to the flavoured imitation kind?"

Brian laughed a jolly laugh, as if this were the most amusing thing he'd heard all morning. "Two orders of waffles with syrup. Coming right up," he said, shaking his head and still chuckling, tearing off their order and returning the notepad to the confines of his waistband from where it was originally retrieved. And with that, Brian headed off to the kitchen, whistling a happy tune as he went.

CHAPTER TEN

"I didn't know I'd said anything funny?" said Libby once Brian had gone, tapping her finger on the table like a telegraph operator. "And was that a bit of flirting going on, Gran? Are you sure it's just the waffles you come in here for?" she asked, giving Gran a look.

"And the special syrup!" replied Gran.

Libby wasn't sure if Gran's response was in answer to the first part of her question, the second part, or both. Either way, she didn't press the issue, and just sat for a few moments instead in silent contemplation. Then, she reached across the table to take her gran's hands in her own, giving them a gentle squeeze. "I love you, Gran!" she said, tilting her head.

"What? What's wrong?" asked Gran, uncertain of where this was coming from all of a sudden, but appreciative nonetheless of the sentiment expressed.

"No, nothing's wrong, Gran," Libby answered her. "No, sorry, I think my emotions have just gone a bit haywire of late, but particularly so from reading Grandad's journal. I feel like a fly on the wall, and it's so strange to think that everything I'm reading about occurred over forty years ago. Oh, and I reached the entry last night where you ended up in hospital, you see. And it's just been playing on my mind, is all."

Gran gave Libby's hands a good squeeze in return. "I'm fine," she assured Libby. "And no need to worry, dear. Because, what happens is—"

Libby promptly pulled her hands away, closed her eyes tightly, and jabbed an index finger into each ear. "La-la-la-la-la!" she said. "I'm not listening!"

For those also in the café waiting for or eating their breakfast, Libby must have appeared very much like a two-year-old having some form of a tantrum. After several seconds or more, Libby opened one eye, tentatively, to see if Gran's lips were still moving. They weren't, and so she felt it safe to unplug her ears. "You mustn't tell me, Gran," said Libby playfully. "You'll ruin the story!"

Gran had a look of bewilderment painted across her face. "But I've told you how I met your grandad before, Libby," she pointed out.

"Yes. Boy meets girl... they get married... they have children," replied Libby, waving her hand in animated fashion as she said this. "But what I haven't known are all the little missing pieces of the puzzle, yeah? Like you ending up in hospital, for instance!"

Gran nodded her head. "Ah. Right, right. I see. Well, just so you know, what happens there is that—" began Gran.

"La-la-la-la-la!" said Libby once again, plugging her ears once more and scrunching her eyes closed. Her general demeanour caused Brian — now with a plate in each hand — to approach with caution.

"She's not had her medication yet this morning," offered Gran, as explanation to Brian.

"A-ha. Right, then..." said Brian, giving Libby as wide a berth as possible.

"So," added Libby once Brian had moved on, her ears now unplugged again. "Promise you won't tell me what happens next?"

Gran nodded in the affirmative, pouring her syrup in spiky wave-shaped motions like the pattern displayed on a heart rate monitor. "Sure, sure," she replied somewhat distractedly, her attention more on the syrup, at present, than anything else. "It's all happened so long ago that you'll probably need to remind me about some of the finer details anyway," she said. But then she raised her head, as she'd just thought of something significant, something important. "I do miss him, Libby," she confided. "He was quite the character, your grandad. And you know what he'd say if he were here now? Sitting right at this very table?"

"No. What would he say?" asked Libby, sitting up straight in her chair, her interest definitely piqued.

"He'd tell you to eat your bloody waffles before they go cold!" Gran answered.

"Fair enough," Libby said with a laugh. And truth be told, once started, she didn't need too much encouragement as, quite to her surprise, she found the waffles to be absolutely sublime. What this little backstreet eatery lacked in sanitation it certainly made up for with its food, she reckoned, and was likely the reason for the constant queue of people she noticed waiting for a table.

CHAPTER TEN

It wasn't long at all before Libby was mopping up the last trace of syrup on her place with her final forkful of waffle. With the last bite devoured, Libby released a contented groan. "That was very good. Very good indeed," she said, leaning back in her chair and caressing her belly. "I think I may have overdone it, and I don't even want to know the amount of calories I just consumed," she added. "Thank goodness I have a fast metabolism," she remarked, "or I'd be done for." She glanced down at her watch. "Oh, fiddlesticks, I'm late!" she exclaimed, now pushing her chair back. "I'm supposed to be meeting James in two minutes at the shop!"

"James?" asked Gran, raising one eyebrow.

"He's helping me with my e-commerce strategy," replied Libby, hands still pressed on tummy. "Bloody hell. I'm supposed to be in training for this race, and I think I've just eaten my own body weight in waffles. Maybe not so smart. Too much of a good thing?" she said, standing up and stretching like a contented cat. She walked over to Gran and placed a kiss on her cheek. "Sorry, but I need to dart. Love you," she said, turning to head towards the exit. "Oh," she added, raising a finger in the air as a thought suddenly occurred to her. "Speaking of this race, Gran," she said, pivoting round. "My entry number was dropped through the letterbox this morning. What confused me was that my number had a little yellow post-it note with my name on it, but there was another number with your name on it as well. My number had the white surround, indicating the 5k run, but the other had a yellow surround, which indicates an entry into the half-marathon."

"Mmm-hmm?" said Gran, mouth full just at the moment.

"Right. So what's all this, then?" asked Libby, placing her hands on her hips. "Were you going to mention this to me at any point?"

Gran raised her fork to indicate she was still mid-chomp, and for Libby to hold that thought for just a moment, as Libby glanced at her watch once more. "You inspired me to enter the race," explained Gran, a moment or two later.

Libby laughed, but of course not in any way unkind. "Gran, you've only gone and entered the half-marathon, now haven't you," she chided her gently. "Now, look, I know you're a sprightly sort and all, but... Gran, you know I'm your biggest supporter in everything you do, yes? But... do you not think you're a little bit too... well... ehm... that is to say..." she said, squirming, searching for a delicate way to say what she wanted to say.

"Old?" replied Gran, saving Libby the trouble.

"Well I didn't want to come right out and say it," Libby told her. "But, well... yeah. That."

"Of course I'm too old! But that's what makes it all the more fun!" Gran happily declared.

After seeing the look of shock and concern on Libby's face, Gran then went on to explain, "I'll not be running that entire distance, silly."

"You're not?" asked a somewhat relieved Libby. "Well thank goodness for that." Then, a look of confusion. "Wait, but how...?"

"I spoke to the organisers, and they're going to allow us to run it in legs," Gran elaborated. "That is, the gang from the Lonely Heart Attack Club. We're going to run it like a relay, see? And if you think I'm old, well, young miss, the average age of those who've signed up is eighty-eight years! Now, I suspect that we're not going to set any records, mind. But if we have a good day out, all of us, and raise some money for the club in the process, then that's just fine, yeah?"

Libby wasn't just fit to burst from overconsumption of waffles, but now also with pride as well. She leaned over and placed her arms around her gran, planting another kiss on her cheek. "You're mad as a hatter, Gran, but I just want you to know what an utterly amazing person you are. I love you lots."

"It runs in the family, kiddo. Being amazing, that is," said Gran, offering up a wink. "And I love you lots as well."

⁂

Libby sprinted from the café, through the narrow streets, and with her stomach churning like a washing machine. She could hear the large coffee she'd drunk earlier sloshing around, bits of waffle no doubt caught up in the swell. She had the *Rocky* theme

CHAPTER TEN

tune running through her head, though — inspired by her earlier conversation — which spurred her on.

She'd been relatively industrious over the previous couple of days, having been given a bit of homework to do by James, homework she could happily attest was completed and that she was hopeful would receive an A+ from teacher. Further motivation to improve the fortunes of her shop was also provided in the form of an invoice received the day before, with that invoice being the current quarter's rent payment on the shop. And on the basis that she'd not yet caught up with the previous quarterly rent, she really did especially value the assistance James continued to offer. Accompanying the invoice was also a covering letter — firm and succinct in tone — advising that further delays to the rent being paid would regrettably not be tolerated, and thirty days' notice was formally issued and would be enforced if all arrears were not rectified. There was further commentary, should the monies not be recovered, regarding eviction, the prospect of which filled Libby with dread.

Confidence of righting the financial ship and getting it sailing smoothly again, however, was reasonably high on account of the new initiatives and improvements that had been made for the shop, all with the help of James. She was also surprised to find that James was also proving to be great company, and Libby found herself actually enjoying their interactions.

Soon...

"Hiya! Sorry!" said Libby, as she came to a halt outside her shop. She leaned over, placing her hands on her thighs, panting to try and catch her breath. "Sorry I'm late," she told James, who was standing leant up against the wall of the shop, waiting patiently, dog lead in hand, familiar friend there at his side.

"Morning. All right?" replied James.

"Sure, sure. All right," Libby answered, straightening herself up now that she'd regulated her breathing to a more respectable level.

"Good, good," said James. "And don't worry, you're fine. Hulk and I were just admiring the lovely view from this side of town. You really are in a splendid location here, overlooking the sea."

During past interactions, Libby would have found herself concerned by James expressing such fond appreciation for her particular locale, suspicious of his intentions. But all fears regarding him possibly having designs on her shop had long since been allayed, and Libby now genuinely valued his counsel. "Right. Well I've completed my assigned research, James, I'm very happy to report," she said to him, unlocking the door. "Come on in, I'll show you."

"Ah. Very good," said James, following her inside.

Libby performed her well-rehearsed morning routine, turning things on, getting things going, and dancing between light switches to bring illumination to her vast retail empire, such as it was.

"Here we are," she said, after all that business was sorted. She was now stood behind her counter, pulling out a printed spreadsheet she'd kept there at the ready in expectation of James's arrival. "I've pored over my records, giving the lot of them a long overdue seeing-to," she said, proud as you like.

"Seeing-to?" asked James, surprised by Libby's phrasing.

"A going-over! I gave them a good going-over!" said Libby, quickly correcting herself. "You know what I meant!"

Fortunately, further embarrassment on Libby's part was alleviated by way of Hulk pressing his nose against her leg, providing a not-unwelcome interruption. "Ah! Hello there, little fellow," she said to the friendly pooch, who'd wandered over to her side of the counter, and she bent down to give him some affection.

Once the ensuing round of generous head-patting to Hulk had run its course and come to its natural conclusion, Libby then stood up and applied her focus back on James. "Now where were we?" she asked, trying to recall where their conversation had left off. "Oh, yes. Here we go," she continued, the paper on the counter in front of her jogging her memory. "Right. So I've detailed my top twenty bestselling books right here," she said, pressing her research forward towards James like a blackjack dealer dishing out a new hand. "Also, as instructed," she went on, "I've cross-referenced my current selling price on each of these titles with that of my main online competitors, in order to

CHAPTER TEN

get some basis for comparison. In addition, as directed, I've been to the post office and, after so many questions I was afraid I was going to make a nuisance of myself, I've now got a proper handle on all the various postage rates as well as shipping and packaging options and such." Libby smiled, pleased with herself for what she'd so ably accomplished. "Oh, and I needn't have worried," she added. "About being a nuisance, I mean, as the people as the post office were perfectly lovely."

"Excellent," said James, nodding his head in approval. "I'm impressed, Libby. And, meanwhile, while you were busy doing that, I've also spent some time thinking about some initiatives for your shop," he told her, removing his jacket as he said this.

Libby couldn't help but notice what was now revealed, there on the front of James's t-shirt. It was an image of Yoda, with a cheeky caption underneath that read: *Offend you I did? My ass you can kiss!*

"Um, aren't you on your way to work after this?" remarked Libby, pointing at the shirt. "I mean it's perhaps not especially, I don't know, customer-friendly, is it...?"

"Hmm?" said James, looking down. "Oh, this," he said, upon seeing what Libby was referring to. "No, it's one of my most popular, actually," he replied. "See, every t-shirt I wear to work, I also sell in the shop. I'm like a walking advertisement!" he explained. "It's probably a similar sort of concept as when you run a book club, I imagine, yeah? In that you recommend a book to your club, and then all your members come in and buy a book to review and discuss, right?"

"When I...?" said Libby, looking back at him blankly.

"When you run a book club," repeated James. "You... do run a book club, yes?" asked James, after the vacant look on Libby's face didn't go away.

"A book club," said Libby in wonderment, turning the idea over in her mind. "Why didn't I think to run a book club?" she asked, as if this were the first time she'd ever thought about it, and this was because it was indeed the first time she'd ever thought about it.

James reached into his leather man bag sat by his feet and whipped out his laptop computer. He joined Libby on her side of the counter. "Scoot over," he said, placing the device in front of them both and opening it up. It took a short moment for the display to wake up, but when it did there was already something queued up on the screen. "Et voilà," announced James with a sweep of the hand, "the Bookshop by the Beach now has its very own website!"

"Oh my goodness!" said Libby. "Already? How have you gone and managed that?"

"I'm a nerd, Libby," James replied with a grin. "My social circle also consists of lots of computer-proficient nerds, and when I put out the call to action to assist a pretty lady in her hour of need, well, they were all only too eager to help," he explained. "Anyway, go ahead and take a gander."

"It looks fantastic!" replied Libby, eyes wide with delight, and having herself a proper look. "And this photo of the shop here on the homepage, I have to say, is so wonderfully inviting. James, you really have a talent for making things appear even more attractive than they are," she observed. "Right! I should have you take my next passport photo, as I look absolutely awful on the current one!" she joked.

"I can't imagine how that would even be possible, you looking bad in any picture ever," replied James, suave as you like.

"Honestly, this all looks brilliant," said Libby, staring straight ahead at the screen. She realised she'd left herself wide open for that remark he'd just made, but she was keen to steer the conversation back to the original topic.

"Right, then," replied James, back to business. "So it's all set up so that you can easily upload images of the books you're wanting to list. And I've taken the liberty of uploading a fair few books for you already, just to get you on the way," he explained. "Just scroll a bit, and... yes, there you are," he said, guiding her along. "And here," he continued, "here's where people can submit reviews, and also use the chatroom feature, so you build a reading community on your website, yeah?"

Libby nodded along, liking what she saw.

"It's fairly straightforward to set or amend pricing, and to add new products, and so forth. And of course you'll be able to take

CHAPTER TEN

payment online now," James told her. "And..." he added teasingly, wiggling his fingers to build suspense.

"And?" asked Libby, now hanging on his every word.

"And," said James, "I've taken the liberty of setting you up with a seller's account on both eBay and Amazon. I've assigned you a username and password for each, which I'll write down for you. Soooo... the only thing for you to do now is to upload the rest of your products to the worldwide web, and start raking in the dosh!"

"My goodness," Libby answered. "I... I don't know what to say."

"Well. And there you have it," said James, clasping his hands together in finality. "You now have an online presence," he concluded. "Simple as that."

"Simple?" replied Libby. "You're far too modest. It hardly looks simple!" she said appreciatively. "Look, I'm no expert," she told him, "but even I can see all of the time and effort that must've gone into this. You must be looking for some kind of compensation, surely? How much money do you want for all of—?"

James placed a finger to his lips, shaking his head. "It's fine," he told Libby. "Ultimately, if you're successful in the shop, then that means the rent gets paid on the shop, which will in turn keep my dad happy, yeah? So you see it's not just myself I'm thinking of here, as it benefits everyone. Still, I hope this demonstrates to you that I'm not the complete scoundrel you thought I was previously?"

"No, you're not a scoundrel at all," Libby agreed. "I'm ashamed to think I ever thought so in the first place," she conceded. "And all of this has come about at the perfect time, as well, as your dad may have mentioned that I'm just a wee bit behind on the rent?" she added with a grimace.

"He did mention something to that effect, yes," James answered. "But I've told him what we're up to, with the website and all, so I wouldn't worry too much if I was you. If he sent you some kind of notice, that's merely a formality. And you shouldn't pay it much attention anyway. Because with you now set up as an online seller, you'll soon be swimming in so many orders you won't know what to do with them all, am I right?"

"I certainly hope you're right," replied Libby, trying her best to share James's confidence.

"I usually am," replied James with a grin. "Aren't I, Hulk?" he asked, looking to his faithful canine companion for confirmation. But Hulk was now dozing.

Libby continued her examination of the new website, navigating here and there, and taking a moment each time to flash James an appreciative smile of approval. It's fair to say that Libby had been on a decent enough number of shopping websites over the years, and she'd certainly seen her share of dodgy-looking sites, as well as those that looked quite nice. And what she saw before her here, right now, looked quite nice. It didn't smack to her of a DIY, makeshift sort of solution thrown together on a budget. No, this was really top drawer, as far as she was concerned, and a small part of her wondered if it was perhaps even too good for her.

For James, watching Libby's face, it was like witnessing a child on Christmas morning. But he still had one bit more of information to pass along, as a surprise...

"Oh. There is something else," he told her, as if just remembering it. He reached into his pocket, pulling out a piece of paper, carefully unfolding it, and he then presented it to Libby ceremoniously. "This," he said, "is your first batch of orders!"

Libby took the paper in hand and ran her eyes over it. "You're serious?" she gasped. "There's nearly... that's... there's got to be over three hundred pounds worth of orders here!"

James lifted his chin, puffing out his chest. He blew on his knuckles, after which he proceeded to polish an imaginary set of medals pinned there.

Libby stared down at the order details on the page in amazement. "That's more than I take in at the shop on a Monday!"

"Right, then. Come on, Hulk. It would appear our work here is done," said James, rousing his pooch from his slumber. "Next, I just need to do a little more search engine optimisation, or SEO as it's called," he added to Libby as he gathered up his things.

"Um... okay? Thanks?" replied Libby, having no idea what James was on about, but assuming it must be something good.

CHAPTER TEN

"Ah. Sorry. By that I mean I just need to try and make your website show up more prominently in search results," explained James. "Which will then of course lead to more purchases, yeah? Or at least that being the desired outcome."

Libby could almost taste the new business. "I don't know what to say, James. Thank you. I really mean that, sincerely."

James offered a salute in return as he headed to the door.

"James, wait!" Libby called out, dashing towards him in pursuit. Once caught up to him, she pressed herself up on her tippy toes and planted a kiss on the side of his face. "Really, James, I can't thank you enough," she told him.

James touched his cheek, and then shrugged. "It's just what we heroes do," he said dismissively. "Some superheroes have super-strength, whereas others fire energy beams from their eyes and such, or what have you. My superpower, on the other hand, just happens to be great facility with a computer mouse. It's my weapon of choice."

"Well if that's the case then I just have to say that as far as handheld weapons go, yours is magnificent!" Libby replied.

It took only about two seconds or so for what she'd just said to replay in her head, and to realise how it might have come across. "I mean your mouse... Your computer mouse is a wonderful weapon, not... I mean, that's not to say also that... I mean it could very well be, of course, but, ah, that's not what I... Oh, dear..."

"I should go," said James with a smirk. "And take my weapon with me."

"Yes, thanks. You should go," said Libby, allowing him to set off and waving him on his way. She was flustered but happy, her mind occupied with thoughts of all the online retail sales that were soon to follow. The proof was in the pudding, she thought to herself as she returned to her position behind the counter — the pudding, in this case, being the sheet of paper set there before her.

Libby picked the printout up again, taking it in her hands, looking it over, and admiring it. "Over three hundred quid!" she said aloud. "This is just too good. I think I need to send Freya a text and convey the good news!"

Libby reached for her phone, but then stopped halfway there, her hand hovering in mid-air. The scent of James's aftershave was caught in her nostrils from when she'd pecked him on the cheek, and it was now distracting her. "Oh, my," she said, as she was considering the effect this was having on her. She placed her hand up to her mouth and pinched her top lip, kneading it like a lump of dough between her fingers. "No…" she said, James still very much at the forefront of her mind. "I don't… do I? Or do I?"

Chapter Eleven

Freya cast a generous and reassuring smile for the benefit of the extended lunchtime queue of people inside the shop waiting to reach the counter. Not that folk seemed to mind, however, as progress was fairly steady, and people were also taking it as an opportunity to have a friendly exchange with friends or visitors to the island. Still, a reassuring smile to indicate that all was in control and well in hand, was a nice little added touch, Freya felt, to put those waiting at ease at the promise they'd soon be fed. This was Freya's domain, and she was queen of all she surveyed. She stood, poised and at the ready, behind the glass counter, and when the next order was relayed, those hands of hers whipped into the glass cabinet with the speed of a serpent strike. In the blink of an eye, requested slice of Madeira cake and sticky iced finger were retrieved, packaged, and handed to another happy, satisfied punter, with that patron being sent along their merry way to make payment and then out the door.

The intimate little shop, despite its relatively modest size, sold nearly every conceivable treat known to man (or known to the Isle of Man, at least). Freya quite liked working there, and what had begun some years back as a Saturday job for her when she was a mere slip of a girl had ended up an actual ongoing career — and one which, in the main, she still enjoyed. While the winter months could be a little slow, being constantly surrounded by delicious things was not so bad a prospect, and having the beach as the view from your office window didn't particularly hurt matters either.

"What'll it be today, boys?" she asked the next in line. She said this politely enough, but also in a tone which suggested the young gentlemen's decision-making time should be kept to a minimum in view of the current length of the queue behind them. The two lads were regulars, who Freya would also often see out and about as one might expect in a small seaside community, and so she was familiar enough with the both of them though couldn't exactly say she knew them well.

The pair leaned in close to the glass cabinet, feasting their eyes upon all the selectable — and quite delectable — sandwich fillings there to be had, with each of the various choices laid out before them. They looked into the cabinet for several very long seconds, glanced at each other, and then looked back into the cabinet yet again.

"Hmm," said one, scratching his chin, taking his time of it, his distinct lack of decision as much on display as the sandwich fillings waiting there to be selected.

"What do you reckon?" said the other, looking to the first lad for direction, his decision-making skills being no better than those of his friend.

"Dunno," came the reply. "Loads to choose from. Not sure what I fancy today, and everything—"

"Everything looks so good," said the second lad, completing his friend's thought for him.

"Yeah," agreed the first.

With the two lads obviously oblivious to the fact their present indecision was throwing a spanner in the works and preventing the line from moving, Freya thought it best to help speed things along by making a helpful suggestion, a suggestion she felt confident was certain to find favour amongst the pair:

"Just had some lovely bacon fresh out of the grill?" she proposed, throwing her thumb over her shoulder to indicate where the bacon resided.

"Mmm, bacon," said the one lad.

"Baaacooon," moaned the other, sounding perfectly amenable to this option.

"Two bacon sarnies it is, then," Freya declared decisively, and, before the two of them had chance to change their mind, leapt

CHAPTER ELEVEN

into action. She turned round to fetch the bacon, busying herself preparing their order. "What kind of sauce would you like?" she asked them. "We've got HP, and also—"

"No sauce," was the curt response from one of them, though Freya couldn't see which as she currently had her back to the pair of them.

"Nah, no sauce," the other chimed in.

Freya thought this was very odd, as what sort of madman doesn't have brown sauce on their bacon butty? But the customer is always right, or so they say, and so all she could do was shrug as she wrapped up their strangely sauceless sandwiches.

"Something sweet for afters?" she asked, turning back to face the two, and handing them their finished orders. It was always a good idea to try and upsell her customers with a nice pastry of some kind, and most people couldn't resist.

One of the lads looked as if he were about to take Freya up on her offer, but the other replied before he could. "Nah," came the answer, "If we wanted something for pudding we could just go and see your mate in the bookshop."

There was something definitely off about these two, thought Freya. First it was no sauce with their bacon, and now this. She had no idea what they were on about with this last crack, and she wasn't sure she even wanted to know. Best to just ignore, she decided.

"Right, then. Pay over there, lads," was all Freya said, pointing to Gemma over by the till, and wishing to push things forward. But while Freya was done with the two lads, it didn't appear they were quite done with her.

"Ehm..." said one of the lads, still standing there before her. "Your mate..."

Freya smiled at the hungry patron next in line and held a finger aloft to let him know that she would help him in just a moment. Then she narrowed her eyes, turning her attention back to the two now-sniggering lads.

"Yes? What about my mate?" said Freya, on the verge of losing her patience.

"Do you have to, you know, like, book in? Or do you just turn up?" asked the braver of the two.

Freya stared at them for one very long moment. "What's the joke, gentlemen?" she asked eventually, as she had not the slightest clue what these two yobs were finding quite so amusing.

"Also..." said the slightly-less-brave, but now-emboldened other of the pair. "Also, does she offer credit?" he asked. "Only I don't get paid until Friday, you see." And with this, the two of them set off to laughing once more.

Freya smiled, but it wasn't a warm sort of smile. Not in the slightest. "What have you two been smoking?" she asked.

"Nothing. We're talking about your mate," said one.

"Your mate at the Bonkshop on the Beach," added the other, for the sake of clarity.

"It's Bookshop by the Beach!" replied Freya, emphasising the *book* in the word *Bookshop*. "It should be quite simple to remember. Even for the likes of you," she told them curtly.

"Sorry. *By* the beach," one of them replied. "But the Bonkshop part is right. And not only that but word on the street is that your mate is ostensibly the most popular tourist attraction in the whole of Peel at present, if not the entire Isle of Man," he went on. "And we're just wondering if she takes advance booking, because—"

"And accepts credit," the other entered in.

"Takes advance booking, and accepts credit," the first one amended. "Because, well, she *is* pretty fit."

"Ostensibly," added the other. Unlike his friend, he didn't seem to know what the word actually meant, but appeared to like the sound of it.

Freya offered another apologetic smile to the fellow waiting next in line, as well as the others waiting in the queue. "Sally!" she then called out to the rear of the shop. "Sally, I need to pop out for two minutes! Would you be a dear and jump onto the counter for just a bit?"

"Ay? What's this?" said Sally, popping her head out from behind the door of the back-kitchen area. "Bit stuffy back there. Happy to help!" she said cheerfully, but then changed her tune slightly once she'd clapped eyes onto the state of the queue there in the outer area. "Oh, dear," she said, eyes like saucers.

CHAPTER ELEVEN

"I'll just be a minute or two, I promise!" Freya assured her helpful-yet-frightened, and now-hesitant co-worker.

Leaving things in Sally's capable hands temporarily, Freya made her way out around the counter, placing a palm squarely between the shoulder blades of each of the two lads in question and asking them politely but firmly for a quick word outside the shop once they'd paid for their items. Ordinarily, for talking such rubbish about her friend, the two lads would be in receipt of one knuckle sandwich apiece, as opposed to the bacon variety in their possession. But they were customers, after all, and so she had to unfortunately maintain at least a modicum of self-control here. As such, she ushered them outside of the bakery and, once clear of the shop, tried her best to address them in as civil a manner as possible.

"So," she said with a smile, dusting off the shoulder of the lad closest to her. "What's going on?"

The lads were now stood with their backs pressed up against the whitewashed walls of the adjacent cottage, appearing apprehensive as Freya — even a smiling Freya — gave the impression that she could make things turn very ugly if need be with only a minimal effort.

"Ehm..." said the lad on the left, with all the piss and vinegar suddenly escaping him like the air from a punctured bicycle tyre. He looked to his friend for assistance, but there was no help to be had there, as his mate was currently burying his head into his chest and leaving explanations to the other. "Well," the first lad continued, "it's just that... well, your friend is a prozzie, isn't she? Though I wasn't really going to use her services, mind, what with it being a small town and word getting around and everything. I mean, if my mum found out, I'd never hear the end of it, right?"

"We could go at night?" suggested his friend, lifting his chin and brightening up a bit, pleased he had something perhaps valuable to contribute. "It'd be dark, and no one would see?"

The two lads glanced over to Freya, and were both startled to see she appeared to have somehow practically doubled in size, rearing up in anger as she was. In response, the two of them sank down like turtles retreating into their shells, fearful a serious dressing-down might soon be approaching. Which, in fact, it was...

"A bloody prozzie?? Seriously, what the hell are you right pair of idiots talking about???" she shouted, with all notions of that the-customer-is-always-right bloody nonsense now firmly dismissed and thrown straight out the window. "Libby a prostitute?? Are you completely mental???" she railed.

It was about this time that a couple of heads poked out from the bakery entrance door, curious to see how the conversation from inside the shop might possibly be playing out. But, seeing what was going on, the heads popped back into the shop just as quickly as they'd appeared, preferring the relative safety of the shop's interior instead of the storm brewing outside.

Afraid violence of the physical variety was imminent, the lad on the left pointed tentatively to his pocket. "Can I... can I reach for my phone?" he asked, feeling it best to request permission.

Freya nodded her assent, her visage stern.

The lad handed his still-wrapped bacon butty to his mate for safekeeping, and then flicked through his phone as a bead of sweat ran down his temple.

"Hurry up," prompted his mate, staring at his sandwich-laden hands. It may have been out of concern for moving things along, explanation-wise. But it appeared equally likely the second lad was simply having great difficulty resisting the siren-like song of all that bacon suddenly in his possession, calling out to him to be eaten.

"Here," said the lad with the phone, finding what he'd been searching for and turning his phone round so that Freya could see.

Freya strained her eyes, trying to make out what was on the screen, before finally just taking the phone in hand for closer inspection. "What the...?" she said.

But the lads — by all appearances, at least, based on what she was seeing — looked to be correct in their unseemly assertion. There on the screen was a website, with a picture of Libby stood outside the bookshop, accompanied by a tariff guide advertising various flesh-based services on offer along with hourly rates.

CHAPTER ELEVEN

"I'm sorry, lads," said Freya, returning the phone. She could see that, horrible as the lads' accusations were, they were at least not cut from whole cloth.

Freya took a step back, craning her neck to glance up the street in the direction of the bookshop. She knew Libby was in financial dire straits, as Libby had told her as much. But was it indeed possible that, out of sheer desperation, Libby had expanded her business model to include the selling of things beyond the mere written word? Things of the more sordid variety? Freya entertained this notion briefly, but only very briefly. "No, I'm sorry, boys. I hate to burst your bubble, but that website is a load of bollocks," she told them, laying the matter to rest. "Someone's having a laugh at Libby's expense, I'm afraid. Though I don't think it's funny at all."

"No, not at all," lad Nº1 agreed, self-preservation in mind.

"Terrible. A terrible thing," said lad Nº2, following his mate's lead.

"So do many people know about it?" asked Freya. "This rubbish website?"

"Oh, quite a few, I expect," said one.

"Lusty Libby's the talk of the town!" added the other, a little too enthusiastically. "I mean… that's what people are calling her. *Other* people, mind. Not me. Never me."

"All right. Piss off, you two. Before I change my mind about kicking your arses," Freya told the pair, extending her arm to indicate they were free to go.

The lads didn't need to be told twice, scampering off, and disappearing from view in two shakes of a lamb's tail.

Freya stood there, hands on hips, thinking. She was wondering how on earth she was going to break the news to Libby — assuming Libby didn't already know — that she was now being advertised on the island as a member of the world's oldest profession. "Bloody Bonkshop by the Beach," she said, with a sort of sad chuckle, shaking her head. But her expression returned to stern almost as quickly. "Why in hell would somebody do such a thing? Why do this to Libby?"

Freya returned to the shop, helping Sally sort out the waiting customers, and as quick as she could, took an early lunch.

Over at the bookshop, Freya pressed her nose up against the glass door, checking to make sure there were no customers inside at the moment, which fortunately there didn't appear to be. "Hiya!" she said, cheerily announcing herself as she walked in.

Libby's head was buried in some sort of reading material or other, Freya couldn't tell what. Libby didn't look up, offering Freya only a perfunctory wave as she kept her eyes glued to the page.

"Oh. Are you terribly busy, then?" asked Freya, wondering if now was really the most opportune time to tell her friend what she was about to tell her.

"Hmm?" answered Libby, still distracted. She looked up, placing a finger down to hold her place in what she was reading, and glanced over to the clock on the wall. "What's going on? Are you on lunch already?" she asked, looking back at Freya.

"I took an early lunch, yeah," replied Freya. "I needed to tell you something."

"To tell me something...?" asked Libby, blinking, and not really understanding what could be so important that Freya had made a special trip over just to see her.

Freya wasn't really one for sugar-coating things, and figured she wasn't going to start now. Suspecting that Libby would think she was crazy if she came right out with it, though, Freya pulled out her phone, loading up the offending website as the two lads had done a short time earlier.

"Are you okay?" asked Libby. "What's this all about?"

"Libby..." began Freya, sucking air in through her teeth. "Libby, word on the street is that you're a call girl, and that this shop of yours here is some kind of house of ill repute, so to speak," she rattled off, exhaling.

Libby just sat there. She blinked again, and Freya could tell she was having trouble digesting what she'd just been told.

"Ehm... come again?" Libby eventually replied.

"Sorry. Here, have a look. Sorry," Freya answered, holding the phone out so Libby could see.

CHAPTER ELEVEN

"That's... that's my shop," said Libby, taking possession of the phone. She pushed her chair back, rising to a standing position, phone still in hand, her eyes held to the screen. "Freya, this isn't my website, so why's it got a picture of me and my shop on the..." she said, trailing off. "Hang on, what the hell is a *bonkshop*?" she asked. "This is definitely not my website!"

"No. No, it's not," agreed Freya.

"And fifty quid for a...?" added Libby, eyes obviously now drawn to the description of services offered.

"Yeah. That's what it says," confirmed Freya — though there was certainly no joy in this confirmation.

"Have you done this for a joke?" pleaded Libby. "Please say you have," she implored.

Freya shook her head. "I wish I could say I have," she answered. "It would be a joke in extremely poor taste. But I wish I could say I'd done it," she told her. "No. It was two young lads at the bakery that put me on to it. Customers. It wasn't their doing either. But they told me about it."

"This doesn't make any sense," said Libby, still staring at the screen.

"No, it doesn't," agreed Freya. "But, according to that website there, which loads of people have now apparently seen, you're a... well, a lady of the evening, to put it politely."

"Are you kidding me?" said Libby, stamping her foot down angrily. "I can't even give it away for bleeding free right at the moment, so what hope could I possibly have in *charging* for it?" Exasperated, she dropped back down into her seat, handing Freya back her phone. "Oh, god," she said, pressing her palm to her forehead.

"Yeah, I know," said Freya sympathetically.

"No, not that," Libby answered. "I mean I just thought of Doreen," she explained. "We need to go and make sure old Doreen at the hairdressers is okay."

"Doreen?" asked Freya, confused. "I don't understand. What, is Doreen a prozzie as well or something?"

"Nobody's a prozzie!" Libby wailed. She then, once calmed down, proceeded to clarify. "No, I received a call about twenty minutes ago from some bloke asking me for a..." she said, beginning to blush. Libby lowered her voice, which was not particularly required on account of the shop being empty apart from the two of them. "He asked me for a *blowie*," she whispered, almost ashamed to be saying it out loud.

This received a smirk from Freya.

"It's not funny, Freya!" insisted Libby. "No, he sounded quite old, and I just assumed the poor dear must've got his words confused and was talking about a haircut. You know, like a cut and blow-dry, that sort of thing. Wait, it just occurred to me, do men even get a blow-dry with their haircuts?"

"I don't think so," Freya offered.

"No, I don't suppose they do," Libby continued. "But I didn't know then what I know now. And so the only thing I could think of at the time, the only thing that made sense to me then, was that he meant blow-dry. So I politely explained that it wasn't a service I could provide, but that Doreen could, and that she was something of an expert at it, in fact, as she did it all the time all day every day!"

"Oh, dear," said Freya, seeing where this was going now.

"Yes," replied Libby. "I was only trying to encourage shopping local, wasn't I? And now look what I've done. Now Doreen will have had some randy old goat phoning her up and asking her for god-only-knows what!"

"Well I think we already know what, actually," Freya pointed out.

"Poor Doreen," sighed Libby.

"Poor Doreen," echoed Freya gravely. Although the truth of it was, the thought of that conversation Doreen might soon be having with the old fella tickled her funny bone, and Freya had to suppress the smirk she felt was in danger of taking over her face again.

"You know I've had some unusual requests in here the last few days, and it's probably because of that damned website," Libby reflected. "I've sold three copies of the bloody Karma Sutra in that span, for god's sake, which I thought was unusual."

"The Kama Sutra, you mean?" Freya entered in.

CHAPTER ELEVEN

"Whatever it's called, yeah," Libby answered. Then she narrowed her eyes for a moment, wondering how Freya was such an expert on the subject. "Anyway, I also had some bloke pop his head around the door yesterday, wanting to make sure that I take cash, he said, as he couldn't use his card in case his wife found out," she went on, back to the original subject. "Freya, I thought he must have been wanting to buy his wife a nice present or something, and that he just didn't want her to be able to tell how much it would have cost him! Now... well, now, in hindsight, I think that's not what he meant at all..."

"Probably not," Freya entered in, though not sure she was really helping matters any by agreeing.

"Aww, how is this happening to me?" Libby asked in despair, dropping her head down to the countertop. "And I was having a relatively good week, too, on account of the seventy online book orders I took in," she moaned, banging her forehead against the hard surface.

"Seventy?" asked Freya. "Wow, that's definitely good, yeah?"

"Well, it is, and it isn't," replied Libby, lifting her head back up and rubbing her sore forehead. She'd only been banging her head against the counter for show, and hadn't meant to actually hurt herself. "The sales are good, yes. But the profit margin on them is very slim, unfortunately."

"Oh? How so?" asked Freya.

"It's the darndest thing," Libby answered. "Somehow, I'm not sure how, a fifty percent discount is being applied to each sale during the checkout and payment process. At least that's what I think is happening, near as I can figure. Because in the individual listings for each book, the prices show up correctly, just as they should. It was only when I received my weekly sales summary that the numbers didn't add up. I didn't make anywhere near as much money as I should have on these overall sales — in fact I'm *losing* money on each of these sales — and I've been trying to work out why."

"Oh," replied Freya, not any wiser to the source of Libby's problem than Libby herself.

"These here," said Libby, picking up the paper she'd been poring over when Freya walked in. "I printed out the summary, and

I'd been going over all the figures just now, trying to get to bottom of it. And then that's when you wandered in, the bearer of even more bad news."

"Don't shoot the messenger!" Freya entreated, throwing up her hands in surrender.

"I don't blame you, don't worry," Libby answered reassuringly. "I appreciate you telling me, of course, even if I don't like what it is you had to tell me."

Freya put her hands down, feeling it safe to do so. "Hmm, as far as the books," she suggested, thinking out loud, "maybe just don't send them, and politely advise those customers that there's been a mistake? Cancel the orders?"

Libby shook her head sadly. "Yeah, I thought of that. But that's bad for business, as the sales have already gone through and I'd probably get accused of fraud or something," she told Freya. "Besides, I've already posted a bunch of them because I didn't even realise at first that something was amiss. It was only once I'd received my weekly summary by email that I noticed there was a problem."

"Ah," said Freya, wishing she had something else to offer but coming up empty.

Libby scrunched her printout into a ball and threw it behind her like a racetrack punter on a losing streak. "I thought things were on the up, Freya, but this has probably cost me upwards of five hundred pounds."

Libby placed her hands to face, and it looked to Freya as if she might start crying. "Hey now," said Freya, moving to Libby's side of the counter and placing a comforting arm around her friend. "It'll all be fine, Libby. You just need to speak with James and have him find out what's going on. I'm sure it's something simple and easily sorted, yeah?" Freya gave her a squeeze of encouragement, and then added, "Put this week down to experience and move on, bigger and stronger, right? There's a girl."

"I suppose so," replied Libby.

But her response clearly lacked enthusiasm, and so Freya rubbed her back a bit.

"Right. I'll speak with James," Libby sighed. "I need to speak to him anyhow, as I don't yet have full access to the site. He still

CHAPTER ELEVEN

hasn't given me my passwords and such, so I couldn't go in and change any settings or what have you even if I knew how," she told Freya. "Ah, bugger," she said, as the printer in the store cupboard behind her kicked into life. "That means another sale has just come in, which I'll make practically no money on," moaned Libby. "Also, I'm now going to be wondering if every customer that comes through that door from now on is looking for a book, or looking for a..."

"Bonk?" suggested Freya.

"Exactly," answered Libby. "You know I hate to admit it. But it's a fairly clever name, in a daft sort of way," she added. "The Bonkshop by the Beach? I mean, *honestly*, right?" she said with a laugh, followed by another sigh.

Freya rubbed her friend's back some more. "Keep smiling, kiddo. Meanwhile, I'm going to make a few enquiries in regard to this dodgy website," she said. "See if I can't work out who's behind it."

"Thanks, Freya," replied Libby. She reached for her handbag, pulling out her keys from within, and then walked with Freya over to the door. "I'll come and see you after work," she told Freya, "and maybe we can come up with some kind of plan of action before this all gets completely out of hand."

"Are you leaving as well? Where are you off to?" asked Freya.

"I need to go and make sure Doreen's not booked that old chap in for a blowie!" Libby reminded her.

"Oh, I almost forgot about that!" replied Freya. "But... who knows? Maybe Doreen does that as well? She could be quite good at it, for all we know, and appreciate the extra business?"

This got a laugh out of Libby, at least, which Freya was happy to see.

"Still. Probably best to warn her, just in case," advised Libby with a chuckle.

"You know best," agreed Freya, chuckling as well.

Chapter Twelve

29th April

Today, I finally got to see Gwen for the first time since the assault. She assured me that she's going to be fine but is still covered in bruises and has a nasty gash on her chin and a chipped tooth. I wanted to cry when I saw how painful her face looked. Considering she's been out of hospital for nearly a week, I was shocked by how swollen she still was.

Seeing her there like that, I felt compelled to tell her how important she'd become to me. I told her just how much I cared for her. And then, I didn't know how it happened, it's like the words came out of my mouth all on their own, but I also told her that I loved her. It wasn't a mistake, though, and I'm glad I told her because I do. Love her, that is.

She cried. I think that's a good thing? At least I hope so.

She told me that it was her arsehole of an ex-boyfriend that attacked her. He punched her to the ground and then kicked her in the face outside the pub when she'd finished work.

I'm so angry that I'm in danger of snapping my pen as I write this. I just want to go around and smash him in the face the exact same way he did to her. Good thing the police got to him first. The bastard has been arrested, and the police also strongly suspect he's behind the arson attack at my house because of what came out of his wretched gob as he was beating her up. Gwen tells me the filthy blighter was yelling and carrying on the whole time about seeing that picture of us in the newspaper – the one where she's got her arms around me. Turns out he doesn't cope with rejection well, the sad sorry maggot, and told her, in typical maggot fashion, that if he couldn't have her then nobody could. His intent, apparently, was to render her so unattractive with the beating to her face that no one would find her appealing ever again. He was of course wrong – and especially so, given that Gwen's beauty shines brightly from within as well as without. But that's something I doubt he could ever understand.

How Gwen could ever get mixed up with someone like him to begin with I don't know. I suppose people like him can pour on the charm when they want to, and Gwen is also so kind hearted and trusting and likes to see only the good in people.

Not the right time just now, but I think I should mention soon to Gwen about going to the Isle of Man next month. It'd be nice for her to have something to look forward to, I think. Something positive, something to take her mind off things. I think she'd look forward to that, wouldn't she?

Gran has insisted on making Gwen some soup for me to take around. Gran swears by it, and apparently, according to her at least, it's the cure for absolutely everything. Not sure how it'll fare when it comes to fixing something like what Gwen's been through, but I'll just have to take Gran's word for it as this is her area of expertise of course and not mine.

30th April

Gwen loved the soup and said it was wonderful. I dropped it off on my way to work and then on the way home I stopped by again with some flowers for her.

She's still not made any reference to me saying that I loved her. I just hope I've not come on too strong and scared her

CHAPTER TWELVE

off. And she seemed a little more quiet than usual today, which worried me. And when I say more quiet than usual, I mean even considering the current state she's in. I told her, for what it was worth, that even though her face was still all swollen and such, she's still the most beautiful woman I've ever clapped my eyes on.

I did manage to drop into conversation about how the TT races were on at the end of the month. I didn't go into too much detail at this stage and just planted the seed. I'll talk to her about it again in a day or two and see what she thinks.

In other news, I received a letter from the insurance company today and they're going to reimburse me for the ruined scooter, which is a result. Dad's also pleased as they're going to stump up for a new shed. The old one had seen better days anyway, so getting a new one's not so bad, Dad told me, looking on the bright side of things, and said he'd get a bigger one this time as well. He also confided in me his vision of creating himself a cosy place where he can sit inside of it, hide from any prospective housework, listen to the radio, and have a beer or two. He made me promise not to tell Mum, especially the part about avoiding housework!

I'll give Auntie Norma on the Isle of Man a quick ring tomorrow to see if it's still okay if we come over and stay with her (assuming we do make the trip, that is). It's not long until the TT, so probably best to give her some notice.

It's my last couple of weeks in work and I cannot wait to leave. It's so boring, and also I'm fairly certain the receptionist there, Barbara, is flirting with me. She keeps winking at me and making suggestive comments, and it's reached the point where it's making me a fair bit uncomfortable. Now I'm all for banter in the workplace and don't have a problem with that as such, but our Barbara must be upwards of sixty years old! Saucy old mare.

2nd May

I mentioned to Terry who Gwen's ex-boyfriend was. I could tell when the blood drained from his face that he knew exactly who I was talking about. Him and his family are all crazy, Terry said, and had done more porridge than Goldilocks.

I'm still so angry that anybody could hurt someone as sweet and gentle and kind as Gwen.

Anyway, had a great chat with my Auntie Norma today and I can't wait to see her as she's a great laugh. She was telling me about her shop which sounds lovely. Apparently, it's so close to the beach that you can smell the sun cream. She also told me all about the local pubs that she'd take us to. Dad always described her as being a little bit prudish, oddly enough, but she came across to me as absolutely the opposite. She described the Isle of Man in TT week and how lively the place gets. I'm actually really excited about going over now, even more than I was before, and Norma said she's delighted to have me stay with her.

I did mention that I may have company, but that I wasn't certain who it would be at this stage. She assured me it's not a problem, though, and said the more the merrier as far as she was concerned.

I've seen another scooter for sale. Like my old one, but in slightly better condition (I mean as compared to the old one before that one had been set on fire, of course). I've not had the insurance payout as yet, but Gran, legend that she is, offered to lend me the cash in advance of receiving the insurance settlement if need be. So, I think I'm going to buy it. After all, I can't go on my first trip to the Isle of Man TT races without a bike of some sort or another. It's just not the done thing!

I do hope that Gwen wants to come on the road trip with me. I think I'll buy another helmet that would fit her, just in case.

CHAPTER TWELVE

4th May

Bloody hell. Barbara, the receptionist in work, asked me out for a drink today. Well, it wasn't really a request and more of a demand, as she told me where to be and at what time. She even told me what drink I should buy for her. When I politely declined, she accused me of leading her on. She's older than Mum for pity's sake and probably not too far away from Gran's age. I'll avoid walking through the reception area at work for the next few days as I think she's somewhat unhinged. The lads in the canteen said she's known to carry a cosh. I can't wait to leave that job.

Terry's romance is off again as the love of his life, as he's referred to her, has now left him for some bloke who owns a Jaguar. (The car variety, I assume, as opposed to the big cat. I'll have to ask him to be sure.) He's now trying to see if he can arrange a refund on the holiday he's already booked, but I don't fancy his chances at this late stage. Poor chap is gutted, and I did manage to resist the urge to say I told you so.

And now that he's no longer going abroad, Terry's naturally asked me what date we're leaving to go to the Isle of Man TT. I bent the truth, just a little, and said that my aunt didn't have the room for us both. I'm horrible, I know, but I'm really hoping to go with Gwen instead. If Gwen doesn't end up wanting to come over with me, I can always just tell Terry that Aunt Norma has managed to sort something for us both and bring him with me as was the original plan.

As for Gwen, I've been working on a little surprise for her. Something to put a smile on her face, I hope. She once told me that she went to Blackpool every summer as a child and how she has such happy memories from her visits there.

And so I've spent the last week painting a watercolour picture of the Blackpool seafront for her, including the famous Blackpool Tower. I didn't think it would take as long as it did, but it's turned out rather splendidly if I do say so myself. I can't wait to see her face and I'm sure it'll cheer her up.

I'll take it around for her tomorrow when I ask her about going to the TT with me.

5th May

Gwen wouldn't see me today. Her mum asked me to give her some space. I don't know what I've done wrong.

I feel sick.

6th May

Gwen doesn't want to see me anymore. She phoned me tonight and told me she wanted to be on her own for a while.

I'm devastated.

22nd May

I'm starting to dislike this year. I've heard nothing from Gwen for weeks.

Last night, Terry convinced me that the only solution for heartache (with him being the expert after being dumped by Sharon with the big tits) was copious amounts of lager, which I stupidly agreed to. After about the seventh pint, Terry, for some idiotic reason, pointed out the bloke in the corner of the bar as being that arsehole ex-boyfriend of Gwen's, who must have been out on bail.

Without even having to think twice about it, I stormed over to him and gripped this bloke, throwing him clean over the table where he'd just been sat. As he struggled to get to his feet, I pulled him up by his collar and then proceeded to punch him numerous times about the face, just so he could get a taste of how Gwen must have felt at his hands.

CHAPTER TWELVE

Well, this is what I WANTED to do in my alcohol fuelled mind, at least. That's how it played out in my head. But what ACTUALLY happened was that I did walk over to him (that part was true), despite Terry's protests, and hurled a load of insults at him, to which he just laughed. At that point, I threw several punches in his vague general direction, all significantly wide of the target and missing the mark entirely. In my drunken state, only one of the punches connected with anything at all – and with that one particular thing unfortunately being a solid oak shelf sticking out behind his big fat head. More laughter from him, and from his mates as well. He then stood up and, unlike me, had not the slightest bit of trouble in landing a flurry of punches, all in quick succession, before Terry was able to drag me away. On the positive side, there were several lads in his group, so the beating could have been significantly worse than it was if they'd opted to join in which fortunately they didn't.

This morning, I woke with a thumping hangover, several cuts to my face, a black eye, and what was later confirmed through this afternoon's subsequent visit to the local A&E as a fracture in the wrist caused by punching that bloody shelf as well as two broken fingers.

I was foolish to do what I did, but Terry shouldn't have allowed me to get so drunk in my fragile state, so I place the blame squarely on him! Alas, poor Terry also received a couple of punches for his trouble also.

In good news, I did manage to pick up my new scooter yesterday before all that unpleasantness at the pub occurred. It's a beauty, but it's all feeling a bit flat now as I'd hoped I was going to be taking it to the Isle of Man with Gwen. Terry however is now reinstated as being my travelling companion. Unfortunately I can't even properly ride the scooter because of this busted hand of mine, so I've no choice but to ride pillion and have him piloting.

24th May

I'm such an utter idiot. My hand (now in a plaster cast, along with the wrist) is the hand I paint with and I'm supposed to be completing a detailed portfolio ahead of joining art college. If I can't use my hand – which I indeed can't – then college have suggested I skip a year.

As an alternative to college, I spoke to work about rescinding my notice, but they've already lined up a replacement for me, so there goes that idea straight out the window.

So, no job, no girlfriend, and now the likelihood of having to skip a year of art college until my hand is on the mend.

I could honestly cry at the minute.

The only positive is that Gwen's ex-boyfriend doesn't appear to have taken too much offence from my useless attack. Terry heard from one of the barmaids that he found it all absolutely hilarious and a great bit of fun. Hopefully, this means that I'm not going to have that lunatic on my case.

Gran knitted me a pair of socks to cheer me up. Which they did, to some extent at least. Bless her soul for thinking of me.

28th May

That's us all packed and ready for the Isle of Man. We only have room for one rucksack apiece, so hopefully I can wash some clothes at Auntie Norma's otherwise I'll be wearing the same undies for two weeks.

I'm really looking forward to our adventure, even if I don't get to ride my new scooter with my hand at the throttle as I'd like.

We've no idea how long it's going to take us to get to the ferry terminal in Liverpool, so we're leaving before dawn tomorrow to make sure we arrive in plenty of time.

CHAPTER TWELVE

I've not mentioned to Terry, of course, but I still wish I was going with Gwen. I've still not heard anything from her. Anyway, I just hope she's safe and feeling better soon.

Next stop, the Isle of Man TT races!

Chapter Thirteen

With most of the town now likely believing she was a bloody hooker, the last thing Libby needed in her life right about now was the 5k race that she'd signed herself and Freya up for. Training had now taken a back seat, as the thought of being on public display under the current circumstances was far from appealing. She'd desperately wanted to pull the plug on their participation, but with all the effort towards training Freya had ended up putting in — surprising, and impressing, Libby in the process — it simply wasn't fair to call it quits, Libby felt, as the two of them had entered as a team.

It was a struggle to find any motivation for anything at present, and Libby was now actively exploring the job prospects back in the UK as she now seriously considered calling it quits here on the Isle of Man. She had no idea how she would go about breaking this news to her gran. After all, when Libby had originally accepted the offer to take over the running of the shop, she'd also accepted with it a weight of responsibility. It was a family-owned business that had operated successfully for over forty years, and that task now sat firmly on her shoulders. When she first moved to the island, bright-eyed and bushy-tailed, thoughts of this adventure being anything other than a roaring success had simply not entered her mind.

Indeed, when she'd arrived, brimming with confidence, she was happy to pick up the mantle and carry on the legacy she was now a custodian of — to nurture and grow it, both for present and also for future generations. How, then, was she supposed to sit her gran down and tell her that not only had she single-handedly run her grandparents' beloved family business into the ground, but that she was potentially leaving the island as well? It was something that kept Libby awake at night, as did the Bonkshop website debacle. As for that nasty bit of business, she had no idea how to go about getting that awful thing taken down, so all she could do, for the time being, was to place several posters in the windows of the bookshop explaining that it was, of course, not a house of ill repute. This explanation was understood by most of the local population, but obviously drew confused reactions from tourists who likely had no prior knowledge of the spurious website. Either way, she wasn't sure the posters were having the desired result regardless, as people (locals and tourists alike) appeared to be taking Libby's vociferous denials only as further proof that such a thing must actually have been true. No matter what she did, she felt she just couldn't win.

On this present evening, with Gran out of the house attending a Silver Sprinters event of some sort, Libby had been faced with the not-entirely-undesirable prospect of having a quiet night in front of the telly on her own. Until, that is, she reluctantly accepted Freya's gentle suggestion of a training run followed by a pint of something cold in an available beer garden. The thought of being outside, in public view was, however, still not overly appealing.

Waiting for Freya at their agreed meeting point near to Peel Castle, Libby stretched out her legs while gazing down to the boats bobbing on the tide in the harbour below. "Come on, Freya," she said to herself, looking impatiently at her watch. Ordinarily, Libby would be quite happy to stand admiring the lovely seaside view, breathing in the wonderful salty air, but in her present paranoid state being out in public was making her rather uneasy. She second-guessed the purpose of every passing glance in her direction and presumed people were talking about her when, in all probability, they likely weren't.

A further ten minutes elapsed, and the tendons in Libby's legs were now at risk of snapping from being stretched so much. Figuring she'd been stood up, Libby, now already thoroughly warmed up, reckoned she'd simply go for a run on her own. But just as she was about to set off...

CHAPTER THIRTEEN

"Libs!" Freya's enthusiastic voice rang out, causing Libby to turn and look to its source. "Hiya, Libby!" Freya called over, followed by an eager wave as she made her way up the pavement in Libby's direction.

Libby couldn't help but notice the distinct absence of running clothes on Freya's person, and the fact that Freya was in fact still sporting her work attire.

"So sorry I'm late!" said Freya cheerily, upon arrival.

"Em... not really the most practical running outfit, I should think...?" offered Libby, only half-jokingly.

Freya smiled in response but didn't appear to register what Libby had said, instead taking a notepad from her pocket and tapping the cover excitedly with the tip of her fingernail. "I have news!" she declared, offering up a knowing wink.

"News... about how you're going to run without your running clothes...?" Libby gamely ventured.

"Hmm? Oh, no. No, nevermind that," Freya replied. "No, listen, the reason I'm late," she pressed on, "is because I've had my detective hat on!"

Libby looked to the top of Freya's head. There was definitely no hat up there, detective or otherwise. She was just about to make another snarky comment, to that very effect, and how a detective hat wouldn't have been suitable for a run anyway, when Freya somewhat read her mind and responded.

"Not a literal hat, silly!" said Freya. "Figuratively speaking, I mean!"

"Ah," replied Libby. She shrugged, then nodded, indicating that Freya may as well just go ahead and say what it was she so desperately wanted to say, then, as there didn't appear to be any point in trying to stop her now.

"Yep, your best friend has been pounding the cobbled streets of this fair town to uncover the answer to a recent mystery!" Freya declared triumphantly. "A mystery, as it should happen, of keen interest to you, in fact!"

"Oh!" replied Libby, suddenly interested. "So you know who set that rubbish website up, is that what you're telling me?" Libby asked, eyes widening in anticipation.

"Ah... well, no," replied Freya. "Not exactly. Not yet, at least."

"Okay. That's a little anticlimactic, then," Libby answered, not quite so interested as she was only a moment ago. "But do go on, I suppose. What information have you got?"

"I have news on Luke!" said Freya, tapping the notepad again, and trotting out another knowing wink for a second go, hoping to recapture Libby's full attention.

"Luke? I don't understand. Why would I care about anything having to do with Luke at this point?" asked a confused Libby, not understanding why she should care about anything having to do with Luke at this point. "Look, are we going for a run or not, Freya?" she said, changing the subject.

"No, no, listen!" said Freya, shaking her head. "This is good, I promise!" she promised, flipping the cover of her notepad over like a seasoned detective and running her finger down her notes. "I've been reliably informed that Luke is not quite the man-whore you've been led to believe he is," Freya reported.

"I see," said Libby, head cocked, and one eyebrow raised. "Continue," she instructed.

"No, he's not," replied Freya, encouraged now by Libby's slightly more receptive reaction. "In the bakery this afternoon, I was speaking to…" she said, pausing as she ran her finger down the page again, as she'd lost her place already.

Libby waited patiently.

"John!" said Freya, finding the note she was looking for. "Yes, that's it. And you'll know John, as he always wears horrendously loud shirts and is an awful gossip."

"Okay," said Libby, not sure she knew who this John fellow was but deciding it didn't really matter anyway if she did or didn't.

"Right. Anyway," Freya carried on. "Anyway, he asked if you and Luke were still together which is when I then made some pointed remark about Luke's womanising ways which took John by surprise. John assured me that Luke wasn't the type at all to have several women on the go. He then added that he'd heard that you, Libby," she said, pointing at Libby, "had several blokes on the go at any given time."

CHAPTER THIRTEEN

"*What?*" screeched Libby. "That's crackers! I don't have several blokes on the go! I've bloody never had several blokes on the go, even if I'd wanted to!"

"Wait. You wanted to?" asked Freya, blinking in surprise, and lowering her notepad for a moment.

"I meant hypothetically!" Libby answered. "I meant even if I'd *wanted* to, which I *didn't*, but even if I'd wanted to, I never did."

"Right. Okay? Well, now that that's perfectly clear... or not... let's move on, shall we?" proposed Freya. "Right. So, back to John. So this is when I asked where he'd heard such nonsense. Anyway, John wasn't too close to the details and so suggested I speak with Pete," she said, again referring to her notepad. "When I phoned Pete, he wasn't too sure either, and so suggested I speak with Stan, but Stan was—"

"Freya," Libby interrupted, tapping her foot and taking a quick glance at her wrist. "Can you get to the point, please, as I'm not getting any younger here."

"Right, well you know how you were led to believe that Luke was the Hugh Hefner of the Isle of Man, with dozens of women in his harem at any given time?" responded Freya.

"Yes? And...?" said Libby, waving her hand to encourage further elaboration.

"Well, it turns out Luke had heard that very same story about you. That story being that you had several men in tow and were, ehm..." Freya told her, pausing ahead of the next point she was about to make. "Well, that you were the town bike, shall we say, according to..." she said, referring to her notes. "Tom," she declared. "It was Tom that told me that."

"What?" replied Libby, screwing up her eyes in anger and disbelief. "I don't understand."

"Oh, sorry. Do you not have that expression from where you're from?" asked Freya. "A town bike means—"

"I know what that means!" Libby cut in.

Freya closed over her notepad, its service to the current investigation now concluded. "Ah. Well. Simply put, Libby, you were told that Luke was playing the field with all and sundry, while Luke was told the same cock-and-bull story about you," she told

Libby. "And as an unfortunate result of this dastardly misinformation campaign, the pair of you ended up not speaking to each other."

"James!" came Libby's immediate reply, spat out like a curse, as she put two and two together.

But Freya pressed on, as she was not yet finished in relaying her fascinating tale of subterfuge and intrigue. "So. After learning what I did, I next set out to determine exactly how this false news had made its way into Luke's ear. Thus, I followed the chain of people in order to trace the malicious rumour to its origin, tracking the flow of information to find out precisely who had told them in the first place. There were quite a few people to interrogate... erm, I mean interview... which is why I needed the notepad, so that I didn't get confused or forget anything."

Libby spun her hand around, motioning to Freya that any time she'd like to finish up her summation would be nice, the sooner the better. She also didn't understand why Freya was still prattling on, as surely the answer had already been presented.

"I actually quite enjoyed being an investigator, and as a further positive, I did obtain a few phone numbers during my enquiries," Freya continued. "Numbers belonging to hunky rugby players, I might add," she added, dreamily. "It took me a while to get there, to the solution. But get there in the end I did!" declared Freya. "Ten points if you can tell me who started the rumour?" she invited, cupping a hand against her ear in anticipation of the forthcoming response.

"Wait. Not James?" asked Libby, confused.

"It was James!" replied Freya, as if the answer had never been previously revealed. "James told one of Luke's mates that you were a bit of a slapper, and being a small town, the word naturally didn't take too long to spread," she explained. "Didn't take too long to spread..." she repeated, a cheeky thought occurring to her. "Didn't take too long to spread, which is a bit like your legs, am I right?" she said, smiling at her own improvised comic genius. "I mean, that is, if one is to believe all they hear, of course," she quickly clarified.

CHAPTER THIRTEEN

"So it's James," said Libby, placing her hands on her hips and completely ignoring what she felt was Freya's inappropriate and rather ill-timed attempt at humour. "James. I don't get it. Why? I mean, why on earth would he...? I just don't get it. What's his motivation? We've been getting on perfectly well lately, and he's even been helping me to get the business on track with the new website. I even thought, the other day, he was going to..."

"To what?" asked Freya, in full investigative mode once again. "Shall I take out my notepad? Will I need to write this down?"

"No, you don't need to write this down," replied Libby, lowering her head. "Kiss me," she said softly.

"What, right now?" replied Freya. "Erm... and like what kind of kiss are we talking about here, exactly?" she asked. Freya loved Libby well enough, of course, but this was new territory and coming as a bit of a surprise.

"James," Libby answered by way of explanation. "I thought James was going to kiss me."

"A-ha! There it is, then!" said Freya, getting the picture now, and adjusting her imaginary detective hat accordingly. "There's the answer, Libs. James has got the hots for you, and he was trying to get rid of any competition!"

Libby took a moment to digest all that had been presented to her. After due consideration, there was only one thing she felt ought to be said at this stage. "That pint we'd planned for after?" she put forth. "Let's say we go for it now rather than later, yes?"

"Good idea," said Freya. "Best to leave the run for another time, as I've just noticed I'm not exactly dressed for it!"

Libby stared, fascinated by a small colony of ants making short work of a discarded sausage in the grass. She'd taken a seat in a secluded area of the Peveril beer garden with her back to the other patrons who were likewise enjoying an early-evening beverage. Her first pint didn't even touch the sides, and so Freya had been swiftly dispatched for a refill.

She couldn't settle, her mind now working in overdrive trying to process what she'd been told by Freya. If James was indeed responsible for the whole false rumour affair, as Private Investigator Freya had indicated, then that really was a rather creepy move on his part. She could certainly understand a bloke sending a bunch of flowers to win a girl over, for instance, as that would be a perfectly normal thing to do. Or, if a fellow wanted to further set himself apart from the herd of potential suitors, he could perhaps serenade the woman he fancied with a Shakespearean sonnet — that would be a cute thing to do, and might even stand a high chance of delivering positive results. But spreading rumours calling someone's virtue into question? Such a thing beggars belief, Libby felt, and she just couldn't understand why he would ever think something like that was a good idea, or how he even thought he'd get away with it without being found out. Surely he must have suspected that Libby would bump into Luke at some point and put two and two together? It was a small town, after all, and he must have known that she'd get wind of it, eventually, one way or another.

Libby shifted her attention from the busy ants to a returning Freya, laden with two freshly poured pints, one in each hand, along with a large packet of crisps secured between her teeth. "So, does this mean that Luke might still actually like me?" Libby wondered aloud, as Freya reclaimed her seat and set her haul down on the table. "I mean," Libby continued, having given this some thought, "the only reason we haven't been in contact with each other was because we both thought, erroneously, that the other was sleeping with half of the island. So if you take that slight complication out of the equation, then technically..."

"I suppose it's certainly possible," ventured Freya, tearing open the packet of crisps and plunging her hand in. "The road to true love is often a long and winding journey, full of unexpected twists and turns," she offered contemplatively, before filling her gob with crisps and munching away merrily.

"Listen to you, going full poet on me," Libby said with a laugh, while gratefully taking possession of her drink and drawing it near. "But I'll tell you, love is a complete pain in the behind is what it is," Libby went on, turning serious again. "It was because of love that Gran has just had her face pummelled, and with her left lying on the side of the road in the gutter to bleed out."

CHAPTER THIRTEEN

"What?" said a horrified Freya.

"Oh, sorry. I mean in the journals," clarified Libby, reaching out to pat Freya's hand to calm her down. "I'm still reading my grandad's journals, you see, and in them Gran has just had her face smashed in. Which is just as horrific as it sounds, yes, but happened a very long time ago. Also, at this point in the journals, my poor grandad now thinks that he's been dumped, and is headed to the Isle of Man TT without her, which he's sad about. So, as you say, the road to love doesn't always follow the straightest of paths."

"Ah," said Freya, relieved that this was an account of things that had happened far in the past, and also feeling it safe now to take another handful of crisps, which she did.

"I do take some inspiration from them both, however, because at least they get there in the end, yeah?" considered Libby. And then a smile washed over her face, as she took her own handful of crisps from the large packet Freya was holding, and continued, "You know, as far back as I can remember, Freya, from my earliest memories as a child, they were always so lovely together. They held hands wherever they went, and I recall him picking her a fresh bunch of flowers from the garden each week to place in the vase on the kitchen table. They were the cutest couple, and as a young girl, if you'd have asked me what true love was, I'd have simply pointed to my grandparents as the perfect example."

Libby's bottom lip was in danger of wobbling at this point as Freya listened on intently.

"If you want something in life, you've got to work bleedin' hard for it," offered Freya. "Nothing comes easy."

Libby nodded as these sage words of Freya's were planted in her ear, where they gradually germinated, sending shoots of positivity throughout her brain. Of course it could just as easily have been the quickly-consumed pints of cider that were having this effect as well, as opposed to Freya's inspiring comments. Whatever the case, Libby started to feel a wave of determination run through her.

"Yes, you've got to take the bull by the horns," Freya carried on, now on a roll. "You've got to take the bull by the horns, wrestle it to the ground, and then, panting, in a heaving, sweating tangle of limbs, once you've got it there, you've got to—"

"Nothing does come easy, does it?" said Libby, a dreamy, faraway expression on her face.

"Oh," said Freya, disappointed Libby was no longer listening, and also disappointed that the time for clever, colourful analogies had now sadly passed.

"I've had a few setbacks of late, but I can get through this, can't I?" Libby asked of her friend, her eyes returning to focus. "I adore living in the Isle of Man, so why would I want to leave?" she added, more rhetorically than anything else. "I'll work harder than I've ever worked," she added, "and I'll prevail! Won't I, Freya?"

"Girl power! You can do it!" said Freya, raising her glass. "Between the normal summer uptick, and now the online sales as well," she offered, "I expect business should improve dramatically, yeah? Also, once Luke realises you're not a... well, you know. Once he realises that, then you never know, do you? Love has a way of always, well, finding a way, I should think."

"Thanks, Freya, that makes me feel better," Libby answered. "Hmm, you know what else would make me feel better?" she asked.

"Another pint of cider?" guessed Freya.

"Yes, that," agreed Libby. "But, no, that's not what I was thinking at the moment," she said. "I was wondering if you'd like to help me beat up James! That would certainly raise my spirits!"

"Sure, I'm in," replied Freya, cracking her neck in anticipation of a scuffle. Freya always did like a good scuffle, skirmish, fracas, brawl, mêlée, or what have you. "Although, you might just be better ignoring him," she offered, upon further consideration. "I mean, as much as I hate to have to be the responsible one here, forced against my nature to say sensible things, I'm not sure a stretch in jail will improve your prospects in either business or love, now will it?"

"You're right, of course," answered Libby, letting out a deep sigh. "Still, it would have been glorious, wouldn't it?"

CHAPTER THIRTEEN

"Agreed," agreed Freya. "And keep in mind, nothing says we couldn't still do it at a later date, yeah?" she added, pointing out the positive side.

"I like your way of thinking," Libby replied with a laugh. "Ugh, but I still need to go and see him, though, as I've got to get the access passwords to my website," she added, after a moment's reflection. "So I can't ignore him completely just now even if I wanted to."

"I'll go," suggested Freya. "And when I do, I'll take a rolling pin from the bakery with me, and if he gives me any trouble, I'll stick it right where the sun doesn't..."

"Shine?" offered Libby, wondering why Freya hadn't finished her thought, and why Freya had her eyes now fixed on someone or something else.

"Speak of the devil, there's James now," said Freya, extending her pinkie finger in the direction of a figure strolling down the road outside the pub.

Libby smiled, assuming Freya was joking, until realising she wasn't. Libby turned her head to see that there indeed was James, walking down the street away from them with Hulk, as usual, for company.

"Want me to jump him from behind?" asked Freya, shaking her fist. "Once I've got him in a headlock, I'll give you the nod, yeah? And you can then come in and rabbit-punch him in the kidneys!"

"Wait, I thought you said fighting him right now was a bad idea?" asked Libby. "I mean I like your plan well enough, don't get me wrong. It's just, you just said..."

"Oh, yeah, I did say that," replied Freya, her shoulders sagging as she lowered her fist.

"Next time," promised Libby.

"Next time," agreed Freya. "Now, aside from James-related issues," she added, "please promise me that you're not leaving the island, because..."

"Yes?" said Libby, wondering why Freya had a funny look on her face all of a sudden.

"Libby," replied Freya, her voice increasing in pitch, "What if it was James who published the website?"

"Ehm, yes. Yes he did," Libby answered. "That's why I need the passwords from him, as I said. Haven't you been listening?"

"Not your one, Libby," said Freya. "The Bonkshop one."

Libby furrowed her brow as she thought this over for a moment. "Nah," she decided, dismissing the idea. "No, James telling people a few lies is one thing. But to do something like that? I don't think he'd stoop that low. Why would he? I mean what would his end game be?" But even as she said these words, she had her doubts. "Nah," she said, tilting her head as she considered it further. "He wouldn't. Would he...?"

"Who else could it possibly be?" Freya put forth. "James has already demonstrated he's not beyond this sort of thing, after the bizarre lies he's spread. He's obviously not right in the head."

"Hmm. You could be correct," said Libby, slowly coming round to Freya's way of thinking.

"We know James has the skillset to do it," Freya pointed out. "So I'd say, all things considered, he's at the top of the list as far as current suspects go. Although, if he is behind it, I can't say at this stage I've any logical reason why he'd do it."

"I think I'm a little scared," said Libby, taking another swig of her pint and then adding, upon reflection, "It must be him, Freya, as I don't know why anybody else would want to do it."

"Yeah," said Freya, nodding her head in agreement, and then taking another sip of her own pint.

"I think I'm a little scared," Libby said again. "Freya, what if he's psychotic or something? What if he's some kind of madman or lunatic?"

Freya dismissed this notion with the wave of a hand. "You're fine, Libs. He's just a skinny streak of piss," she said by way of assurance. "Oi, I just had a thought," she added. "What if he's ruining your reputation so that no other men want to be with you, and he can then have you all to himself?" she submitted. "If that's the case, you have to sort of oddly admire all the trouble he's gone through to produce that desired result, weird though it may be," she mused.

"I can't exactly say admiration is anywhere near what I'm feeling right now," Libby noted, fearing she might soon be rolled up in carpeting and thrown in a car boot.

CHAPTER THIRTEEN

Before Freya could offer anything in response, Libby's pride was suddenly served another blow when a group of smirking lads glanced over in the direction of their table. One of the group had his mobile phone on display to the rest of his mates, a round of raucous sniggers ensuing. "Bonkshop," said the less-than-discreet owner of the phone, huddled over the screen. "Eighty quid," he commented further, flicking his eyes towards Libby and then back to his phone.

The discourteous lad with the phone didn't elaborate as to what particular service the amount of eighty quid was supposedly meant to purchase, or for what duration, though Libby wasn't sure she really wanted to know anyway.

"If you're not in the shop tonight, do you do house calls?" the cheeky lad with the phone called over in Libby's direction, and loud enough, unfortunately, for the entire pub to hear.

"How about I do a house call on your face!" replied Freya, giving the lad an icy stare.

The young fellow's friends all laughed again, but it was unclear if they were laughing *with* him this time or *at* him.

Freya's eyes remained fixed on the lad with the mouth. "Oi. That you, Graham?" asked Freya, narrowing her eyes.

"Em... yeah?" replied Graham, all the confidence in his voice dropping away.

"I thought that was you, Graham. Funny, I don't remember you being quite so cocky when I used to babysit your sorry arse," Freya called over. "Just wondering. Did you ever get past that horrible bedwetting stage of yours? How old were you then? Twelve? Thirteen? Terrible thing for a boy that age to still be wetting himself, don't you think?"

Graham buried his chin into his chest, pulling the peak of his cap down over his face. It looked like he hoped the ground would open up and swallow him whole, as his friends were now pissing themselves laughing at his expense. Which was rather ironic, Freya considered, given the subject matter in question.

"Thanks, Freya," said Libby.

"It's just what I do," said Freya, looking pleased with herself. "Oh, hang on, I had a thought just now," she continued, moving on to something else now she'd finished humiliating Graham.

"Maybe James has left your passwords written down somewhere in his shop?"

"I suppose it's possible," replied Libby, unsure how this suggestion helped her predicament.

Freya leaned over to Libby from across the table. "We could go and break into his shop and find them, yeah?" Freya whispered conspiratorially.

Libby was a bit disturbed by this idea of Freya's. "So let me get this straight," she said. "Assault is a bad idea, but breaking and entering is a good idea?"

"It was just a suggestion!" insisted Freya. "Just throwing it out there as a, you know, hypothetical."

"All right, then," laughed Libby. "But, no. No, what I'll do is pop around to his shop in the morning and be as nice as you like. I won't let on that I know about him badmouthing me, or our suspicions about his involvement in the other dodgy website. I'll politely, but firmly, request the passwords from him, and once received—"

"Then we can tear him a new one?" Freya cut in.

"Then, and only then, can we tear him a new one," Libby answered, adding, "I must say, I'm starting to get concerned about your levels of aggression, Freya."

Freya laughed, shrugging this off, then said, "No, but seriously. I'm coming with you tomorrow. I'm not letting you go near that nutter unaccompanied."

"Nutter?" said Libby. "Weren't you the one trying to convince me James was harmless?"

"Best not to take any chances," replied Freya.

Libby ruminated on this for a moment, then answered, "I don't know. I'm not sure I can trust you to keep those fists of yours in check, Freya, and you might end up hitting him before I've got what I need."

"Fine," conceded Freya, "I'll just stand across the street. And if you give me the signal, then I'll be in there before you can say—"

"Hang on. Signal? What signal?" asked Libby.

"Hmm?" said Freya.

"What signal should I give if I need rescuing?" asked Libby.

CHAPTER THIRTEEN

"Oi, let's not get too hung up on the details, right? We can always work that out later," replied Freya, taking a large sip of cider and then licking her lips.

"If things turn ugly, I could just scream?" suggested Libby.

"No need to overthink things. But, sure, that'll work," said Freya.

"Okay, then," replied Libby, resigned to the fact that Freya, bless her heart, was going to be coming along whether Libby liked it or not.

"Right, then. So, moving on to other matters..." said Freya. "Training run in the morning?"

"What? Training run?" asked Libby, trying to get her bearings after this sudden change of subject.

"Yes! Training run!" insisted Freya. "After all, it's not long until this 5k and we don't want to make fools out of ourselves, now do we? We've got to get our training in! We can't just sit around and drink cider all the time, you know!"

"No. No, I don't expect we can," Libby answered, shaking her head and laughing to herself. "Anyway. Another pint?" asked Libby. "Shall I get them this time?"

"Oh, yes, please! Cheers!" came Freya's enthusiastic reply, all thoughts of anything else apparently having disappeared. "And another packet of crisps! Salt and vinegar, same as the last!"

Chapter Fourteen

Libby sat motionless, staring intently, like a dog willing its owner to throw them a ball.

"Am I particularly interesting today?" Gran enquired, peering over the rim of her spectacles across the breakfast table. "Libby, wakey-wakey, eggs and bakey," she added, although this served to produce no immediate results either.

"What? Sorry. No, I've already got cereal," replied Libby, finally jumping back into the moment. "Actually, can I give you a cuddle, Gran?" she asked, but then didn't even wait for an answer as she rose and walked around to the other side of the table in order to dole out the mentioned embrace.

"Not that I'm complaining, Libby, but what's all this for?" said Gran, patting one of the arms currently wrapped around her shoulders.

Libby squeezed a little tighter. "It's those journals," she explained, before releasing her constrictor-like grip and then returning to her cornflakes on her side of the table. "I'm finding it all rather emotional, Gran, reading through the entries. I was just looking your face over to see if you had any scars remaining after what that horrid boy did to you."

"Ah, I see. Plenty of moisturiser is the secret," said Gran, running her fingers down one cheek, caressing the skin there that a woman twenty years her junior might kill for. "Hardly noticeable now, and in fact I'd not thought about that for many a year," she added. "So. Has your grandad headed off to the Isle of Man at this point in his journal?" she asked, sipping her morning tea.

"Only just," answered Libby. "Don't say any more, though! Don't give anything away!" she admonished, raising her spoon and brandishing it about.

"All right, I promise," said Gran, with a knowing smile. "Anyway, you were out rather early this morning, weren't you? Earlier than usual. Were you out there on your training run the whole time?"

"Yes I was," Libby was happy to confirm.

"My goodness. You're taking this race very seriously, aren't you?" Gran observed.

"Ah. Well. Yes and no," replied Libby. "I mean, yes, I am. But it was mostly to work off the extra calories the two of us, me and Freya, took in from consuming too many pints of cider over the course of the previous evening, to be perfectly honest. It wasn't so bad, though, being out extra early. It was lovely out there, actually. The town was empty, and it felt like we had the island all to ourselves."

"Ah," said Gran.

"You know," Libby added, "and speaking of Freya. There's a girl that couldn't run the length of herself not too long ago, and yet here she is now not only able to run 5k but doing it in rather a respectable time as well."

"Lovely, lovely," said Gran, taking another sip of tea.

"And then there's you lot!" Libby continued. "You and your friends signing up to the half-marathon, no less! Look at you! Well done!"

"We're all having a day off from the running today, actually, as we need to give our legs a little recovery time," replied Gran, waving away the impressive scale of their group's collective endeavour. "Helen suggested we try something nice and relaxing this afternoon, like boat yoga. So that's what we're doing. I've no idea what that is, but I'll certainly try anything at least once," she said with a shrug of her shoulders.

"Wait, hang on," said Libby, upon registering what Gran had just told her. "Boat yoga? What on earth is that?"

"I've not got the faintest idea," Gran answered. "Apparently, we're getting the club bus out to a farm on the outskirts of Peel.

CHAPTER FOURTEEN

Which I thought was more than a little curious, because that'll be nowhere near any boats at all, now will it?"

"How peculiar," agreed Libby. "Hmm, boat yoga..." she said, rolling this around in her head. "I wonder... Are you sure it's not maybe... goat yoga? That's actually a thing, apparently."

"I suppose it could be, yes. Helen isn't very good with text messages, so she could very well have spelt it wrong," replied Gran, pursing her lips. "That would explain the farm location, at least. Although I've no idea how we're going to coax those wee devils into performing yoga. Those are wilful creatures, goats, and not really inclined to be doing as they're told, I expect."

"I'm afraid I'm a bit short on the details," Libby offered. "I've heard of it, goat yoga, but beyond that know nothing about it."

"It should be fun," Gran said brightly. "Maybe that's where the exercise enters in, by chasing the goats around!"

"They *are* cute little things," remarked Libby. "Be sure to take some pictures of your escapade, will you, Gran?"

It was at this point that Libby felt the need to replenish her large coffee mug, which was currently empty. It'd been a fitful night following Freya's revelation about James spreading false rumours, and also him being the prime suspect in the whole sordid Bonkshop mess. She was frustrated she'd not trusted the original gut feeling she'd had about James, and she also found herself worrying how she'd get on without his help, moving forward, as she obviously couldn't associate with him any longer after this. She could really have done without him being such a sorry misfit, because he was otherwise exactly what she needed right now — a business mentor, and someone she could bounce ideas off of. But, at this point, it looked as if all he was likely to become was the subject of a restraining order.

Without the continued availability of James's expertise or input, Libby's thoughts had turned, once again, to the actual viability of her making the business successful. Her fears haunted her, both when she was awake and when she slept. She had a recurring nightmare, in fact, in which she was turning the lights off in the shop for the final time. She could see herself taking one last look around the shop, sobbing, as she placed a sign in the window saying The Bookshop by the Beach was now closed. Outside the shop stood her gran, dressed all in black, wiping away her own tears of sorrow. Ryan Reynolds would then often make an appearance, oddly enough, but, to be fair, that was because he was often queueing up for the next dream or was sometimes still hanging about from the previous one.

Unfortunately, even thoughts of the lovely Ryan Reynolds couldn't cheer Libby up at present, and as she sat back down at the breakfast table with her coffee she began to feel a mite overwhelmed, afraid that all her hopes and dreams would soon come crashing down.

"Libby? Whatever is the matter, dear?" asked Gran, lowering her tea, faced as she was by the sudden presence of tears running down Libby's cheeks. "Hey now," she said, moving over and reciprocating Libby's cuddle from earlier. Gran rubbed Libby's shoulders, and then stroked her cheek with the back of her hand. "It's okay, darling."

"I just want to make you proud, Gran," said Libby, her voice breaking.

Gran rubbed and patted Libby's back like she was burping an infant. "What's all this about, Libby? You make me proud every single day," she assured her.

Gran was tough as old boots, but Libby figured the troubles she was having with the shop and the problems she was having with James would only worry her unnecessarily, and so, up until now, Libby had kept it all to herself. Also now fearing that Gran would hear about the Bonkshop website second-hand, she updated her, through the sobs, on everything that had been going on. "I didn't want you to find out and think I was actually selling my body!" Libby cried, at the conclusion of this explanation.

Gran had just been given an awful lot of information to process. But the most important thing for now, as far as she was concerned, was to comfort her granddaughter. "Oh, Libby, you poor thing," she said. "You mustn't bottle these types of things up. It's not healthy, dear!"

"I-I didn't want to burden you," Libby stammered.

Gran took stock of the situation, having a moment to both collect her thoughts and to choose her next words carefully be-

CHAPTER FOURTEEN

fore continuing. "Libby..." she began. "Libby, the shop is something that's very important to me, as your Grandad and I spent our entire working careers building it up."

Libby's tears only intensified at this point.

"Wait, I'm not finished!" said Gran. "I'm not saying this to upset you, Libby, I promise," she went on. "What I was going to say was that, yes, it's very important to me. *But*, it's just a shop, yeah? It's only a building, and what gives it its personality is those people associated with it. If for any reason the business does fold, Libby, then of course I'd be disappointed. But my priority is you, my dear. Your happiness is all that matters to me, and if the bookshop is ever too much stress, and you're losing sleep over it, well, perhaps it's the time to look at other options, okay?"

Gran then blew Libby a kiss, sending it on its way across the table.

"I don't deserve somebody as wonderful as you," sobbed Libby. "I love you so much!"

"Do keep me in the loop, though, all right?" Gran cautioned. "It's not so I can criticise how you run the shop, but so that I can help you. Don't forget, I ran it for over forty years, and there's a lot of knowledge stored in this noggin!" Gran pointed out, quite literally, by tapping at her right temple. "Oh, and for what it's worth, I'm pleased that you're not a prostitute," she added cheerfully.

"Thanks, Gran," replied Libby, spitting a tear as she laughed. "I might need to become one if the shop fails, though," she said with a shrug.

"Oh, and do let me know if this James fellow causes you any more trouble," Gran offered. "If he does, me and a few of my friends can pay him a visit at that shop of his and rough him up a bit?" she suggested.

"Gran!" replied a shocked but somewhat impressed Libby.

"We can make it look like an accident!" insisted Gran. "And two of our group know taekwondo, so I'm sure they'll be more than happy to put their skills to good use!"

"I'll keep the offer in mind," Libby said with a laugh, and then stood and drained the remaining contents of her coffee mug. "Freya and I are heading over to his shop right now, as a matter of fact, in hopes of retrieving my passwords. Wish us luck! Oh, and enjoy your boat yoga, or goat yoga, or whatever it turns out to be."

"That reminds me," said Gran, frowning, and reaching for her phone.

"About?" asked Libby.

"Helen sent another text message, saying she's booked us in for a sax lesson," explained Gran. "I need to re-read it and make sure it actually is a sax lesson and not something else, as I'm now a bit worried!"

"I've a feeling you'll enjoy it either way," suggested Libby, offering this up with a cheeky wink.

Freya marched through the narrow streets of Peel with purpose, a fierce determination fixed onto her face. "Just say the word," she told Libby, "and I'll be in that shop in no time and dragging him over the countertop by his hair."

Libby followed behind. She was much less enthusiastic about their current endeavour. She did want her passwords, of course, but wasn't particularly looking forward to what lay ahead.

"Libby? Did you hear me?" asked Freya, wondering why she wasn't receiving any sort of answer from her comrade-in-arms. Upon turning her head round, she discovered Libby to be at least several paces to the rear, straggling behind like a reluctant toddler. "Oi! Let's go! Let's do this thing!" Freya called out, clapping her hands smartly.

"I know, I know," moaned Libby. "But you do realise I'm useless with conflict, Freya."

"You'll be fine, Libs," Freya assured her.

"I'm not certain I will," replied Libby, drawing up alongside Freya with a heavy lower lip. "Maybe I should just text him or something?"

"You've already done that, Libby, and he's not bothered to reply, has he?" Freya pointed out. "Not even any sort of response at all, much less comply with your request. No, you need to go and

CHAPTER FOURTEEN

see him face to face, playing it nice initially of course but firmly standing your ground to get what you want."

"I suppose," said Libby, rather noncommittally.

Sensing her friend was on the verge of losing her nerve, Freya stopped, plonking her hands down on Libby's shoulders. "Libby," she began, in a calm, measured tone, "Not to put too fine a point on it, Libby, but James has been telling all and sundry that you're a woman of questionable virtue. This, in turn, sent Luke, who you really liked, and I believe still like, running for the hills. It's also a pretty secure bet that he designed and put up a website with the sole intention of even further impugning your character, indicating to everyone in town that you were, to put it politely, a fille de joie."

"A what?" asked Libby.

"*Fille de joie*," repeated Freya. "It's a nice way of saying hooker or prostitute," she explained.

"Well why didn't you just say that, then?" asked a confused Libby.

"I was trying to be nice," Freya offered. "You know, so as not to offend you."

"No I don't know," countered Libby. "How would just saying the proper word offend me?"

"Ah. Well there's no shame in doing what you're doing, is there?" Freya answered. "It's the world's oldest profession, after all. So I was just trying to be polite, so as not to hurt your feelings or anything."

"But I'm not a prostitute!" said Libby.

"Right, right. But if you were," Freya answered.

"But I'm not!" said Libby.

"Right, but still," offered Freya.

"Freya, I'm not a prostitute!" Libby shouted.

"Right, and that's the whole point, isn't it?" said Freya, patting Libby on her shoulders.

Freya was rather adept at getting people riled up, it would appear, as evidenced by Libby currently grinding her teeth in anger.

"You're right!" Libby replied, setting off once again, picking up the pace, and even leading from the front this time. "He's a complete bellend!" Libby declared, leaving Freya now trailing in her wake and struggling to catch up.

A few expletive-laden minutes later filled with a variety of ever more colourful curses as they went along, and the girls had reached their destination.

"I think I'll need to come with you, Libby," decided Freya, now that they were in position standing opposite to James's shop. "I mean, we should have worked out some kind of signal for if you run into trouble and need saving, yes?"

"If only we'd had time to discuss that previously," said Libby, rolling her eyes at the recollection of having made precisely this point back at the pub the day before.

"Right. No need to dwell on that now," replied Freya, oblivious to Libby's gentle sarcasm. "We'll just have to think these things properly through next time around if we should find ourselves planning for a similar circumstance, yeah?" she continued. "I mean, you could scratch your nose or something, but from this distance, and with you inside, I don't think I'd see you," Freya said, thinking aloud. "I suppose you could simply scream if you got in trouble…" Freya considered, brainstorming on the spot.

"Gosh, I never would have thought of that," Libby entered in, though once again Freya was too distracted to notice the gentle ribbing or the animated eye-rolling being directed her way.

"Still, if he attacks you, it could be all over by the time I cover the distance from here to there," Freya carried on. "So, as I say, I think the wisest course of action is for me to come with you, yes? And I'll linger by the front door close by, right?"

Libby shifted her weight from one foot to the other uneasily. "He's not going to attack me, is he?" she worried.

"Let's err on the side of caution," suggested Freya.

"You should linger, Freya. Close by," agreed Libby, deciding this to be the safest approach. "Right!" she said, holding her fists up. "Don't try and sully my good name and think you can get away with it!" she said, rallying herself. And then, "I'm going in!" she declared, with a final look of determination to Freya now she'd finally, eventually, plucked up the courage to tackle this issue head-on.

CHAPTER FOURTEEN

"Wait! Stop!" Freya whispered, taking a quick hold of Libby's shirtsleeve in order to halt any forward progress.

"Ah, hell, Freya, I was good to go then," protested Libby, wondering why Freya was suddenly interfering with her mojo just as that mojo had got flowing good and properly.

"Over there," said Freya, pointing to the front of James's shop.

Libby had been so busy working herself up into a lather that she hadn't even been paying attention. But James had appeared at some point in the interim and was now stood outside his shop with a rather pretentious-looking chap in a garish blue suit by his side. This other fellow had his hair gelled back with so much grease that he looked as if he could well have lubricated the undercarriage of a commercial lorry with it. Whoever he was, the two of them engaged in some sort of deep conversation, with the chap in the suit nodding along and taking notes.

"Damn," said Libby, with her adrenalin levels decreasing. "Do you think James saw us skulking about? If he's spotted us, he might know that something's up or that we're on to him?"

Freya shook her head. "I don't think they saw us," she said. "They're not looking this way."

"All my bravery's up and left now, rolled back like the tide," said Libby, taking a few steps back in search of a better spot that might provide them with a bit of cover. "All that's left, I think, are barnacles and stranded starfish," she told Freya.

"Don't fret. Give it two minutes for them to finish talking and we'll proceed with the original plan. Simples," replied Freya.

The two women retreated from view, standing in the doorway of a locksmiths that wasn't yet open for the day, around the corner from where they'd been stood a moment ago. "We should be fine for now, as long as we don't draw any attention to ourselves," remarked Freya.

Their attempts to remain inconspicuous, however, were dealt a blow in short order when a BMW in shiny metallic bronze pulled up directly in front of where they were hiding out. The window of the passenger side door rolled smoothly open with the gentle hum of an electric motor, and the driver — a seedy-looking middle-aged man with a noticeable paunch and an abysmal combover — stretched himself over the seat for a better view of the girls.

"Ah, I thought it was you. Fancy spotting you here. I was going to drop by your shop later, in fact," said the fellow, his voice gravelly, as if he smoked far too many cigarettes and drank entirely too much whiskey. "Later, when the wife goes out to the bingo, you see," explained the man, wetting his lips with his tongue. He looked up and down the street, checking to see if the coast was clear — and perhaps that his wife wasn't in the area as well — before engaging them both once more. "You've saved me a trip! Eighty quid, it said on your website, correct?" he directed towards Libby, retrieving his wallet from the glovebox, opening the clasp, and then proceeding to count through a stack of notes. "I didn't know there were two of you, though," he added, looking to the pair of them and then running his eyes up and down Freya admiringly. "Is there any discount offered if I purchase both your services at once?"

In hindsight, Libby decided that standing in the doorway of a closed shop, appearing decidedly shifty, was probably not the best of moves, especially given the present atmosphere, rife as it was with persistent rumours swirling about in regard to her supposed shady activities pursuant to sketchy supplemental income.

Freya stepped forward, placing a hand on the roof of the car of the bargain-hungry shopper, and then lowering her head so she could address him directly. Fortunately, she was still hidden from view of James and his associate provided they didn't suddenly change position. The man in the car was getting a nice close-up view of her, though, and appeared to like what he saw.

"This isn't Aldi," Freya growled, bursting the fellow's bubble, upset more about the request for a discount than the implication that she looked like a prostitute. "I'll have you know, that if I was selling *this*..." she said, waving her hand over the goods in question. "If I was selling this, with her, then it'd be for a damn sight more than eighty quid!"

"I can go to the cashpoint for more money!" the fellow quickly suggested, his interest piqued and his libido aroused by Freya's

CHAPTER FOURTEEN

aggressive, domineering manner. It seemed like he was eager, now more than ever, to enter into a negotiation.

"Hmm. How much are you offering, exactly?" asked Freya, seemingly not quite as averse to the prospect as she was only a moment before.

"Freya!" Libby called out in a loud whisper. "The two of us are not for sale!" she scolded her. "We're not for sale at any price!" she stressed, lest there be any confusion in the matter on the part of either Freya or the man sat in the shiny BMW.

Sadly, for Freya, she wouldn't get to find out this day just how much her time might possibly be worth in exchange for certain services rendered. "Right. Shame on you. Off you go, then!" Freya said, tapping the roof of the car. "On your way, you mucky old devil, before I tell your wife what you've been up to!" she added, shaking her head in a show of disapproval and disgust that she hoped looked convincing.

"Eww," said Libby, as the car sped away. "You really think he was married?" she wondered aloud.

"So he said," replied Freya distractedly, her thoughts still on the previous proposed transaction, it would appear, and what might have been.

"Freya, you wouldn't really have…?" asked Libby, not wishing to even utter the rest of the thought out loud.

"You didn't see how many notes he had in his wallet," replied Freya. "And he said he was going to get more!"

"I'm going to have to assume you're joking, Freya," Libby responded, shaking her head sadly. "Anyway," she added, "I reckon we should really get back on track with our goal." And with this, Libby took the lead once again, creeping up to the end of the street to sneak a gander at James's shop. "Darn it, he's still talking to that other chap," she reported in frustration.

"Mr Slick?" said Freya, as she tucked in behind Libby, propping her chin atop Libby's head to also have a look. Their two heads, peering around the corner as they were, might well have appeared to be floating, like ghosts, to any motorists driving by. "You know, that chap in the blue suit James is speaking to looks awfully familiar," Freya observed. "I'm sure I've seen him somewhere before…"

"Before?" asked Libby.

"Before now," Freya clarified.

"Ah. From where?" replied Libby with a grimace, due to the increased pressure from behind. "Oi, I'm about to topple over!" Libby cautioned, pushing back against the weight of Freya so that she could try and remain concealed from view.

Freya sucked in air through her nose as she ran Mr Slick's face through the database of information stored in her cranium. "Hmm," she said, searching her memory. "Hmm," she said again, still searching, taking her time of it.

"Any chance?" said Libby, beginning to crumple like a wet cardboard box.

"Nah, sorry, I thought it was coming to me. But then it was gone," said Freya, pulling her head away and moving back towards the doorway of the locksmith as Libby followed. "It'll come back to me eventually, I expect, as I'm usually good with faces," Freya remarked.

"Good with faces in what way? Kissing them?" Libby joked, leaning against the wall of the recessed doorway once they'd returned to their previous position.

"That too," Freya answered with a laugh. "But, no, I meant good at remembering them," she explained. "Anyway, what do you reckon? Do you want to hang about and wait for them to finish whatever it is they're doing?" Freya asked.

"No, they're taking blooming ages, and to be honest I'm not sure it's such a good idea to be standing around in this doorway again as we saw what happened last time," responded Libby. "Come on, we'll leave him for now before we get arrested for soliciting or whatever they call it. I'll send him another text later asking him, yet again, to send over the passwords. I'll just have to hope that he does. And then, once the passwords are in my possession, I can finally unload both barrels on him and give him a piece of my mind."

"And I'll give him a knuckle sandwich," promised Freya.

The two of them aborted their current mission, heading off, back towards the beach area from whence they came. James would not have to face the wrath of either Libby or Freya just

CHAPTER FOURTEEN

yet, be it in the form of a tongue-lashing from Libby or the knuckle sandwich pledged by Freya.

"What if he didn't set up that website?" wondered Libby, thinking out loud as they made their way along.

"What, the dodgy one?" asked Freya, walking beside her.

"Yeah. If James denies it, or it really actually wasn't him, then what am I supposed to do?" Libby asked. "I've no idea how I go about getting a website taken down. Do I go to the police?"

"Sure, I guess you do," offered Freya, but, like Libby, this was a subject in which she held no real expertise. "It can't be anybody else but James," Freya added with renewed assurance. "It's just too much of a coincidence, and... and..." said Freya, trailing off in her speech, and then coming to an abrupt, unexpected halt as well.

"What is it?" asked Libby, stopping alongside her suddenly stationary friend. "Did you have a thought?"

"I had a thought!" confirmed Freya, wagging a raised finger in the air to indicate that this thought of hers was currently in the midst of being processed.

It seemed to Libby as if the wagging finger might also somehow be meant to help facilitate her partner's thought process, though she couldn't be certain.

"That bloke..." said Freya, staring off into the distance. "That bloke with James..."

"Bloody hell, is that what you're still thinking about?" Libby asked with a laugh.

Freya continued to waggle her finger as she wracked her brain, trying to place him. "No, no, this could be important. I know I've seen him before. It was right on the tip of my tongue... It was..." Freya thought for a moment longer, but her sterling recall, once again, let her down.

"Come on. I'll shout you a coffee," offered Libby, setting off without her. "The caffeine might help you think better," she called behind her.

"And cake?" enquired Freya, and this time it was her that was catching up in order to keep pace alongside. "There should always be cake to go with the coffee, yes? You need the addition of cake in order to receive the complete nutritional benefit!" Freya advised.

"Ah, is that so," replied a sceptical, but amused, Libby. "Is that really true, you think?"

"What is truth?" said Freya, turning suddenly philosophical. "If you believe something strongly enough, then surely it becomes true."

"Is that the way it works, then? How interesting," chuckled Libby.

"This is indeed the way it works," Freya was happy to confirm. "Oh! Unrelated, I went to pick something up from the post office this morning before I met up with you," Freya added.

"Something interesting?" asked Libby, noticing how Freya had really perked up at mentioning it.

"It's our outfits for the race!" said Freya giddily. "We're going to look amazing, and these costumes will certainly put the *fun* in the fun run!"

"Wait, what?" said Libby, stopping dead in her tracks. "What costumes?" she asked.

But Freya hadn't stopped short as Libby had, and was still merrily ploughing on ahead.

"Freya! *What* costumes?" Libby shouted after her.

"I'll tell you all about it over coffee and cake!" Freya answered gaily, calling out behind her. "Now come on, stop dawdling! You said you were buying, after all, and cake always tastes better when someone else pays for it!"

Chapter Fifteen

10th June

I had every intention of being regular with my journal entries whilst on the Isle of Man. I wanted to capture every sight, smell, and sound of my first trip to the iconic TT races so I could look back on it in years to come.

Well, looking at today's date I can see that didn't go exactly to plan. I can't even blame my tardiness on this blasted cast on my hand as I can still write, albeit with my penmanship suffering as I can't write quite so neatly as I ordinarily would.

No, the reason I've not written for a number of days is because being here in the Isle of Man at the TT races is the most incredible experience of my life and I've been a bit overwhelmed by it all!

As soon as we arrived at the ferry terminal in Liverpool, I was astounded by the sheer volume of bikers waiting for the boat over. Motorbikes were dotted around like pebbles on the beach there were so many of them. There were some spectacular looking bikes on display, and they were everywhere.

And what a splendid bunch of people the motorcycling fraternity are! Granted, their riders did like to poke fun at my little scooter, but it was all done in high spirits. I could only describe it as a party atmosphere, with grown men as excited as small children on Christmas Eve. Terry and I spent the entire voyage over listening to tales from bikers as they painted a picture for us of what the Isle of Man was like for the fortnight of racing. As we listened to them, neither of us could wait to find out for ourselves. One good thing was that having a designated rider as I did on account of my injury, I was able to enjoy a couple of pints of bitter on the way over as the bikers regaled us. A most pleasurable way to travel and fortunately the Irish Sea was calm.

Aunt Norma couldn't have been a more considerate host if she'd tried. What a wonderful, salt-of-the-earth woman she is. To think that Terry and I were worried about disturbing her with our drunken antics. Well, she was out with us for three nights running and can respectably hold her own in the drinking department as it turns out!

Her house is just off the beach in Peel, which is an absolutely perfect location. It was like something from a picture postcard, with golden shores, glorious sunshine for the most part, plenty of pubs to be had, and people walking around in a state of utter euphoria at being in such a splendid place at TT time.

Aunt Norma told us about all the best places to go and watch the racing and she wasn't wrong. I could write a thousand pages trying to explain how enthralling an experience it was to witness men and machine hurtling past mere inches from your face. You could smell the exhaust fumes and I swear some of the riders were that close that you could have reached out and touched the bikes if you were foolish enough to try.

I do think that I'll need a liver transplant in the not-too-distant future due to the quantity of alcohol consumed. I'm blaming Aunt Norma as it's important to blame someone in these types of situations!

We must have covered every square mile of the island and each town we visited was delightful in its own unique way.

CHAPTER FIFTEEN

One minute you were by the seaside, the next up a mountain. It really is an island of contrast which is remarkable in a place that's only thirty miles long. They've certainly managed to cram an awful lot in. As an artist, I could spend a lifetime using it as a study.

I wrote Gwen a postcard from one of the places we visited as well. Despite this being the most wonderful holiday I've ever had, I still thought about her every day wishing she was a part of it. I've shed a good number of tears thinking about her, I'm not ashamed to admit, usually after one-too-many shandies. I wish she was here with me now. I just hope she's feeling better, of course, and is happy in whatever she does and wherever life leads her.

As for myself and where things will lead, I know some people like to place their trust in some form of higher power when deciding what to do next with their lives. I always thought it was a load of rubbish, looking for some kind of sign or searching for some sort of meaning in some random circumstance. That was, until I sat on a famous part of the TT course called Bray Hill with a cold beer in my hand and the sun beating down. It was then that I had a moment of clarity and could understand this whole business about the universe giving you a sign. That sign being the situation with Gwen, and the delay in going to college because of my hand. I closed my eyes, and lay on the grass, listening to the birdsong while waiting for the next race to begin. In that moment, I had an epiphany.

I'm not going home.

I realised that I don't actually have anything to go back for or back to. I'm out of a job in three weeks. I can't go to college until my hand is properly healed, because I can hardly paint right now. I've got no girlfriend, and for all I know Gwen's crazy ex-boyfriend is going to want to beat the stuffing out of me at some point in retaliation for my assault on him, inept and unsuccessful though it was.

When I came to this decision to stay here, it wasn't a sombre moment but rather a happy one. Terry is going to take my scooter back home as I can't ride it at the moment anyway. He loved the place as much as I did, so when my hand is on the mend he's going to come back over for another trip and give me the scooter back. We've not figured out how he'll get back on the return leg of his trip after getting back off the boat. I suppose we'll sort that out later.

Aunt Norma was thrilled when I suggested staying, as it turned out. And not the polite version of thrilled like when you say your mum's homemade Bakewell tart is terrific, for instance, when secretly she's somehow managed to muck it up and it's truly awful. No, Norma was genuinely delighted at the prospect. She even said she'd hoped Terry was also staying as she'd had so much fun lately with the two of us.

She's pretty much on her own after my uncle died and said she'd therefore be grateful for some company around the house. It's not a massive house but it's lovely and only a short walk away from the beach. She's even offered me a part-time job in her shop, which she says could be permanent if I wanted. She said I can call myself the manager!

She has one eye on retiring, she confided in me, and so would be grateful for the help and says it's actually good timing that I'm here. It's a bookshop called Moby Dickens. It's certainly nice enough but could do with a bit of sprucing up, I think, which I told her I'd help take care of if she liked. The shop enjoys a decent amount of foot traffic, it would seem, especially in the summer season with the steady stream of tourists coming over. But I think there's real opportunity in the place and a chance for even greater success if it just had a bit of fixing up here and there. I was worried Aunt Norma might be offended when I suggested it but on the contrary she's very willing to hear any suggestions and open to implementing them if she thinks they're good ones.

CHAPTER FIFTEEN

I spoke with Mum and Dad and they're in agreement that it sounds like a fine enough thing to do, me staying and helping at the bookshop. Dad's already said that he's going to turn my room into a gym. I knew he was joking of course as that corpulent old bugger's never been near a gym in his life! More than likely he'll just put another telly in there for someplace else to relax. Or maybe Mum will beat him to the punch and turn it into a sewing room or something.

Gran was a little upset at not being able to see me so much. I told her that she'll now have an excuse to come over for a couple of days which she did seem quite excited about.

Also, from a self preservational emotional perspective, I probably need to be somewhere that I'm not going to bump into Gwen. I love her so much but the thought of seeing her and having to engage in nothing more than meaningless small talk is too much to bear when I know she doesn't want to be with me now.

Still, I'm rather proud of myself for being so impulsive as I think I've made the right choice in the end.

Bert Tebbit – Manager of Moby Dickens. I do think that it has a certain ring to it, if I'm not being too immodest, and I'm rather looking forward to my new life in the Isle of Man.

Chapter Sixteen

"Ow, ow, ow," complained Libby with every step taken. "I thought you were joking when you suggested this," she said, casting Freya a frosty look. "These feather knickers or whatever you call them are prickly, and scratching me every time I walk, and just how am I supposed to be able to breathe with this beak on?" she asked, holding up the plastic beak in question, secured in place over her mouth by virtue of a sturdy elastic cord around the back of her head.

"Have I got these on straight?" asked Freya, adjusting the rubber ears atop her head as part of her own costume. "Anyhow, that's a bill, not a beak," she insisted. "Since when do ducks have beaks?" she scoffed, but then paused, uncertain if in fact she'd got it right. "Anyway," she pressed on, "I can make some adjustments to your outfit easily enough, I think, in order to make it more comfortable for you. And at least we're ironing out any teething problems now rather than the day of the race, right?"

Libby adjusted her yellow bill, positioning it up and out of the way so that she could continue to speak unimpeded. "I was hoping to break my personal-best time in this race, Freya. I've not much chance of that dressed like this, as Daisy Duck," she said, giving a quick glance down at herself and then shaking her head in dismay. "I'll be lucky if I even complete the race at all, especially with this thing on me," she complained, looking up at the bill now jutting out from her forehead like some oddly shaped unicorn horn. "I could die of asphyxiation!"

"*Pfft*. You worry too much," replied Freya. "By the time I've done the adjustments, it'll be nearly as comfortable as your running gear. And, also, a few strategically placed holes poked into that beak will sort out the breathing well enough," she declared. "See? Simples."

"Beak? I thought you said it was a bill?" Libby pointed out.

"Beak, bill, what's the difference, it's all the same. No need to get so hung up on small details," replied Freya with a dismissive wave of the hand.

"Silly me, what was I thinking?" said Libby, shaking her head again, and chuckling softly.

But Freya could neither see nor hear Libby especially well at the moment, the polka-dotted dress of her costume currently being bunched up about her neck and head. "Oi, give us a hand with this, will you?" came Freya's muffled voice through the fabric, her arms flailing wildly.

"What on earth are you trying to do? Put it on, or take it off?" asked Libby, wondering if she should offer aid immediately or hold position and enjoy the show for a bit longer.

"Put it on, obviously!" answered an increasingly frustrated and panicked Freya.

"But why would you try to put it on *after* you've placed those big ears on top of your head? Wouldn't it have been much easier doing it the other way round?" asked Libby, finally stepping forward and rendering the appropriate assistance as required — after which Daisy Duck was soon joined, once entirely sorted, by her esteemed associate Minnie Mouse.

"I don't see any need to bring logic into this," remarked Freya as she looked herself over.

"You know," said Libby, tilting her head and sizing her friend up, "I have to say you actually look rather adorable in that outfit, Freya."

"I do, don't I?" responded Freya, tittering as how she imagined a bashful Minnie Mouse might do, along with giving a dainty little curtsy. "Hmm, we'll just have to make sure we don't get too near any naked flames, yeah?" she added, giving a cautionary glance at the tag on her dress in search of the country of

CHAPTER SIXTEEN

origin. "I reckon this material is likely as flame retardant as a firework doused in petrol."

"That could be a good thing, though. Might make us run faster?" Libby suggested with a cockeyed grin. "But you're sure I actually agreed to fancy dress?" she asked, becoming more dour. "I'm certain I would've remembered such a thing."

"We'll look lovely!" insisted Freya. "And, yes. Yes, I'm sure you did. We'd had a couple of ciders when you agreed, but..." she said, nodding her head to draw a line under that particular detail, in hopes of hindering further discussion.

Libby eyed Freya with suspicion as enjoying a few ciders was definitely not the same thing at all as being blackout drunk and unable to remember things, and she had zero recollection of agreeing to these costumes they were presently wearing. But she found it decidedly difficult to remain stony-faced with Minnie Mouse performing deep lunges right in front of her.

"Just testing for give," explained Freya, easing into another stretch. "The fabric, that is, not my legs."

"I need to go, dearest," Libby said a few minutes later, giving her costume one final glance, having removed it and placing it on Freya's bed. "I should get to work, Freya," she went on. "I've got the pleasure of a meeting with the landlord. Which is always something to look forward to," she said, with no attempt to hide the obvious sarcasm. "And I'll be sure to let him know how his son has royally cocked up my ability to make money."

"Have fun!" Freya answered.

"Speaking of fun, it's probably best if you hide those," Libby added, pointing at both costumes now lying on the bed. "I'm thinking that if you have any gentlemen callers, they might get their hopes up of a little Disney-themed roleplay party," she explained.

"Chance would be a fine thing," submitted Freya. "Very fine."

⋆

Libby had left Freya's flat not overly keen on the idea of wearing outfits for the race, nor convinced it was such a good idea. Still, she admired Freya's passion for getting into the spirit of things.

And at least they'd certainly stand out in the crowd, the two of them, dressed as they were. All she could now do was pray that Saturday wouldn't be too terribly warm a day, as the thought of running a 5k race in full feather knickers under the afternoon sun was not one she found appealing.

It'd been four days since Libby had seen James outside his shop with Mr Slick (as Freya liked to call him), and not one iota of communication had been received from James in that time. Libby had tried phoning, texting, and emailing him. But, again, nothing. She'd even gone round to his shop, but every time she had, his shop assistant simply fobbed her off, with James likely hiding out in the back. Not only was her website still processing inaccurately priced orders, but now her computerised till system, which he'd helped her install, was also on the fritz as well. With the till on the verge of completely giving up the ghost, she'd even resorted to using an empty biscuit tin as her cash drawer just to be on the safe side.

As far as e-commerce gurus went, or business mentors in general, Libby was not entirely satisfied with James's services to date. Unfortunately, the lone website of the two that appeared to be operating without difficulty was the one still offering flesh-based services on her behalf. She'd spoken to the police who, to their credit, were taking the matter seriously, but it was simply not an area they'd been called upon to investigate previously and were thus taking more time than desired in coming up with a resolution. But as to her genuine business, with the current technological issues Libby was facing in both the shop's physical location and website, Libby wasn't exactly flush with cash right at the moment. And of course the bogus website only exacerbated things further, with the negative word of mouth generated from it putting an additional damper on what should have been a decent overall time for trade.

As she made the journey to her shop from Freya's flat, Libby enjoyed a few short detours along the way through the winding, narrow streets of Peel. It gave her the opportunity to admire the flowerboxes outside the quaint stone cottages, and also the opportunity to have a sneaky peek inside the occasional window.

CHAPTER SIXTEEN

She adored living with her gran, but the thought of one day perhaps being able to buy her own place held a definite attraction, particularly something close to the beach. Such properties, however, came at a premium, she knew, and were sadly a little out of her reach. Well, *a little* was definitely a fair bit of an understatement, she reckoned, especially with everything going on at present. *Significantly* out of reach would have been a more accurate description. Still, it didn't stop her from dreaming, and wishing. Towards this end, Libby also had a regular glance in the estate agent's window whenever she walked by, as she was on this occasion as well. It was rather like a pleasure-pain exercise, but she did like to torture herself now and again. Eric would be fine if he had to wait a few minutes longer for her, she reasoned.

Libby flicked her eyes between the postcard-sized adverts hung between strips of wire in the window of the estate agent, imagining herself occupying the various properties featured therein. She could easily see herself in one of these homes, attending to the blooms in her outdoor garden and offering a cheerful smile to those tourists or locals alike who should happen upon her happy abode whilst out enjoying a stroll.

She was snapped out of her reverie, however, when her eyes continued past the adverts in the window and through to the shop inside where the salespeople were attending to other folk with property on their mind. Libby pushed her nose up against the glass to catch a better look, certain that one of the salespersons looked awfully familiar to her. The man in question was scribbling furiously on a pad, a phone held between his ear and shoulder. Libby struggled to place the face, which she was certain she recognised. There was something about the cocky expression and the slicked-back hair.

"A-ha! Mr Slick!" she said, realisation finally striking her. She hadn't been able to place him initially because he wasn't wearing the same blue suit he'd worn the other day when she'd first seen him, but that gelled hair of his was a dead giveaway. And at least now she could put Freya out of her misery and tell her where she may have recognised him from herself.

"Oh, sugar," said Libby, catching a glimpse of the clock on the wall inside over Mr Slick's head, which told her it was time to get a move on. She had no particular desire to meet with her landlord Eric, of course, but she wanted to get it done and over with as she knew she was in for a tongue-lashing about the constant overdue rent, a tongue-lashing which, to be fair, Libby understood to be completely warranted.

Libby had tried previously to crack through Eric's crusty exterior, but there didn't appear to be much warmth hiding beneath the surface no matter how deep she attempted to dig. He seemed harmless enough, at least, if not a little unique in his ways. He was a short, portly fellow that tended to shuffle rather than walk, bald on top with a monk's hairstyle that was often in need of a trim. Libby always had a spray bottle of air freshener on hand for when he'd been in the shop, on account of the pungent odour of mothballs he left in his wake. Also, being short in stature often resulted in his eyeline landing directly on Libby's chest, and he never bothered making any attempt to disguise the fact he was having a good look. He was an acquired taste, was Eric, but as he owned the building a diplomatic relationship was required.

Libby dashed along the promenade and towards her shop, where she could see Eric hovering just outside of it. "Sorry, Eric!" said Libby upon arrival, grabbing the keys from her handbag. She'd not even opened the door and he was already looking at her chest. Perhaps a snug-fitting practically see-through white t-shirt was not the wisest choice of clothing items in preparation for a meeting with him, she thought, and made a mental note to keep this in mind for future reference. "I got caught up along the way!" Libby elaborated as she stepped inside, reaching for the light switch. "You see," she continued, without taking a breath, "we're doing this fun run and my crazy friend had this batty idea of buying us costumes so that we'd stand out in the crowd and we had to try the costumes on you see only mine wasn't all that comfortable so we were talking about…"

Libby prattled on, steaming full speed ahead, the words tumbling out of her mouth at a rate of knots. But Eric was currently paying her absolutely no mind, so she soon drew the small talk to a close. Instead of listening to her, in fact, Eric was presently examining the doorframe for some odd reason, going over it and

CHAPTER SIXTEEN

rapping it here and there with his knuckles as if checking for structural integrity. It almost looked as if by successfully tapping out the right combination of knocks, thought Libby, Eric perhaps hoped to open up a portal to another dimension or something similar — or at least this was precisely how peculiar his actions came across to her.

"Erm... you okay, Eric?" asked Libby, smiling politely.

But again, he was paying her no attention at present. After a bit more time attending to the door, as a matter of fact, he then proceeded to wander around the interior of the shop, continuing to ignore Libby and this time looking upward towards the ceiling.

Confused by this strange behaviour, Libby wondered if he'd suffered some sort of funny turn. "Hello? Eric?" she said, laughing nervously. "You all right?"

Without explanation, Eric retrieved a tape measure that was attached to his belt and then, without saying a word, began measuring the width of the shop window nearest to him.

"*Ahem*," said Libby. "Hello, Eric? What's going on?" she asked, getting somewhat impatient by this point.

Eric retracted the tape, and then holstered the device like a professional gunslinger — or, that is, like a podgy, unfit gunslinger smelling slightly of mothballs.

"Measuring up," Eric replied simply, finally answering her.

Libby smiled, though not as amiably this time. "Yes, I can see that," she told him. "But I'm just not entirely sure why?"

Eric pointed a stout finger towards the window. "I need to get new signage on the windowpane here," he explained, at which point he then produced his mobile phone from his pocket in order — presumably, as near as Libby could tell — to capture a picture of the window for the benefit of the signwriters.

"Ohh-kaayyy..." said Libby, drawing the word out as she tried to make sense of what was happening. When she was unable to do that, she came straight out with it. "And why do I need new signage?" she asked.

"Not for you," remarked Eric. "I need to start getting organised for when you leave," he said flatly.

"Right," said Libby, dispensing with cordiality. "Right, Eric, what exactly are you on about exactly? I'd hoped we were going to discuss the overdue rent, and possibly work out a repayment plan. I was also going to update you regarding the various initiatives being put in place to improve the business, and how that will with any luck result in my rent being paid on time moving forward."

Eric stopped what he was doing and turned to face Libby directly, partaking in a long, lingering look at her chest as he did so. "You have three days left of your notice period, and as I've not received..." he said, rubbing his thumb and forefinger together indicatively, as if he was counting cash. "Well, then I'll need to start making preparations for the next tenant."

"Next tenant??" wailed Libby. "What do you mean, *next tenant*? Eric, please, there's got to be some..." she said desperately. "Look, Eric, I mean... Eric, please..."

Eric, judging by the expression on his face, clearly wasn't expecting to receive the sort of earache today as he was getting just now. "Libby, you've not paid your rent, and I've given you notice to rectify the situation, which you haven't done. Therefore, in three days' time, you will need to vacate the shop per the details of the letter you received," he explained and instructed. "Libby, I believe I've been extremely patient with you up until now," he told her, "but enough is enough. You can't expect to keep the shop when your rent is constantly in arrears."

Libby placed her hands to her cheeks, like in Edvard Munch's painting *The Scream*, as she tried to steady herself, realising the gravity of the situation. "Eric, I've spoken to James at length about the overdue rent," she told him. "He told me not to worry about the letter, and that it was just a formality, and that he'd speak with you on my behalf," she pleaded. "You can't evict me," she went on. "Eric, I'll be able to catch up soon, I promise. James has even helped me with a new website, and I've got so many ideas to put in motion that are sure to increase trade, yeah?"

"James? Why would James help you?" asked Eric, this news coming to him as an obvious surprise. "I don't know anything about that. And why would he be helping you when he's the one

CHAPTER SIXTEEN

who'll be moving in?" he replied. "That wouldn't make any sense at all, now would it?"

Libby paused, allowing Eric's words to sink in. "James is moving in here?" she asked, after a long moment. "Your son is moving his business into my shop?" she asked, just to be completely clear.

Eric nodded his head in the affirmative.

"Eric," began Libby, through gritted teeth. "Eric, James promised me he'd speak to you about the rent delay and that you'd be fine with it. He also assured me that he'd update you on all the initiatives we were taking in order to turn the fortunes of the shop around," she told him. "Please tell me he told you like he said he would, Eric," she said, though the answer by this point seemed unfortunately well evident.

"I have absolutely no idea what you're going on about, Libby," replied Eric, his face contorting like he could suddenly smell his own essence du mothballs. "As I said, I'm completely in the dark as to whatever it is you and James may have been up to. James has told me nothing. And I can't see it making any difference even if he had, because the only way James could have truly helped is if he'd paid up your rent himself, and I can assure you that he most certainly has not."

Libby didn't say anything in response, as she was too angry at James just then to even speak.

"What James did mention to me, however, was your other business interest, a business interest of the more unsavoury variety and one that you're apparently operating out of this very same premises," Eric continued, shaking his head in dismay. "I have to say, that's probably a breach of your tenancy agreement in and of itself. I mean, granted, it's not specifically mentioned in the tenancy agreement. But that's only because I never imagined I'd ever need to spell such a thing out, as we've never before had a tenant operating as a... as a..."

"I'm not a prostitute!" Libby interjected.

"Now, you're an attractive young girl, Libby," said Eric, apparently not finished yet in the point he wished to make. "You're an attractive young lady, to be sure, but I dare say that this is not a suitable career move for you at all. No, not at all."

The funny thing was, even as Eric was telling Libby about how shameful it was that she would be prostituting herself, he seemed to enjoy rolling the idea around in his mind just the same. "I'm not a prostitute!" Libby insisted again, this time adding a firm stamp of her foot to the floor for emphasis. "Look, Eric," she went on, "James, your son, has apparently played me for a fool. He said he was going to help me. He said he'd speak to you on my behalf. But it's obvious he hasn't. I don't... I don't know what to do."

Libby felt lost and betrayed. She wanted nothing more than to run over to James's shop with a cricket bat, putting it to exceptionally good use over his head. But, alas, she had more pressing matters currently at hand.

"Please, you can't evict me, Eric," said Libby, pleading again. "My grandparents have had this shop for over forty years!"

"Good people, the both of them," replied Eric. "I used to play darts with your grandad," he said wistfully. "Helluva nice fellow."

"I know, right?" said Libby, encouraged by Eric's nostalgic reminiscence. "So how about a little more time, then? I'm certain things are on the up, and if you could see your way clear to just giving me a bit more time, I promise that..."

Eric looked at Libby, waiting for her to finish whatever it was she was going to say.

"I don't believe it," she said instead. "Oh my god, Eric. I can't believe I didn't see this before now. I've been such a fool." She lowered herself down, slowly bending her knees until her bum was sat on her heels, her face cupped in her hands. "Your son is a snake in the grass. A complete snake in the grass," she said to an increasingly befuddled Eric.

"Should I phone someone for you?" asked Eric.

Libby lifted her head to look up at Eric, which didn't take too long, even in her current pose, on account of him being rather short. "Eric," she answered, pushing herself to an upright position once more. "Eric," she said again, but this time with determination. "Your son came into this shop with promises of how he could help me turn the business around. And yet all he's actually done is to try his best to sabotage it," she continued, now circling Eric like a lioness stalking its prey. "Not only that. Oh,

CHAPTER SIXTEEN

no, not only that. Not content in merely destroying my business, he's also ruined any hopes I had of a relationship with a man I really liked, and then..." she told him, punching her fist into the palm of her other outstretched hand. "And then, I'm fairly certain it was your own dear son who also set up that dodgy website to impugn my character, all with the aim of thoroughly destroying my reputation so that he could force me out and worm his way in, relocating his little tat emporium for nerds into the shop that my family has been operating for forty some-odd years!"

Eric gulped, glancing about to see how close he was to the exit, working out just how quickly he might make good his escape if push came to shove and he had to make a run for it. "Anyway..." he said tentatively, testing those very waters. "I think maybe... I should go...?"

"Wait, hold on!" barked Libby, having a thought. She then bolted over to the shop counter, riffling through a messy pile of papers that were in desperate need of being organised. "Don't move!" she commanded further, as she flicked through the pile hastily.

Eric did as he was told, not knowing what else to do.

"Ah! Here!" Libby said eventually, now holding up the paper she'd been looking for. "This is your letter of notice!" she said for Eric's benefit, as it didn't appear Eric dared venture any closer to her at this point in time. She ran her finger along one particular paragraph until she found the line she was looking for, which she then read aloud. "Here it is," she said, reciting:

"Unless all outstanding monies owed are settled in full, the management company reserves the right to commence and instigate eviction proceedings at the conclusion of such time period as indicated."

Eric nodded, although he was of course already aware of the contents of the letter as he was the one who'd written it. "Yes, but I don't see what—" he began.

"So!" interrupted Libby, brandishing the document like a defence lawyer holding up a piece of critical evidence in a murder trial. "According to your notice, and as you've yourself admitted," she said, waving the letter in the air, "I've still got three days left! You've still got to give me three days!" She took a breath, refilling her lungs, and was right on the cusp, additionally, of visiting upon Eric a good-sized speech as to the virtues of him doing the right thing. But, before she could even begin, Eric held up his hand.

"I agree," Eric entered in.

"I... Wait, you do?" Libby answered, half relieved, and half disappointed she didn't have the opportunity to deliver her impassioned oratory as intended.

"Of course I do," said Eric. "At the end of the day, Libby, I just want my rent. And eviction means legal bills and all sorts of other associated unpleasantness that I neither want nor need."

"Oh," said Libby, blinking, and surprised their little talk had gone so much easier, in the end, than she'd ever anticipated.

"Also, may I suggest, in future, that you speak to me directly in regard to matters of rent rather than conducting your business through James?" Eric proposed, not unreasonably. "Anyway, so we're clear, all outstanding rent by Monday, yes?" he told her. "I'm happy to work with you, Libby, but Monday is the deadline. Otherwise..."

"Right. I understand," replied Libby, getting the picture. "I'd very much like to keep this shop, and also, no offence, prevent James from setting up shop here himself."

"No offence taken, as I'd prefer it if he stayed where he was, actually," offered Eric.

"You would?" asked Libby, this admission of Eric's taking her by surprise. He was, it would seem, a man who didn't allow loyalty to family muddy the waters in business decisions, though Libby had to admit she didn't understand Eric's reasoning on this.

"You see, this property..." Eric explained, sweeping his arm across the interior of Libby's shop. "This property, I could rent out in an instant if need be. It's a prime location, situated where it is. James's shop, on the other hand, is a pokey little place on the outskirts of town. And if he leaves, then I'll struggle to find new tenants to fill it," he told her.

"Ah," said Libby.

CHAPTER SIXTEEN

"So, just so we're on the same page here," said Eric, "you do understand that both your outstanding arrears and this quarter's rent all need to be paid in full by Monday, yes? You're confident you can arrange that?"

"Of course!" Libby assured him. Although even as she uttered these words, she knew she had very little money in her bank account, and so where precisely she was going to gain this windfall in order to cover the amount needed to settle up with Eric, she had not a clue.

"Right, then. I should go," said Eric, preparing himself to leave. "Libby," he added, pausing for a moment. "Libby, keep what I said about James and his shop to yourself, if you don't mind?"

Libby mimed herself zippering her lips, and then, for good measure, turning a key to lock them, and then tossing that key away.

"Oh, and please sort out that other website, as I don't want anyone thinking that I'm allowing a house of ill repute on my premises," said Eric, giving Libby a weird sort of half-wave that she wasn't sure was a command for her to stop the whole prostitution thing or just him saying goodbye.

Libby offered a cheery wave in return as Eric shuffled out, leaving his trademark scent of mothballs behind him. Once he was out the door and off on his way, Libby breathed a sigh of relief. But then she thought of James, clenching and unclenching her fists several times as she did so. "James, I promise you, you've made a powerful enemy," she declared, looking off into the distance in the general direction of James's shop. "A powerful enemy indeed."

Chapter Seventeen

The Silver Sprinters were ramping up their training ahead of the half-marathon relay endeavour. Eleven hardy souls had so far volunteered but, even then, with an aggregate age nearing four figures, the challenge they faced was still a significant one. The training regime thus far had been rigorous, but enjoyable, and today's effort involved an early morning boxercise class, which was always a treat. Whilst some of the gang could still throw a mean right hook, there were those who could hit a fly on the punch bag and the fly would still get away without so much as a mild concussion. Either way, it didn't matter, as the main aim was to have some fun.

Eager to engage in a spot of fitness training themselves, Libby and Freya had also tagged along, last minute, as they quite fancied the idea of a bit of boxercise. Plus, spending time with the Silver Sprinters was something that always brought a smile to their faces.

The previous evening, Libby — as she'd promised she would keep Gran in the loop — had updated her gran on the rent arrears and all the current James-related matters including his industrial sabotage efforts. For a moment, Libby feared that her gran was going to head out and put a brick through his shop window. Gran was feisty as it was, but hurt her only granddaughter and god help you.

Unfortunately, whilst she owned her own home, Gran was not exactly cash-rich, with little to spare beyond her modest pensions. Despite this, she'd immediately offered to speak with the bank to re-mortgage her property, though this was a suggestion rejected in short order by Libby. Libby appreciated the gesture, of course, but risking her gran's house, on top of all her other worries, wasn't something she was willing to do. Libby assured her gran that something would come up. She was hopeful that an emergency appointment with the small-business manager at the local bank would produce the desired result, with the manager seeing his way clear to extend a temporary overdraft. Failing that, the only other option Libby could imagine involved a gun and a mask at the very same bank, but this possibility was dismissed, at least for the time being.

Presently, Frank, the muscular proprietor of the gym they were at, strutted over to Freya and Libby, who were taking a two-minute breather from their rope-skipping training. He was the perfect advert for his establishment — you could grate cheese on his abdomen, and his arms were so big around that they could well have generated their own gravitational field.

"Here's Frank," said Libby through the corner of her mouth, smirking as Freya sucked her stomach in, thrust her shoulders back, and pushed her chest out.

"Yes, I can see that," Freya whispered back.

"Hiya, ladies!" said Frank, clasping his hands together with enthusiasm. "Top job on the rope-skipping! Excellent form!" he told them, a twinkle in his eyes.

Frank sported a beard that was manicured with the care and attention of the playing surface at Wimbledon Centre Court, and whenever he spoke his perfect white teeth left Freya weak in the knees. As such, it was probably a good thing Freya was already sitting down.

"Em, Libby... is your gran okay?" Frank asked of Libby, turning slightly more serious now. "Only I've been doing a little bit of sparring with her just now, and she's gone and done this to me," he said, pointing to the swelling below his left eye.

"Gran did *that*?" asked Libby, horrified, yet at the same time impressed.

"Yeah," said Frank, rubbing the affected area. "She shouted, *Mess with my family, will you? Get into the sea!* At which point she then delivered a devastating left jab rather out of nowhere. I didn't even see it coming."

"Oh my goodness," replied Libby, putting her hand to her mouth.

"I'm a little confused," said Frank. "Have I offended either of you in some way?" he asked.

"You couldn't offend anyone, Frank," said a doe-eyed Freya. "Not even if you tried," she cooed.

Libby smiled at Freya, chuckling and shaking her head sadly, before giving her attention back over to Frank. "She's just a bit tightly wound at the minute, Frank, so I wouldn't take it personally," Libby offered. "I'm having a few issues bedevilling me at the moment, you see — nothing at all to do with you, Frank, I promise! — and Gran is just upset about it, I imagine, and has unfortunately been unloading some of that aggression," Libby explained. "And she's obviously got a little carried away, by the looks of things. Sorry about your eye, Frank, I'm sure she didn't mean to do that," she added sympathetically.

"Is it about that whole prostitution claptrap?" sighed Frank.

"No, but I'm really just *so* pleased that you've heard about that too, along with everybody *else* on the island," replied Libby, releasing a sigh of her own.

"Luke told me," revealed Frank. "But don't worry, Libby, he wasn't having a dig at your expense or anything. He was laughing it off because he found it so completely absurd."

"He said that?" asked Libby, her ears perking up. "He spoke about me?"

"Sure. Yeah," said Frank. "He was speaking about you at rugby practice."

"He was?" Libby replied brightly. But then, not wishing to appear undignified and overeager, she proceeded to tone it down several notches. "Hmm, so what was he saying?" she asked, completely nonchalant, in an I'm-not-that-bothered-at-all sort of way (even though she was, in fact, entirely bothered).

"Oh, not much, Libby," Frank answered. "A bunch of the guys had heard about that website and were, you know, making the types of off-colour jokes about it that lads tend to do. Luke told them to stop talking rubbish, that's all, insisting that any claims made by the website were absolute nonsense."

"So he leapt to her defence," noted Freya. "Interesting," she said, offering up a grinning side-eyed glance to Libby.

"Anyway, I best get going. I just wanted to make sure your gran wasn't angry with me for some reason, Libby," Frank submitted. "I'll leave you lot to your training, as I think I should go and check on Herbert over there," he added, hooking his thumb across his shoulder in the direction of Herbert. "He's getting a little too impassioned with the speed ball, and I don't want him to get another hernia," Frank said with a smile, flashing his teeth at Freya. "Oh, and Libby? You might want to consider getting that other website taken down. The dodgy one, I mean, yes?" he put forth, as an afterthought, as if Libby hadn't already contemplated this very thing herself.

"Not as easy as you'd think, sad to say," Libby answered him. "You wouldn't happen to be any good with websites and such, would you, Frank, by any chance? Know how to hack one and take it down?" she asked hopefully, as one never knows.

"Nope, I spend all my time in here," replied Frank, flexing his muscles illustratively, sending Freya all aquiver in the process.

"Ah well. I figured it wouldn't hurt to ask, at least," remarked Libby, shoulders dropping.

Frank turned in order to go and attend to Herbert, but then he stopped before he'd even quite set off, rubbing his manicured beard as he pivoted back around. "It just occurred to me that you might give James over at the local comicbook shop a try," he said. "He's fairly good with websites and all that computer kind of stuff, I reckon. I've never actually stopped in there, but if I remember correctly, his shop is the one on the other side of town, over near—"

"Yeah, I know exactly where his shop is," Libby politely cut in. "Thanks, Frank, I do appreciate it. But let's just say, working with James is not such a viable option right now for me."

"Hmm, well in that case, you might try his friend Giles, then?" Frank offered. "He's also good with all that sort of thing. In fact, it was Giles and James who came here and set the website up for this place of mine," he said, introducing the gym with his hand.

CHAPTER SEVENTEEN

Libby nodded appreciatively. "Thanks, I might just do that, Frank," she told him. "And where might I...?"

"Just pop into the estate agents," said Frank. "He's the one with the slicked-back hair."

And with that, Frank was off to save Herbert before Herbert could get himself into too much trouble with the speed ball as Frank feared.

"Slicked-back hair? That can only be..." began Libby, speaking to herself now that Frank was gone.

"Mr Slick," Freya entered in, finishing Libby's thought for her.

"Mr Slick," agreed Libby.

"James and Mr Slick were laughing and joking together last week," remarked Freya. "Thick as thieves, they were."

"Indeed," replied Libby.

"What do you reckon they were up to?" asked Freya. "You were telling me James was planning on moving into your shop. You think he was talking to Giles about putting his current location on the market? Was he that confident he'd be leaving?"

"That can't be it," Libby countered. "His dad owns the property, same as he owns mine. So James couldn't sell it even if he wanted to."

"Hmm," said Freya, fresh out of possible explanations.

"No, if I were to hazard a guess as to why Mr Slick was up at James's shop," Libby proposed, "I'd say they were having a good laugh about their handiwork."

"Their handiwork?" asked Freya, attempting to join in on Libby's current train of thought, but not quite reaching. "How do you mean?"

"Well, if they work on websites as a team, then I believe it's a fair bet this Giles character is involved in mucking up my real website, creating the false one, or both," explained Libby.

"I see, I see," said Freya, nodding along.

"And I think we ought to do just as Frank suggested, and go and see this Giles fellow," Libby added.

"Oh?" said Freya, liking the sound of this idea. "Will there be physical violence involved? Punishment perpetrated?" she asked

THE BOOKSHOP BY THE BEACH

optimistically. "Or threats of physical violence meted out, at the very least?"

"Possibly," responded Libby. "But we'll see if we can get some information out of him first. Maybe even get him to help us, get him over and onto our side."

"Really? You think he'd help us?" replied Freya, wanting to believe this might be true and yet sceptical. "I mean, if he's a friend of James, then why would he do that?"

"Because our cause is righteous!" cried Libby, balling up a fist and thrusting it into the air.

"And if he doesn't help us? If he doesn't, *then* I can belt him around the mouth?" asked Freya, ever hopeful.

"I suppose so. Yes," Libby granted.

"Brilliant! I like this idea!" exclaimed Freya.

"Right. I've got an appointment at the bank, before work," Libby related. "God, I do so hope the bank gives me an overdraft," she added, pressing her palms together in prayer. "So, anyway, should we go to the estate agents on your lunch hour, then? I could close up shop for my own lunch break at the same time?" Libby mused, thinking out loud.

"Sounds like a plan," agreed Freya.

"I've got eight hundred pounds squirreled away," said Freya. "It's yours to put towards the rent."

Libby stopped walking and took her friend's hand. "What? That's amazing, but... no, I couldn't."

"You can and you will. I insist," Freya insisted.

"I don't really know what to say, how to thank you," Libby answered. "Honestly, Freya, for all you've done for me, you're the most selfless, loveliest of friends I could ever have wished for, you know that?"

"Aww, it's nothing," Freya replied with a sniff, resuming their walk. "I was going to use that money for electrolysis," she added, rubbing her upper lip. "But your need is greater than mine."

"Eight hundred pounds just to sort out your upper lip?" asked a surprised Libby.

CHAPTER SEVENTEEN

"Not just that. Other areas as well," admitted Freya. "And if you find the right person, they'll also do your—"

"Anyway, thanks so much!" Libby cut in, not needing to hear about quite *all* of the areas Freya was planning to get electrolysis on. "I need every bit of help I can possibly get after that car-crash of a meeting at the bank earlier," she said.

"That bad?" asked Freya.

"Yep. The bank manager actually laughed out loud, right in my face, when I enquired about an overdraft or a loan," Libby answered.

"Oh. That's a bit rude, yeah?" replied Freya sympathetically.

"To be fair, she'd heard about that rubbish Bonkshop website and assumed I was wanting it for that, to expand that side of my business," explained Libby. "To take more ladies in, I guess, and turn it into a proper brothel rather than just a solo operation."

"A full-blown operation?" said Freya. "Egad."

"You could say that, yes," replied Libby. "Anyway, I had to explain to her that it was for the bookshop itself, as opposed to the side business, and that the side business *didn't actually exist*. She then looked over my figures and, though she was more polite this time, promptly declined my request for aid."

"Blimey, they've got loads and loads of money in there, don't they? They're a bank! They couldn't give you just a little slice of it? Break a tiny piece of it off?" Freya offered helpfully.

"You would think," agreed Libby, before suddenly extending her arm across Freya's chest to bring them both to a halt. She used her spare hand to point to the estate agents, their destination within view a bit further up the street. "Here we are. It's that one I saw him in," she told Freya. Libby then leaned back against the brick wall behind her, taking several deep breaths to compose herself. "Right. How do we play this?" she asked.

"Dunno," replied Freya, as she didn't know, though was of course up for anything. "What do we need to achieve? What's our objective here?" she asked.

"Well..." began Libby, setting her stall out. "Well, assuming he was a party to setting up that false website, then I just need him to take the bloody thing down, as it's destroying my actual, genuine business."

"And your reputation," added Freya.

"And my reputation," agreed Libby. "There's a lot riding on this," continued Libby, staring at her feet. "We should probably play it calm at first, try and get him onside if we can, before…"

But Freya didn't hang about for the conclusion of whatever Libby was going to say, heading straight for the entrance of the estate agents instead. "Come on, then! What are we waiting for!" she called over her shoulder.

With them both soon inside, Libby could see the premises were empty at present save for themselves, Giles (aka Mr Slick), and one other, older gentleman sitting behind his desk talking over the phone. Freya was in front of Giles's desk, having already taken up a position there before Libby had herself entered. Giles had the handset of his phone to his ear, just as the other fellow did, but it looked as if Giles was just ending his call.

"Must go," said Giles into the receiver, holding his finger up for Freya's benefit, indicating that she should hold on for just a moment. "Two lovely ladies have come into the shop just now. I'll speak to you later. *Ciao*," he said, concluding his call.

Freya was stood there staring at him, which Giles seemed to mistake for interest. He got up, ran his hand lightly over his glossy hair, and then came out from behind his desk, extending his hand. Freya wasn't about to take it, however, and continued to just stand there. Undaunted, Giles wiped his hand on his suit — the very same loud blue suit they'd seem him in previously — casually leaning back against his desk, parking both of his bum cheeks there.

"Are we in the market for something special, ladies?" Giles asked, his manner suave, polished, and slightly smarmy. "If so, you're in the right place," he added, with an overly familiar wink, like a true salesman.

Freya grabbed a large stapler from a desk nearby. "I'll tell you what I'm in the market for, sunshine," she said, glowering, and holding the stapler up to his chin. "I'm looking for a new home for this," she told him. "And I've got a prime location already in mind, if you take my meaning."

Libby had a funny feeling the go-easy-and-get-him-onside approach they'd discussed earlier was now off the cards.

CHAPTER SEVENTEEN

"Uh... pardon?" said a slightly uneasy Giles, obviously having no idea what to make of all this. Freya advanced a step closer to him — which was remarkable, as she'd been standing toe-to-toe with him already — resulting in Giles bending back at a thirty-degree angle over his desk and likely to lose his balance and topple over momentarily.

At this stage, neither Freya nor Libby actually knew, with absolute certainty, that Giles had anything to do with the false website other than an educated guess. Freya, apparently, however, had assumed the offensive approach to be the better course of action in the circumstance, dispensing with niceties entirely.

"You and that tosspot in the little toy shop up the road..." said Freya, waving the stapler about in Giles's face. "You and him have been up to a whole lot of no good! We know that you're involved in that website, so either you help us rectify the situation or so help me god I'll stick this stapler so far up your bottom you'll have staples for earrings! Do I make myself clear??"

Giles's associate, the mature chap on the phone, had spun around in his chair to watch the unfolding mêlée, with both the glimmer of a smile on his face and absolutely no intention it would seem of ending his call in order to come to the aid of his collapsing colleague.

"I don't know what you're on about. Honestly, I don't," Giles protested to Freya weakly, before turning to Libby in the desperate hope that she might offer him some protection.

"Recognise her, do you?" asked Freya, in reference to him looking over to Libby. "That's right, Slick. You and that comicbook cretin have nearly destroyed that poor girl's business and reputation with that rubbish little website of yours, and I can assure you, the police are taking the matter very seriously," she warned.

Libby looked back at Giles, returning his gaze, and just gave him a shrug that said, *Well?*

Freya then took a step back, allowing Giles to right himself and also to take stock and reassess the situation as, after all, he'd just received an earful.

"Can we...?" Giles whispered, motioning for the two women to please join him outside, away from his grinning colleague, so that he could speak with the two of them more privately.

The two ladies agreed, and once they had all moved outside, Giles offered them up a cheesy grin. But this had little effect on Freya, who merely stood there perfecting her glower.

"Ehm, now what's all this about bringing the police in?" Giles asked, looking more than a little bit worried.

And it was at that precise moment when Freya knew she had him on the ropes. "That's right, slimeball. The *police*," she happily confirmed, hammering the point home.

"The *police*," Libby reiterated, further confirming the confirmation that Freya had just confirmed.

"Look," said Giles, correctly sensing that this was no laughing matter, and holding his hands up in surrender. He continued to smile, however, just enough to give those who might happen to walk by the impression that everything was business as usual. "The police, seriously? Look, ladies, it's relatively simple coding that I did for James. I can easily undo it," he told them.

Freya didn't have much of a clue about website coding, or what website coding might have to do with anything anyway, for that matter, so she pressed out her bottom lip and nodded her head, encouraging him to carry on. Which he did.

"I can just log on as the system admin, and then simply change the bits that require changing so that it starts to charge the correct price," explained Giles. "No need for the police. Really," he said to them, loosening his tie and undoing the top button of his shirt.

Freya stared at him for a moment, and then turned to Libby. "Any idea what he's on about?" she asked Libby.

Libby released an audible gasp as the penny dropped. "Wait," she said, stepping forward. "You're saying it was *you* who sabotaged my bookshop's website, making it charge the wrong price for each sale no matter what I do?"

"Well I wouldn't say *sabotage*, exactly. But, yes," replied Giles, confused as to why they were both confused. "Although I only did it at James's direction."

CHAPTER SEVENTEEN

"You bastard!" said Libby, pointing an accusatory finger at him. "That website was supposed to save my business, and all it's done is make me lose money!"

"Wait, hang on," Freya entered in. "So then what about the *Bonkshop* website?"

"The what?" asked Giles, laughing, assuming this to be some form of joke or other. The look on the women's faces, however, told him it was not. "Sorry. *What* Bonkshop website?" said Giles, looking fairly clueless. And the reason for this was because, right at the moment, Giles was indeed clueless.

"So you didn't help James create *this*?" demanded Libby, reaching for her phone to bring up the offending website in question.

"May I?" asked Giles, taking the phone, having a look, and then scrolling through the website there on the screen. "Oh, goodness no. No, I didn't do this," remarked Giles, continuing to scroll.

Freya reared up, unconvinced, ready and willing to administer a beating should a beating become necessary.

"No, honestly," pleaded Giles, handing the phone back to Libby. "That website is truly substandard work," he explained. "I have much better skills than that, let me tell you. And, also, I would never do something as unkind as that. I don't go in for that sort of thing, as that's just childish."

"Yet you'd sabotage my website, which could easily go a long way towards destroying my business??" Libby scolded him.

Giles shook his head, not entirely following Libby's line of reasoning. "Look, you keep using that word. But I didn't sabotage anything. Or at least it was never my intention to do so," he answered. "See, James knows I'm good at this kind of thing, better than him in fact, so he pays me for assistance from time to time including helping him on your new shop website," he explained. "Your *real* shop website, that is. I just assumed you were having a sale, or that you were running some sort of special in order to commemorate the new online business or what have you. I didn't ask, not imagining there was ever any *need* for me to ask. And, you have to believe me, I had no idea that what I was doing for James was being used for nefarious purposes."

Libby motioned to Freya that she could now stand down, as physical violence or threats thereof would no longer be the order of the day, the need for them having well passed. Freya seemed to Libby disappointed, but it had worked out better this way in the end, Libby reckoned.

"Okay, I believe you," said Libby to Giles, softening her tone to something a touch more gentle. "Can you at least help me to fix my shop website?" she asked him. "Would that be possible?"

"Sure," replied Giles with a shrug, eager enough to help. "I'd just need the system admin passwords. I didn't save them, and James has likely changed them by now anyway."

"I don't have them. James has never handed them over to me despite repeated requests," Libby answered Giles with a frustrated sigh. "And what about the other website, the Bonkshop one? Would you be able to…?" she started to ask, although already suspecting the answer.

"Sorry, yeah, I'd need the passwords for that as well," replied Giles. "But for what it's worth, I'm fairly certain that Bonkshop website is the result of James, if that's of any use to you at all," Giles added.

"We figured as much," said Libby. "Though you're sure?"

"Fairly sure, yeah. I can tell by the style," said Giles. "But if you can somehow manage to get both sets of passwords from him, though, then I can get rid of that fake website and fix your real one as well, no problem."

"I don't know how we'll do that, but we'll certainly try," said Libby.

"Try, we will," said Freya, cracking her knuckles.

Giles, happy Freya's ire was no longer directed at him, sorted himself out by buttoning up his shirt, setting his tie right, and checking that his hair was still secured in place. "Could you do me one favour?" he asked the both of them. "I'm all set to post the rental listing for James's shop, so please don't mention what I've said? I'm having something of a lean spell at the moment, so this upcoming sale will do me a world of good, yeah?"

"I hate to break it to you, Giles, but I suspect James won't be moving shop anytime soon," Freya told him. "Not if we can help it."

CHAPTER SEVENTEEN

"Not only that, but it isn't even his property to rent out," Libby pointed out.

"W-what?" said Giles, clearly taken by surprise.

"It's his father's property," Libby informed him, as gently as she could. She felt a little sorry for him now. The poor lad was as pale as a ghost, and he wasn't actually guilty of anything, as it turned out, aside from being overly cheesy, possessing a garish dress sense, and having questionable hair styling.

"B-but, why would he...?" asked a rattled Giles.

"Because he is a flatulence," said Libby. "A flatulence in human form."

"A flatulence," Freya echoed, just to make Libby's point eminently clear.

"A flatulence," Giles repeated back, shaking his head in disappointment and dismay. "In human form."

As they were all in perfect agreement at this point, and with this particular portion of Libby and Freya's investigation having been completed, the two girls decided to leave poor Giles to his own devices. Soon enough, they set about on their journey back from their respective lunch breaks.

As they made their way along, pleased with each other's efforts, they fancied themselves rather a modern-day Cagney & Lacey. "Nice work," remarked Libby. "It wasn't what I'd initially intended. But you were right to go on the offensive, as it totally caught him off-guard."

"It's what I do," said Freya, her investigative credentials still firmly intact. "On reflection, though, I should have kept that stapler. Only thing I regret," she said.

"Oh? Why's that?" asked Libby.

"Because I'd like to use it on James!" Freya answered, propelling her hand upwards in an enthusiastic, thrusting motion. "I've got to place it up *someone's* derrière, don't I?"

Chapter Eighteen

27th June

This delightful little island is still playing havoc with my regular diary entries as there is just too much going on. It's a nice problem to have, though, and I'm sure that I'll pick up the pace again soon. My hand is still on the mend, getting better bit by bit, and I'm able to move it a little more freely now.

As for recent news, it's funny how a new opportunity can present itself unexpectedly as I discovered today. I was sat on the wooden bench just outside the shop soaking up the sunshine, paper and pencil in hand, enjoying sips of lemonade between doing a bit of drawing. I couldn't really do anything more than quick sketches on account of my hand but I figured it was good exercise for it and would help stretch out the tendons.

Right so anyway there I was sketching when a young girl came from the beach across the way chasing after this beach ball that'd got away from her. I recognised her as she'd been in the bookshop with her mum a little earlier on their way to the beach. I smiled and waved and she moseyed on over to see what I was doing. When she saw what I was doing, she got very excited and asked if I could possibly draw a picture of her. I told her sure but she'd have to ask her mum first to see if it was okay.

So then here comes her mum shortly after. She'd been reading her new book, she told me, and had looked up to find that her daughter had gone missing. She was relieved at having found her easily enough and she told her daughter to leave that poor fellow (me) alone. I laughed and said I didn't mind and then explained how the girl had wanted her picture drawn but that I'd said it had to be okay with her mum first.

Here's where it gets interesting. Her mum thought it was a splendid idea, and even said she'd pay me! I refused the kind offer of payment, however, as they'd already spent money in the bookshop and it's nice to be nice.

So I drew a simple caricature of the girl. Nothing fancy as my hand wouldn't allow me to draw anything too complicated even if I'd wanted. I embellished her blonde pigtails and had her proudly holding that large beach ball of hers she seemed so very fond of, a big smile on her face. The whole thing probably didn't take much more than five minutes or so to accomplish, but I was quite pleased with the results as were the little girl and her mum. It gave them a nice memento of their trip to the beach, and I liked the idea that she'd cherish her picture and perhaps pin it to her wall when she got home.

Anyway, whilst I was drawing the little girl a crowd gathered and before you knew it I had a queue of people wanting all to have their caricatures done and all of them wanting to pay me for the privilege. Well I'd refused payment for that first little girl, hadn't I, but I wasn't going to make that same mistake twice!

As an added bonus it was also leading additional people into the bookshop seeing as how I was sitting right outside of it, which Aunt Norma didn't appear to mind one least little bit.

I kept at it for the better part of the afternoon, with one customer following another, until my hand got too sore to

CHAPTER EIGHTEEN

continue and I had to promise people I'd be back at it again the next day.

And thus my new sideline was formed!

And a blooming lucrative one it is at that as I've made more money in one day doing it than I would've earned in a week back at my old job!

It's a funny old world, isn't it? Can't complain about the view from my new office either, that view being a gloriously sandy beach with gentle waves lapping the shore.

Terry phoned me this evening, and when I told him about the huge piles of cash I'd made from drawing he offered to return straight away in order to be my glamorous assistant. I had to remind the silly sod that artists don't tend to have assistants glamorous or otherwise and that he was probably thinking of magicians or similar.

Whilst he was on the phone, Terry also mentioned in passing that he'd seen Gwen. My heart sank as I thought for sure he was going to say he'd spotted her out and about with some other fella, obviously having given up on and having moved on from yours truly. But, no, it was her asking after me and if I was okay and such. Which was good, actually.

It was nice of her to think of me and I'd be lying if I said I'd not been thinking about her as well, especially as the thought of someone laying a hand on her in anger as they did still twists my insides into knots.

As Gwen was kind enough to ask after me, I decided to send her another postcard. It was an image of the bay at sunset with the silhouette of the castle shrouded in an orange glow. I told her how this was such a magical place and about my newish career, and I also told her I hoped she was safe and happy. I didn't tell her how I wished she was here with me now although of course I wanted to.

THE BOOKSHOP BY THE BEACH

30th June

It's fortunate we have a bit of room outside the entrance of the bookshop, enough for me to be able to place a few folding chairs there for anyone waiting to have their picture drawn. My hand is feeling stronger by the day, and I hope to be able to get out to fully explore the differing landscape of this gorgeous island and soon commence painting something a little more challenging than quick portraits. Not that I'm knocking the caricature drawings, mind, as my wallet has never been so stuffed full of notes.

In my spare time (if I have any!) I'm going to give the shop a bit of a refurb. The exterior has faded over time by the looks of it and is long overdue a good lick of paint. Aunt Norma has done a splendid job in running the shop on her own for a good while but even so I'm sure there are some improvements we can look at inside also. The carpeting for instance is threadbare in parts and the finish on most of the wooden shelving units looks a bit dull having long since lost its lustre.

I don't blame Aunt Norma as there's only so much one person can do all by themselves. She's a special lady, is Norma, and what a worker she is. Aside from a Sunday, she's not had a day's holiday in twenty-six years, she tells me. I suspect the shop hasn't made her an awful lot of money over the course of its history but with a little fixing up here and there I'm confident it could be a goldmine for her particularly considering the town is packed with tourists every day in the summertime.

When I finished work today, I treated the both of us to fish and chips and then ice cream for afters as we sat on the sea wall watching the waves.

I feel at home here. I feel like this is just where I belong.

CHAPTER EIGHTEEN

3rd July

Aunt Norma has only gone and arranged a blind date for me with her friend's daughter, Susan. Norma informs me that Susan is supposedly a charming girl who can sew and is tall. I'm not sure why I'm meant to view her being able to sew as a positive trait although of course there's absolutely nothing wrong with being able to sew. But this, along with the strange emphasis from Norma on the fact that Susan is tall, suggests to me this girl is not exactly a looker. Not that I'm so shallow that all I consider in a girl is looks, mind. It's just that I'm not in the market for a girlfriend at the moment anyway, and any girl I meet I'd only end up comparing to Gwen which wouldn't be fair on them as no one could ever measure up to Gwen in any category at all looks or otherwise. I suppose I'll need to be going along on this date however as a courtesy to Norma.

I spoke with Terry again today. I do miss the daft bugger, and the good news is that he's coming back in a few weeks. He asked if Aunt Norma could put him up and also if he can bring his new lady friend along. Terry didn't tell me this new bird's name, so not sure if I know her or not. I just hope she's better than his last one. Aunt Norma said that it's fine to put them both up but told me to relay to Terry that there's to be no hanky-panky under her roof. She was smiling when she said that part though so I'm not sure if she really actually meant it.

Terry is also going to bring my scooter back over with him, which is great, and with my hand improving hopefully I'll even be able to ride it well enough by then. Still don't know how he's going to manage without my scooter to ride once he gets off the ferry on his return trip home. I guess neither of us has really thought that far ahead on it.

In other news, after getting the landlord's OK to do so (and he was only too happy to agree, as it turned out!) I sanded down the outside of the shop in preparation for painting it, hiring one of the neighbourhood kids to help me. Well

I say kid but he's really only a few years younger than me. Also when I say he helped me what I really mean is that he ended up doing most of the work and I helped him. I'd intended to contribute more but despite my best intentions there was only so much I could do because of this blasted hand of mine. It's healing, yes, but sanding is bloody hard work as I was to find out in short order. Anyway, we finished up the sanding portion today and the boy was happy to earn some money and did a very fine job. The outside of the shop will be looking brand new soon and I can't wait to view the finished results. I'm sure Aunt Norma will be pleased as well.

7th July

Oh dear lord. I've managed to survive that blind date, but only by the skin of my teeth. I had hoped Aunt Norma might forget all about it as long as I didn't bring up the subject again. Unfortunately I was wrong and so had no choice but to go. She'd confirmed to me this morning that it was all arranged, and that I was to meet Susan outside the bookshop at 7pm. I didn't have the heart to tell Norma that I wasn't interested and plus it was too late for me at that point to pull out anyway.

Susan was stood outside the shop as arranged. I nearly walked straight past her as she must have been close to forty and I thought well that couldn't possibly be her. Only it was. There had to have been some communication error between Norma and her friend, surely? And I'm also working under the assumption that Aunt Norma has never had an opportunity to actually meet this friend's daughter. Because if she had met Susan and yet still proceeded to arrange this date well then I'd need to be having some serious words with my aunt.

As for the date, Susan has three teenage children, I was to learn. Which is nice, I guess? Although I have to imagine I'm only a few years away from her oldest, which is a little

CHAPTER EIGHTEEN

worrying. Oh, and Susan drinks quite a lot. And when I say quite a lot, I mean QUITE a lot. She dragged me around to what must have been every single pub in Peel including those I didn't even know existed and proceeded to get progressively and increasingly drunker in each and every one we landed in. She also smoked like a chimney and smelt like an ashtray. To make matters even worse she didn't even bring any money with her and expected me to pay for absolutely everything. Looks like I'll be working a double shift on caricature portraits tomorrow in order to make up for all the money I ended up spending this evening.

Anyway after all the pub hopping Susan insisted we go to the chip shop. She was ravenous she said and explained that drinking always increased her appetite immensely. She also gave me a peculiar look when she said this which made me very uncomfortable. Then, after her dispatching a large portion of chips, two battered sausage – which she ate very suggestively, dropping one of them down her gullet whole like a bloody gannet gulping down a fish – and a steak and kidney pie, she suggested a nightcap back at hers thereby confirming my deepest fears. Now forgive me but an emotionally unhinged woman old enough to be my mum, with laddered tights, a tattoo across her knuckles, bloodshot eyes, and dried gravy on her chin is not my idea of the perfect date and not someone I particularly want to go home with. What is it with the older women fancying me anyway? First there was Barbara at work and now this!

When we left the chip shop, I searched desperately for some means to flee as all she kept talking about was what she was going to do to me once we got back to hers (the details of which I don't care to repeat here as I wish to erase them from my memory). I eventually stopped at the public toilets by the yacht club on the pretence that I had to go to the loo, and once inside I promptly climbed out the rear window and made good my escape. A horrible thing to do, I know, but I just couldn't see any other course of action at the time.

Aunt Norma waited up to see how it went, which was nice of her. I told her as gently as I could that Susan and I just didn't appear to be compatible. I also suggested to Norma that, for future reference, I wasn't really in the market for a girlfriend just now. I thanked her and told her I knew she of course meant well.

What a night. What an expensive night (for both my wallet and the toll it's taken on my soul). Right now I just want to go to sleep and hope I wake up tomorrow morning forgetting this evening ever happened.

13th July

It's been a busy handful of days but the bookshop now looks wonderful. It's amazing what a coat of paint and a new sign can do, amongst other things.

It's not just a new sign either but a new name on the sign as well. I'd never been overly keen on the existing name of the shop, Moby Dickens, so Norma and I came up with some alternatives. New beginnings and all that. We had a shortlist of about ten names and Norma said that she wanted me to make the final decision which I did.

I brought her along tonight to unveil the new sign and covered it up with a sheet so that I didn't ruin the surprise. I attached a piece of cord to the sheet so that she could pull it down for the grand unveiling, a bit like the Queen does when formally opening up a new building. Norma stood there staring at the sign. She didn't speak. And then she walked across the road to get a better look and then she started crying.

I rushed over and assured her I could rip the sign down if she didn't like it or if she wasn't pleased by the name I'd chosen. Fortunately hers were tears of joy. She said it looked absolutely lovely, thanked me for all my help, and then told me she was certain the business would thrive with the both of us at the helm.

CHAPTER EIGHTEEN

I do hope she's correct. I've even taken the liberty of having a pair of name badges made for the two of us. I was exceptionally proud of mine which reads:

Bert Tebbit – Manager
The Bookshop by the Beach

18th July

Ah, there are days in your life that you simply won't forget and are certain will be with you until the day you die. And for me, this was one of those days.

I got out of bed early to prepare the spare room for Terry and his new lady friend. I then took Aunt Norma for a slap-up breakfast where we chatted about plans for the shop. She was very receptive to every one of my suggestions including a delivery service. I figured that once I'd got my scooter back it'd be great fun darting around the island dropping books off. Plus the scooter runs on next to no fuel so it won't cost hardly anything at all.

It's so nice to see the shop so busy at the moment. It was a huge responsibility to make any changes so to see the increased footfall was an enormous relief. Activity outside at my easel has been equally as frantic as well. Today I don't think I had less than four people waiting in the queue at any one given time.

I was halfway through a picture this afternoon of a young lad who insisted on telling me amongst many other things where he was visiting from, what his school was like there, and what he wanted to be once he got older, and also that he loves sharks. He was a pleasant enough little chap if not a bit overly chatty. With his love for sharks, he asked me to draw him swimming with a shark chasing after him and about to eat him for tea. I don't think there are any sharks in these waters, or at least not any of them being of the man – or boy – eating variety, but of course I was happy to oblige. And I was just finishing up the shark's fin, as it should happen, when I heard the distinctive toot-toot of my scooter's horn. It was Terry and his lady friend, who wore the brightest yellow jacket I'd ever seen. She was like a lemon sat there on the seat behind him. I couldn't get a good look at her though as she had her helmet's tinted visor down over her face. Even so, she seemed oddly familiar to me somehow.

I offered a generous wave and indicated for Terry and his passenger to park up. I only had two more portraits to finish after my current one and I could already taste our first pint. I'd been really looking forward to seeing Terry, I have to admit. I've met quite a few people on the island but it's not the same as the friends you grew up with.

Terry offered a quick hello but could see I was very busy and so told me the two of them would pop off for a bit to stretch their legs. I then set to work at finishing up with my clients while the two of them buggered off.

I finished up with Shark Boy, then with the next client as well, and was on my last client of the day when I caught sight of that dazzling yellow jacket once again out of the corner of my eye. It was Terry's passenger, who'd returned. Terry didn't appear to be with her although I wasn't sure because I was focussing on my drawing right then more than anything else.

Anyway I called out a hello and told her to have a seat. I asked jokingly if Terry had perhaps gone on to the pub by himself without us, and then I asked her if she'd like her portrait done.

Now, I'd asked her about having a portrait done only to be polite. I was already on my last customer of the day and I'd put up a little sign and everything that said I wasn't taking anybody else and to please come back and see me the next day. But this was Terry's guest, so of course I extended the invitation, though secretly hoped she'd decline as I was really thirsty for enjoying that pint instead.

CHAPTER EIGHTEEN

But then Terry's passenger said that yes she WOULD like to have her picture done actually if it wasn't too awfully much trouble.

This should have been a bad thing, right? But instead it was a very, very GOOD thing. Because I recognised that voice!

Could it really be Gwen? My sweet, sweet Gwen?

It was! It really, really was!!!

I looked up from my drawing and saw that it was her. I couldn't believe my eyes, and my drawing hand started shaking so much that my customer asked me if I was okay.

Of course I was more than okay. Much, much more.

Chapter Nineteen

The image hung in the hallway was one that Libby had walked past quite a good number of times but had never paid all that much attention to previously. It was nice enough, of course, but in the past had never struck her as being in any way especially noteworthy.

Today, however, was a different matter. She'd spent so long staring at the picture that she wondered if she ought to take a chair from the dining room and position it so she could sit in comfort like in a plush art gallery as she admired it. The previously unremarkable picture had now taken on new meaning. No, it was not any sort of great masterpiece. Rather, the picture was just a basic, colour-pencil drawing of a much-younger Gran smiling, holding an ice cream with a drip running down the cone, and with a backdrop of Peel Castle. She'd been drawn with twinkling oversized eyes, and a broad grin stretched across her face. It was a relatively simple drawing and didn't look as if it could have taken particularly long to draw. But for Libby, having read about its origin in her grandad's journal and thus gaining an understanding as to its significance, it looked more beautiful to her now than anything she'd ever seen before.

Libby didn't need any reminders, necessarily, about the importance of the shop, either to her gran or to herself. The picture on the wall, though, did serve nevertheless to bring into sharp relief how central to her family's history the bookshop had been. She thought warmly about all the people who must have come through the shop's doors over the years, all the happy customers, many of them no doubt on their way to the beach, plucking their next read from the bookshop's shelves.

And then her emotions turned from fondness to anger at the thought of James possibly getting his grubby mitts on their beloved shop and the very real prospect of him taking over the property for himself. His evil designs were strictly selfish in nature, of this Libby had no doubt, with him having not the slightest care or consideration for all the love her family had invested into the place over the years, no concern for the great wealth of memories associated with it. "Knob," declared Libby. "Tremendous, oversized knob," she revised, honing her declaration further into something she felt described James even better.

Libby took one last look at the picture of her gran on the wall before her. "Nope. Not on *my* watch," she proclaimed, and flush with determination and resolve, she then produced her mobile from out of her pocket and set about dialling a certain special someone at the top of her phone's contact list.

"Freya, it's me," said Libby, after Freya had finally picked up on the other end after a few or more rings. "Right, then. I've got a mission for us...

"... Yes, sorry to call so early, I know it's Sunday morning...

"... Yes, sorry, I know you like to sleep in on Sundays... Yes, I know *this* is a Sunday... Yes, I...

"... No, look, it's James, you see...

"... No, he hasn't done anything else. Rather, it's what he hasn't done...

"... Right, right, he still hasn't got back to me, and I can't seem to get hold of him no matter what I do...

"... Yes, Freya, I've tried going round to his shop. Multiple times, in fact. I think the bastard's gone into bloody hiding...

"... Yeah, I think the blighter's doing it on purpose, trying to run the clock down until my eviction takes place...

"... Yes, luv, I promise physical violence perpetrated upon his person could well be on the menu should the need arise...

"... Yes, I'm going round to his home right now, as a matter of fact...

"... Great! You're in, then? Brilliant! And I think you were telling me previously that you'd tracked down his address...?

CHAPTER NINETEEN

"... Excellent. You're absolutely indispensable... No, really... No you are... No, *you* are...

"... So you'll be here in a few minutes? Excellent... You're a dear...

"... No, *you're* a dear. And, yes, you can punch him in the gob if need be... Yes... Yes you can...

"... Yes... Yes to that as well... Right, see you soon."

Freya, for her part, didn't seem to need asking twice once she knew the score. Libby would have gone it alone if she'd had to, of course, but was happy her friend was following her into battle. As far as allies went, Freya was a valuable asset, and Libby was grateful that Freya always had her back. As far as friends went she couldn't have picked a better one, and only a short time later, as a matter of fact, Freya was on Libby's doorstep.

"So I wasn't sure if I should just use my bare fists, or if I should bring a weapon," Freya told Libby after she'd been invited in to discuss strategy before setting off.

"A weapon?" asked Libby. She wasn't sure if Freya was joking or serious.

"Yeah, I was going to bring my knuckle dusters but I couldn't find them," Freya continued.

"Freya, are you trying to get us *arrested*?" asked Libby, slightly more alarmed now.

"What? I said I don't have them on me. I told you I couldn't *find* them," Freya replied, not really understanding the problem. "But to be clear, you *did* indicate over the phone that there'd be violence involved, yeah?"

"Gordon Bennett, Freya, I said *maybe* there'd be violence should the need arise!" Libby admonished. "And I was only half-serious at that!"

"Well if you were only half-serious, then that means you're still *partly* serious, yes?" replied an ever-hopeful Freya, choosing to see the glass half full, so to speak, as opposed to half empty.

"Freya, we're just going to have a little word with him, okay?" answered Libby, patting her on the shoulder to calm her friend down. "We're using violence only as an absolute last resort, all right?"

Freya sighed. "Fine. Very well," she said in response, though unbeknownst to Libby she did have her fingers crossed behind her back as she answered.

"Besides, weren't you trying to talk me *out* of using violence before? Presenting yourself as the sensible one between the two of us?" noted Libby.

"Oh, that. Yeah, that was only the one time," Freya pointed out. "Plus I didn't really mean it," she further pointed out.

"I just need him to get rid of that Bonkshop website, and also give me access to my own, the real one," Libby informed Freya. "We'll play it nice at the start, similar plan of action as we've done in the past. Give him a chance to do the right thing," she instructed.

"Okay, don't worry, I get it," Freya assured her.

Freya had a huge smile on her face when telling Libby not to worry. Which only served to make Libby worry. But she moved on, ignoring this, and asked, "So you know where he lives, then?"

"Yeah, yeah. Like I said," Freya replied, holding an envelope up for Libby's inspection in response.

"What is it?" asked Libby, struggling to read what was printed on the face of it because Freya kept waving the thing around so much.

"His gas bill! I intercepted it, and it's got his address printed right on it!" explained Freya, quite pleased with herself.

"How on earth did you...?" began Libby. "No, in fact, never mind. I don't want to know," she said, switching gears, figuring the less she knew about how Freya had procured it the better.

"Right. You and me, on a mission, ready to crack some skulls before breakfast!" said Freya enthusiastically as she headed towards the door.

"No cracking of skulls!" advised Libby. "Remember, Freya, we're simply on a mission to get some passwords," she reminded her. "You can, I suppose, stomp on a few flowers in his garden if you like...?" Libby considered upon reflection.

"I think he lives in a flat. One of the upper floors by the looks of it," Freya answered, examining the address on the letter she'd found. "Alas, no flowers to stomp, I expect," she reported, clearly disappointed.

CHAPTER NINETEEN

"Okay, maybe..." said Libby, taking on this new bit of information into consideration and thinking a moment. "Maybe you can throw some rocks at his window instead?" she offered.

"Hmm, I like it," agreed Freya. "Wouldn't that break his window, though?" she asked, surprised by Libby's bold suggestion but still totally up for it.

"I meant very small rocks," Libby clarified.

"You never let me have any fun," Freya pouted. "But, fine. Let's get a move on, shall we? What are we waiting for? Tally-ho!"

Freya ran her eyes over the polished brass plate which housed the selection of entrance buzzers for the block of flats, checking against the address of the gas bill held in her hand. "Here we go. This is him," she said, pointing to number ten.

"Top floor? Penthouse flat?" said Libby, taking a few steps back from the doorway and having a gander. "Blimey, he must have a fair few quid to live here," she remarked. "I had no idea selling comicbooks was so bloody lucrative a business!"

"It can't be, though, can it?" asked Freya. And yet there was the evidence right there before them.

"Dunno. He must have a hand in other things as well, is all I can think, because these flats are downright luxurious," Libby observed. "I can only imagine the view he must have from that balcony of his up there," she remarked, staring up.

Freya didn't feel a need to wait any further at this point, and so proceeded to press her finger right then on buzzer № 10. And she didn't just press and release, either. Oh no. She pressed that button long and hard.

She pressed that button for so long, in fact, that Libby had to eventually try and shush her. "What are you doing?" asked Libby, alarmed, putting her finger to her lips. "You're making enough noise with that thing to raise the dead!" she whispered.

"Well we *want* to wake him up, don't we?" Freya answered with a shrug.

"But the neighbours..." Libby protested, giving a cautionary glance up to the group of flats.

There was no immediate response from anyone within the building in answer to Freya's liberal, enthusiastic application of James's buzzer. So Freya joined Libby away from the entrance, and the two of them looked up to see if there might perhaps be any sort of visible movement from any of the balconies above.

"Hmm, I think I see a creature stirring..." said Freya.

"James?" Libby asked hopefully.

"No, I mean an actual creature," Freya answered. "I think it's his dog. What's its name? Hulk, wasn't it?"

"Yeah. Hulk," confirmed Libby.

There was no human movement that either of them could ascertain, but there did indeed appear to be a moderate canine reaction to their presence. They could both make out the figure of James's dog there on the top floor, visible to them through the glass screen surrounding the balcony. The pooch appeared to have been having a nap, from the looks of things, just there on the other side of the glass, as he lazily raised his head to greet them. After which, unfortunately, he promptly set his head back down in order to resume his nap.

"Well that won't do," declared Freya, at which point she then cupped her hands about her mouth. "Oh Huuulllk!" she shouted up. "Rise and shine, little Hulkster!" she continued, a bit louder this time.

This seemed to have the desired effect, as the wee rascal was now upright, front paws pressed up against the glass. "Woof?" said Hulk tentatively.

"I'm not sure, it's hard to tell from here, but I think I just saw something from behind the sliding glass door leading out to James's balcony?" Libby informed her compatriot. "Keep doing what you're doing, Freya!" she encouraged.

"Who's a good boy, buddy? Who's a good boy?" Freya carried on, waving her arms and shouting at the now alert and responsive Hulk. "That's right, wake Daddy up! Wake up your daddy! You can do it!" she called up to him.

Hulk took to the challenge magnificently. He let out a yip, and then a yap, and deciding this to be great fun, continued on with a frenzied assortment of more of the same in quick unbridled succession. He'd moved on from his initial tentative woof

CHAPTER NINETEEN

and was truly getting into the spirit of things, with the sharp barks he was now producing echoing off the glass and piercing the still morning air.

It wasn't long before James's head loomed over the edge of the glass screen on his balcony, rubbing his eyes as he attempted to gather his wits about him. "Oi. Quiet, Hulk," he said to his dog.

"Morning, Sunshine!" Freya called up.

"Oh! Morning!" James called down, casually, as if he'd only just noticed Libby and Freya standing there. "So lovely of you to stop by!" he added. "Sorry, I'm a bit tied up today!" he continued. "But if you need me, I'll be at the shop next week in my plush new premises, yeah?" he told them, thumbs raised.

"That's it, it's become official," said Libby privately to Freya. "I officially hate him."

By this time, a few of James's neighbours didn't seem to be too pleased with James right at the moment either. With Hulk's incessant yapping from a few moments earlier having woken them, a collection of heads poked out onto their own balconies to try and work out what the fuss was all about.

"Well, that's me! Must be off! Busy, busy! Lots of arrangements to be made!" James called down to the women. "Cheerio!" he concluded, giving them an overly enthusiastic wave, and then promptly disappearing and returning from whence he came.

"Aww, nuts," said Libby, as her chin dropped to her chest. She sighed a heavy sigh, disappointed that their mission had turned out, by all appearances, to be an abject failure.

But Freya hadn't given up just yet. Not on your nelly. "Excuse me, sir!" she screamed at the top of her lungs, loud enough for all of James's neighbours to very clearly hear her. "Sir, it's just us from the Bonkshop in town! We're here to let you know that when we attempted to charge your credit card last night, for your booking of one of our lovely ladies, it was declined! As you should be aware from your many past purchases, full payment must be made up front in order to procure the services of one of our special girls!"

No response from James. But Freya soldiered on...

"The owner of the establishment has asked us to come round to let you know about the discrepancy!" she said. "We could have phoned you of course, but we do like to offer a personal touch!"

"And we know how much you like our personal touch, you filthy thing!" Libby entered in, picking up on Freya's lead. She wasn't sure she liked the idea of lending the Bonkshop website any credence, necessarily, by pretending in front of James's neighbours that they were its representatives. They wanted to dissuade people of the notion that it was legitimate, after all. But she could see where Freya was going with this, and so she was happy to play along in this one instance.

"What's all this?" demanded a well-groomed chap, coming into full view on the balcony below James. "Do I need to phone the police?" he shouted, adjusting his dressing gown and then his spectacles.

James quickly reappeared, as if by magic, flapping his arms to try and hush the girls. He seemed at this point resigned to the fact that they weren't going away, and he pointed to his wrist and then held up his hand, extending all five digits. The girls took this to mean he'd meet them in five minutes, and so they both made their way back over to the entrance.

It was considerably less than five minutes, as it should happen, when a harried, embarrassed-looking James appeared before them, throwing open the front door. "What in hell are you two doing?" he began. "Are you mad? This is a nice area, and you lot making out like I'm a—"

"Button your hole, you slimy puke," Freya cut in, not bothering to mince words. "I've got my Doc Martens on and you should know, James, that I'm about six seconds or so away from putting them to very good use!" she advised.

Libby stepped forward, now that James could see they meant business. "James, I'm not sure how to put this delicately. So I'm just going to ask point-blank," she told him. "James, why did you set that website up?" she asked gravely.

"Look..." said James, drawing in a big breath in preparation for what he was about to say.

Libby assumed this was the part where James would come up with some kind of ridiculous excuse as to how this whole thing

CHAPTER NINETEEN

was some form of huge misunderstanding, that he'd played absolutely no part in what she was accusing him of, and that he was completely innocent of any and all charges laid against him. Or some similar sort of rubbish to this effect.

"Look, I'm guilty," James said instead, quite to the surprise of both Libby and Freya.

"Wait. About what, exactly?" asked a confused Freya, believing this admission of guilt of his to be a little too easily obtained and wanting to make sure they were all on the same page in regard to whatever it was exactly he may have been confessing to.

"The Bonkshop website. The erroneously discounted pricing on your real website. All of it," replied James, perfectly matter-of-fact, a Cheshire grin emerging.

Freya clenched her fists. "Bloody hell, James, you're not even the *slightest* bit ashamed at what you've done?" she asked him.

"Not really, no," replied James, with an indifferent shrug of the shoulders. Then he turned to address Libby. "It's just business. Nothing personal, you understand," he told her. "For what it's worth, though, I really like you, Libby," James offered. "Well, liked you, that is to say. Past tense," he added quickly. "I actually thought we had something of a chance, romantically, at one stage," he explained. "But that was my mistake, as it only clouded my judgement in relation to reaching my objective."

"Your *objective*?" gasped Libby. "Ruining my life was your objective??" she asked, very much wishing she'd worn a pair of Doc Martens herself.

"You set out to ruin a family business by destroying the reputation of my very best friend? Are you really for real?" asked an incredulous Freya. "Are you seriously this seriously deplorable??"

"*Ahem*. Don't forget the entire rent arrears situation. It's not all on me," said James dismissively, not giving Freya the courtesy of looking at her as he replied and directing his answer towards Libby instead. "My business is on the up, Libby. Surely you can see that. I now need larger premises, and your shop just happens to be ideal for my growth aspirations. Personal feelings aside, you can understand that, yes?"

"Can you please just shut that bogus website down, James, if nothing else? Please?" implored Libby, fighting back the tears and once again starting to give in to despair.

James gave another shrug. "Maybe. Dunno," he said noncommittally. "Perhaps if I was asked very, very nicely," he pondered. "But, even then, I still don't know," he added, quickly waving the idea away.

"You're not getting my shop!" snapped Libby, the fight back in her. "It doesn't matter what you do or don't do, you're still not getting my shop either way!" she declared defiantly.

James smiled sympathetically, though it was obviously insincere. "Libby," he said condescendingly, "Libby, you're months behind on the rent and you're due to be evicted in a matter of days. When that happens, once you've moved out and I've moved in, then it's certainly possible that website will simply disappear."

"Oh? Well it just so happens that I've *got* all the money to pay the rent! What do you think of that!" Libby answered, lying. Or it was a partial lie, at least. She'd managed to accumulate about two-thirds of the outstanding amount thus far. But she was determined to beg, borrow or steal the rest. Whatever it took to thwart James's plans.

"I don't believe you. You're bluffing," insisted James, though with his confidence wavering just a touch.

"Only I'm *not*, though, am I?" Libby insisted right back. "No, your dad will have all his rent come Monday, you'll see," she told him. "So a bit of advice," she suggested, "if you've hired yourself a removal van, now might be a good time to cancel it!"

This was now a game of poker and James, though wavering, still believed he was in firm possession of the stronger hand. "It hardly matters," he answered. "With your reputation in tatters, Libby, you can't expect more than a small handful of people to be walking through your door. As such, you're only delaying the inevitable. At this point I'd say your shop is like a horse that's gone lame, and the only decent and humane thing to do at this stage is to put the poor miserable beast out of its misery and let it go," he told her.

CHAPTER NINETEEN

Libby couldn't see what James was trying to accomplish by saying this, as it only served to infuriate her and motivate her further.

"Tell you what, Libby, I've got a deal for you," James put forth, sweetening the pot. "If you just walk away from the shop, Libby, right now, today, with no hard feelings, I'll even pay off the outstanding rent you owe my father so that you can walk away from this debt-free. You can make yourself a nice clean start, yeah?" he told her. "That's a right generous offer, I reckon, and one that I suggest you accept before I go and change my mind," he said. "Because I could change my mind at any moment."

"Are you deaf or just stupid?" Freya entered in, indignant. "You don't seem to be getting the message here. She's already got the money for the rent, so she'll be keeping the shop, done and done, whether you like it or not."

While Libby may have bent the truth just slightly regarding the rent, James certainly had no way of knowing that. His master plan — which was akin to the zany dream of a James Bond scriptwriter — was under threat if Libby could simply pay the monies that were due. Rent paid equalled eviction proceedings ceased, and he knew that. Still, he had a few cards in his hand left to play...

"Fine, you've got the money to pay the rent. Well done," he said, as if this concerned him not one jot. "But..." he added, pausing for dramatic effect. "But, even if you do pay the rent," he resumed, "you can't very well operate without books, now can you? How can your bookshop run if you don't have any stock?"

"What?" asked Libby. "What the blue bloody blazes are you wittering on about?"

"Well, I felt it only my duty to advise your wholesalers that you were having trouble with your rent and eviction was imminent, and that, as such, they ought not to extend you credit for shipments of stock for the foreseeable future," James answered, laying his hand out on the table. "As one business owner to the others, I felt it was strictly the right thing to do, you know? I was just doing my civic duty, I suppose you could say."

Libby opened her mouth to speak. But before she could reply, James continued on, as he wasn't quite finished.

"Also, Libby, I'm pleased that you've managed to get the rent together. However, don't forget the small matter of my fee. I'll be happy to drop an invoice in the post, if you like?" James said.

"Fee?" asked Libby, nonplussed. "*What* fee? I don't owe you a bloody thing!"

"Ah, but I built you a website," James stated, as if what he was saying should have been obvious. "You don't think those come for free, do you?" he asked her. "That's very fine craftsmanship as well, that is. One of the best e-commerce websites you'd ever expect to find, I reckon," he declared, high on his own self-importance.

"And one that charges the wrong prices and makes me lose money!" Libby was quick to mention.

"A moot point," replied James with a sniff. "The fact of the matter is that you agreed to my fee when you signed the paperwork that was presented to you."

"You told me that paperwork was just for domain names and other technical stuff I didn't need to worry myself about or concern myself over!" Libby answered through gritted teeth.

"But surely you wouldn't sign a contract without first reading it carefully over, would you?" asked James in mock surprise. "No, of *course* you wouldn't," he said, making no attempt to mask his overly patronising tone. "Anyway, as it states in the contract very clearly if you'd bothered to read it, the total due is to be calculated at my discretion. Now I've not totted it up completely thus far, but I'd estimate it to be at around seven or eight or so as it now stands," he told her. "*Thousand*, that is, not hundred. Just to be clear," he added. "So, if you can settle that in addition to my father's rent, then Bob's your uncle, as they say."

Libby lurched forward, having to be promptly restrained by Freya. "I-I don't even know what to say!" Libby sputtered. "That you could be so underhanded and despicable!"

"It's simply business," James replied coolly.

"Try saying it's just business one more time and see what I do!" Freya seethed, threatening to let go her grip on Libby and join her in a bout of vigorously applied battery.

CHAPTER NINETEEN

The blood drained from Libby's cheeks, however, as she now came to realise that James wasn't so poor of a poker player as she'd previously imagined.

"You may survive for a bit, if you do manage to come up with the rent money as you claim," said James with a casual shrug, and with this directed at Libby. "But without books to sell and saddled with debt from the money you currently owe me, I don't fancy you'll last the summer. Then, I'll simply take over the shop when your business inevitably fails."

"You're quite the charmer," observed Freya, the sarcasm conveyed in her voice well evident. "You always know precisely the right thing to say in order to win a girl over, don't you?"

While James would never admit it to the two women, the truth of it was that he and Libby were actually at a bit of a stalemate. Libby could conceivably muddle on for months, he knew. Also, if she could miraculously come up with all the money she owed for rent, then it was possible, however unlikely, that she could do the same for the money she now owed him as well. James had immediate plans he sincerely wished to fulfil, and the prospect of this problem dragging on for an indeterminate amount of time was not one that held any sort of appeal. "Tell you what, Libs," he said, once again ignoring Freya's comments and addressing Libby directly. "And may I call you Libs?"

"No," came Libby's rather immediate response. "No, you most certainly may not."

"Right, then. So, Libs," continued James, undaunted. "So, Libs, how about an old-fashioned toss of the coin? If I win, you walk away. If you win, then I walk away."

"You're deranged," remarked Freya.

"Completely deranged," agreed Libby, aghast.

"No, hear me out," suggested James. "If you win, Libby, then I'll restore everything to as it should be. You'll have one of the finest websites ever designed, and I'll fix the pricing errors. I'll also tell your wholesalers you're in the clear, and I'll even pay off the rent you owe my father," he explained. "I'll also forgive the money you owe to me, so that you'll have an entirely clean slate. Onwards and upwards."

"And if I lose?" asked Libby.

"Ah, well I think you already know the answer to that one," replied James.

"You're mad if you think she'll ever agree to gambling the fate of her shop on the toss of a flippin' coin," Freya told him, her face twisted up in disgust. "Tell him, Libs," she invited to Libby, releasing Libby from her grip so that Libby could more easily confront James over this abject nonsense. "Libs...?" said Freya, when no response was immediately forthcoming. "Libs, tell him," she invited again.

"All of what you said, plus five thousand pounds, if I win," Libby directed to James.

"*What?*" Freya squealed in surprise and horror. "Libby, please tell me you're not actually considering what this bloody tosspot here is offering!"

"I'm not sure there's any better option, Freya, if I'm to have a chance of keeping the shop going," Libby answered with a sigh. "And one more thing," she went on, speaking to James again. "You're to take an advert out in the newspaper to tell everyone I'm not, and have never been, a prostitute," she insisted.

"My pleasure," James agreed. "If you win, you'll have a full spread in the paper. Ehm... double-page spread, I mean. As in advert, and not—"

"Yes, I get it," Libby replied curtly, cutting James short before he could say any more.

Freya stared at the both of them, incredulous. "Libby, please! Think this through! You can't do this! You can't bet your entire future on the flip of a bloody coin. Libby, please...!"

Chapter Twenty

25th July

Gwen has told me she loves me! She's also apologised for having ever pushed me away and keeping me at a distance. Doing so, she confided, had been a dreadful mistake, she realised – and thus her recent trip over with Terry had been devised. And Terry deserves a bloody medal for being able to keep that one particular secret and ensuring it was a huge monumental surprise. What shouldn't have come as any sort of surprise, on the other hand, is that Aunt Norma absolutely adores Gwen. This of course was to be expected as everyone adores Gwen when they meet her because it's impossible not to!

I've had to pinch myself every day since Gwen has arrived in order to be absolutely certain I wasn't dreaming. I constantly find myself looking at Gwen with a big stupid grin on my face because I simply cannot believe she's here and I know it's a big stupid grin because I can feel it stretched all the way across my face. We've all had such a wonderful week, and Aunt Norma was kind enough to loan me her car – with all of us not being able to fit on my scooter – on several occasions so that the three of us, me Gwen and Terry, could properly explore the island.

Gwen's ex-boyfriend has still been making a nuisance of himself back home, she told me. She said that's the reason she'd told me she didn't want to see me anymore. It wasn't because she didn't want to be with me but because she was afraid for me and she didn't want to expose me to any sort of danger on her account. Her heart was in the right place obviously but I can't believe she'd even have thought that because I'd walk over a bed of broken glass and brave any kind of danger for her!

As for Terry, I suspect it's going to be a bit of a struggle to get him to leave come the end of his visit. He's in love with the island and is also particularly fond of a sweet Irish girl he met at one of the pubs on the seafront.

In other matters, I've arranged the official grand reopening of the bookshop for the end of the week. I'd started to make the plans before Gwen had even arrived, so to have her here now and present for such a special day is an absolute treat. The mayor of Peel is invited, as are an assortment of Aunt Norma's friends along with select customers old and new. I've even managed to secure a pair of oversized scissors and some yellow ribbon to tie across the door so that the Mayor can do his bit by cutting it. I've also pushed the boat out by purchasing loads and loads of fizz because we'll need to properly toast the future of the Bookshop by the Beach now won't we.

28th July

Aunt Norma has been so generous to me since I arrived on the island and I wanted to do something nice to repay her. The money from the drawings I've been doing has been great and I'd managed to save enough to pay for her to go on holiday to see my mum and dad for a few days further on in August. I knew she hasn't seen them in ages and she was just telling me recently how much she missed them, so I thought this might make her happy and it did. She was thrilled and even had a couple of tears.

She was worried about the shop though and how I'd cope on my own for the better part of a week at the height of summer rush. I told her not to worry because I'd managed to secure the services of a helper in the shape of Terry who

CHAPTER TWENTY

has decided he wants to stay. He adores the island and not one to dwell on big decisions has phoned back home and quit his job without notice. It's surely impulsive on his part but I really don't blame him as once you've been to the Isle of Man it gets under your skin (in a good way) and makes it incredibly difficult to leave. Also I seem to recall making that very decision myself! So again I can't really fault him for doing the same. And him staying on is quite useful as it turns out in that he can help in the shop before he goes looking for a more permanent job.

And speaking of staying or leaving, Gwen was due to return home next Tuesday but I couldn't bear the thought of being without her. I spoke with her about how much I adore this place and how much more I'd adore it additionally if she was in it. I told her what a wonderful opportunity I felt it would be to make a new life over here not just for me but for the both of us. I told her straight out that I don't want to let her go.

She said yes! Oh my lord she said yes!

Aunt Norma was so happy to hear the news and even said she'd be delighted for Gwen to come on board to help man the shop should that be something Gwen was interested in doing.

I'm writing all this with a massive smile on my face. Again, I know I'm smiling because I can feel the tugging at either end of my mouth and if I were to smile any wider I think my head might quite possibly split in two!

Funny how things turn out, how things you never could have foreseen happening end up being the most perfect thing to happen. Only a few short weeks ago I could never have imagined myself helping to run a bookshop on the Isle of Man. And yet here I am happy as a clam faced with the prospect of running this quaint little shop by the sea with the girl I love by my side and I don't think I could ever have wished for anything better. Oh and having Terry here is a bonus as well of course, daft lovable plonker that he is!

THE BOOKSHOP BY THE BEACH

30th July

Gwen and Terry helped me prepare the catering for the grand relaunch. We got a little bit carried away, I reckon, because we ended up making enough sandwiches to feed practically the entire island.

With its now pristine paintwork and such, I believe the newly christened Bookshop by the Beach strikes a rather commanding presence on the seafront. I even managed to procure a red carpet for the day's occasion. Aunt Norma was well chuffed to have the town Mayor coming along to her little shop for the event, and it was lovely to see her so incredibly happy today.

Gwen bought a new dress specifically for the big occasion. As she hadn't given any thought to staying when she initially came over, she had of course travelled light. I suspect she'll be dragging me around the shops to replenish even more of her wardrobe over the course of the next few days but I don't mind so much as I enjoy being with her at all times even and including shopping for clothes. Anyway new start new clothes she said, and she looked lovely today and by that I mean even more lovely than usual.

Oh I nearly forgot to mention I'd had a bit of a worrying situation at the shop right before the start of the festivities! That Susan one only went and turned up, didn't she, having tracked me down. She came sailing in wanting to know where I'd gone off to that night and why I haven't phoned her since then. She seemed to think the date went fairly well astonishingly enough and was actually expecting a second one it would appear.

She's even fiercer in daylight. I told her I was awfully sorry I had to run out on her that evening but that was because an emergency had come up rather unexpectedly (which is sort of true???) I also informed her as gently as I could that, most regrettably, I was now seeing someone and that as a result of this I was, very sadly, unable to extend an offer to her of the pleasure of any future dates. She seemed to take

CHAPTER TWENTY

this amazingly well, thank goodness, with her even referring to me as a real Casanova (which I'm certain I've never been called before) and with the cheeky thing then turning her attention straight to the snacks table and filling up her handbag with sandwiches on her way out the door.

Naturally Terry was pissing himself watching me squirm throughout this entire ordeal. Gwen, for her part, didn't appear to know quite what to make of it all and watched on in astonishment. Once Susan departed with her lunch I had to explain what had happened with the whole blind date thing. Gwen laughed about it but also chastised me for ditching Susan the way I did regardless of how badly the evening went. I had to reluctantly admit that she was right, although inside my head I have to say I was privately rationalising my prior actions by insisting to myself that desperate times simply called for desperate measures!

Aside from the Susan incident, the day couldn't have gone any better, and we all enjoyed the fizz. Everyone was suitably impressed with the revamped shop, and the commotion of people coming and going even caused traffic to slow on the road outside with drivers I imagine wondering what all the fuss was about. The mayor was in fine form, and as I stood with Gwen and Aunt Norma as he cut the yellow ribbon I think I could easily have been the happiest and proudest fellow alive.

31st July

Hello journal, this is Gwen. We've not met before. I watch Bert diligently writing in you most days and I think it's a wonderful thing to chart your life as he does, but I promise I've not read you as that would be very rude and a dreadful intrusion of privacy.

Bert was just about to excitedly write in you this evening but instead offered to go to the chip shop first in order to pick up supper for the both of us, lovely lad that he is. Well, when I saw you lying open there on the table, I hoped Bert wouldn't mind so terribly much if I took the slight liberty of making a minor journal entry of my own. I wanted to take a moment to write to you, Bert, in your own journal, to get my thoughts down knowing that you'd see them.

Bert, from the moment I first met you I think deep down I knew in my heart that I was going to be with you always. You're a wonderful talented kind-hearted gentleman and one who makes me smile each and every day.

I think there's a reason we end up meeting the people we do in our lives and certain people especially, call it fate or what have you. I don't know exactly how I became blessed enough to have the amazing good fortune of getting to eventually meet you, dear Bert, but each night before I go to sleep I thank my lucky stars that I have.

We're going to have a marvellous life, you and me, in the Isle of Man. I cannot wait to see what's in store for us and what lies ahead, and I'm also pleased as punch that I'll be working by your side in the Bookshop by the Beach and in fact honoured to do so.

Now, Bert Tebbit, as to the quite remarkable thing you've asked me today, I never expected that you'd ask me so soon, or even at all. But of course I'd be lying if I were to suggest that I wasn't happy you did!

Bert, I've already responded to you in person directly after you posed the question, but I'll let you read this as well once you've come home with our fish and chips (and I hope you haven't forgotten the mushy peas this time as you know it's my favourite part!) So, just so there's absolutely no mistaking my answer, let me reiterate it here:

Bert, I cannot wait to be your wife, and I feel both pleased and privileged that you've chosen me to accompany you on your life's journey! Mr Tebbit, I very much look forward to soon becoming Mrs Tebbit, and I love you with all my heart!

Yours forever and ever,
Your dearest darling Gwen

Chapter Twenty-One

The day of the Peel fun run was one of the most hotly anticipated dates in the town's social calendar. Not simply about the running, it was also an excuse for the community to come together. With a few hundred plucky souls donning their shorts to participate in either the half-marathon, or the shorter but just as competitive 5k race, it was the perfect opportunity — and some might even say excuse! — for the community to rally together, and the pubs, eateries, ice cream shops, beach, and every imaginable venue were packed out from early in the morning until late into the night. Supporters arrived in droves both to cheer the competitors on and, as they did so, enjoy a jolly pleasant day out by the seaside as well.

With the current year's race due to commence at noon, the normally busy roads were now closed to traffic and participants began milling around for final registration a good couple of hours before the starting pistol fired.

The start/finish line for the race was on the promenade and within easy viewing distance from Libby's shop. If Libby, Freya, and Gran hadn't been racing themselves they'd have taken up position there outside to cheer on the runners. Right now, Libby stood outside the bookshop and was looking up, with trepidation, at the sign. She couldn't help but wonder with dread if, despite her very best efforts, the name of James's business would soon be hung on the sign above the door rather than hers. Her thoughts were interrupted, however, as Freya rejoined her.

"Won't be long now!" Freya said cheerfully, pinning her race number to her chest. "You know, I have to admit, I thought this whole idea was crazy at first!"

"What?" replied Libby. "Oh, you mean the race," she added, realising what Freya was referring to. "Yeah, I know, right? And you got off to a bit of a rocky start when we first began training, didn't you?" observed Libby, offering Freya a crooked grin. "Well, more than a *bit* of a rocky start, actually. No offence."

"None taken," laughed Freya. "It's a fair cop."

"But look at all the effort you've put in! Seriously impressive, that," remarked Libby, rubbing her friend's shoulder affectionately. "Well done, you!"

"It's been loads of fun, actually, Libs," Freya answered happily. "Spending quality time with your bestie, losing a few pounds along the way, enjoying the great outdoors? What's not to like?" Freya's cheery demeanour eased, however, and turned a bit more serious for just a moment. "Just so you know, I've had a word at work," she said. "They told me they'd be happy to take you on if... well, if, you know, your business went tits-up?" she told Libby, taking a glance at the bookshop's sign as Libby had done only a short time earlier.

Libby's instinctive reaction was at first to be offended. How could Freya have so lost confidence in her, she wondered. But of course she understood that Freya was only looking out for her and wished only the best for her. "Thanks, Freya, but I think I'll be okay," Libby answered, trying to sound reasonably optimistic.

Freya pulled Libby to one side as what looked like an industrial-sized hairdryer suddenly burst into life inflating a giant red arch which was to span the start/finish line near to where they were standing. "Libby," Freya continued, once the two of them were clear. "Libby, look, it's not too late to drop this bet with James," she whispered confidentially. "I mean, it might be a slightly better option than the coin toss thing? But, still..."

"At least this way it's not down to pure luck, though, right?" Libby suggested. "And I got him to agree to the revised bet by appealing to his bloody ego. Typical male! I knew he wouldn't be able to resist, and this way I at least have some control over the outcome, yes?"

CHAPTER TWENTY-ONE

"Even so..." Freya answered. "I dunno, Libby, even so, having a bet on who finishes with the quickest race time? I'm not sure that's entirely too much better in the end. I mean you've never run a half-marathon, have you? And James, comicbook nerd though he is, has already done this multiple times. So, again, I'm not exactly sure—"

"Freya, it's done," Libby gently cut in, offering her a smile of reassurance. "It's done. James has agreed to the amended bet, and all I can do at this stage is to go and give him the good drubbing that he so richly deserves," she went on. "Also, Freya, don't forget that it's precisely *because* I've never run this distance and he has that he's stupidly agreed to giving me a half-hour handicap advantage over his own race time," Libby added. "That just shows you how cocky and arrogant he is! And I can finish within half an hour of his race time, I'm certain of it. Yes, I know he's a capable runner. But I'm no slouch myself, and I've been training hard. I know I can beat him, Freya. I *know* I can!"

Libby was doing a splendid job of offering up an air of confidence. Freya wasn't sure if it was meant to convince her, to convince Libby herself, or perhaps if it was maybe a bit of both. Whatever the case, she decided it wasn't worth fighting over. "Fine," she said with a shrug. "Right, you go and get our timing bands, then, all right?" she suggested. "Meanwhile, I'll go and get the two of us some energy smoothies, get us both fuelled up for the race. How's that sound?"

"Sure, okay. Sounds good," Libby agreed.

Freya turned to scoot off, but then immediately pivoted back around. "Oi, your best mate has just turned up," said Freya, cupping a hand over her mouth and whispering furtively as she said this. "Over there," she clarified.

"What?" asked Libby, craning her neck. "Who's turned up, exactly? Over where?"

"No, don't look!" Freya told her. "I meant it's bloody Captain Underpants. Just ignore him and hopefully he won't notice us, right?" she advised. "Or do you want I should go over there and give him what for?" offered Freya.

Libby chewed this kind offer of Freya's over for a moment or two, and then replied, "Naw, you were right the first time. We'll just ignore the tosser."

After this, Freya set forth to fetch the smoothies as promised, and Libby made her way over to the registration table as she'd herself promised. She waited patiently in line, happily absorbing the positive energy from those competitors around her as if by osmosis. It was truly an event for all ages, abilities, shapes, and sizes, she could see, with everyone coming together for a common goal — to have some fun, and to raise some money for the charity of their choice in the process. The day couldn't have been any better for it, Libby was pleased to note, with the afternoon temps warm and yet relatively mild, and with also plenty of big fluffy clouds in the sky to keep the sun from directly beating down on them.

"Lovely day for it!" said someone from behind, without warning, and in seeming agreeance with Libby's own thoughts.

It was, quite sadly, an all-too-familiar voice, and Libby knew precisely who it belonged to, unfortunately, her attempts at remaining inconspicuous having obviously failed. And while this certain someone's sentiments might coincidentally have echoed her own, drenched in sarcasm as they were the words from this fellow were clearly not meant in the same way. Without bothering to turn around, she replied, "It is indeed a lovely day, James. But it could've been an even lovelier day, I would think, if only you'd suddenly fallen gravely ill and hadn't been able to make it along."

"Ha! Unlucky for you, then, that I'm as fit as a fiddle!" James declared gleefully. "Why? Worried, are we?"

"*Pfft.* I *hardly* think so," replied Libby, as if James's tired, pathetic taunts bothered her not in the slightest. "I could still beat you even if I *didn't* have the advantage of a half-hour handicap, James, so I'm afraid *you're* the one who should be worried," she told him.

Beyond this brief exchange, Libby was hoping that by ignoring him thereafter, James might somehow disappear. With the participants before her having been sorted, it was soon her turn

CHAPTER TWENTY-ONE

to step forward. She gave her full attention now to the girl, bubbly as a lovely glass of champagne, sat behind the table armed with both an infectious smile and a clipboard. "Registering as a team, or individual?" the girl asked brightly, her pen poised.

"As a team," Libby answered. "The name is the Book Runners."

The girl, in response, began running a finger down the long list of alphabetised names in hand. "Hmm, let's just see here..." she murmured. "Would it be under *B* for Book Runners, or T for *The* Book Runners... and would Book Runners be listed here as one word or two..."

"Book Runners? Cute name," James whispered to Libby, leaning in to confidentially deliver his snarky observation and yet saying it loud enough that anyone standing nearby could obviously hear it anyway.

Libby didn't bother answering him. She just swatted the air as if she were shooing away an annoying insect buzzing about her ear, which in essence she was.

"Yes, here we are. Found you!" said the cheerful girl, checking Libby off the list and then looking up and handing several timing bands over to her. "Right, then. Just place these little beauties here over your wrists, okey-dokey?" she instructed, and after which adding, "And that's you all registered! Very best of luck!"

"You'll certainly need it," suggested James from the rear. "Oh, and just as a friendly reminder, Libby, should you even *consider* reneging on our bet I've got the whole exchange recorded and saved to my phone."

"You're such a...!" began Libby, finally turning around this time in order to look at James while speaking to him. But she caught herself in what she was about to say, not wishing to grant him the sort of reaction he was no doubt looking for. "Yes, as do I," she told him instead, more calmly now. "I've got it saved to *my* phone as well, just in case *you* decide you can weasel out of our arrangement once I win the race, which I will."

James opened his mouth to respond, but Libby raised her hand to shush him before he could utter another word. And here, also, was Freya, as it should happen, fortuitously heading straight towards them and thereby doing her part to save Libby from any further James-related unpleasantness as well.

"Don't worry about this one. Better yet, take a gander over here," said Freya, quickly ushering Libby well away from James's general proximity and conveying that Libby should presently be directing her attention elsewhere instead. She handed Libby the smoothie that had been recently procured for her benefit, and then asked, "There, now does that not melt your heart?"

"What, the smoothie?" asked Libby, but then, after following Freya's eyeline over to the beach, revised her answer accordingly by saying, "Is that Gran? Ah, it *is* Gran!" and, "Aww, and doesn't she look fab!"

The Silver Sprinters, as it turned out, were all lined up on the beach. They wore matching blue shorts and white t-shirts, and with the t-shirts bearing their club logo emblazoned across the front. The gang, as it should happen, were currently partaking in a warmup yoga session in order to loosen up any tight muscles or stubborn joints — of which, at their advanced age, there was likely to be a good number. If any inspiration were required ahead of the race, all Libby need do was admire that lovely crew performing an assortment of various yoga poses like the Downward Dog, amongst other strange contortions of both body and limb. Libby wasn't even sure she herself could accomplish some of the more difficult poses they were doing, and yet here were a group of oldies pulling them off just fine.

Gran and the gang had been putting in a fair old shift these last few weeks and in fact were a common sight in and around Peel as they trained for their half-marathon effort. As for the race itself, there were concessions afforded the group in that they were being allowed to run the race in legs, with their runners being swopped out at regular intervals. There had been concern expressed as to what the course of action might be if they had a retirement halfway through a lap. And to assist in this regard, the organisers had also kindly arranged a golf cart that would follow their team around to facilitate a substitution should such need arise.

They were quite the news story locally, with several members of the crew invited on the radio to talk about their training regime, diet, and other such matters. Their Facebook group had

CHAPTER TWENTY-ONE

attracted over six hundred followers, which Gwen liked to imagine was due in large part to the personal morning workout videos of hers that she'd been uploading regularly. The lot of them were an inspiration not only to Libby but to everyone else as well, encouraging the rest of the island's population young and old alike to get off their rumps, put their trainers on, and get out and stay active and make new friends.

"What a bunch," observed Freya.

"I know, right? Melts your heart indeed," replied Libby, smiling fondly. "And Gran happened to tell me earlier they've managed to raise a pretty decent amount of money for their organisation because of today's race, so there's that as well," Libby added. "Nearly eight thousand pounds so far, I think she said?"

"That's a fair bit of dosh," said Freya, duly impressed.

"Hang on, is that not…?" asked Libby, spying someone else amidst the group on the beach. "Oh my goodness, it is," she said, in answer to her own question. "It's Eric, James's dad. My landlord," she told Freya. "I'd no idea he was a Silver Sprinter."

"But, hold on a moment, what exactly *is* it that he's doing out there?" remarked Freya, narrowing her eyes and trying her best to make sense of what she was seeing. "Is he performing… erm, I mean, is he doing some sort of interpretive dance…?"

"No. No, I think that's just him attempting a couple of star jumps," Libby answered with a laugh.

"Ah, okay," replied Freya, tilting her head oddly, as if she were trying to shake water out of her ear. "I think I can *sort* of see it now? I mean, if you look at him from just the right angle…?" she said. "Anyway," she went on, "if that's James's dad, I'm surprised he's able to do anything at all, all things considered. I would've expected you to bash in his kneecaps with a cricket bat or something by now, Libby."

"Yes, but it's not necessarily his fault, I suppose, that his son is a right so-and-so, now is it?" Libby offered graciously.

But Freya didn't answer. She appeared to be distracted right at the present moment.

"Freya…?" enquired Libby.

"Ahoy. New person of interest spotted at two o'clock," Freya reported, filling Libby in as to what had caught her attention. "It's Luke," Freya reported further.

"So it is," Libby replied, giving Luke a wave hello.

"I don't think he sees us," observed Freya.

"No, but we can certainly see *him*," Libby offered. "And that's not such a bad thing, either."

"Blimey, he's got a pair of legs on him that go all the way to the floor!" Freya was only too happy to agree.

Libby laughed. "That's one way to put it, I guess. He *does* look awfully good in those shorts, doesn't he?"

"I like the cut of his jib," Freya once again agreed. "Anyway, it's nice that you two are talking again," she added.

Libby took another long, lingering look towards the beach before responding. "Yes, and that's no thanks to James, either," she answered after a few moments. "Although I suppose it's fortunate in a weird sort of way that Luke had heard all the rubbish James has been spreading around," she told Freya. "Because the more ridiculous it got, the more Luke became convinced it was precisely that."

"Ridiculous? Or rubbish?" asked Freya, seeking clarification.

"Ridiculous rubbish," said Libby.

The more elite and ultra-competitive of the runners jostled for position under the inflatable arch as the start time approached. The race, although a charity fun run, was taken very seriously by some, eager to have a clear road ahead of them and avoid the congested carnage of the opening few-hundred metres

Amongst those barging their way through to the front was James, who'd clearly sharpened his elbows such was his desire to eke out any advantage. The race was, however, a time trial, with each competitor breaking the timing beam on the start line when they advanced through the arch. For that reason, it didn't really matter which position one started from, necessarily, as the stopwatch only began on your race when the computer registered the electronic tag on your wrist. Still, having a

CHAPTER TWENTY-ONE

clear road and no people to get in your way was not something that would be in any way unwelcome.

The route for the race took participants on a circular path around the historic seaside town of Peel, with plenty of viewing points available for spectators to offer up encouragement. Each full lap was a little over 2k in distance, and so the half-marathon would be completed in ten laps. The route was varied and not always level, incorporating a couple of hills into the mix for good measure, offering a good challenge to the runners.

"You've got this, Libs," said Freya, taking her friend's hand.

They'd both taken up a position at the rear of the field, using the opposite strategy to James, Libby's reasoning being that by the time the field spread out there would be fewer people to obstruct her path. She would have preferred to keep James in her sights during the entirety of the race but she knew this may not really be possible. When they were on friendlier terms James had discussed with her his racing times, and so she knew he was quick enough, quicker than one ever might expect of a comicbook nerd. And also, while he had raced dressed as Wonder Woman previously, unconcerned about that particular year's race time, today's race was of course a different matter. With everything at stake, Libby knew he'd be in top form. Still, she remained fairly optimistic as to her own results.

As for Freya, she was at present receiving a number of admiring glances as a result of the absolutely adorable Minnie Mouse costume she was wearing, with her having changed into it just before the start of the race. It had the effect of setting a fair few pulses racing already in and of itself, by the looks of things, before the race had even begun.

Freya was taking part in the 5k race, although under the same team name as Libby, and had her own target time in which to finish, subject to her oversized ears not causing too much wind resistance. In view of the particular gravity of Libby's race, special dispensation had been granted by Freya for Libby to wear running attire instead of her Daisy Duck costume as originally planned. Fortunately Gwen had taken a fancy to it, however, and was happy to put the costume to good use. She was always up for a bit of fun, she said, and hoped the sight of it might possibly induce the public to be even more generous towards her collection bucket when she ran her leg of the race.

Libby closed her eyes momentarily as the crowd, prompted by the timer on the digital scoreboard, called out excitedly, with everyone collectively counting down from ten. Libby thought of the photograph of her grandparents stood outside their shop all those years ago. This business of hers was both her history and her future, and she wasn't giving up on it.

When the clock finally reached zero, the crack of a starting pistol sent those at the front, now unleashed, surging forward in a huge wave. Libby cannily held back, waiting for clear tarmac in front of her so that when she broke the starting beam she'd be at full pace rather than tarrying, impeded. Each individual second would count if she hoped to have any chance of securing the shop. She shook her arms and legs out as the hordes in front of her rolled out. As the crowd thinned, she could see a route through, and took a further look over to her shop, and then to the path ahead.

"Go get that maggot, Libs!" said Freya.

"Oh, bloody right I will!" responded Libby. "I love you, Minnie Mouse!"

"I know you do!" replied a cheeky Freya. "Now give him what for!"

Libby stamped her right foot to the ground like an angry bull, snorting through her nose, and focusing on the task ahead. The gap in the crowd she was waiting for eventually presented itself, and with a throaty roar, setting off like a shot, she quickly transformed herself from angry bull to stabbed rat.

The race was on.

Chapter Twenty-Two

Horace was eighty-six years young, in possession of both an arthritic hip and, right at present, also a huge smile. Firmly carrying the responsibility of the Silver Sprinters opening leg, he pumped his arms to propel himself forward whilst also managing the occasional wave to the cheering spectators urging him on. Horace wasn't likely about to break any land speed records, that was well evident, and in fact had only progressed a few hundred metres from the starting line when those runners who'd set off first came past him, with them having already completed their first lap and now into their second. Those passing Horace gave whoops of encouragement, though, with many of them offering enthusiastic, two-fisted thumbs-up to him as they ran by.

Following just behind Horace, at an unhurried rate of speed that kept time with Horace's own protracted pace, was the petrol-powered golf cart carrying the next two runners in the team — one of whom would step in when Horace's energy levels had depleted and Horace was in need of replacing.

Horace's effort was admirable, but as he rounded the corner at the end of the promenade — adjacent to the boats bobbing lazily in the waters of the quay — his pace decreased from slow to slower and for a moment it looked as if he might raise his hand to show his leg in the race was at its end. Before he had a chance to do this, however, a young lad, three or four years of age, broke free from his mother's grip and ran straight towards Horace. He took hold of Horace's hand as he joined him, running alongside. For the eager child it was only a gentle trot, and for the boy's mother who followed behind no more than a brisk stroll. But it hardly mattered how quickly or not they progressed because, in that moment, they demonstrated wonderfully the perfect spirit of community that the day's event was ostensibly all about.

Horace offered the lad a grateful wink, pressing on, now motivated to continue on for just a little while longer. Meanwhile, however, further ahead in the race and at the opposite end of the charitable spectrum, there was James.

"Out of my way, you bloody idiot!" James bellowed, berating anybody who dared obstruct his path. He wasn't a professional runner by any means but he could certainly move along at a decent clip when the mood struck, and on this day in particular with the fate of Libby's shop at stake — a prime-location premises he very much wished to claim for himself — the mood had well and truly taken.

The male's race category was fairly competitive overall, with many club runners taking part and also plenty of others who weren't part of any running club, necessarily, but were in top form and wished to challenge themselves, pushing to test their own limits. While James could never have been considered a top physical specimen by any reasonable measure, he nevertheless usually managed to place respectably in these things and he was confident of a decent time in today's race. In fact he was rather *insisting* on a decent time in today's race.

"Get out the bleedin' way, slowpoke!" he hollered at the poor woman now directly ahead of him. The woman was participating in the wheelchair race, and she had the apparent temerity to keep her wheeled chariot in James's way when James was very much wishing to pass. "Coming through!" James shouted, and then tut-tutted at her loudly, thoroughly inconvenienced at the terrible trouble of having to make an ever-so-slight course correction in order to navigate round a fellow competitor.

At the upcoming water station, a good-natured schoolgirl — jolly pleased to be one of the dozens of volunteers doing their part for the day's event — held out a plastic cup for the next of the parched runners that should come by to, she felt certain,

CHAPTER TWENTY-TWO

gratefully take up from her hand. She caught sight of the rapidly approaching James, and judging by the colour of his cheeks and the look on his face not unreasonably assumed he was in desperate need of such fluids as she was graciously providing.

James didn't break his stride as he passed, however, rejecting the girl's hospitality and instead knocking the drink of water from her outstretched hand as he ploughed by. Why he didn't accept it was anyone's guess. The only thing anybody might have agreed upon after witnessing James's crass performance is that, if they'd been bestowing racing medals for the runners deemed "Most Deplorable Character" or "Hugest Twit" or the like, then James would surely have secured one of these quite handily.

Also running flat out, although significantly further behind, was Libby, giving it her all, albeit in a rather more orderly and polite fashion than James. As a competent short-distance runner, she was able to turn her legs over at an impressive rate and was picking off the field in front of her at will, but she knew this was a marathon — or half-marathon, at least — and not a sprint, and told herself she therefore really ought to be pacing herself. She thrived on the energy provided by the fervent spectators, though, and harnessed it to propel herself forward. Her lungs were burning by this point in time and the muscles in her legs screaming for her to stop, but she was giving this everything she could. She knew she must, as there was so much riding on the outcome.

With each new lap bringing her through the start/finish line near to her bookshop, she could almost hear the ghost of her grandad cheering her on from over there. She'd just completed her second lap, in fact, and was moving through the familiar inflatable arch once again in order to commence with her third. A quick glance to the digital scoreboard confirmed that she was indeed on track for the overall finish time she was hoping for — two hours and twenty minutes, or less. If she could finish in this time, with her agreed-upon handicap, this meant that James would have to finish in less than one hour and fifty minutes if he had any hope of winning. Naturally, it was of course Libby's fervent wish that James should *not* win.

Having reached the present milestone of entering her third lap, she felt like she'd worked past the pain. She was easing into her stride, it seemed to her, and she even allowed herself a smile as her gran — who'd yet to head out on her own leg of the race — jumped up and down like a jackhammer, yelling over in her direction. "You can do it!" Gran shouted, accompanied by a chorus of similar such encouragement from the other members of the Lonely Heart Attack Club/Silver Sprinters that were standing there as well.

Libby raised a clenched fist into the air in acknowledgement and solidarity, as she headed towards the end of the promenade in the direction of the magnificent castle. "Come on, Libby, my sweet," she said to herself, setting her jaw in determination and steeling herself against any remaining pain.

With 4k now completed, Libby was approaching the upper limits of her usual running distance. She was pleased with her efforts so far, and she was finding the entire experience rather surreal at times on account of the array of unusual characters she was encountering along the course. She'd already overtaken an exceptionally tall Chewbacca, for instance, who must have been sweltering burdened under all that hair, she reckoned, and was coming up on an older lady dressed as a teapot, and with both of these people appearing to be having a thoroughly good day out despite the obvious restrictions of their respective costumes. At least Libby certainly hoped these were people dressed up in costumes — otherwise, she worried, her current exertion had obviously resulted in some rather curious hallucinations!

Laps three, four, and five passed by in a hazy blur. Libby kept her concentration mostly on her breathing, and she tried her best to remember to take up the cups of water and packets of energy gel so obligingly offered at regular intervals along the route. Her feet were starting to chafe as the moisture built up in her socks, and by lap five she could also feel the onset of friction burns on her inner thighs. Libby's discomfort was forgotten for a moment, at least, when she spotted Freya who having completed her own, shorter race, was waiting for Libby near to the start line as Libby commenced lap six.

CHAPTER TWENTY-TWO

Freya, despite her own fatigued legs, jogged alongside to offer Libby some welcome encouragement. "You're doing brilliantly!" Freya cheered. "Libby, you're smashing this!" she told her. The two of them exchanged waves and traded smiles as Freya then pulled away, allowing Libby to carry on with the task at hand — or rather the task at foot, as the case may be.

Libby definitely appreciated Freya's support and praise, but even in her current weary state she couldn't help but marvel at Freya herself. Here was her friend who'd never even run a race before today — any race at all, of any length or duration — and yet there she was completing her first 5k, and having acquitted herself quite well in it by all appearances no less.

Libby presently dug in her heels, determined, as she kept on keeping on. Even so, despite her fortitude, she eventually found herself, after some time, beginning to lose steam. Her legs were starting to get heavier the further she progressed, feeling as if she were running in wet sand, and her body began to ache. She worried about how long she could possibly keep up her desired pace, and her anxiety was only compounded when James sped past her, offering mocking taunts as he did so. He was currently sprinting like a gazelle, giving no indication of any more exertion being expended than if he were simply out for a mere jog.

Libby had to imagine that James's current performance was just that, a performance, and one that was meant to demotivate her. Still, it was doing its job well enough. And the fact James had now lapped her didn't help, either, as it meant he'd already eaten into her time advantage with still three laps left for them to run. Libby knew her pace was slowing, while it very much appeared that James was unfortunately experiencing the opposite.

When next she found herself heading towards the distinctive inflatable arch, Libby's fears were only confirmed as she noticed her lap time. It had exceeded sixteen minutes, her slowest so far. It was a kick to the stomach, to be sure, and she fought the urge to collapse in a heap at the side of the road. She couldn't even bring herself to look over to her shop, which felt like it was disappearing from her control quicker than James was from her view.

Completing the race over several relatively short circuits at least had its advantages over, say, a longer race with only one lap. It meant one had the opportunity to frequently see many of the same faces as you circulated, those faces belonging to a dedicated set of supporters who were ready and willing to provide aid by way of enthusiastic encouragement. This was a lift for Libby, and she in turn, despite her own fatigue, was quick to offer similar words of motivation to any of her fellow runners who appeared to be flagging.

The Silver Sprinters' golf cart soon came into view once more, with Gran now aboard as a passenger, still dressed up as Daisy Duck and raring to go for her particular leg of the race. It was a sight for Libby's sore eyes (and for her sore everything else, as well, for that matter), and it was rather amusing seeing a giant duck in feather shorts being chauffeured around shouting excitedly to her fellow club member out in front. It helped buoy Libby's spirits, at least temporarily, and she clapped her hands in delight as she passed.

Hopes of keeping James in view on the other hand had long since been abandoned, with him likely extending his advantage, Libby worried, with each stride. Libby was on her eighth lap right now, and it was proper agony. Every step resulted in shooting pains in her legs, with her shins throbbing. Only the thought of James hanging his new sign over her former shopfront kept her going, as she steadfastly wished to avoid this possible outcome. She'd given up on monitoring her lap times as without knowing how James was progressing it was a futile exercise. She couldn't control his race. But what she could control was her own, however, and to that end she got her head down and gave it her all. Also, she contemplated rather hopefully, if James were to suffer some sort of catastrophic race-ending injury, then that wouldn't be so bad, would it? No, she reckoned it wouldn't. She felt a little guilty for wishing such a thing, but not all *that* guilty.

As she made it through to the end of lap nine, she deliberately avoided looking at the timing board as she passed by the shop

CHAPTER TWENTY-TWO

for the penultimate occasion in the race. There was now little point in knowing her lap time, not only because she had nothing to compare it against but also because she had very little left in the tank to give. She was running on empty right about now, with her legs in real danger of buckling at any given moment. James hadn't lapped her again, so there was that as a positive, at least. But on the other hand, he would very probably have finished his race by now, she imagined. In fact she was surprised he wasn't right there, milling about, waiting for her to come by so that he could offer his own idiotic brand of special so-called encouragement. Freya was there by the shop, though, good old Freya, and had secured a giant foam hand from somewhere or other and was now waving it furiously as Libby passed. "We love you, Libby!" Freya called over, as Libby headed out onto her last lap. "Give 'em hell, Libs!"

Gran was there as well. Libby wasn't sure whether or not Gran was yet to complete her leg of the Silver Sprinters' collective endeavour, but she saw that her gran was still decked out in her Daisy Duck costume. Libby watched as Gran lifted up her yellow bill and then cupped her hands around her mouth. "I love you so much, Libby!" shouted Gran. "Whatever happens today, you'll always have it, dear! No matter what!"

Libby blew a kiss over to the both of them, sending it on its way as she tucked in for the final stretch. A tear or two appeared on her cheeks as she pressed on. She certainly appreciated her gran's kind words to the effect that her love was unconditional and forever there, regardless of the outcome of Libby's race. Still, that very same generous, unselfish sentiment expressed encouraged Libby only to be that much more determined to succeed.

The tears continued to flow, and the spectators along the route could easily have been forgiven if they'd imagined them to be tears of joy and relief as Libby made her way ever closer to the finish line. There *was* a bit of that, of course. But, mostly, it was on account of Libby thinking about what was at stake — and with what was at stake being literally everything. So much was riding on the outcome of this race, and she absolutely could not let Gran down. Nor, for that matter, could she let herself down either. She *had* to win.

Every muscle and joint in Libby's body was screaming for mercy, however, and in a moment of panic she feared she might vomit. As embarrassing as that might have been if it were to happen, Libby, funnily enough, was more horrified about the idea of someone having to clean up her mess. She didn't want that. Fortunately, rescue from that unwanted fate came in the form of that same cheerful schoolgirl James had nearly taken off her feet when he'd bulldozed his way past her earlier.

Libby was far more receptive to the girl's overtures, gratefully accepting the cup of cold water on offer, gulping down half of it and then splashing the remaining portion over her face. "Thank you!" she called over her shoulder, wiping her eyes as she continued along her way.

Libby soldiered on, pleased that she'd soon be completing a race of this distance, something she'd never before attempted. But her delight at this accomplishment was also mixed with a fair bit of trepidation, as she knew her life could be changing significantly for the worse based on the results.

In not too terribly long of a time, she reached the next water station situated at the midway point of the circuit, and then, refuelled once more, she pushed ahead. It was a little quieter in this region, as most of the crowd had by this time moved towards the general area of the finish line to support those runners concluding their race.

And with that very conclusion of the race in mind, Libby somehow managed to summon enough energy to pick up the pace for the final stretch. She pictured James waiting at the end, looking down at his watch, mocking her. Naturally, she would much prefer it if he were looking down at his watch in horror and disbelief at the realisation of his defeat. Had she done enough to make that possibility a reality? She wasn't sure. She certainly hoped so, of course. But, either way, she would find out soon enough.

Currently a short way ahead, a grey-haired chap was happily consumed in his own race, with Libby soon to overtake him. Passing him would mean she was that one step closer to the finish line. She recognised the fellow from the bright lime-green trainers he was wearing. She'd encountered the man before,

CHAPTER TWENTY-TWO

having passed him several times around the circuit over the course of the race. She told herself that, after this whole thing was over and done with, she'd have to ask him where he'd found such lovely footwear.

But then something terrible happened. Libby watched as the man faltered, veering slightly off course, resulting in one of his feet clipping the curb and snapping back on itself, sending him face-first to the ground. The fellow hit the pavement with a sickening crunch, and he laid there on the ground moaning in pain.

This isn't the way things were meant to happen. Yes, she'd prayed to the pantheon of race gods for some sort of race-ending incident to befall James. But, cruelly, through incompetence or spite, they'd mucked it up and apparently chosen this unfortunate fellow instead.

Libby, all thoughts of the race now pushed to the side for the moment, stopped dead in her tracks. She went over and knelt by the older gentleman, tending to him as best she was able, attempting to comfort him. "You're all right," she told him. "You'll be fine, my lovely," she said reassuringly. "I'll get you some help, yeah?"

However, the truth of it was she wasn't sure at all if he'd be all right. Libby knew his ankle must be in a frightful state, but as to the full extent of the injury she couldn't be exactly certain. More immediately obvious was his face, which was very clearly damaged. The poor man had taken the brunt of his fall directly onto it, resulting in it currently looking as if a butcher had a go at it with a meat-tenderising mallet. She had to resist the urge to grimace, as she didn't want to alarm him

"You'll be fine," Libby said again, very calmly, in hopes of putting not only the fellow at ease but also, to some extent, herself as well. "I'll get you some help," she repeated.

Libby stood up, scanning the surrounding area. Saints be praised, she could see the yellow high-vis vest of a marshal at the bottom of the hill, about fifty or so metres away. "Over here!" she shouted, waving her hands high in the air to help attract the attention of the marshal. "We need help!"

She said this with enough urgency, she hoped, to convey the seriousness of the situation — but not so much urgency, she also hoped, that she should alarm the injured man, who she was trying her best to keep calm.

Fortunately the marshal seemed to receive the message well enough and began sprinting up the hill momentarily, speaking into her radio as she did so.

Libby knelt down, returning her attention once more to the stricken runner, who by this time had been able to turn over onto his back. He was obviously in quite a bit of distress, holding his hands to his face as he was, but he did nevertheless manage to produce a smile for Libby's benefit.

"The things I'll do... to get... a pretty girl... to stop... and talk to me," the man joked, gasping this out between winces of pain.

"I've called for additional assistance," advised the marshal, arriving on scene only a short minute later. She pulled out a first aid kit and set to work, thanking Libby for her help and assuring her that the man would be properly cared for.

Libby lingered for a moment, smiling warmly at her fellow runner. "Ah. Well I suppose I should probably be getting myself back into the race, then..." she offered apologetically.

She really didn't want to leave him, but she knew there wasn't much she could do. The marshal, on the other hand, had significantly more medical experience than her own (with Libby's expertise in this area being limited to little more than, say, the application of a plaster or removal of a splinter), and with more help on the way besides.

Libby rose to her feet. Although she didn't blame the current circumstance for causing her present delay, she also knew that this extended interruption had cost her some valuable time. And so, with that, she decided she shouldn't waste any more of it, and then set off once again.

It wasn't far to go now.

As Libby pumped her legs, getting into her final rhythm, she took stock of her current situation. She'd absolutely given it her all, but she still didn't know if it was enough to prevail over James. Realistically, she feared she hadn't done enough to beat James's time, and this recently added delay certainly wouldn't

CHAPTER TWENTY-TWO

have helped matters any. Still, she vowed to run through the inflatable arch confident and strong. If James should be there watching her, she didn't want to afford him the satisfaction of looking in any way broken in morale.

The final stretch wasn't really that long, technically speaking. However, throw into the mix fatigued legs, burning lungs, and friction burns and running this last distance felt like an eternity to Libby. She was accompanied by a small number of other runners who happened to be concluding their own race at the same time, all of whom looked similarly exhausted but mostly in high spirits from knowing the end was drawing very near. The group exchanged smiles, and one by one they crossed the finish line, Libby included.

It was over. With her race now finally, blessedly complete, Libby leaned forward, seeking to catch her breath. She grasped her throbbing knees, panting, and wondered how long it would take to bring her pulse rate back to some semblance of normality. A quick glance at the scoreboard as she'd pulled in had given her a general indication of her race time, but she'd need to check with the organisers in order to get her final results. All she could do at this point was to hope for the best.

"Over here! Coming through!" and, "Libby, I'm on my way!" the familiar voice of Freya could soon be heard.

Libby looked up and, sure enough, there was Freya making her way through the crowd, water bottle in hand. Libby wasn't sure what she found a more welcome sight right then, Freya or that bottle of water she was holding. "Is that for me, I hope?" she asked, upon Freya's arrival. Fortunately, it was, and Libby took a long, grateful guzzle.

"You did it, Libs! You did it!" said Freya excitedly.

Libby pulled the water bottle from her lips. "What? I did it? I beat his time?" she gasped, daring to believe.

"Ah... whoopsie! Maybe a poor choice of words there on my part," replied Freya, biting her bottom lip in contrition. "Sorry. I just meant good job on finishing the race," she offered apologetically. "I've actually no idea about your final race results. Sorry about that."

"Aww, it's fine, don't worry," Libby answered, laughing gently. "Come on, let's go to the timing station and see how I got on, then, shall we?" proposed Libby. She put her arm around Freya and the two of them began to make their way over, shoulder to shoulder. "A-ha! Well done yourself, by the way," offered Libby, upon noticing the finishers medal placed around Freya's neck. "Bloody well done indeed," she said, thoroughly delighted for her friend.

"Fuelled by cider!" Freya asserted proudly, fingering her medal as they walked.

A sea of people hovered about the beleaguered but forever cheerful group of volunteers informing the participants of their individual finishing times. Some runners were waiting to see if they'd smashed their personal best, whilst others were happy to simply have the printed piece of paper confirming they'd managed to finish the race. Libby, with Freya at her side, joined the line of people. They waited patiently for their turn at the front of the queue, happy to tarry amongst their fellow comrades-in-arms and enjoying the company.

Unfortunately, this wonderfully conducive atmosphere of peace and harmony was soon interrupted by the yapping of a small dog. This prompted Freya to remark, rather presciently, "Oi, that sounds very much like…"

"Hulk! Who's over there, Hulk?" said James, in that cloying, cooing, treacly voice that pet owners and parents of very young children quite often used. "Why, look, it's Aunty Libby and Aunty Freya!" James then added, answering his own rhetorical question as he and Hulk headed in their direction. This produced an audible groan from both Freya and Libby alike.

The fact that James had by this time already changed out of his running gear, that he had a coffee cup placed casually in his hand, and that he was now accompanied by his faithful furry companion, told Libby he must've concluded his race some time earlier. No matter. When it was her turn, she handed her wristband over to be scanned, doing her best to ignore James for just a little while longer.

"Good job! Jolly good show!" the chap behind the table told her, checking his monitor and then writing the time on a piece

CHAPTER TWENTY-TWO

of paper. "Your split times will be on the website in a day or two, if you'd like to check them then?" he suggested helpfully. "We can only hope to see you back for next year's race, at which point you'll likely be even quicker! Although, to be fair, that is a fantastic time and one that'll be tough to beat!"

Libby appreciated the fellow's enthusiasm. "We'll see," she told him, offering up a grin, and then folding the paper and closing her fingers around it without reading it. She took a deep breath, leaving the queue so as not to impede the other runners from gathering their own race times as well.

"Right. Time to blow this clambake?" asked Freya.

"Yep. Make like a tree and leave," agreed Libby.

"Put an egg in our shoe and beat it?" proposed Freya.

"Make like a banana and split," concurred Libby.

"So where are we off to now?" enquired a curious Freya.

"I was actually thinking a coffee wouldn't be such a bad idea," Libby answered.

"Hmm. Along with some sort of pastry or confection?" Freya put forth optimistically. "After all, we should probably replenish our blood sugar levels I should think?" she pointed out helpfully.

With the pair of them in perfect agreeance, the two girls set off, deliberately ignoring James and Hulk and leaving both behind, although James unfortunately had other ideas.

"Libby! Ohhh, Libby! Well...?" said James, calling after them. "Don't keep us in suspense!"

Libby sighed, and then came to a halt. She had hoped to have a quiet coffee and review her time in peace, but she knew James wasn't about to leave her be. Best to simply get it over and done with, she thought, reconsidering, and so stood there waiting for James to catch up. She looked down, unfolding the paper in her hand and reading silently to herself what was written there on it, after which she then scrunched the paper into a ball. Her eyes closed, and with her other hand she covered her brow, wondering what the next few moments were to bring.

"Libby?" asked Freya, rubbing her back in support. "Whatever happens, you'll be fine," Freya assured her.

"Well? What's it say, then?" a self-assured James demanded giddily, now standing before them and shifting his weight from one foot to another like an excitable idiot.

"Yours first," instructed Libby.

James shrugged, and then retrieved his own slip of paper from his pocket. He held it out to Libby for her to take from him, a big stupid grin on his face.

She shook her head, unwilling to play his game. "Will you have a look?" Libby asked of Freya. "Do you mind?"

Freya did as requested, snatching up the paper from James's hand. She read to herself what it said, and then turned to Libby. "Ready?" she asked.

"Hit me," said Libby, nodding.

Freya cleared her throat, hesitant, ignorant as she was as to whether the next words from her mouth might possibly destroy her friend's future.

"Go on," said Libby, nodding again.

"One hour, forty-seven minutes, and seven seconds," Freya recited. She looked up, searching Libby's face for any noticeable reaction, any indication as to whether this was good or bad news she'd just delivered. "Libby...?" Freya prompted, unclear if she'd soon be joining Libby in either celebration or commiseration.

"Libby?" pressed James, more forcefully. "*Well...?*"

Libby didn't answer straight off, which only appeared to frustrate James even further. "Come on, Libby, out with it, I haven't got all day," he insisted. "What was your time? Did I beat you? I did, didn't I? I *know* I must've beaten you. It's okay, just *say* it," he demanded.

James seemed to Libby to be overly confident and yet terribly fearful, both at once. Seeing his uncertainty brought a smile to her face, and she knew she was going to only compound his unease as her smile graduated to an outright laugh.

"Here now, what's so funny? You think this is all a joke?" responded James, entirely nonplussed.

Libby's laugh increased in volume and intensity, evolving to the point where she placed her palms down on her thighs to steady herself, her shoulders heaving. James took a cautionary step back.

CHAPTER TWENTY-TWO

"You, ehm, you okay, Libs?" asked Freya, not entirely sure what to do.

"I'm fine! Ab-so-lute-ly wonderful, in fact! I'm just terrific!" Libby answered, and then promptly resumed laughing.

"Uh... that's good?" Freya replied, tentatively.

Libby stood upright once more. She pressed her shoulders back, finally pulling herself together, though her cheeks were still wet with tears. "Don't worry," she said, in reference to Freya's look of concern. "No, really. This is a wonderful day. It really is," she promised her.

"Has she gone mad or something?" James cut in, his expression dour and disapproving.

"Okay... Libby...?" Freya said slowly, while deliberately ignoring James. "Should I go and get help for you? Are you suffering from dehydration, perhaps? Do you need first aid assistance...?"

"No, I don't need any first aid," Libby answered, wiping the tears of laughter away from her face. "No, honestly, it really is all right," she assured her friend. And then she let out an extended sigh, happy and contented.

James looked on, his eyes narrowing. He appeared to be very displeased.

"James," said Libby, addressing him now that she'd left him to stew a bit. "The answer to your question is *no*, I'm not mad. At least I don't believe I am."

"And?" said James.

"You beat me. And by quite a wide margin, as it should happen," she replied, getting more to the point with this answer, the point with which James was of course most concerned. "In fact you beat me by..." she added, running her tongue over her lips as she waved her finger through the air, using an imaginary blackboard as she worked the figure out in her head. "Yes, in fact you beat me by fifty-two minutes and some-odd seconds!" she declared triumphantly, after a few moments of quick calculation.

"I... I think I'm going to find that medic for you after all," Freya's offered in response.

"She's gone completely crackers, hasn't she?" observed a thoroughly bewildered James, shaking his head in dismay and looking as if he almost very nearly (but not quite) felt sorry for Libby.

Chapter Twenty-Three

The race for the majority of the runners was complete for another year. For some of the slower participants, however, there was still a little way to go before crossing the finish line. Among those still out on track, doing quite magnificently, were the gang from the Lonely Heart Attack Club, Silver Sprinters division. Gwen was several strides in front of the golf cart, still going strongly in her leg of the race, as she completed their fifth lap and headed into their sixth. She was rather enjoying being dressed as an oversized duck, and her comparatively sedate pace gave those remaining spectators an opportunity to admire it also — and an added opportunity, as well, for them to throw their change into her charity bucket, which of course the group didn't mind at all. Gwen was indeed enjoying her run, but she was also desperate for an update from Libby.

Also thoroughly enjoying themselves were the crowds in general, many of whom could now be found congregated outside the town's pubs to toast the day with a glass of their beverage of choice, be that beverage of choice beer, cider, or something else. With the waves lapping the golden beach, it was a splendid backdrop to the party atmosphere.

The atmosphere near to Libby, meanwhile, was still one of abject confusion, at least on the part of James, and to an only slightly less extent in Freya. Libby, for her part, however, seemed unworried at present...

"Freya, there's Gran!" shouted Libby with delight, ignoring James for the moment as Gran came into view, the sight of Gran naturally taking precedent over James's annoyingly persistent pestering. "Go, Gran!" she screamed, startling those in her vicinity. "That's my gran!" she announced by way of explanation and for the benefit of anyone who may have been looking in her direction as a result of all the sudden shouting.

James looked like he'd found himself as the main character in an episode of *The Twilight Zone*. "Yes... wonderful...?" he said, somewhat dazed, in response to Libby. He was struggling to understand why Libby was so upbeat considering the marked difference in their respective race times to his obvious favour and to her obviously very large detriment given the nature of their mutual bet.

"Isn't it, though?" replied Libby dreamily, more to herself, really, than in answer to James.

James had no choice but to wait until Gwen and her coven of Silver Sprinters associates had made their slow-but-steady way by. It was the only way he'd regain Libby's ear. "Right. Well," he began, once the procession had passed by and he felt it safe to speak. "Right, so Libby. We had a deal, yes?" he said as more of a statement than a question. "You agreed to this bet, if you recall. In fact this current variant was your own idea, no less! I was quite happy with the coin toss, remember, until you suggested this instead, which I then very graciously went along with."

"Sure... Yeah, I remember..." replied Libby, still distracted as she watched Gran & Co fade off into the distance.

James's cocky arrogance had, by this point, given way to a sort of exasperated bafflement. Here he was faced with someone who'd just lost a bet — and a rather significant one at that — and there was Libby acting as if she'd lost nothing more than, say, ten pence down the back of the sofa. Sensing that something was gravely amiss, he pulled out his phone in desperation and held it aloft, gripping it with both hands like it was the hilt of a mighty broadsword that would surely save the day. "I've got the entire bet recorded, Libby!" he said. "Right here!"

"Hmm? Oh, yes. Yes, I'm sure you do," Libby answered, disinterested and only half-listening.

"Now see here," said James. "You don't seem to be taking this as seriously as you should, and I don't think you at all appreciate the gravity of the situation," he told her. "I've got every detail of

CHAPTER TWENTY-THREE

the bet recorded, and more importantly your agreement to the bet. So don't be thinking you can somehow wriggle your way out of it, as I beat you fair and square!" he railed. "And if I'd lost the bet, you can be damned sure I would have honoured every detail! But I *didn't* lose the bet, did I? No, I didn't!"

James then lowered his phone from the air, hovering his finger over the touchscreen poised and ready to play the video in question should Libby refuse to cooperate. As he did this, Libby, however, not the slightest bit bothered by James's ranting, took up her own phone, casually pressing the screen a few times and then placing the phone gently to her ear. "It's good to know that you're so honourable," she told James with a wink and a nod as she waited a moment for the call she'd just made to connect. "Hold that thought for a tick, will you?" she instructed, raising a finger in the air to keep him quiet, before then shifting her attention back over to her phone.

"Oh, hi there," Libby spoke into her mobile once she'd got through. "Yes, it's me... Right, right... Yes, if you wouldn't mind terribly... Only if it's not too much trouble, of course, and you could possibly see your way clear? ... Okay, in that case, you can find us near the timing station..." Libby said to the person on the other end. "Right, then... Yes, cheers... Cheers. See you soon."

Libby placed her phone back into her pocket, completely disregarding the daggers James was shooting at her with his eyes. She then unscrewed the cap from the water bottle Freya had so kindly given to her a little earlier. She took a dainty sip, pinkie finger extended, and then waited one very long moment before taking another tiny little sip, at which point she then repeated this same process yet again, making sure to exclaim, "Ah! Refreshing!" between each and every sip. And then, with this most unhurried procedure having thus been successfully completed, she very, very leisurely screwed the top back on the bottle.

This protracted performance of course infuriated James, which was entirely Libby's intent. He stood there glaring at her, much to Libby's great amusement. To throw salt in the wound, she figured she'd wind him up even more. "I do love your medal, Freya," she said, turning her attention once again to the medal around Freya's neck, whilst paying James no heed. She took up

Freya's medal between her thumb and forefinger for closer inspection, caressing the surface admiringly.

"Libby...?" said Freya. "Okay, but seriously, Libby, what gives?" Of course Freya was as happy as anyone to see Libby grinding James's gears. But she was at a complete loss herself, unable to explain Libby's bizarre behaviour and wondering just what on earth had got into her dear friend.

But any answer Libby might have offered was interrupted by an amiable-sounding voice coming from nearby...

"Heya! Here I am!" Luke called over from only a short distance away. He headed straight to them, giving Libby a squeeze once there and planting a quick kiss on her cheek. "Hiya, Freya!" he said cheerfully, turning to face her. "I spotted the two of you out there on the field today, and I have to say I was impressed by what I saw! You were both cruising along at a fairly decent clip!"

"Yeah, it... felt good to be out there?" answered Freya. She was a little confused as to Luke's sudden appearance. She was aware that he and Libby were actively talking again, but even so, the public display of affection had still caught her off guard. It was more than that, though. Luke was obviously the one Libby had just called, she reasoned, summoned there upon Libby's request. But Freya still didn't know why Libby would have done so, having no clue as to how Luke might somehow fit into this current puzzle.

"Ah! Nice medal!" Luke said, noticing Freya's medal still in Libby's hand, and taking it up in his own in order to admire it. "Libby said this was your first race, Freya?" he asked her.

"It was. And the first of many, I expect," declared Libby on her friend's behalf.

"Yes, yes, it's a lovely medal! Now enough about the damnable medal!" interjected a frustrated and agitated James.

This prompted a stern look from Luke, which worried James as Luke was twice his size and had arms the size of bloody tree trunks. Freya also shot James a look, which James didn't treat lightly either. While she may have been quite a bit smaller in size as compared to Luke, James got the impression that Freya wasn't to be messed with herself, and wasn't someone he wished to be on the bad side of or rub the wrong way.

CHAPTER TWENTY-THREE

James made a quick, judicious attitude adjustment, smartly shifting his tone accordingly to something a fair bit milder as he tapped the watch on his wrist and said, "Look, Libby, I really need to get on. So, I'll call you later to make the arrangements to vacate the shop, yes?"

"Yes," replied Libby, a little too quickly and much more easily than James was likely expecting. "Oh, wait..." she added, stroking her chin. "How about, well, *NO?*" she said, upon further immediate consideration.

"Ehm... what?" replied James, blinking.

"Yeah. Yeah, I'd say it's definitely a no," Libby told James, reiterating the amended response she'd just given him. "Yep, no question," she said cheerily. "Absolutely a no!"

A rattled James took a step forward, but as that appeared to antagonise Luke, James stepped back to where he was previously in short order. "Libby, we had a bet," he said to her from what he hoped was a safe enough distance. "I've got the whole thing recorded, as I've said, so there's no way you can possibly worm your way out of this. The deal's right there for all to see, clear as day, and I've beaten you."

"Well yes and no," Libby answered him matter-of-factly.

"Yes and no?" asked James. "What does that mean, yes and no? I'm not following your—"

"You beat my time, yes," Libby cut in. "BUT, you didn't beat *his* time, now did you?" she said, giving Luke's beefy arm a gentle squeeze to let James know just who she was referring to should there be any doubt.

"But what's that got to do with...?" James began, but then didn't know what else to say.

Libby watched as James's mouth opened and closed like a flapper valve, with air rushing in and out but no words issuing forth, and she figured now would be as good a time as any to put the dear boy out of his misery. "When you agreed to our little bet, as you should be able to recall, and please do refer to your video recording if need be, right there on your phone..." she told him. "But when you agreed to our little bet, I said that in order for me to win, your time couldn't be any quicker than that of the Book Runners, correct?"

"But I *was* quicker than you," James was eager to point out. "And you can't very well include *her* time," he objected, nodding over to Freya. "She was in the 5k race, so of *course* her time was going to be much quicker than mine. There's no way you could count her time, then, as that wouldn't be the slightest bit fair!"

"No, that wouldn't be fair at all," Libby agreed readily. "But Luke, as it should happen, *did* race in the half-marathon," she advised. "And judging by the size of his medal, which is quite a bit larger than yours, I'd say he obviously placed considerably better than you did."

"What are you even on about?" James protested. "I'm not even wearing my medal, so how would you know what size it was! And what's his time got to do with anything anyway!"

"Ah. Silly me," said Libby. "I just assumed your medal must be on there somewhere but was, as would sadly only be typical in your case, so small that it couldn't be seen with the naked eye. Sorry. My mistake."

Luke chuckled at this, while James's face grew very red.

Before James could say anything else, Libby continued on. "Luke is a proud member of the Book Runners charity team," she informed James, finally laying it all out there and revealing her winning hand. "The bet was that your time, in order for you to win, would have to be quicker than that of the Book Runners charity team. And Luke, coincidentally enough, is part of that very team. And what Luke did, as it turned out, was to beat your time by a HUGE margin."

"But... but..." James sputtered.

"You can check on your phone the details of the bet, if you like?" offered Libby. She was enjoying all this, feeling rather like a lawyer summing up the case in a murder trial once again, this time for the prosecution.

"But he doesn't count! Surely he doesn't count!" James answered, pointing his finger franticly in Luke's direction. "I didn't know he was in your team! How could I?" he asked, glancing desperately about, like a school snitch looking for the teacher, in hopes of some authority figure intervening.

"I'd say that's *your* problem, James," Libby answered, offering him little sympathy. "Because as of last week Luke here became

CHAPTER TWENTY-THREE

part of our charity team and is formally registered with the organisers," she told him, with a satisfied grin. "Feel free to check if you like? And in fact you were standing right there when I got my timing bands. They handed me three of them, though you didn't seem to notice at the time."

"You can't do this!" shouted James. "This is cheating! I'll have a word with my father, tell him he's got to evict you from the shop as you're nothing but trouble! He'll do it, you know! He already wants you gone anyway!"

Libby didn't have the heart to recount to James the conversation she'd had with his father, and the fact that Eric much preferred it if James's shop would remain precisely where it was. She could tell him, but then Eric would know where the information came from, and Libby wanted Eric onside and friendly in their future relationship. Instead, Libby simply shrugged her shoulders and said to James, "Go right ahead. Knock yourself out. Talk to him to your heart's content. I doubt it'll do you any good."

"I just might do," insisted James defiantly. "So we'll see what's what in the end, just you wait," he pouted.

"Anyway, now that that's all settled, back to the terms of the bet for a moment, just so we're clear on everything," said Libby, breezily sailing onward despite James's firm objections. "As I recall, you agreed to restore my debit balance with your father to zero. In addition, I owe you nothing for the work you did establishing my website, and you also fix it so that normal prices are charged and I'm not losing money on every darned sale. *And*, you take down that stupid rubbish website proclaiming me to be a bloody prozzie, and then you also take out a double-page spread in the local newspaper clearing my name." She paused for a moment, trying to think if she'd remembered it all. "Hmm, is that everything?" she asked, wondering to herself aloud.

"Don't forget the extra five thousand pounds he promised on top of everything else!" Freya offered helpfully, tapping her nose.

"Ah, yes! Thanks for that," answered Libby. "How could I have forgotten that juicy little morsel? So, James, you also need to throw in an extra five thousand pounds, because you're SUCH a nice guy. So cheers for that as well."

James's left eye was twitching, and there was a vein throbbing on one side of his forehead that very much looked as if it was in imminent danger of rupturing. "You can kiss my ass!" he said after due consideration. "You've bloody had me over, is what you've done. So if you think I'm doing all that, then you can... well, you can kiss my ass!" he told her, not being able to think of anything wittier right at the moment and so sticking with his tried-and-true kiss-my-ass theme. And with that, James extended his finger into the air both for emphasis and to hold his place, fully intending to continue his tirade once he'd thought of something clever to add.

But James never got a chance to say anything more, as Luke promptly reached out, clamping hold of James's raised digit and squeezing it in his vice-like grip. "You shouldn't ever swear at a lady," Luke admonished, torquing James's finger a bit for good measure. "Especially if that lady happens to be my girlfriend," Luke added pointedly.

"S-sorry?" was all James could manage to say, as he grimaced in pain.

Luke leaned in, moving his face closer to James's ear. "Right. When I release your finger, get lost, yeah?" he whispered with menace. "And if I ever hear you've designs on Libby's shop again, or that you're bothering her at all in any way, then I might recall how you slagged me off all over town saying I'd been with half the female population. I might also remember that you very nearly managed to break me and Libby up. And if I do happen to remember these things, well then I might get very angry, won't I? And if I get angry, then something else might just be getting broken, if you take my meaning."

Luke gave James's finger one final twist and then set him free, leaving James to scarper off, which he did.

As James executed his hasty retreat, he could be heard chastising his dog. One supposes that, with his ego bruised, James had to direct his ire somewhere. "Whole lot of good you were back there!" he scolded poor Hulk. "You'll bark at a butterfly, but you just sit there doing nothing while your master is being assaulted!"

CHAPTER TWENTY-THREE

After watching James bugger off, Libby turned her attention back to Luke and Freya, and was horrified to see the present look of consternation on Freya's face.

Freya, for her part, had watched this entire preceding scene unfold, standing quietly by for the most of it. She was, of course, delighted to learn that Libby was going to be keeping her shop. But, as Libby's best friend, she was left feeling slighted by the fact that she'd seemingly been intentionally kept out of the loop in regard to Libby's master plan, and she couldn't help but be somewhat offended and a little wounded.

"I'm so sorry!" said Libby, sensing her friend's disappointment and correctly surmising the cause of it. She reached in and gave Freya a big hug. "I wanted to tell you about this, honestly I did, but I just couldn't," she told her. "Will you ever forgive me?"

"You could have trusted me," replied Freya, clearly unsatisfied at Libby's feeble consolation. "Surely by now you should know that you can trust me with anything?" she sulked, perfectly willing to forgive her bestie but still unhappy about it.

Libby puffed out her cheeks. "I know I can, Freya," she replied, after the deep exhale. "I just needed you to be utterly convincing in how you might have interacted with James in this last week or so. I didn't want to somehow give the game away, you know?" she told her, arguing her case. "I thought this was the best way," she said, frowning, and now not entirely convinced herself that she'd pursued the most reasonable course of action. "I love you loads, Freya, and would trust you with my life. If I had it all to do over again, I'd, well... Forgive me...?" she implored.

"Eh, I suppose. Sure," Freya answered with a shrug, and just like that, letting bygones be bygones. "Anyway, what now?" she asked.

"You mean *now*, now? Like, immediately? Hmm, how about we go and catch up with the Silver Sprinters?" Libby proposed. "We could follow them around for a lap or two and help them with their collection buckets!"

"Okey-doke. Sounds like a plan!" answered Freya, perking up, and thus instantly forgiving and forgetting any offences that Libby might possibly have perpetrated.

"Luke, you in?" asked Libby.

"Sure, count me in, let's go!" Luke responded.

With that having been decided, Libby linked arms with both Luke and Freya, the three of them heading in the direction of the circuit.

"I reckon at this point it's only the Silver Sprinters remaining out on track?" Libby remarked along the way.

"Well, them and probably that one chap who'd decided on hopping the entire distance for charity for some reason," offered Freya. "Remember him?"

"Ah, yes! Of course!" Libby answered.

"Yeah, I expect he's likely not finished yet either," Freya commented, using her free hand to straighten up the Minnie Mouse ears she'd never bothered to take off after finishing her own run. "Anyway, while we're on our way there, perhaps you can also tell me how your very best friend in the whole world knew nothing about you and Luke formally getting back together!"

"Aww, nuts," said Libby, lowering her head in shame for a moment or two. "Sorry, Freya, it all happened so quickly, and I just didn't want to jinx anything, you know what I mean?" But Libby knew as soon as the words escaped her lips that this was a pretty lame excuse. To make things right, she made Freya a vow. "From now on, I'll tell you absolutely everything that happens in our relationship!" she steadfastly declared. "Deal?"

"Wait. Everything?" asked Luke, unsure if he liked this idea quite so much. "Everything, as in *everything*?"

"Yes, it must be absolutely everything!" Freya stressed giddily. "It's what best friends do!"

"Guess what?" said Libby, apropos of nothing. She picked up the pace and started to skip gaily, with the others feeling obliged to replicate this as well — even Luke, such was the occasion — and with the three of them looking like they were marching up the Yellow Brick Road on their way to Oz.

"What?" Freya and Luke answered together.

"I get to stay in my shop!" Libby announced to her friends, and also to the world. "The Bookshop by the Beach is going nowhere!" she shouted with delight. "I cannot wait to tell Gran the good news!"

Chapter Twenty-Four

One week later...

Today's front page is tomorrow's chip wrapper, or so the saying goes. On a small island where people often knew each other's business, Libby was doing all she could to help quash the rumours stemming from her shop's more seedy — and false — online alter ego. The fact that the Bonkshop website was still up was of course doing her genuine shop absolutely no favours. Her public announcement, as a result, advising that she'd been the victim of a viciously cruel smear campaign came in the form of a relatively modest 16cm × 25cm advert in the local newspaper.

Libby's advert wasn't the expensive double-page spread that James had committed to as per the terms of the bet he'd lost, and this was because James had in fact failed to follow through on that promise. And the reason he'd failed to follow through on that promise of his was because he was, in Libby's estimation, a giant flapdoodle, amongst other things. But flapdoodle was the current term of the day, at least, taken from a book of insults Libby had in stock at her shop. She and Freya had been poring through it, finding it to be a wonderful stress reliever, and taking great delight in appropriating each and every term they encountered and applying it to James, with flapdoodle being the present word du jour.

The previous few weeks, with everything that had been going on, had been challenging to say the least. Libby had been on the verge of throwing in the towel on both the business and the life she now adored. After considerable reflection, however, she'd ultimately concluded that the prospect of leaving this beautiful rock in the middle of the Irish Sea to return to her former home in a big, bustling, overcrowded city was not one she cared to embrace. Now, with the entire James situation consigned to history, she could look forward to building her business and securing her future. Every night, in bed, just when she closed her eyes, she could still see the expression on James's gormless face at the moment he realised he'd lost the bet. It was a most pleasant image to drift off to sleep to.

By way of reaction, to say that James had thrown his toys out of his pram was, perhaps, an understatement. Threats of legal action were bandied about. He then refused to pay for the newspaper advert or stump up the monies he'd promised. Eric was sympathetic to Libby's plight, especially once shown the video of his son making the bet he'd lost and the associated promises that were made in service of that bet. Unfortunately, though sympathising, Eric did still want and expect his rent from Libby.

Fortunately, Libby had managed to scrape together a good portion of the money due by begging, borrowing, but fortunately not stealing, and her saviour in paying the remainder of the rent came in the form of Luke, who she was now delighted and honoured to call her boyfriend. Luke was the grateful beneficiary, as it turned out, of the rugby club sweepstake for being the highest-placed runner in the race. With each club member throwing a hundred quid into the pot, Luke had won a little over two grand for his efforts, which he then, prince among men that he was, happily contributed to Libby's rent fund.

With the rent sorted, that left one particularly vexing problem Libby wasn't able to resolve in any sort of way, with the creepy counterfeit website still being live and there for all the world to see. Amazingly, James was denying all involvement despite his previous private admission of guilt and categorically refused to offer any help at all in removing the bookshop's salacious sister site. James was, the girls decided, a hornswoggler — their second favourite word from their book of insults.

CHAPTER TWENTY-FOUR

Libby held a deep abiding affection for her bookshop, which was strengthened only further on account of her nearly losing it. With her getting a new fresh start, she also wanted the shop to have one as well, she decided. So, with the assistance of Freya and Luke — and with inspiration taken from her grandad's journal — they'd given the exterior of the shop a well-deserved lick of paint. And of course no fresh start was complete without a little party, which they were also in the process of organising. She wanted to really show her gratitude to her loyal customers, and also to all of those people who'd helped her along the way.

One of those people who *hadn't* helped — but was very eager to try and make amends for the part he'd inadvertently played in Libby's troubles — was James's former associate Mr Slick, aka Giles. Currently, on this particular afternoon, Giles was offering up his time to aid Libby in resolving the various technological difficulties in her shop. Even though any involvement Giles had in implementing these very difficulties hadn't been in any way intentional or done with malice on Giles's part, he still felt guilty about it, and was therefore only too happy to try and rectify the situation in any way and as best he could.

"I brought you a cuppa, Giles!" said an affable Libby, generous host that she was. "I'm going to pop up to the bakery in a bit and get us a couple of cakes as well, if that's all right?"

"Hmm? Oh, sorry, Libby," said Giles, breaking his attention away from Libby's laptop after a moment. He was a man on a mission, and so hadn't registered at first what Libby had said. "Sorry, was just in the zone," he explained. "Ah! Thanks for this!" he added, finally noticing the tea on offer, and then picking it up and taking a sip.

"Have you managed to make any progress?" Libby enquired amiably.

"Well, I've not been able to restore quite all of the settings on your website just yet, but I'm getting there, and at least it's not charging the wrong prices anymore. Also, I've taken the liberty of making some general improvements to the site as I've gone along as well, tweaking a handful of little things here and there," Giles was happy to report.

"Oh! I didn't realise you'd be this successful!" Libby replied, surprised but not in any way displeased. "You were able to get in and do all this without James's passwords?" she asked. "I mean, I thought—?"

"James isn't nearly half as clever as he believes himself to be," Giles answered, gently cutting in. "Wasn't too difficult at all to get around his security protocols, as it turns out."

"Brilliant! So the website's now as good as it should've been at the start?" replied a delighted Libby.

"As good? Oh, I should think not," Giles answered, wrinkling up his nose. "It's not *as* good, Libby. It's a helluva lot *better* than what James originally cobbled together," he informed her. "Here, have a butcher's," he offered, turning the screen to face her.

Libby had a gander, not entirely sure what the improvements were other than having the pricing issue sorted out, but she was certainly happy to take Giles's word for it. "Looks amazing!" she said, beyond thrilled that she now had access to technology that actually worked as it was meant to.

"I've also fixed your till system here in the shop. So that won't be causing you any further trouble," Giles related. "And you can now go back to using your biscuit tin for biscuits," he said with a grin. "Oh, and as far as your website goes, I can assure you that, unlike James, I'll make sure to give you a note with your new passwords for it once I'm finished," he added, taking another sip of tea. "Mmm, this is good. Earl Grey?" he asked.

"Earl Grey, yes," Libby cheerfully confirmed. "And thank you, Giles! I don't honestly know what I'd have done without you. I know you said you don't want any money, but is there anything else I can do to thank you? Is there anything you need?"

"Well…" Giles answered with a laugh. "How about a date?"

Libby waited for a further laugh from Giles, after the date part, but he simply looked up at her with a serious, hopeful expression. "Ehm… Giles? I'm not quite sure what you're asking me," Libby replied hesitantly, worried this conversation was quickly taking a turn to the decidedly awkward. "You know I'm already dating Luke, yes? And you also know I'm not *actually* a

CHAPTER TWENTY-FOUR

prostitute, regardless of what that dodgy doppelgänger website's claims are to the contrary, right...?"

"W-what? No. I-I mean, yes, yes of course I know that," Giles stammered in response, blushing. "No, I meant Freya. About the date, I mean," he said. "And I know she's not a prostitute either!" he added quickly. "I was just wondering if a date with Freya, you know, a proper date, might be possible...?"

Libby wiped her forehead in exaggerated, comical fashion. "*Phew!*" she said, exhaling in relief. "Right, then. In that case, I'll have a word," she promised him.

It wasn't a difficult promise to make, nor was the idea of Giles and Freya together so far-fetched. Freya hadn't come right out and said anything to Libby, but she didn't really need to. The fact that she'd been in the shop several times over the course of the last few days, mysteriously appearing when it just so happened Giles was in there working, and then Freya lingering about for no specified reason, told Libby all she needed to know. Somehow or other, Freya had gone from making fun of Giles, as she'd done previously, to now obviously fancying him. Libby could only surmise that now Giles was clearly one of the good guys, Freya was seeing him in an entirely new light.

"One more thing," added Giles. He leaned back in his chair as he said this, locking his fingers together behind his head and looking quite satisfied, similar to just having eaten a very substantial meal. A sinister smile crept across his face, as if he had something deliciously devious in mind. "About that Bonkshop website..." he began.

"Yes? replied Libby, her interest piqued.

"Well, it's not exactly been created with too much care or attention to detail. Even so, I've still not been able to take it down," Giles told her.

"Oh," said Libby, disappointed, shoulders sagging, and certainly wondering what the sinister smile was all about. "Sorry. Bit of an anti-climax there, Giles, no pun intended...?"

"Well, I haven't been able to take it down, necessarily, but what I *have* been able to do is hack it," Giles clarified.

"Oh?" replied Libby, interest duly regained.

"Yes, and I'd say James is in for a bit of a rude surprise next time he looks at it," Giles offered, sly grin firmly intact. "And I'll wager that once he does look at it, it's very likely he'll find himself motivated to take the thing down himself."

"Indeed?" answered Libby, keen to know the details.

"Here, I'll show you," said Giles, loading up the offending website in question and then once again turning the laptop so that Libby could have a look.

"Oh! Oh, you cheeky devil!" replied Libby. "I love it!"

With the use of technological wizardry that was alien to Libby, Giles had somehow managed to amend the Bonkshop's featured image so that it was now a photo of James as opposed to one of her. In addition, instead of Libby's shopfront being the background image, James's shop was now substituted. Also, any references to Libby on the site had been removed and replaced accordingly. The result of all these changes, of course, was that the price list of adult services on offer now pertained specifically to James. There he was, the sad, sorry prat, for the whole world to see, grinning invitingly to all comers.

"I was going to include his dog in the picture, at first," Giles continued. "After all, the two of them are practically inseparable. And where there's one there's always the other, right? But then I reconsidered as I didn't want to give people the wrong idea, you know? I mean, I didn't want anyone to get the impression poor Hulk was up for sale also, now did I? That would just be wrong. And of course it's not the pooch's fault his owner is an arsehole, either, so in the end I just..."

"Yes?" asked Libby, waiting to hear the rest of the story. But it seemed Giles was now distracted, as the lovely Freya, coincidentally enough, had just popped in yet again.

"Right-ho!" said Freya, holding her trowel up for inspection. "I've filled all the flower boxes outside the shop, and it looks bloody marvellous," she said, pretending to look at Libby but a little less-than-discreetly looking right past. "Oh, hello there, Giles," Freya added nonchalantly, as if she'd noticed Giles sitting there only just now. "I had no idea you were in here," she said, batting her eyelids innocently. "No idea at all."

CHAPTER TWENTY-FOUR

Giles flashed her a smile. "Heya," he replied, with a wink that sent Freya all giggly.

Libby then pulled Freya aside, on the pretext of some trowel-related matter or another, and once carefully out of Giles's earshot asked, "Thanks for that, but I didn't ask you to come here on your lunch break and do this?"

"Oh, it's no trouble! Just doing my part!" Freya offered gaily.

"I see," answered Libby, trying her best to suppress a grin.

"Anyway, while we've got each other's ear, you think you could have a word?" said Freya, sneaking another glance over at Giles.

"Hmm? What sort of word?" Libby asked coyly, knowing full well what Freya was on about but playing dumb nonetheless.

"About Giles," Freya answered, tipping her head in his direction. "Perhaps have a word with him on my behalf?"

"Giles? Really? My goodness, I never would've imagined!" replied Libby, pretending to be surprised. "Wait, hold on, I thought you didn't like his hair?" she asked.

"Yeah, but that was before," Freya pointed out.

"Before?" asked Libby, not letting Freya off so easily.

"Right. That was before. This is now," Freya explained, as if that should clear matters up nicely. Noticing Libby's look of scepticism, Freya elaborated, "I changed my mind. I like it now. It's kind of sexy, in an Italian sort of way, you know?"

"Ah," Libby replied, satisfied enough.

"Right. Anyway. So you think you could have a word?" Freya asked, reiterating her previous request.

"Hmm, I don't know..." said Libby, playing up like this was something she really had to think hard about and thoroughly consider. Finally, eventually, she nodded in assent. "Well, okay, Freya. But only because you're my absolute bestest friend, yeah? And because you've helped me out so much," she told her. "No promises, of course. But I'll give it a go and see what he has to say, all right?" said Libby, as if the outcome were not in any way foreseeable.

"Thanks, mate. Appreciate it!" replied a hopeful Freya, casting another flirtatious glance in Giles's direction, before then turning her attention back to Libby. "Oh, unrelated, did you get that supplier situation of yours all straightened out, by the way?" she asked.

"All sorted," Libby responded. "Eric was true to his word and was kind enough to write me an official letter that I could then provide to my suppliers confirming that I was good for credit and not in arrears. So, yeah, all sorted," she said. "Also, speaking of credit, on a rather sad note, I've cut all of my credit cards up," she added. "It was a rough day to get through, Freya, as we've been through so much together, my credit cards and me. It was so very hard to say goodbye," declared Libby, giving a heavy sigh of seemingly deep loss and regret.

Freya laughed, as she knew Libby's sigh of despair was only slightly serious. "You did the right thing, Libs," she assured her, giving Libby some pats on the back consolingly. "Don't worry, the pain will ease over time eventually," she assured her with a crooked grin.

"Thanks for the support," Libby answered with a chuckle.

"Anyway, can't stand here chatting all day," Freya told her. "Gotta get back to work soon, so I'm going to give those flowers a nice little drink and then I'm off."

With Freya soon outside, watering can in hand, Giles popped his head up over the computer screen. "So you'll have a word? You know, with Freya?" he asked. "Or did you just...?"

"Not yet, no. But, yes, I suppose so," Libby answered him, as if she were really putting herself out there but would make a very special effort just for him. "Although no promises, of course. All I can do is put in a good word for you, Giles, and see what she has to say, yeah?"

"Cheers! Appreciate it!" replied a sunny-faced Giles optimistically.

The Bookshop by the Beach was like a child on the first day of the new school year, in that it was immaculately presented. Fresh paintwork, polished brass, some new shelves, a little red carpet, and Libby had even managed to secure a yellow ribbon

CHAPTER TWENTY-FOUR

and an oversized pair of scissors, just like her gran and grandad had done all those years before.

It wasn't exactly a formal reopening, but the shop had played such a pivotal role in her family's life, and now her own, that she wanted to pamper it and show it off to close friends and loyal customers alike. With the event presently in full swing, Libby was the consummate host, working the room like a seasoned socialite, closely shadowed by Luke who was doing a splendid job helping her by dispensing refreshments. She'd even donned a red velvet dress for the occasion, which was perhaps a little too fancy but had ended up complementing Luke's tuxedo perfectly nonetheless as he'd arrived somewhat overdressed for the event himself.

"He's lovely, Libby," declared Gran, pulling Libby aside as she came near, raising her champagne glass to toast her observation. "I spoke to him earlier, and what a polite young man," she said. "Do you know who he puts me in mind of?" she asked, but without even waiting for a response, immediately answered her own question with, "Your grandad. Your grandad was also a perfect gentleman."

Libby bit her lower lip, as she'd been rather emotional of late and her tear ducts were presently possessed of a hair-trigger response. She took her gran's hand. "Thanks, Gran, that means a lot to me," she said. "And thank you for having faith in me, also. I won't let you down, I promise."

"You never do," Gran assured her. "Oh. Here, hold this for a moment, will you?" she added, handing her glass to Libby, and then rummaging through her bag. "You've reminded me that I wanted to give you something," she explained. "Ah, here we are!" she said, holding up the item in question that she'd been looking for. "I thought you could maybe use this as a good luck charm in the shop?"

Libby placed the champagne glass in her hand onto a nearby surface so that she could attend to her eyes. "Oh, Gran!" she replied, tears about to destroy her perfectly applied makeup. She then reached out to accept the crocheted love heart her grandad had inadvertently left in Gran's care on their very first date all those years ago.

"I always meant to give it back to him," said Gran. "But..."

"I'll cherish it, Gran. And every time I look at it, I'll think of..." said Libby, but she couldn't finish as she was now blubbing.

"Everything okay?" asked Luke, appearing on scene, platter of sandwiches now in hand for consideration.

"Fine, fine," Libby answered him, passing on the kind offer of sandwiches but taking up a napkin from the tray instead and using it to remove the moisture there on her cheeks. "Absolutely fine," she added, tucking her head into Luke's shoulder. "It's just an emotional day."

"I can well imagine," replied Luke, placing a kiss on the top of her head. "It's the start of the next chapter for both you and the shop, so plenty to look forward to, I reckon," he offered sympathetically.

"Mmm-hmm," Libby murmured into his shoulder.

"Libby, sorry, but other than the sandwiches, I did come over here to inform you that there's a chap arrived who's looking for you," said Luke, pointing off to a grey-haired man in a three-piece suit and a black fedora.

"Oh?" said Libby, straightening up and eying the stranger. There was something familiar about him, perhaps, but she couldn't quite place him. On first inspection, he looked rather like an old-time Chicago gangster who'd just been released from a lengthy prison term.

Sensing he was being spoken about, the fellow who was the topic of discussion took the liberty of approaching the three of them, removing his hat with one hand and then presenting a lovely bunch of flowers from behind his back to Libby with the other.

Libby was pleased enough to receive the flowers — and in fact quite relieved they weren't a weapon of some kind as she'd for a moment feared! — but she smiled politely, wondering what the flowers were for. She couldn't help but wonder if this gentleman might perhaps be confusing her with someone else.

"It took me a little while to find you," the fellow offered. "But find you I did!"

Libby wondered if this was going to be similar to one of those Hollywood movie moments in which a long-lost dad turns up at

CHAPTER TWENTY-FOUR

the tail end of the film. Only she knew who her father was, or at least she thought she did.

"I'm still sporting a few cuts and scrapes about the face, still healing up," said the man, running his hand around his chin. "So, I'm afraid I'm not as presentable as I should like to be. But I just wanted to come round and thank you for stopping to look after me as you did."

Libby raised her eyebrows in a sudden lightbulb moment. "Oh! You're the chap who fell in the race!" she said.

"That would be me!" said the fellow, in a proud affirmative. "Sam," said Sam by way of introduction, holding out his hand.

"Well, Sam, it's a pleasure to properly meet you," Libby responded, shaking Sam's hand. "Sorry. I didn't recognise you at first, looking like this," she told him.

"Like this?" asked Sam, puzzled.

"I meant without those bright lime-green trainers of yours on!" Libby explained. What she'd really meant was that she didn't recognise seeing him vertical, as opposed to horizontal on the ground and bloodied, and also with him now dressed to the nines rather than in his running gear. But of course she didn't want to cause offence. "Won't you stay for a drink and some food?" she suggested. "You're more than welcome here, Sam," she told him, as she found a home in the form of a tall, empty champagne flute for the flowers he'd so graciously given her.

"Of course he'll stay," declared Gran on Sam's behalf, stepping forward and linking his arm. "Come on, Sam, allow me to find you a drink of something bubbly!" she said, ushering him away.

"Oh aye," Libby remarked to Luke, as she watched her gran escort Sam straight over to the table doubling as the temporary bar area for the afternoon.

"She's certainly not wasting any time, is she?" agreed Luke, with a gentle laugh. "Well, I suppose when you're that little bit older, you don't have an awful lot of time to dilly-dally around with such things," he considered thoughtfully. "Time is of the essence, yes?"

"Yeah, I know. As opposed to us, right?" Libby replied with a chuckle. "I mean, how long did it eventually take for us to become a couple? We took our sweet time about it, didn't we?"

"The best things come to those who wait!" proclaimed Luke.

"Wait, so you're saying you're the best? I can't do any better than you?" Libby answered, giving Luke a good-natured ribbing.

"I'll let you decide that," Luke said with a grin. "Anyway, it just occurred to me, I know this place isn't a knocking shop and all, but it *is* almost like a dating service, isn't it?" he observed wryly.

"Oh? How so?" asked Libby, not quite following Luke's train of thought.

"Well, there's us, of course. And then there's Freya and Giles, who I understand are now an item. And, presently, it looks like your gran may have found herself a possible new love interest as well," Luke answered. "I wonder who's next?" he mused.

"Dunno. But I've already found mine, and that's all that matters," said Libby, reaching around and giving one of Luke's bum cheeks a surreptitious squeeze.

"Oi! Don't make me drop this platter of sandwiches!" Luke responded in mock protest.

"And how, exactly, am I meant to help myself?" answered Libby, pleading her case. "After all, you look just so damned good in that tux, now don't you!"

"It's a rental," Luke informed her. "Sadly, it needs to be back by six."

"Ah, what a shame. I would love for you to have worn it later on tonight," Libby told him. "Well, at least until I'd torn it off you," she then clarified.

"Well, I suppose I could just pay the extra for bringing it back a day late?" offered Luke.

"Whatever you think is the best course of action," said Libby, giving him the sort of wink that suggested they both knew full well what course of action that ought to be.

Cajoling people to pose together for a group photograph was a challenge at the best of times. Insert alcohol into the equation, with those people being very well lubricated, and it was about as easy as trying to herd cats. Sensing the fizz was starting to flow a little too easily, the photographer that Libby had secured for

CHAPTER TWENTY-FOUR

the afternoon coaxed everyone to the street outside accordingly. "Come on, you lot," he said cheerily, "I promise I won't keep you from the refreshments for too long!"

With everyone in place, more or less, the photographer took up a position across the road from the shop and reached into his pocket for the piece of paper he'd kept for reference. Libby had furnished him with this printed-out copy of her gran's photograph from the bookshop's opening day over forty years prior, and he was under strict instructions that no matter how distracted Libby may become over the course of the afternoon, or how crazy things might possibly get, they simply had to have the group picture done to replicate the original.

"Libby, if you'd like to move just there?" he called over, using his arms like a conductor trying to organise the brass section. He took a further peek into his viewfinder, and more instructions of a similar nature were issued forth to the wider group.

Libby and her gran, for their part, each took a grip on the pair of oversized scissors procured for the occasion, placing the blades of it on the yellow ribbon as directed. The photographer took another look at the image from forty years earlier and, once confident he'd managed to recreate it to his satisfaction, raised up a hand to get the group's attention and have them hold position for the shot.

"Wait!" shouted Libby, waving her hand to Luke and Freya, who had both, out of modesty, remained on the periphery. "I want the two of you at the centre of this picture!" she said, inviting them in.

Luke took up a position next to Libby, and Freya next to Gran, and with this slight adjustment to the composition now sorted, the photographer was once again prepared to snap the shot.

"Are we ready to say cheese...?" the photographer asked tentatively, wanting to be absolutely certain everything was now in order and exactly as it should be.

"Not cheese!" Freya shouted out. "The Bookshop by the Beach instead!"

"Should we go with that?" asked the photographer, looking to Libby for approval. With Libby nodding her assent, he then addressed the group. "Right, then. Shall we? Let's all say..."

"The Bookshop by the Beach!" came the collective cheer, no further instruction needed.

The photographer, perfectionist that he was, wasn't quite finished with them, capturing several more shots. He knew how important this photograph was to Libby. She'd told him what the photo she'd provided to him meant to her, and how it encapsulated the start of her grandparents' grand journey together in both business and life, theirs being a life spent filled with love, happiness, and a complete devotion to each other.

"You're positively aglow," said Luke to Libby, placing his arm around her once the photographer signalled that his duties had been fulfilled and everyone could now move about as they pleased.

"I know," she replied. "And that's because..." she began, but again, was an emotional wreck and overcome by emotion.

"Because?" asked Luke, taking a handkerchief from his jacket pocket.

"Yes, because," Libby answered, after sorting herself out. "Because I'm just so grateful about how things have turned out, Luke," she elaborated, arching her neck and stealing a kiss. "I very nearly lost the shop, and to make matters even worse, I very nearly lost you too."

"Well, you found me again," replied Luke. "So you're stuck with me now, I'm afraid," he said with a grin.

"I wouldn't want it any other way," said Libby, a gleam in her eye. "Oh, and, ehm, I just had a thought..." she added, caressing his arm.

"Yes?" said Luke.

"Maybe tell the rental company you might be a *couple* of days late with their tux?"

"Done and done," Luke answered.

"Splendid," said Libby, beaming. "Everything is splendid now."

The End

Also by the Author

If you've enjoyed this book, the author would be very grateful if you would be so kind as to leave feedback on Amazon. You can subscribe for author updates and news on new releases at:
www.authorjcwilliams.com

J C Williams
Author

authorjcwilliams@gmail.com
@jcwilliamsbooks
@jcwilliamsauthor

And also, if you've enjoyed this book, then please check out the author's other offerings!

The *Frank 'n' Stan's Bucket List* series:

The Lonely Heart Attack Club series!

And *The Seaside Detective Agency*, and *The Flip of a Coin*:

You may also wish to check out my other books aimed at a younger audience...

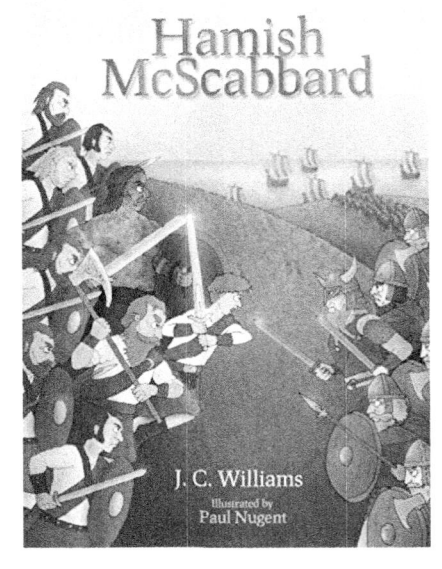

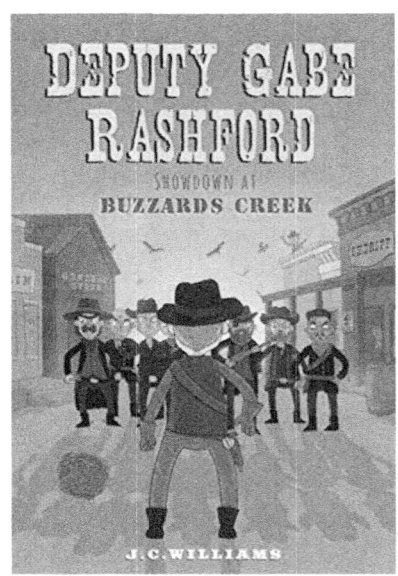

All jolly good fun!

Printed in Great Britain
by Amazon